Fourbodings

A QUARTET OF UNEASY TALES
FROM FOUR MEMBERS OF THE MACABRE

This special signed edition of
Fourbodings
is limited to 1,000 copies.

FourBodings

Edited By
Peter Crowther

FourBodings

Simon Clark
Terry Lamsley
Tim Lebbon
Mark Morris

Edited By
Peter Crowther

CEMETERY DANCE PUBLICATIONS
BALTIMORE
- 2005 -

FOURBODINGS

"Introduction" © 2005 Peter Crowther
"So Long Gerry" © 2005 Terry Lamsley
"Langthwaite Road" © 2005 Simon Clark
"In the Valley Where Belladonna Grows" © 2005 Tim Lebbon
"Stumps" © 2005 Mark Morris

Cemetery Dance Publications 2005
ISBN: 1-58767-090-9

Dust Jacket Art: © 2005 by Edward Miller
Dust Jacket Design: Gail Cross
Typesetting and Design: David G. Barnett
Printed in the United States of America

Cemetery Dance Publications
132-B Industry Lane
Unit #7
Forest Hill, MD 21050
http://www.cemeterydance.com

10 9 8 7 6 5 4 3 2 1

First Edition

INTRODUCTION

PETER CROWTHER

WHOSE HAND
WAS I HOLDING?

RANDOM THOUGHTS BY WAY OF
AN INTRODUCTION TO *FOURBODINGS*

LET'S TALK ABOUT subtlety. Face it: it's not the kind of topic you'd usually associate with horror fiction but that's an unfortunate oversight. Because, for my money, subtlety is the biggest and most overlooked strength of the whole genre.

The vast body of macabre fiction [*1] and all of its myriad practitioners can be divided into two very distinct groups: the effective and…well, let's be gentle and simply call the second group the 'less than effective'.

The way we can separate these tales and these tale-tellers is generally fairly simple: once the knee-jerk reaction to the *BOO!* factor has died down, you have to ask yourself this: does the image or the concept surrounding or supplementing that *BOO!* factor stick in your head…and, better still, even when it's faded away, does it return, deep in the middle of the night, when the house is quiet and the wind is rattling the shutters and you wonder whether maybe that creak you hear is the sound of a rotting foot taking one step at a time up the stairs towards your bedroom.

The sad reality is, they rarely do.

Like everyone, I covered myself in popcorn and soda when the partially-chomped head appeared suddenly in *Jaws*…and, of course, we've all enjoyed (or endured!) many more great *BOO!* moments in movies, all the way from those wonderfully shlocky William Castle movies from the 1950s up to shameless (but hugely entertaining) paro-

---

[*Footnote #1: I guess the same could be said about any other artistic field and its practitioners but it just seems more apposite where the 'spooky' is concerned.]

dies such as the *Scream and Scary Movie* series. But the most memorable pieces are not those that make you jump but rather the ones which make you think…and, alas, neither *The Tingler* nor *Scream* itself provides much in the way of cerebral stimulation [*2].

There are two fine examples of what I'm thinking of in 1963's *The Haunting* [*3], Robert Wise's extraordinarily excellent adaptation of Shirley Jackson's *The Haunting of Hill House:* the first is where Eleanor (played by Julie Harris), terrified at the noises outside her room, holds onto Theo's (Claire Bloom's) hand, eventually complaining that Theo is holding it too tightly…until the lights come on and Eleanor discovers Theo is still in bed across the room; and the second is the sequence where Dr. Markway (played by Richard

---

[*Footnote #2: John Carpenter's magnificent *Halloween* however provides massive amounts of cerebral stimulation in that it suggests the existence of a real bona fide boogeyman…a creature, seemingly constructed of flesh and shadow, that you just don't seem able to kill.]

[*Footnote #3: In *Danse Macabre*, Stephen King describes Wise's *The Haunting* as "the world's first radio horror movie" and it's easy to see why: the whole thing is aimed at stimulating the audience's imagination rather than on thinking for them. Thus, instead of over-egging the old BOO! factor —"Here's a 'knife-in-the-eye-socket' scene for you!" —Wise insinuates the story into your subconscious in a way that few other movies have managed. In fact, there are only two other examples that occur to me 'top of the head'.

The first is *The Blair Witch Project*, purely because of that final frame —just what had he seen that would cause him simply to turn his back while 'the witch' dealt with the girl, knowing full well that he himself would then be top of the playlist? It demonstrates better than any other movie just how sweet life is that we might consider calm acceptance of the promise of utter horror so long as it meant we got a few extra minutes…all of which is eerily reminiscent of the images of people jumping from the twin towers because what they were leaving behind them was a damn sight worse than the rapidly approaching concrete sidewalk.

The second is the original European version of *The Vanishing*: once again, it's the final revelatory scene that clinches it. You could pile a thousand BOO! setpieces against that one scene and *The Vanishing* would win hands down. And that's because it gets us where we live…we can empathise, we can imagine all too well what it would be like to be lying there waiting for the air to be getting stale, hard to breathe. All of which comes down to this: in the final analysis, death always comes second place to the knowledge that you're going to die…which is why plane crashes top the chart over all other methods of checking out —because, in all too many instances, you have as long as several minutes knowing the end is nigh.]

Johnson) and Luke (Russ Tamblyn) watch the room door buckle inwards beneath a torrent of blows in the corridor outside the room. In each instance, one can only guess at the entity involved…either the one squeezing the woman's hand or the one causing a thick wooden door to bend like taffy. And the truly scary thing in each case is that if we had seen either of the culprits, or even if we had had the character of Hill House painstakingly explained to us, we'd have been all the poorer for it.

It's all about subtlety and imagination.

Which leads us nicely to the book you're now holding.

On the back of the critically acclaimed series of *Foursight* collections (put out from 2000 to 2003 by the UK publisher Gollancz) gathering some of the best novellas from my PS Publishing imprint, I talked with Richard Chizmar about the possibility of doing something similar for CD…but this time with collections of brand new, specially commissioned long stories of unease from some of the best people currently working in the field. Aside from anything else, it gave me an opportunity to use another groan-inducing piece of wordplay utilising a word that relates to the theme and tone of the stories and the fact that there are four of them. (Heck, when you find something that works, brothers and sisters, you have to milk it for all its worth!)

So, where we had *Foursight* (for, of course, 'foresight', defined as "the act of looking forward"…which was appropriate for the genre-bending semi-SF strangeness of those 16 novellas), we could have *Fourbodings* [*4], for 'Forebodings'…defined as "omens, portents and feelings of impending evil or disaster".

What we wanted was just that…a sense of impending doom. And we got it in spades.

But let's get things straight right from the off: there aren't too many *BOO!* moments in the quartet of novellas which make up *Fourbodings*. And that isn't a mistake or an oversight; it's intentional.

What there *is* in here, however—and in generous quantities—is mystery, disorientation and fear.

Like that experienced by the man in Terry Lamsley's exceedingly

---

[*Footnote #4: This of course means that all you smartasses who thought, 'Boy, Chizmar and Crowther have really screwed up this time: what chance have we got when they can't even proofcheck the goddam title!'…well, enough said.]

strange apartment building who just doesn't seem to hear you when you holler at him to get out *now*, to forget his clothes and other belongings…to just hightail it out onto the street—because there's a reason for his friend seeing someone in the room with him when he stays the night, and there's a reason why those obnoxious kids from the next apartment are so clued in all the time, and there's a reason—a very good one, as it turns out—why the landlord doesn't seem too worried about collecting the rent.

For minutes footsteps had been audible as someone had been running up and down the thinly carpeted stairs below, in high heels by the sound of it, and now a man's shrill, demanding voice could be heard arguing at well above the normal conversational level, though not loud enough to be clearly understood. A woman snarled back in a language that, if it was English, was so heavily accented as to be equally incomprehensible.

Things aren't a whole lot easier for the man who lives in fear of Simon Clark's stretch of Langthwaite Road. He just doesn't seem able to grasp the connection between his friend's guitar and all the deaths the road has chalked up over the years…and so he doesn't see the danger of walking that lonely piece of blacktop on a dark evening…

"It's funny isn't it? The decision you make in the next ten minutes could result in you dying. Doesn't have to be a big LIFE or DEATH decision. You might choose to take a bath. You slip on the soap, break your neck. You might decide to fix the downspout on the guttering. Only you fall off the bloody ladder. In our case it was the walk."

And then there's the old woman in Tim Lebbon's strangely familiar yet somewhat alien valley who fights against a succession of strangers who travel from the post-apocalyptic land beyond the mountains in an effort to get her to return…at first, pleadingly and later, decidedly more determined. Here comes the first one now…

She'd spotted him almost half an hour before. A smudge on the ridge surrounding the valley, an imperfection to the skyline that she'd noticed instantly, so familiar was she with the horizon. He disappeared for a while, and she hoped that he'd turned around and gone back. But then, heading down the dusty yellow road that still connected her with the outside—a useless vein, an artery carrying nothing that could give life—she saw movement.

And finally, there's the luckless family in Mark Morris's fine short novel who discover a series of strange stumps in the back garden of the house they moved into just a few days ago…odd wooden sculptures, either natural or hand-carved (nobody really knows), on whose surfaces shadows and sunlight seem to vie for prominence:

Here, for example, was a rudimentary face, the mouth gaping open as if struggling for air; here was a foetus in a womb; here a squatting, simian figure.

So, here are mysteries and strangeness, menace and dread, and things you can see going wrong or slightly-off-kilter…but you just don't seem to be able to do anything about them. And that's a shame because, as a direct result for all of our characters here, there'll be tears before bedtime. Then, of course, there's just the night and the darkness and the silence to look forward to.

Now…whose *was* that hand you were holding?

Peter Crowther
Harrogate, England
January 2004

So Long Gerry

Terry Lamsley

— ONE —

THE MAN FROM the flat agency was standing in the hallway, staring out through the open door at the withered leaves swirling by in the bitter wind. It was only ten in the morning but he seemed weary, as though he'd been on the go all night. Dark suited and gaunt, he looked like an undertaker who had undertaken too much. As Gerry approached him he flicked away a half-smoked cigarette and grunted, "Mr. Royal?"

Gerry nodded. "I'm a bit late," he acknowledged. He glanced up at the building in front of him. It didn't look at all promising. Like most property in the area it showed depressing signs of twenty or more years of neglect. "I had a lot of trouble finding this place. Somehow kept missing the street. Sorry."

Without giving any sign that he accepted this apology the man gave Gerry a solemn look then turned and led the way up to the second floor. He climbed the stairs awkwardly, as though knees were stiff or his feet hurt. Even so, Gerry had to make an effort to keep up with him. The man was in a hurry.

They came to a halt outside a yellow painted door. "This is it," the agent said, dipping his hand into a plastic bag full of keys. "Number Eleven."

When the agent got the door open he wafted Gerry into the flat with a wave of his hand and stepped back, as if reluctant to enter himself.

Gerry couldn't believe his luck. The place was habitable. Large living room, bedroom, tiny spare room for overnight guests, and a decent sized kitchen. The furniture was okay, though there wasn't much of it. A drop-leaf table would serve as a desk to work on, and there were shelves on one of the walls for his books. He wandered about, poking the big double bed to test it for comfort, dropping experimentally into one of two armchairs, and inspecting the kitchen, trying not to let his excitement show in case the rent went up. At last, he went to the living room window and looked out.

"Not much of a view," he said.

Behind him, the agent agreed. "And the television needs attention, I believe," he added. "It's always going wrong."

"How about a new one, then?"

The man shook his head in a way that made it clear that was out of the question. "I'll try to get someone to fix it," he said. "Shared bathroom across the passage outside and the gas is metered. The rent covers heating and lighting." His rather refined way of speaking and dry, disinterested tone made him sound preoccupied and dismissive of everything. A man who's come down in the world, Gerry decided.

"And the rent is how much?" he asked. He knew, but wanted to hear it again for confirmation.

The man quoted the amazingly low sum. During the last couple of days Gerry had seen worse flats for more than twice that amount, and in more sordid and less convenient parts of the city.

"That seems okay," he admitted. "I'll take it."

"One week's rent in advance and the rest paid weekly," the agent said. "In cash."

"That's unusual nowadays, isn't it?"

"Not round here it isn't."

"Well, it suits me, anyway."

The agent ventured a little way into the room and gave the impression he was determined to go no further. He looked more than tired now; he appeared worn out, as though the climb upstairs had used up the last of his energy. Gerry asked him if he was alright.

The man shrugged, implying it was none of Gerry's business, and looked pointedly at his watch. "I'm fine. Except that I've got to be somewhere else five minutes ago," he said.

"Always on the go, eh?"

"I never stop," the man agreed. "You'll have to sign these," he added, handing over a couple of densely printed forms. "The tenancy agreement."

Gerry wrote his name on the sheets of paper after giving them a cursory inspection, then pulled out his wallet and laid a few notes on the table. While the man laboriously made out a receipt, Gerry had another look round the flat and became more aware of something he had only half-noticed before. There were a number of personal items lying about; left, presumably, by a previous occupant. A woman, that must have been, because there were tights draped over a radiator and blouses and a couple of skirts on plastic hangers in the wardrobe in the bedroom. There were other things too—piles of newspapers and magazines, a scatter of inexpensive cosmetics and make-up equipment on the seat of a chair, and dirty mugs, wine glasses and plates on most horizontal surfaces, including the floor.

The agent seemed relieved when he had secured the rent. He even smiled slightly. "Well, good luck to you, then," he said, as though Gerry was about to set out on a perilous journey. "Don't hesitate to contact our office if there are any problems."

Gerry listened as the agent's footsteps clicked down the stairs, then, when all was silent, threw himself down on his back on the bed and laughed with relief. His search for accommodation, that had been beginning to get him down because the flats he had viewed had been so uniformly bloody awful and depressing, was over. The place he'd found was ideal for study, and the University buildings were only ten minutes away! His savings would just about stretch the distance though he would probably still have to find a part-time job somewhere a few evenings a week to put butter on his bread. But if he was careful he could survive the course. He'd scrape through. It was worth putting up with a spell of poverty if, in two years time, he ended up with the qualifications he so badly needed.

He remembered noticing there were some scraps of food left in the cupboard in the kitchen. After locating coffee and sugar, he boiled water in a pan, swilled out a mug, and made a drink.

He held the steaming mug up to an invisible crowd of admirers and friends, said, "Cheers," and tried to take a sip, but the coffee was too hot to drink.

Too impatient to wait and let it cool, he left it and went out to fetch his belongings.

«‹——››»

Less than an hour later he returned from the wretched bed-and-breakfast dump he'd been staying at since he had arrived in the city. He threw his bag of overnight luggage down on the floor and, since his cellphone was flat, went back out at once to phone the friend who had agreed to bring the rest of his things down when he had established himself somewhere suitable. He could tell Alister thought he was exaggerating or drunk when he described his new home.

"It's so bloody *central*," he said when he'd given his address. "No bus journey to the University, so that's a big saving. It's close to a few shops and restaurants, yet *out of it*, if you know what I mean. And quiet. A backwater, but surrounded by some of the main streets."

"I'll believe it when I see it," Alister said, dour as ever.

"Stay over when you come up on Saturday with my stuff."

"I'm not used to roughing it these days."

"Come on. We'll make a night of it."

"And you'll show me the bright lights? You sound like the sophisticated city dweller already, and you've only just got there."

"Piss off, Alister. We'll paint the town."

"Okay. I can't refuse your tempting offer."

"My change has run out. See you then."

"Sure. Saturday afternoon. Early."

Still elated, Gerry went into a supermarket for basic provisions then hurried back to his flat,

Something about the atmosphere of the place when he had first walked in had made him think it had been untenanted for quite a while. The air had been stale and muzzy and dead. It was too cold outside to open a window, but the air cleared when he gave it a few squirts from a *pot-pourri* scented freshener. He picked up some of the plastic shopping bags that were lying about and stuffed the most-likely-to-be-tripped-over heaps of papers and periodicals into them, along with the half a dozen or so pairs of snagged tights and other ruined clothes, dumped the lot next to an over-full and stinking bin at the back of the house, then gathered up all the dirty crockery and left it to soak in the sink.

It wasn't until he started to take the articles of clothing out of the wardrobe that he began to wonder who had owned them and why they had been left behind. It was cheap stuff—the sort of thing Joanne, his erstwhile girlfriend, wouldn't have been seen dead in—not at all sophisticated, but recently fashionable in a teeny, girly sort of way. The two skirts were tiny, and would have been tight on a pair of walking sticks, the handful of blouses and t-shirts were too colourful for his taste, but nothing showed much sign of wear. Indeed, it all looked quite new. Far too good to leave behind, or, he decided, to throw away.

Then it occurred to him that perhaps the owner intended coming back for her things. Perhaps she just hadn't been able to take all her possessions away at once, as he had not been able to bring all his belongings with him from home, and, for some reason, she had not yet gotten round to collect them. In which case, he ought to hang on to everything for a while. He began folding up and bagging the abandoned items of clothing more carefully then, wondering again, as he did so, about the identity of their owner.

His thoughts were interrupted by a series of bangs and shrieks from the corridor outside his room, that shattered his peace and made him start up from the floor where he had been kneeling. Something pressed against the flat door, that he had not bothered to shut properly, forcing it open. The door swung towards him slowly, and he could hear scraping noises behind it. He went to investigate, and saw a stocky, hard-faced child, a boy with a slightly wrinkled face that made it difficult to guess his age, staring up at him from the platform of a shiny metal scooter it was attempting to drive into the room. The vehicle had a shrill electric bell on the handlebar that the child started ringing urgently.

When he got over his surprise Gerry said. "I'm sorry, but you can't come in here. It's private." He tried to make his voice jolly and avuncular, but he realised he sounded harsh and heavy. He wasn't used to talking to anyone under the age of twenty-five. There were no children in his family.

The boy's reaction surprised him. He gave Gerry a contemptuous, belligerent look and tried to manoeuvre the scooter further forward into the room. "No, no," Gerry said, blocking the gap with his legs. "This is *my* flat." He felt foolish, especially when another, similarly constituted child, drawn by the sound of his voice, appeared from somewhere and called out, "Mom, there's a man shouting at Andy."

A woman yelled back, "Alright Bobby. I'll be out in a moment."

The first child took this as a signal that it was okay to attempt another, deeper intrusion into Gerry's territory. Gerry continued to resist.

"Don't you push Andy," the second child said, when Gerry stooped and gently put his hand on the front of the older child's toy to curb its progress. "You leave him alone."

"Mom," Andy called out dolefully, as though he had to put up with a lot of this sort of thing, "Come and see. Someone's trying to steal my scooter."

Gerry let go of the toy, stood up, and sighed.

"Ring your bell at him again, Andy," the other boy suggested, at the top of his voice. "Make him get out of the way."

A woman with short, dyed black hair, dressed in black jeans and a extra-large purple sweatshirt, came out of a door on the other side of the corridor and marched towards the disputants. She looked Gerry up and down as though she was astonished to see him there, wiped sweat from her forehead with the butt of her hand, then pulled a disapproving face at the boys. "What *do* you two think you're doing?" she demanded. "Leave the man alone and come here. *At once.*"

Both children looked outraged, the victims of terrible injustice, but they did as they were told. They went and stood behind the woman, as though they thought they might need her protection from the terrible man, and sulked.

"I've just moved in," Gerry said, emerging from his room. "A couple of hours ago."

"I'm sorry the boy's have been troubling you. I didn't know that flat was taken."

"It's okay. I shouldn't have left my door open."

"I just brought them back from their daily outing in the back garden, a bit of exercise, you know, and there's nowhere else for them to play in the fresh air at home. You can't let kids outdoors nowadays and not keep an eye on them. The boys get fed up, hanging around inside all the time."

"It must be frustrating for them."

"For all of us."

"I can imagine."

The woman stepped forward and held out her hand. "Cynthia Bendix," she said. "Some people call me Cyn but I don't like it."

"Okay. I'll try to remember." Gerry grasped her hot, slightly greasy fingers, and told her his name.

"Alone are you?" the woman asked, staring beyond him into his rooms.

"You mean, in the flat?"

"Well, it is a big place."

"Well, yes; I guess it is. But no, there's just me."

"And what do you do for a living, Gerry?" the woman asked bluntly. Gerry was already feeling a little overwhelmed by her.

"Nothing. At the moment, I mean. I'm going to be a student."

"You look old for that."

"I started College when I left school, but dropped out because I had…financial problems. Now I'm trying again. I'm a *mature* student, Mrs. Bendix," Gerry explained, feeling his store of politeness might soon run out if the woman didn't ease up.

"Not too mature, by the look of you," she said, giving Gerry a sharp stare and a disconcerting smile. From her looks Gerry reckoned he and she were about the same age. Or so it appeared but something about her manner made her seem older. "And don't call me by my surname, please," the woman continued. "I don't like to be reminded of the Bendix side of things. He's out of my life for good, thank God."

"Ah," was all Gerry could think to say in response to that information.

"People say the kids of a single parent are disadvantaged, but I look after my boys. They're good kids."

Gerry looked at them doubtfully, and bit his lip.

"They want for nothing, Gerry, I see to that, in spite of the fact the bastard pays me nothing."

By which Gerry assumed she meant her ex had done a runner. He thought he could understand why.

Andy and Bobby were getting restless. Andy asked his mother to tell the man to let him have his scooter back. It was leaning against the frame of Gerry's door. Gerry picked it up and handed it over to its owner, who fled away on it down the corridor, furiously ringing its bell. Cynthia Bendix gathered up other toys her sons had been playing with, then asked Gerry if he needed any help moving in. He was appalled by the idea of allowing this pushy woman to invade his new domain, but touched by the offer.

"It's good of you, but I've hardly anything to unpack. I've just got to finish clearing the place up."

"Well, that shouldn't take long. I expect the last tenant left the place in good order. She was obsessive about tidiness. I couldn't stand her, nor she me. She invited me in once, and that was enough. I kept away then. Neurotic old cow."

"You mean the last person to occupy my flat was elderly?"

Mrs. Bendix pursed her lips, frowned slightly, and nodded.

"How old?"

"Oh, I don't know." She seemed to be finding it hard to remember. It was the first time Gerry had caught his neighbour in any kind of uncertainty. "*Well* into middle age. Know what I mean? Past it."

"Did she have a daughter living with her?"

"No. Why?"

"Because there are personal effects that must have belonged to a young woman lying about. Clothes and things."

Cynthia Bendix gave a stiff smile and shook her head. "Couldn't be hers. She used to dress beyond her years, if anything. Like a bloody granny."

"How long ago did she move out?"

"Oh, I don't know. I'm not good with time. A year, is it, since I saw her? Could be more. Could be a lot more."

"And it's been empty ever since?"

"I expect the boys would have told me if anyone new turned up. They don't miss much."

"I noticed a NO VACANCIES sign on the front door that looked as though it had been there a long time."

Mrs. Bendix agreed. "Ages."

"I assumed it had just been nailed up there and forgotten about, but maybe not. That's strange. People who own these places usually like to screw as much money as possible from them."

"There are enquiries about flats from time to time—a few people come knocking at the front door on the off-chance, I suppose—but I just tell them to contact the agency." Mrs. Bendix gave a smile of grim satisfaction. "Everything goes through the agency."

"That's where I found out about it."

"The agency? Oh, really. Well, it sounds as though somebody there has slipped up, then, letting you in."

"The man who showed me round seemed pleased enough to take my money."

"Oh, did he? And who was that then? What did he look like?"

Gerry described the over-stretched undertaker.

"*Him,*" said Mrs. Bendix. "There'll be ructions about that. Nobody there knows better than him what the situation here is. He's the senior member. He should be setting an example. All agency staff are under instructions to turn a blind eye to this place; to leave us alone."

Gerry tried to wipe a smile from his face, or hide it, with the back of his hand. "Why is that, for heaven's sake? That's their job, to fill the flats. Someone must have to get enough money out of this building to keep it maintained, if nothing else. That can't come cheap, a place this size."

"Do you think so? Even though it's always caused them a lot of trouble, one way and another, particularly with the electrics, it looks after itself pretty well, this old building. It endures. And it's settled. Well established, if you know what I mean?"

Gerry wasn't sure he did, really, but he wasn't in the mood to pursue the matter further. He said, "It seems I've been even luckier than I thought then, getting rooms here."

"I don't know about that," the woman said. "If he let you in then you must be here to stay I suppose but, as I said, I think someone's made a mistake. But there always have been plenty of them. We'll just have to wait and see."

Andy and Bobby started punching each other's heads.

"It's my turn, bugger," Bobby screamed. "You've had the scooter *all morning*. I want a go."

"*What* did you say, Bobby?" Cynthia hissed.

"Bugger—he said bugger," Andy confirmed.

"Go into your room and get into bed. I won't have you using that sort of language."

Gerry thought the boys might put up some opposition, but he was wrong. They trudged back into their flat meekly enough.

"Don't let the boys trouble you again, Gerry," their mother said. Her tone made the request sound like a challenge. She gave Gerry a brisk, valedictory nod and vanished with her brood, shutting the door behind her.

Gerry could still hear the muffled rumble of Mrs. Bendix's parental disapproval in the distance, but peace of a kind had returned and he was thankful for that. He guessed it probably wouldn't last long.

«« —— »»

When he started to stash away the few things of his own he had brought with him, Gerry found the chest of drawers in the bedroom was not empty, as he'd expected. The top two drawers contained articles of skimpy, grubby looking underwear, and more torn tights; the sort of thing that might well have been left behind on purpose; but the deepest, at the bottom of the set, was half full of more almost new articles of clothing under which were half a dozen pairs of good shoes. So why didn't their owner take them with her?

He was trying to build up a picture of the woman in his mind now, from the rather impersonal evidence of her existence he had discovered, but wasn't getting very far. He could reasonably speculate a little about her life style, but nothing he had found gave him a clue to her appearance, or told him much about what sort of person she was. He thought she was almost certainly young, but not even that was guaranteed. He knew that mutton often dressed as lamb.

Late in the afternoon he heard the Bendix trio leave their flat and the building. The front door slammed behind them. Less than ten minutes later, someone started rattling the letter box and ringing the bell down below. Gerry, spooning up soup he'd just heated, was reluctant to go down to attend to the situation himself, sure the visitor could not have come to see him. He took his time finishing the snack, then, because the would-be caller was still audibly and irritatingly active, his curiosity got the better of the slight lethargy that had come over him, and he went down to see who was there.

It was a skinny, grey-faced diminutive man in a padded leather jacket, ripped jeans and motor-cycle boots. The top, sides and back of his head were almost bald, but a few long hairs had been allowed to sprout over his ears and the back of his neck, and two sparse locks curled down, one over each eye, at the front. Two bright silk scarves were tied loosely round his throat, and a luminous green plastic bone had been stuck through his nose. His appearance was merely ludicrous until he moved and spoke. Then Gerry realised the man was some kind of desperado, a maniac even.

"Maggie," he said, staring wildly past Gerry into the house and twisting his head round slowly, in an exaggerated way. "I want to see Maggie. *Got* to see her." He slapped his hands together and rubbed them energetically, then made two fists of them. He ducked his head, and waved his fists about in front of his face in a way that Gerry assumed was meant to be threatening.

"I don't know her," Gerry explained. "If she lives here, she must be out, or she'd have answered the door."

"Maggie *never* answers the door," the man said, as though that was one of her finest qualities. He suddenly stowed his hands away in his jacket and hunched his shoulders. "Look, I got to see her. Don't be the hard man. Get out of the way. Let me in."

To make it clear he wasn't trying to keep this possibly dangerous man out Gerry stepped aside at once. The visitor bounded past him and, even though his legs were well short of the average length and appeared to be bent or bowed, ran up the stairs two at a time. Gerry heard him thumping a door on the first floor, or maybe kicking it, and shouting, "Maggie. It's me. I'm back. Let me in."

This sort of thing went on for some time as Gerry climbed the stairs, until he was sure Maggie, whoever she was, was off the premises, if, indeed, she did live there. Just when he was thinking her would-be guest was sure to batter the door down, he heard a low female voice call out, and the man yelled in response.

"I *knew* you were there Maggie," he shouted, so Gerry would hear. "Crazy bastard who let me in said you didn't live here. Wouldn't let me through the door."

The woman said something, then the pair of them must have gone into her room, because Gerry heard no more.

He went back up to his own flat slowly, wondering now about the nature of the house he had moved into. In his living room again, to pass the time, he turned on the television, and found everyone on it had green faces. There were no reds anywhere. And the sound was awful. He guessed he was watching some kind of discussion programme but couldn't understand a word anyone said. Well, the agent had warned him about that.

He'd brought a couple of his thinnest, lightest text books with him, dutifully intending to look through them to prepare himself for the commencement of his course. He opened one at the first chapter and started to read. Not for long though. The Bendix family returned, and the boys started bounding backwards and forwards along the passage outside his room again. From the sound of it, they were fighting with iron chains and dustbin lids.

«« — »»

Signing on at college on Tuesday morning, and finding his way around that shambolic institution during the next few days, was more complicated and frustrating than Gerry had anticipated, and kept him out of his flat during most daylight hours.

The evenings were hard, though. He wanted to save as much as possible from the weekly allowance he had calculated out for himself, so he could treat Alister to a drink when he arrived, and essential purchases at the local supermarket had already made a big hole in that sum. Meanwhile going out was not an option as the idea of drifting about unfamiliar streets alone did not appeal, so he hung about listlessly in his room, waiting to feel tired enough to go to bed. From time to time, quite frequently, in fact, he heard people at the front door, but he made no effort to let them in. He'd discovered that if he waited long enough someone else always did. He had a vision of the other tenants, and he had no idea how many of them there were, sitting tight and still in their separate rooms, waiting to see who among them would crack first. The woman on the floor below seemed to have most visitors, as far as he could judge, and they came and went at all hours of the night. Once, he was woken at three in the morning by the clatter of boots on the first flight of stairs and someone shouting to gain entry. The biker back, he guessed, or someone like him. He became seriously worried about what kind of establishment he'd moved into.

On the Friday evening, on his way to the bathroom, he passed the Bendix flat when the door was open. He paused and sneaked a sideways look inside at the sparsely furnished, disordered interior. The two boys were playing under a table with a racing-car track they had extended out onto the corridor. As he carefully stepped over this, one of them spotted him. A harsh little voice said, "That man's back, mom. He's outside the door."

"What do you want?" the other one demanded. "You can't come in."

Mrs. Bendix appeared at the door at once. She gave Gerry a sharp-eyed but weary smile. "Ignore them," she suggested. "They don't mean it."

Not easy, and not true, Gerry thought, but he said nothing.

"You settling in okay then?" the woman asked, after a short but awkward silence.

Gerry took the opportunity to ask where the cleaning materials and carpet sweeper were. His copy of the tenancy agreement he had signed told him he had use of a selection of such stuff but so far he had not been able to locate it. The woman showed him where it was hidden, in a cupboard under the first floor stairs.

"We keep it locked," she said. "People steal anything. You should have been given a key."

"Got it here."

He opened the door and peered inside the cupboard. A couple of plastic buckets, many piles of dusty, faded rags, some boxes of empty bottles, and a broom and mop had been stowed untidily away inside, along with a twenty-year-old carpet sweeper. Gerry reached out for the latter item.

"The Hoover's useless," Mrs. Bendix said. "If you need to use one, you can borrow mine."

He took up this offer. She dragged her sweeper out of the flat, pushed it into his rooms, plugged it in, and showed him how to operate it. The thing moaned like a sleeping dragon, and tugged hungrily at his rugs and carpets. When she'd finished her demonstration she stared speculatively around Gerry's flat. Her eyes darted about like lasers, missing nothing. It occurred to Gerry that perhaps she had offered to lend him the Hoover just to get a chance to give his room the once-over. "You've not got much stuff," she observed. "This place is too big for you. You could do with somewhere smaller and snugger."

"There's more to come," Gerry said. From what he had seen, her flat was considerably smaller than his. "You find it cramped in your place, with the two boys, I expect," he added sympathetically.

She dismissed this suggestion. "Ah, they don't take up much space. I don't let them. I keep them in hand."

Gerry decided to try to pick her brain while he had the opportunity, and asked her who else lived in the building. "I've not met anyone yet, but I've heard them often enough," he explained. "People on the stairs, I mean, coming and going."

"There's only a few occupied flats besides ours, as far as I know," Mrs. Bendix said. "I expect the empty ones are not fit to live in. Anyhow, I don't have much to do with the people who live here. I keep myself to myself. I don't stick my nose in."

"The flat below mine gets lots of visitors. A girl lives there, or a woman. I've heard her voice. Her name's Maggie, I think."

"Maggie Sumpter. Poor kid. She's had it hard."

"Really?"

"Like the rest of us, she got stranded here."

"How's that?"

"She's a single parent, like me. Lives there with her baby, but she daren't take it out of the building."

"Why not, for God's sake?"

"The Social are looking for her. Or so she says. She's hiding out. She told me they tried to take her kid away and put it with foster parents. Said Maggie was neglecting the child."

"Was she?"

"I expect so. She's no money coming in, and she's got bad habits that must cost her plenty. How did they expect her to manage, and keep the kid properly, on Benefits? She did the best she could."

"What sort of 'bad habits'?" Gerry asked uneasily.

"The usual things. She drinks and smokes stuff. Uses a little speed occasionally I expect, from the look of her. The kind of life she leads, cooped-up all the time, who wouldn't?"

Gerry remained thoughtfully silent for a couple of seconds, then said, "So what *does* she live on, then? She can't be getting anything at all from the Government, under the circumstances."

"She's still got friends. Plenty of them, as you said. I expect they keep her supplied."

Gerry thought about the biker. "It doesn't sound too good a life for the kid," he objected.

Mrs. Bendix curled her lip. "Not perfect," she admitted. "But a child is better off with its mother. Don't you agree?"

"I never really thought about it," Gerry said doubtfully.

"Take my word for it. I know. Let me have the sweeper back as soon as you've finished," she added, making for the door, leaving him to it. The boys were kicking up a row outside somewhere and one of them was calling out for her.

Gerry realised he felt a need to make some kind of impression on Cynthia Bendix, something he was sure he had failed to do so far. He suspected she thought he was a dull wimp, and had come to this conclusion on their first meeting, when, he had to admit, he had been somewhat over-awed by her. But she had been kind, helpful even, since. She'd taken time out to talk to him, so obviously didn't despise him utterly. It was up to him now to make the running if any friendship were to develop between them. It occurred to him that he certainly would not want her as an enemy.

He followed her out of the door.

The boys were rolling on the floor nearby, pulling each other's hair and attempting to knee each other in the groin. They resembled two electronic toys locked in combat. Their tussle had an unrelenting look, as though they'd been at it for years, or even decades. Their mother spoke to them once firmly, without raising her voice. They separated, jerked to their feet, and glowered at Gerry as though he had insulted them. Andy had a cut over his left eye. Blood trickled down from this injury and dripped onto his Wacky Warlords T-shirt.

Gerry found some fairly clean tissues in his pocket, and offered them to Andy to staunch the wound. Andy stepped back and shook his head violently, spraying droplets of blood on either side. Some of them landed on Gerry's outstretched hand. He transferred the tissue to his other hand to mop them up.

Andy gave him a defiant, contemptuous look. The blood flowed into his eyes now, but he didn't blink.

Gerry said, "That looks bad. Does it hurt?" The boy's expression didn't change. He shook his head again, and said nothing.

"He could need stitches" Gerry said to the woman behind him. "Is there a hospital nearby with an Emergency Unit?"

Mrs. Bendix's hard eyes crinkled at the edges. She looked amused.

"Things like that happen to kids all the time. Boys have to get used to taking a few bumps. Weren't you the same once?"

"I can't remember that far back, but I don't think so. I used to hate getting into fights."

"You have any brothers and sisters?"

Gerry admitted not.

"Huh, well, there you are then," she said, with what Gerry felt was quite unnecessary emphasis. "Anyway, my kids aren't coddled; they have to get used to a bit of rough and tumble. I don't want them to grow up soft."

The implication could not have been more obvious. Gerry *was* soft.

He'd had enough of Mrs. Bendix and her warlike family, for the time being at least. He wanted to get back to his room and lock himself in.

Nothing was stopping him from doing that so, after making another feeble protestation about the need for medical attention for Andy's cut, which was ignored by the three of them, he withdrew.

Back home again, he swept the rest of his carpets furiously. When he returned the machine an hour later, Mrs. Bendix took it in without comment, and shut the door in his face.

– TWO –

"It's *really good* to see you, Alister," Gerry said.

Alister looked askance at his friend's enthusiastic greeting. "That good?"

"Christ, yes. A familiar face at last. It's a lonely life, being a student."

"I've done my time, remember," Alister said, hauling a box of his friend's possessions out of the spacious boot of his shiny new car. "It wasn't so bad."

"You were younger, the same age as the others in your year. They seem like kids to me, the ones I've met so far, and they treat me like a grey-bearded oldie."

"Just your imagination."

"No, really. I'm not one of their tribe."

"You're not one of anybody's tribe, Gerry. That's your problem. How far up do we have to take this stuff?"

"Top floor."

"I thought it would be."

It didn't take long to transfer all Gerry's worldly goods from the car to the flat—about twenty minutes.

Gerry dutifully set about putting his belongings away in cupboards and drawers. He said, "Plug the CD in will you, Al? There's too much silence round here sometimes in the daytime. More than I can stand. Let's have some music."

Alister obediently fiddled with the machine for a few minutes, then swore. "Something's wrong," he said. "It keeps ejecting the disc."

"What?"

"See for yourself."

Gerry bent forward over the player and pushed the remote button. The disc drawer slid shut then gaped opened at once, as though the CD had been a bitter taste in its mouth. After getting the same result three times with different discs, Gerry said, "Bastard thing," in a tone of disgusted incredulity.

"Try the radio. FM should be okay."

Gerry did, but it wasn't okay. There was nothing anywhere on the dial, not even static.

"It's just out of guarantee, too."

"Check that the plug is in properly."

"I just did. It's fine. And I used the socket for a carpet sweeper the other day."

Alister said, "Take it easy. Maybe we can fix it."

Gerry shook his head gloomily. "You don't know any more about these things than I do, and I know nothing."

Surprised and alarmed at the extent of his friend depressive reaction to this fairly minor misfortune, Alister suggested they took a break.

"You owe me drink. I didn't stop for lunch on the way here. I need refuelling."

Making an obvious effort to lighten up, Gerry apologised for neglecting his friend's needs, and led him out of the building. On the way downstairs they met the Bendix family coming up. The two boys, ahead of their mother, were climbing shoulder to shoulder, blocking the stairs. When they saw the two men descending towards them they seemed to accelerate a little and lowered their heads, as though they were considering the possibility of making a charge. Gerry held back at the sight of them, but Alister, by nature more belligerent, didn't slacken his own steady pace. If Mrs. Dexter noticed that there could be a collision in the offing, she gave no sign. Weighed down with heavy shopping bags, straining with effort, she was probably hardly aware of her surroundings. A sixth sense, or some aspect of her maternal instinct must have alerted her to what was about to happen, however, because she suddenly stopped in her tracks, glared up ahead of her and barked, "Bobby. Andy. Stop. What are you doing?"

Too late. Alister, almost on top of the boys, astonished that they had not moved aside to let him pass, grabbed each by a shoulder, forced them apart, and stepped between them. Whereupon Andy, loudly calling for his brother's assistance, squirmed forward and round and pushed Alister from behind, causing him to stumble and almost fall against Mrs. Dexter, who would probably have tumbled back herself had it not been for the anchoring effect of the weighty bags hanging from her arms.

She shouted at the boys again as she and Alister recovered their equilibrium—a wordless cry that froze them stiff for a moment. Then they continued on their way, passing Gerry in single file without looking at him. He saw they both had smug smiles on their faces and were very bright-eyed.

Mrs. Dexter apologised to Alister for their behaviour, but he was in no mood to listen. He stared for a moment into her face, as though transfixed, glowered beyond her at the boys, then stepped away, heading for the front door. Outside he waited for his anger to subside and for Gerry to join him.

Minutes later, after the two men had stretched their legs some way in silence, Alister said, "What the fuck was that about, then?"

"My neighbours," Gerry explained. "In the flat across the corridor." When he got no response, he added, "She's a single parent."

After another brief period of silence Alister said, "She's a good looking woman."

"You think so?"

"Not your type?"

"I hadn't thought of her in that way."

"Then she isn't."

"She's yours, though?"

Alister grunted. "You know me," implying his taste was wide. He'd had a tangled string of relationships with a remarkably various range of women in the past, before he had married five years ago. The fact that he seemed happy with his wife and three daughters had not blinded his wandering eye, however, and he kept up at least the pretence of being a connoisseur of the other sex. "Pity about those kids though."

"Hard-faced little brats."

"Hard's the word. And not just their faces. Their arms felt like solid muscle when I grabbed them to make them get out of my way. Do you think they do bodybuilding exercises?"

"Wouldn't be surprised."

"I wonder what she feeds them on?"

"No sweets or crisps or anything like that. They're not the sort of children you see with lollipop sticks jutting out of their mouths. In fact I've never seen them eat anything," Gerry admitted.

"You a friend of the family, then?"

"No. But I do see quite a lot of them. Too much. She lets them run pretty wild. Leaves the door open most of the time so they can go in and out when they like. Almost every time I come out of my room, there they are, hanging about somewhere near by."

"A lack of discipline there, then?"

"I wouldn't say that. They come to heel when she wants them to. They take notice of her quickly enough when she calls them to order, though I get the impression they're sometimes reluctant to do so. A couple of times I had a funny feeling about them..."

Gerry paused because they had come to a pub called *The Bricklayer's Arms* and Alister had marched in without consulting him. Inside the long, narrow bar a couple of dozen men and a few women, sitting in ones and twos, were staring up at a large television set high on the wall, watching a boxing match. The sound was loud and the picture quality poor, but that didn't matter because the fight had taken place two days previously and anyone with the slightest interest in the sport knew the result. The customers were watching the screen out of habit, because it was there; because that was what they did at home.

Alister ordered two pints of the best bitter, and got a lizard's sneer from the landlord. "That's the only kind we sell," he said; satirically, as it turned out.

The beer was over-hopped and thin, and not what the two men were used to. Nevertheless, after staring at the screen in stunned silence for a while, they smiled ruefully at each other and drank deeply.

"You were saying about a feeling you had about those kids," Alister reminded Gerry, his voice high as he tried to speak above the near hysterical fight commentary.

"Yeah, well, it's silly really, but it occurred to me that she puts them out in the same way people let out guard dogs. To patrol the area, if you see what I mean?"

Alister scratched the side of his nose ruminatively.

"It's not that she's negligent, and can't be bothered with them," Gerry continued. "Not at all. She keeps an eye on them and an ear open. But a couple of times I've wondered if she encourages them to roam so she gets to know what's going on in the rest of the building."

"Why should she want to do that?"

"Ah," Gerry shook his head. "I don't know."

"She's scared of something?"

"Could be. But the boys certainly aren't. They're fearless. Don't give a fuck about anybody."

"I noticed."

"And you know, Al, there's something about the way they go about together that I've never seen in other kids. Sometimes their movements are synchronised, like highly trained soldiers. I could understand it if they were twins…"

"But they're not."

"And as you must have noticed, their faces have got that lived-in look. That worries me."

"That's a strange place you're staying at," Alister said ominously, implying wider peculiarities than those they had just discussed.

"You think so?"

"Felt it as soon as I walked through the door."

"Really? It seemed okay to me."

"Seemed?"

"I'm having doubts now."

"There's something there. The atmosphere: it's an uneasy place to be at."

"You're more sensitive to that kind of thing than I am."

Alister acknowledged this fact.

Gerry was getting tired of the subject. Possibly his flat, though convenient in many ways, was not all he had first thought it would crack up to be, but it was too late to do anything about that now and he had no intention of wasting time traipsing round in pursuit of something better. At that moment he wanted, badly needed, the forgetfulness that can be brought about by the easy enjoyment of simple pleasures and casual companionship. He gulped down the last drop of his thin beer and suggested they search out a better brew, in more salubrious surroundings. Alister readily agreed.

They failed to find either, but after a couple more drinks it didn't matter. They became less aware of where they were and of what they were pouring into themselves. Unseasonably early snow and restless crowds of clammy, loud-mouthed Saturday night revellers swirled around them as they trudged from one dismal, crowded pub to another. Alister professed himself disgusted with his friend for not reconnoitering the area beforehand to find some quieter quarter, but he was unable to conceal the fact that he was clearly getting a kick out of the 'sordid city slumming' as he described their peregrination. He seemed happiest in a garish little club where three dazed, topless girls pulled pints behind the bar while another, wearing nothing at all, squirmed around in a transparent plastic sack on an adjacent table. Ear-bleeding music slammed the air and the constant passage of people passing to and fro made it difficult to hang on to a drink. Alister gripped his glass like a hero and tried to make personal contact with one of the bar-girls, without success. "It was like trying to communicate with an alien life form," he protested, when his friend had finally managed to winkle him out of the place. "Their brains are not like ours, Gerry."

"That one's brains were fried," Gerry opined. "Did you see her eyes?"

"Beautiful, weren't they?"

"If you go for dead girls, Alister."

"They're my type too, pal," Alister said, and laughed when he saw his friend's expression. "Only kidding," he said.

"I think," he added more thoughtfully.

Somewhere, they bought an armful of tins of beer, something like they made back home, and a brown paper bag full of take-away Mexican food. When they realised they had no idea where they were, and failed to get credible directions from the drunks around them, they called a taxi to take them home. They must have been circling round on themselves all evening, because the journey took less than five minutes. After passing the building containing Gerry's new home and complaining that he couldn't even see it, the taxi driver insisted on dropping them off at the end of the street, a good way from the house, despite Alister's vigorous threats and objections from the back seat. To nip the ugly scene that seemed inevitable in the bud Gerry over-tipped the driver, who sped off instantly, just as Alister realised they had left the bag of food on the back seat.

"At least we've got the beer."

"There's nothing to eat in the flat," Gerry confessed.

"As it happens," Alister said, rather pompous in drink now, "as it *just so happens*, there's a bag of sandwiches in the car, that Mary got me from M & S before I set out. I've not touched them. They may have got a bit dry in there, up front near the heater, but we've plenty to moisten them with."

So they sat in Gerry's flat munching cheese and pickle sandwiches and glugging tins of 'Poacher's Pocket'. When he discovered it was surprisingly early, not yet eleven, Alister decided he was ready to go out and do it all again, or something very like it—perhaps a return visit to the dead girls?—but Gerry complained he was too tired.

Again, half-heartedly, Gerry tried to get the CD player working, to provide entertainment and diversion for the two of them. He found a knife in the kitchen, poked it under the plate at the back of the machine and gave it an experimental twist. When he saw the casing begin to crack he realised how drunk he was.

By then the evening's consumption was having a soporific effect on Alister, whose eyes and shoulders began to droop. Nevertheless, he became quite loquacious. The conversation turned anecdotal. Friends of a lifetime, the two men talked about school and teenage days together, and how awful life had been then. Alister, proud of his self-destructive streak, said he was surprised to be still alive. All those drugs and the drink! Gerry, who had never over-indulged in the consumption of poisonous substances, said he wasn't sure he wanted to be, things had not worked out anything like the way he'd planned and expected when they had both been young. Counting on his fingers he complained that Alister had a wife, three bright, happy children, one large new house with extensive gardens, two cars and a van, a thriving business employing nine people, two or more foreign holidays a year etc. etc; whereas he, Gerry—what had he got? He gazed listlessly round the room at the sum total of his possessions, and shook his head disconsolately.

Alister smiled in tipsy self-satisfaction. He'd heard this sort of thing before many times, and slipped easily into a patronising mode.

"It's your own fault, Gerry," he said. "You could have had it all. You were the clever one, I was the dunce, at University. If you hadn't screwed up and married a girl who was about as good for you as rat poison for breakfast, halfway through your second year, and dropped out of the course so you could earn money to keep her, you'd have flown far higher than I ever could have done. You were on the up elevator, and you had the exam results to prove it. Then, when you get rid of Ms. Wolfrin, or rather, she got rid of you, and you shacked up with your parents again, what do you do but take up with someone worse."

"Oh, come on Al…"

"You know it's true."

"It's all over between Joanne and me now," Gerry said, sounding as though it wasn't just his friend he was trying to convince.

"I should hope so. After how long was it?"

"Nearly four years."

"Shit, as long as that? Four years of hell."

Gerry reached for another tin of 'Poacher's'. "You exaggerate. It wasn't that bad."

Alister gave a snort that went wrong and nearly choked him. Later he shuddered and said, "Christ, it's getting cold in here!"

"The central heating goes off at midnight. I don't think whoever owns this place gets enough out of it to pay his bills. Has to economise."

"Economise! You're joking. Let's turn it on."

"Can't do that. Every radiator in the house works on a timer somewhere."

"We'll go and find the bloody thing and re-set it."

"Leave it, Al," Gerry said. "We can't go racketing about at this time."

"Why not? Someone is. What the hell is going on down there? Some sort of international skirmish."

For minutes footsteps had been audible as someone had been running up and down the thinly carpeted stairs below, in high heels by the sound of it, and now a man's shrill, demanding voice could be heard arguing at well above the normal conversational level, though not loud enough to be clearly understood. A woman snarled back in a language that, if it was English, was so heavily accented as to be equally incomprehensible.

"Most nights are like this," Gerry said. "There's usually comings and goings down there from about midnight. A girl in one of the flats gets a lot of late visitors."

Alister acted exaggerated interest. "So that's the way it is. So I wasn't wrong about this place. What's she like? I might go and call on her myself."

Gerry told him what Mrs. Bendix had revealed about Maggie Sumpter and mentioned the child she was hiding. The last piece of information in particular cooled Alister's ardour.

"The more I hear about this building and it's occupants, the less I like it," he said, and yawned hugely. "Don't know how you put up with it."

"Have to, don't I?" Gerry drawled. "After a few days flat hunting you learn to compromise. It's the same all over. Every city has somewhere like it. Lots of cheap, shitty apartments, where people don't want to live, but have to, because they can't afford anything better elsewhere. People like me, for instance," he added after a moment, with an edge of drunken self-pity. "They find themselves herded together, they hate their environment and get to hate each other and end up like that." He pointed a thumb over his shoulder, presumably at the people downstairs.

All the beer cans were empty and it looked as though the evening was over. Not so, however, because Alister produced a half full bottle of Cognac from his coat pocket and poured tall measures into a couple of mugs. Things deteriorated fast after that. Conversation became disjointed, oblique or, so the two men thought, witty and hilarious. Gerry fell into a doze first, sitting up in his chair, but Alister woke him at once to discuss his own sleeping accommodation.

"I don't know how the hell I'm going to sleep at all with that din going on downstairs," he complained, as Gerry lurched to his feet. An assortment of voices were screeching at each other on the floor below, and doors banged like cannon fire. "If they don't shut up soon, I'm going down to sort them out."

Gerry showed Alister the little spare room. "Shut yourself in here and you shouldn't hear a thing. Wha'd'y'think?" He was finding it increasingly hard to speak. He was much less used to drink than his friend.

Alister flung his expensive ultra-comfortable sleeping bag on the floor and kicked at one of the many plastic shopping bags containing the property of the previous occupant of the flat, that Gerry had stashed away there and almost forgotten about. "What's that?" he asked, prodding the softness with the toe of his shoe.

"Nothing special. Bits of old clothes, things like that."

"Okay if I use it as a pillow?"

"Course you can. Good idea."

Alister dropped to his knees and started crawling about, arranging his makeshift bedding.

Gerry left him to it, shut him in, and wormed his way into his own bed, falling instantly into a deep pit of sleep as he did so.

«« — »»

"What was that?"

Gerry found he was awake in the gloomy dark shouting the question to himself, or to one of the already half-forgotten creatures in the dreams he had been sentenced to as a punishment for his alcoholic over-indulgence.

He lay on his back, eyes wide open, staring up, until he realised there was more light than there should have been in the room, and elbowed himself into a sitting position so he could look around for its source. He saw at once that the door of the flat was half open. Illumination from the corridor beyond, where strip lighting burned uneconomically all night every night, partially lit the most distant corner of the room.

Burglars, he thought someone has broken into the room!

He had no doubt that the door had been closed earlier. He remembered locking it soon after he and Alister had returned from their pub-crawl. His recent experiences with the Bendix kids had made him security conscious.

He listened for the slightest sound of movement or breathing in the room, but all was silent. Even the disputatious night-hawks on the floors below had ended their quarrelling at last.

He swung his legs out of bed, stood up, crossed the room, and switched on the light. The first thing he noticed was that the door to Alister's room was also wide open, the light was on in there, and the room was unoccupied. Gerry's first thought was that some kind of struggle had taken place. The empty sleeping bag was in a sprawling heap, as though it had been spun round after it had been vacated, and the contents of some of the bags of female belongings were strewn wildly about. One bag was empty, the one Alister had used as a pillow, and it appeared that some attempt had been made to turn it inside out.

After checking that the kitchen and the rest of the apartment was empty, Gerry, still mussy and confused by drink—still drunk, in fact— blundered out into the corridor outside.

Alister was standing facing him a few feet from the door, dressed in his boxer shorts and a crumpled T-shirt. He was holding his hands on either side of the back of his head, scratching irritably at a bald spot that had started to appear there a some year earlier, just before his marriage.

"Al what's wrong?" Gerry thought his friend might have been in some kind of fight. "It's freezing out here. You'd better come back inside. Christ, you look rough."

Alister glanced at Gerry's face and laughed humourlessly. "Take a look in the mirror, pal," he said.

Back in the flat Alister went over to the door of the room where he'd been sleeping, peered in, growled discontentedly, and said, "Who turned on the light in here? You?"

"No. I was fast asleep. You must have woken me when you went outside."

"I'm sure I didn't switch the light on."

"What were you doing out on the corridor, anyway?"

"Trying to get away from her."

"Who?"

"The woman."

"In there? In your room?"

"Right."

"I don't think so." Gerry concealed a yawn behind his hand. His head felt terrible, and he wanted to get back to sleep, but he could see Alister was still in considerable distress, and wide awake with it. "Tell me about her, then," he said, trying to sound more interested than he felt.

After a few moments deliberation Alister said, "I woke up and knew at once there was someone with me in the room. Even before I saw her; before I'd even opened my eyes. When I did open them the light blinded me at first. Then I turned and saw *her*, sitting with her back to me on a chair close to the wall. She had a mirror hanging on a nail in front of her, and I could see her face reflected in it…"

Gerry said, "There's no chair in there. Not much room for one, either, if you were stretched out on the floor."

Alister gave him a haggard look and seemed unable to continue.

"Okay, Al, so there was a woman there, sitting on a chair. What was she like?"

"Like no one at all Gerry. She was faceless, or rather her face was a blank. Just an oval, tight-skinned blob, under a tangle of curly dark hair…

"I must have made some kind of noise, perhaps I called out, because she turned her head slightly, perhaps to see my reflection better in her mirror—except, of course, she had no eyes. Anyway, when she knew she had my attention, she put her hand up to her face, like any woman about to put make-up on would do, and that was what I assumed she *was* going to do, in spite of the fact there was nothing to make-up. No features.

"Well, what she did do, Gerry, was to make a face with her finger-tips, as though she was moulding clay. Very quickly, without hesitation, as though she knew exactly what to do because she'd done it many times before.

"The eyes came last, then she smiled. At first I think she was smiling in satisfaction at her own reflection, then, I'm sure, she was smiling at mine."

"How nice for both of you," Gerry said. "So she pulled a face at you." Was that funny? Probably not, he decided. Not kind, either. He was starting to feel sick now. "Then you woke up and ran out of the room to try to get away from your nightmare. It's those dead girls we saw, preying on your imagination. That's an unhealthy state of mind you're in. Well, under the circumstances, I don't blame you for waking me but please, for Christ's sake, let's go back to bed before we freeze, Al. This is not wise, what we're doing, standing here. The temperature outside is way below zero, it's snowing, let me remind you. I'm going to sleep right now—standing up if I have to. I can't help it."

"I'm not going back in that room. I'll sit in the armchair."

"For the rest of the night? Okay. Please yourself.'"

Gerry, in bed, started snoring immediately, as Alister moved a big easy chair round to face the little room he had occupied. He'd left the door open and the light burning so he could see what was going on in there.

Wrapped in his sleeping bag and occasionally taking sips from the now almost empty bottle of brandy he prepared himself to remain awake and on guard until daybreak, still some hours away.

— THREE —

IN THE EARLY MORNING Sunday silence Gerry returned to consciousness slowly and with reluctance. His waking thoughts were that the next day he had the first of the many lectures he had undertaken to attend and that he had done almost none of the background reading he had promised himself he would do to prepare for it. At the back of his mind all the time nowadays was the fear that he might have lost the knack of applying himself to study, that had once come so easy to him, and that he would not be able to keep up with the younger and probably keener minds of the other students in his group. Sweating under his extra blankets (the heating came on at 8am) he moaned to himself about the misery building up inside his aching head and tried to blot everything out by a return to sleep, which would not come.

Thirst drove him out of bed at last. In the kitchen he filled a glass with water, drank it, and repeated the procedure. After a pause, did it again. He went back to his bed and stretched out on top of it for half an hour until the urge to go to the toilet got him up on his feet again. He tried to move about the flat quietly, so as not to disturb Alister who he assumed was still asleep.

When, an hour or so later, he accidentally kicked an empty Cognac bottle noisily across the room and his friend had not so much as stirred, Gerry, feeling the need of company, went to the armchair that Alister had shifted the night before and tugged cautiously at the sleeping bag draped over it. Because of its position Gerry realised that Alister's legs should have been sticking out from under the lower part of it, but they weren't. And there was no bulk under the bag where the rest of Alister should have been. Gerry flicked the bag up and away.

No one there.

Puzzled, Gerry looked into the little room where Alister had tried to sleep. The light was still on in that almost empty space. The woman's clothing that had been scattered about previously had been put back into the shopping bags, which had been placed tidily together against the far wall. Other than that there was no evidence that Alister had ever been there.

Except for a mirror in a cheap frame hanging on the wall at about chest height from a rusty stump of nail, that Gerry had not noticed before, but that had figured, he remembered, in the nightmare or whatever it was that Alister had described to him in the middle of the night. The nail, far too big for the purpose, had split the plaster of the unpapered wall when it had been banged in. Pushing his face close to the mirror, Gerry peered into it, but immediately looked away from the liverish, slightly bloated image he saw there, and absentmindedly picked at the loose plaster around the nail. A triangular chunk fell away, the nail tipped forward, and the mirror slid down and off it towards the floor. Even under the enervating influence of a hangover, however, there was nothing wrong with Gerry's physical coordination and he caught the mirror, just, by the top of the frame. The dislodged nail tumbled and hit the floor with a loud, startling clang, then, as if in response to a signal, the light bulb hanging above Gerry's head flickered twice and blew with a barely audible click.

In near darkness, clutching the mirror to his chest, Gerry scuttled out into his living room.

It took just a few seconds for him to inspect every part of the flat. Alister was not there. And he wasn't in the corridor outside.

Gerry went downstairs to the front door. No sign of his friend.

Not even a note left to say where he had gone and why, Gerry soon established, even though there were plenty of pens and pads of note paper on his work table.

Hungry now, Gerry crept out to a local shop and bought tins of soup, bread, a Sunday paper and something for stomach acidity.

He was back in his kitchen waiting for the Cream of Chicken to warm when he heard his cellphone ringing somewhere in the flat. He had taken it out of one of the bags he had brought with him from the bed and breakfast place he had previously stayed at to recharge it and it took a few seconds to remember where he'd left it.

"Yeah, hello. Gerry here."

There was a sound in the little instrument like someone frantically scratching sharp metal over stone for a few moments, then fragments of mangled human speech. No chance of understanding more than a little of what was being said though, as the words were rendered unintelligible by intermittent stabbing seconds of silence. But Gerry thought he recognised Alister's voice.

"Al, is that you? Speak more slowly. I can't understand what you're saying."

Another string of words with holes in, chittering away against Gerry's ear like angry insects in jungle undergrowth. Straining to make sense of what he was hearing Gerry thought he might have been able to make out—

"don't know...(or *"don't, no..."*)

"loss...

"forms part...

"with me...

"get back...

"meet" (or *"meat"*)

—each word with a big gap in between. He scribbled them down on a paper pad until the voice abruptly lost its human qualities and became a mechanical stammer that quickly became painful to hear.

Gerry cupped the phone in front of his mouth and said, "Alister, you're wasting your time. If you can hear me, you're *breaking up*, so get off the fucking line. I'll try and call you back."

On the cooker his chicken soup boiled over, filling the kitchen with the smell of burning bird and milk.

Gerry snatched at the handle of the hot saucepan.

It took him ten minutes to deal with the resulting mess and the burns on his fingers, by which time the phone was sounding its tinkling tune again. He didn't bother answering. When it stopped ringing he picked it up and called Alister. After half a minute his friend had not answered, so he put the phone down and started to read his copy of *The Independent* which, however, made little sense, because it seemed to contain reports from and about people and places he'd never heard of— news from nowhere.

He was expecting the cellphone to ring again at any moment and a build-up of guilty feelings about the background work he should have done for the start of his course was making him miserable, or more miserable than he was already, so he put the newspaper down, took up a couple of textbooks instead, and forced himself to study. In this he was surprisingly successful. Two hours of useful concentration passed before his phone rang again. This time, he answered it.

It said, "Hi, Gerry. How are you? How are you settling into your new home?"

"Who's that?"

"Mary."

"Mary?"

"Alister's wife, for Christ's sake."

"Oh, right didn't recognise your voice at all."

"Is it that long since you heard it?"

"I guess it is. And thanks, I'm settling in reasonably well, I suppose."

"You suppose?"

"Well, there have been a few snags."

"There always are when you try to change your life or move into somewhere new. You'll get over them. Anyway, you know why I'm calling."

"You want to speak to Alister?"

"I tried to call him earlier but he's not answering. So, yes, please, If he's not still asleep. Or drunk."

"You know your man."

"Of course."

"As far as I'm aware he's neither of those things."

"Good."

"But actually, he's not here."

"*What!* He said he was staying with you?"

"He was here, but he's gone. I thought he might have returned home to you early, without waking me. He can be considerate like that. Occasionally."

"No. No sign of him here."

"My other thought was that he'd just slipped out for a while for some reason. I've been expecting him back all morning."

Mary held her breath for a while before saying, "Where might he have slipped to, do you suppose?"

Gerry had previously considered the possibility of Mrs. Bendix across the corridor or Maggie, the single mother in the first floor flat below, both of whom Alister had expressed lewd interest in. He also remembered Al had threatened to go down to sort out the noisy neighbours but he decided not to mention any of that to Mary.

"No idea. Don't worry though. He called earlier, so he must be alright. At least, I think it was him."

"What the hell does that mean, Gerry?"

"I couldn't be absolutely sure. There was something wrong with his phone. I guess his card was running out."

"Card? Don't be silly. He doesn't bother with things like that. He's a businessman, remember. That phone is his lifeline. Now tell me, just what have you and he been doing?"

"Nothing at all, Mary. Nothing untoward, anyway."

"I don't believe you. You don't sound too perky yourself. What have you two been up to?"

Gerry described to her what had happened during the last twenty-four hours or so, which was, as he told it, nothing much. He gave a lightly censored account of the peregrinations the previous evening. He even mentioned Alister's disturbance in the small hours of the night. "That was the last time I saw him, preparing to go to sleep on a chair.

He'd gone by the time I woke up. But, come to think of it, he probably does intend coming back here. He's left his sleeping bag and his overnight bag."

"I'm sorry, Gerry, but it doesn't add up. I don't believe you're telling me the whole truth. You always did protect him."

"Not this time," Gerry lied. "Honestly. When were you expecting him back?"

"Late afternoon at the earliest. He'd have let me know if he'd changed his plans and intended returning before that. You've got me worried."

"Sorry. But what did you want to speak to him about? Anything urgent?"

"No. Just to check him out. I always call him when he's away at the weekend."

"I'll let you know when he turns up."

"Oh, thank you Gerry—that *is* good of you."

"I don't think I deserve the sarcasm, Mary. It's not my fault he's not here."

"True, if what you say is to be believed. But do me a favour. You must know where he parked his car. Go and look to see if it's still there, will you? Then call me back."

Relieved to be able to put the phone down, Gerry did as he was bidden.

«« — »»

As he left his flat Gerry found the Bendix boys staring across at each other from both sides of his door frame. They each had big, futuristic looking lime green and shocking pink toy guns at the ready. Gerry guessed they were measuring up to shoot each other in the stomach. They didn't look at him as he stepped out onto the corridor. As far as he could tell neither of them so much as blinked as he passed between them—he wasn't there. He had to walk round Bobby to get to the stairs. As he did so he said, "Hi, boys, how's it going?" but didn't expect or get an answer.

Even so, he turned and said, "Um…have either of you seen a friend of mine? Tall guy with a little beard just here." Gerry tickled his lower lip.

– 49 –

Bobby let the question dangle for a while then said, "Course we did. Yesterday, on the stairs. You were with him."

"No, I mean since then."

Andy said, "Why? Have you lost him? That's stupid."

Both boys were watching Gerry with identical casual but crafty expressions on their faces. Standing with their feet apart in an almost military stance, with their arms held slightly away from their sides, Gerry thought they resembled two jowled, bright eyed little pug-dogs on the scent of serious mischief. Though maybe *not* so little. Gerry had no idea how old they were, and was no judge of such things, but he guessed they were big for their age. They had an overgrown look. They bulged.

"But you've not seen him today?" Gerry patiently enquired.

They shook their heads—chins left, chins right, chins left, in perfect time.

"Well, if he turns up, tell him I've stepped out for a little while, please. Ask him to wait here until I get back," Gerry said, knowing he was wasting his breath, sure they would do no such thing.

Outside the building the day had brightened up considerably since he had gone out for his soup and paper. Some scattered patches of wet snow from the previous evening remained but the clouds had cleared and the sun was painfully bright on his eyes. Gleefully, it drilled its beams into his skull and danced about on what was left of his hangover.

Alister had parked as close as he could get to the flat—on the far side of the road, but near enough, so they hadn't had to carry Gerry's possessions far. There was a different vehicle in that space now, a rackety old Ford that conspicuously prosperous Alister would not have been seen standing adjacent to. Gerry walked up and down the street for a good distance in both directions to see if his friend had parked up somewhere else for some reason, but that was not the case.

He walked back to the original parking spot, bent down and inspected the Ford. It had not had an easy life. The body work was extensively scratched and dented along both sides where there was almost as much rust visible as there was paintwork. The vehicle had been stripped to less than its essentials. The seating at the back had been ripped out and been replaced with a large open-topped cardboard box containing a couple of thick, sky blue blankets. Very dirty blankets.

Otherwise, there was nothing else of any interest to see. The inside of the windows were slightly cloudy with what could have been condensation and the air in the interior of the vehicle even appeared misty and humid, like the domain of some tropical creature in a reptile house.

As he moved away Gerry spotted something shining in the gutter beside the Ford. Glass. Crystal fragments of a shattered windscreen. The car, ramshackled as it was, was in that way undamaged. Gerry scraped at the glass with his foot and saw something else. Spots of something red. He hunkered down to take a closer look and saw they were flakes of paint similar in colour, as far as he could remember, to Alister's vehicle.

As he pondered the possible implications of this discovery he began to feel he was being watched by somebody close behind him. And, in the position he was in, bending down close to the ground, almost off balance, with his back, as it were, unprotected, he felt vulnerable. He leaned to his left, pushed down his hand on the pavement to give himself leverage for his knees and clumsily straightened up and turned round.

The Bendix boys were leaning against the wall of a nearby garden, watching him with keen interest. They were, in fact, looking not just at him but beyond, towards someone else who had come out of the building they lived in, and was heading towards them and Gerry with awkward, speedy, disjointed strides. Gerry recognised him at once. He was unmistakable. It was the man Gerry had met on his first day in his new flat; the half-demented creature he had let in to visit his neighbour Maggie, the single mother with the hidden child.

Gerry had assumed the man was a biker but, no, he drove a car. He whipped a bunch of keys on a heavy chain from a belt loop of his severely distressed black jeans, used one to open the door of the car Gerry was standing next to, and with a further display of his over-fast and barely coordinated movements, shifted himself down, section by section, into the driving seat, like a wounded spider tucking itself into a crack in a wall. He didn't, however, close the door after him. Indeed, the bottom end of one of his legs remained protruding outside, foot on the ground, as though he had not quite got space or the dexterity to fit it in.

After fitting a pair of unfashionably heavy and dark shades on his pierced nose he put both hands on the top of the steering wheel, hunched his shoulders a few times to loosen up, opened his mouth, belched, then sighed. He snapped his head round, tipped his chin up and pointed his nose, with its green bone insertion, at Gerry in what could only have been intended as a deliberately pugnacious gesture. Watching him in action was like observing the performance of a slightly malfunctioning automaton, Gerry thought. The man seemed to be struggling with the fairly advanced stages of an overall breakdown in communication between his limbs and his brain.

"Just now you were staring at my car, now you're doing the same to me," he said. "What are you, some kind of snooper?"

"Who, me? No. Not at all," Gerry said.

He noticed that the man did not, as he had assumed, have a radically cut hairstyle, but some kind of disease of the scalp. Most of his head was coated with a thin frizzle of dry dead skin underneath which could be seen an underlay of red raw flesh that looked as though it had been methodically and painfully scratched all over. In fact there was hardly any hair left on his head, except for the two wisps at the front, and Gerry speculated that the man might have pulled most of it out himself in his battle with whatever complaint he had.

"I live in the house you've just come from," Gerry said. "We met there before, remember? I let you in."

"What I remember is that you tried to *stop* me getting in," the man said. "I know who you are. The student. I've heard about you. You sit in your room doing nothing most of the time, is what I've been told. Call yourself a student, yeah?" He took his right hand of the steering wheel, raised it, made a fist, stuck the middle finger in the air and said, "Well, study that."

He tried to smile sarcastically at Gerry but as the corners of his lips drew back his right hand took an obviously unintended jump in the air off the steering wheel, then the sides of his mouth went into a spasm of tics that briefly turned his face into something a gargoyle would not have been ashamed to own. The episode didn't last long but while the man was recovering from it Gerry said, "I came out here to look for a car. Not yours. Nothing to do with you at all. So mind your own business."

Voices from behind Gerry chanted, "He told us he'd lost a friend, Jax, not a car." Bobby and Andy speaking.

"I saw you snooping up and down the street and round *my* car," the man called Jax said. "I was watching you for five minutes. So don't give me any 'mind your own business' shit." He started to push his leg further out the vehicle and laboriously repositioned his body, ready to climb back on to the pavement.

Both boys gave a murmur of approval and anticipation.

"We saw him snooping," Andy said, to force things along.

"Staring and staring." Bobby's contribution.

Jax ignored them but kept a fairly steady eye on Gerry. "This is where I park," he said. "My space. Always has been and always will be. Nobody else round here uses it, so get to know *that*, student. Anyone parks here but me, he's asking for fucking trouble. We have our ways of doing things round here and we stick to them."

Gerry said, "If that's the case—if you're handicapped in some way, for instance—you should put up a sign to let people know you have special parking rights. My friend left his car here yesterday. In this exact spot. Now it's gone. Did you have it towed away?"

"Handicapped! Me? What're you trying to say? There's something wrong with me?" Jax was talking faster and faster and there was evidence that his mouth was also finding it difficult to keep up with the demands of his brain. His jaw was sliding about sideways as he spoke and Gerry could hear his teeth clicking.

Gerry said, "Okay, so you're perfectly normal in every way. My mistake. But where's Alister's car? If you've had it moved and it's been damaged, *you* are in trouble. It's this year's model."

"Are you threatening me, hard man? Fucking student! Listen," Jax leaned forward and managed to extend his neck considerably as he thrust his head closer to Gerry, "This year's, next year's, any year's model, nobody cares about that round here so forget it." He moved his protruding leg further out of the vehicle and laboriously started to squirm back onto the pavement.

He was thin, small, and looked none too well. But he was more than just a little angry and gave the impression he was capable of doing wild, foolish things on the spur of the moment. Gerry was sure he himself would come out best in any tussle between the two of them; in fact he thought his main problem might be stopping Jax from hurting himself, so puny and physically helpless did he appear to be. But Gerry had never been one for fighting in the street or anywhere else, if he could avoid it, and he decided to try a little pacification.

Jax twitched and fidgeted himself out of his car and edged up close to Gerry with what might just have passed as a fighter's shuffle. He pushed his shades up onto his head, where the nose piece left two crimson skid marks in his skin condition. The top of him was level with Gerry's breast bone. He smelled of sweat or his breath was bad. He waved his clenched hands in front of his face and shoved his chest up against Gerry's stomach.

Gerry's first thoughts were for his dignity. He particularly did not want to be made a fool of in front of the Bendix boys which he was sure was, in itself, a foolish thing to allow to concern him at that moment. But he couldn't help it. He lifted his head high to remove it further from Jax's odours and said as calmly as he was able, "Come *on*. There's no need to take that attitude. Stand off. I'm not interested in your bloody car. *At all*."

"*Bloody* car, is it?" Jax was stooping slightly and swinging punches with both fists now. Some of them landed dangerously close to Gerry's groin. "Don't you take the piss out of my car, you s-s-s-student shit."

Jax's arms jerked and whirled like broken saplings in a gale. There was almost no strength in his blows but Gerry found himself instinctively drawing away to avoid them. Sensing this partial retreat on Gerry's part, Jax was encouraged to increase his attack. He spat at Gerry's face. He kicked his shins when he could which did hurt, because Jax was wearing hard toed boots.

Grimly, as though the task was distasteful to him, Gerry took tight hold of Jax's shoulders and held him off at arm's length. Jax redoubled his attempts to strike blows with his hands and feet but his efforts came to nothing now. With his opponent out of reach he became more furious by the second and once again his face contorted, became hideous.

"Right, that's enough," Gerry said, deciding he had seen more than he could take of those unhandsome features. Perhaps the last passing remnants of his hangover had something to do with it. He reached forward with his right arm, slipped it round Jax's trunk, scooped the man off his feet and held him, face down and wriggling and cursing, against his side.

Gerry was surprised to find that the little man weighed almost nothing—in fact, his clothes were probably heavier than he was.

Meanwhile Jax began to jerk and shake. His head swivelled back so vigorously it seemed possible he might break his own neck. Every part of him was convulsing in quick, tense movements.

Alarmed, Gerry laid him down on the pavement as gently as he could.

Jax's kicking legs hit against the ground and caused him to rotate slowly on the paving stones.

"Look what you've done to him now," one of the Bendix boys said. "You've broken him."

The other one said, "Is he going to be dead?"

Gerry, in spite of everything, was relieved to find them still present. If necessary they could bear witness that it was he who had been attacked. There was nobody else around.

"He's ill, that's all," he said. "I think he's having what they call a fit. I'll go and get help. You stay here with him."

"They'll do no such thing," their mother shouted as she came out through the front gate of the apartment building onto the pavement. "What are you doing out here anyway, the pair of you? How many times have I told you *never* to play outside the house without taking me with you? Get inside. At once. Go to your beds and wait for me."

"It's not our fault," said Bobby.

"That man," Andy pointed at Gerry, "asked us to look for someone he'd lost. We came out with him."

"He *lured* us out," Bobby suggested, clearly pleased with the word.

"They must have followed me downstairs," Gerry said sheepishly.

Mrs. Bendix said, "Never mind."

She strolled across to Jax's supine and still juddering body and gave him an experimental jab in the abdomen with a moccasined foot.

"He's in a bad way. I've not seen him like that for a long time."

"That man," Andy pointed at Gerry again, "Picked Jax up and shook him until he had a fit."

"*I told you two to get inside!*" Mrs. Bendix didn't raise her voice but it had an extra edge that was as good as a shout. She took two firm steps towards her brood and they fled.

"I'll go and call an ambulance," Gerry said.

"No you won't," Mrs. Bendix said, matter-of-factly. "Bring him inside. I know what he needs and they don't hand that out in hospitals. Not to just anybody, anyway."

"What he needs is professional attention."

"He'll be okay. He'll be *fine.*"

"Are you some kind of nurse?"

She laughed. "We'll take him up to Maggie," she said. "She knows how to handle him when he's like this. Can you carry him that far?"

"Easily," Gerry said, and he lifted Jax up into his arms. The man hadn't quite stopped twitching and he seemed lighter than ever. His arms and legs were about as thin as Gerry imagined limbs could get on a living person. The smell of him was getting worse. Some kind of secretion problem? Something to do with his glands? Gerry almost ran upstairs to the first floor, so eager was he to be unburdened.

Mrs. Bendix knocked on Maggie's door a couple of times to no effect. The door, deeply split in places, was also scratched and gouged over its surface, revealing different layers and colours of paint going back years, apparently. A long procession of people had taken out a lot of anger against it during that time. It was evident that the lock had been changed frequently too, but the one in place held firm against Mrs. Bendix's assault. After knocking with the back of her fist again, she swore, took hold of Jax's bone-skinny legs, pulled off one of his biker's boots, and set about bashing the heel of it against the door.

There was a lot of noise then in the confined space of the corridor and Gerry was certain any person inside the flat, who was not stone deaf or in a coma, would long ago have come to answer if they were going to at all. He was proved wrong, though, because finally there came evidence of some response. Someone began to fiddle clumsily with chains and bolts, by the sound of it, on the other side. This in itself was a slow process, but one that delighted Mrs. Bendix, who gave Gerry a tight, bright smile with a lot of I-told-you-so in it. He made some attempt to give her his best winning grin back and adjusted the position of Jax, who, still in his arms, was beginning to wriggle again. His eyes were shut and he was breathing deeply through his mouth, but there were signs that, mentally, he was coming back out of whatever state he had fallen into.

When the door was free it opened slowly inwards. A young, fragile, tiny woman in a pale yellow nightdress edged round from behind it and blinked out. She looked more than half asleep. She passed the tips of the fingers of her hand slowly round and round her cheek, pinching and pulling at the flesh, then wiped her lips, which were pale, wet and shiny. They remained that way after she'd wiped them. Her eyes were damp, too, and her nose was running. In a 'before and after' advertisement for a flu cure, she would have been the ideal model for the first picture.

Gerry's first thought when he saw her was, *I hope it's not contagious.*

"Hi, Maggie," Mrs. Bendix said. "What have you been doing with Jax? You're wearing him out. Look at the state he's in."

Gerry offered Jax up a little, as though he thought the man might be due to receive a blessing. Maggie took a step forward and obligingly held out a hand in what could have been a gesture of benediction over Jax's forehead.

Then, cautiously, she touched the skin on the bridge of Jax's nose. "He's cold," she said. "You shouldn't have let him get cold." Her voice was that of a lifelong complainer, used to expecting and getting the worst of everything. "You'd better bring him in, I suppose."

"That *was* the idea," Gerry said, desperately anxious by this time to put Jax down somewhere, anywhere.

"Who's this?" Maggie said, meaning Gerry, as she turned and withdrew into her room. "Why bring *him* here?"

"It's him from opposite me upstairs, the one I told you about."

"That pesters your kids and tries to steal their toys?"

"That's it. The 'mature student'."

"He doesn't look like one of those that goes creeping about messing with children, but it just shows you can't go by looks."

"Never trust appearances," Mrs. Bendix confirmed. "That way you can't go wrong."

Gerry couldn't quite believe the evidence of his ears to hear himself being spoken about so blatantly and unfairly, and he was shocked to discover that Mrs. Bendix could be so two-faced; he'd taken her for a truthful person, at least, but any protest he might have been inclined to make did not reach his lips because he was rendered speechless by what he was beginning to make out in the dark, damp, overheated room, which seemed to be occupied in places by wraiths of grey smoke or, more likely, steam.

The air in there was thick and scented with the kind of odour that comes from the cheapest perfume—sweet and rank, without subtlety—

under which Gerry thought he could detect, among many other things, traces of dope, gin and the ammoniac whiff of soiled nappies. That didn't trouble Gerry too much—it was certainly preferable to the stench that Jax continued to emit—but it was unpleasant enough to set his teeth on edge.

"Where do you want him?" he said, peering round for some likely spot to drop his load.

The room was poorly illuminated by two fat candle stumps set on top of volcano-like mounds of multi-coloured wax drippings squatting on and overflowing a pair of china plates. Webs of heavy web-like net curtains hung at the solitary window, through which it was just possible to discern a hint of the presence of the winter sun shining somewhere outside. What little light there was from these sources revealed, everywhere over the floor, piled knee high in places, what appeared to be soiled clothing, thoughtlessly discarded and carelessly left where it had fallen. It looked like a year's delivery of debagged dirty laundry waiting to be sorted and flung into washing vats. There were narrow pathways through it, where it had been kicked aside, one of which led to a table covered with a chaos of tiny jars of liquidised food, gaping king-size packs of incontinence pads, plastic plates and beakers, grubby toys, mingling with an assortment of full and empty bottles of medicinal and other drugs and alcoholic drinks. Other pathways led to a very large pale blue cot and an unmade bed. The widest path led through to the kitchen where, on top of a cooker, the contents of three saucepans, their lids jingling noisily, simmered over low gas. A huge television set on a low pedestal crouched in one corner of the room. Gerry wasn't surprised to see that no pathway led to it, though. In fact, it was half submerged in a mound of garments.

Maggie stood still and silent amid all this bounty with her palms pressed together between her fallen breasts, gazing all the while up towards heaven with a much put-upon expression, like a moody Christian martyr facing imminent immolation.

"Where do you want me to put him?" Gerry repeated, angry at being so blatantly ignored.

Maggie remained motionless in the middle of the room for far too long, without answering Gerry's question. At last she gave a shudder that ran up and down the length of her body, then stooped, picked up a man's grey overcoat from the floor, and drapen it over her shoulders.

Then, sounding as though she had been seriously inconvenienced, she whined, "On the bed, I suppose. Where else?"

"And be careful," Maggie pleaded as Gerry stumbled through the heaps of clothes. "Don't you drop him."

Gerry was careful not to make too close an inspection of the state of the stained and crumpled sheets as he eased Jax gently down on top of them. As he stretched out his arms his sleeves drew back and the sight of his watch reminded him that it was now almost three quarters of an hour since he had promised Mary he would ring her back immediately.

"I've got to go," he said. "If you're sure Jax'll be okay, I'll leave you to it." He must have spoken too loud into the silence because his voice woke the baby, that he had assumed was somewhere in the flat, but had as yet seen no actual sign of.

Sounds of something squirming came from the cot, which was in a dim corner of the room, away from where Gerry was standing. Vocal noises followed—a long and anguished yawn and wordless mutterings, followed by a muffled rasping explosion that could have emitted from either end of any red-blooded creature's anatomy.

"I'm on my way too, Maggie," Mrs. Bendix said. "My kids will be expecting their punishment. I mustn't keep them waiting."

Gerry wondered about her sense of humour. Did she have one?

The cot began to rattle and shake. Through the gaps between the rails along its sides Gerry could see bedding heaving as a bulbous shape turned, then moved ponderously up, inch by inch, beneath them. When the blankets almost reached the top of the cot they slid away to reveal the upper portion of an unexpectedly large and very hairy head. A hand, similarly larger than Gerry had anticipated, emerged from the interior of the cot, curled over the top rail, grasped the horizontal wooden strut firmly, and took the strain. Then the body of the baby lurched heavily to the left and almost went down again as it lost its balance in an ill-judged attempt to haul itself to its knees.

It appeared to Gerry that during the last minute or so the cot had become extraordinarily full, as though the baby had not only elevated itself, but inflated at the same time. As far as he could make out the naked infant was well on the flabby side of chubby. Its skin, in the candle light, had a pale yellow glow, and was mottled with reddish patches that Gerry thought made it look like something fashioned out of the soft flesh of an over-ripe and enormous apple. As it continued to ascend he turned his back on it and glanced round the room.

Maggie was taking no notice of the baby in spite of the fact that it was beginning to make whining, demanding, 'do-something-for-me' sounds in the back of its throat. She had pulled Jax into a half seated position on the bed, removed his leather jacket, and was pulling his t-shirt up over his head, revealing a slightly concave, hairless chest covered with marks that could have been bruises but looked to Gerry more like suction marks or maybe bites. And not insect bites. Too big. Something else bites.

Gerry realised that his mouth was hanging open, had been for some time. He was stunned, in a daze. Most of the activity in his brain seemed to have closed down—he was afraid there was even a danger he might stop thinking altogether. What would happen to him then?

As he shook his head to try to clear it and get things going again in there, the baby started screaming.

Mrs. Bendix hooked her arm round Gerry's and pulled him firmly towards the door and out into the corridor. Thankfully, he shut his eyes and let himself be led away.

"Best to leave her to it," Mrs. Bendix said as Gerry followed her up the stairs. "We'd only get under her feet in there."

Gerry opened his eyes. "Under her *what*?"

"You know what I mean it's only an expression."

"Yeah—sorry. Just one I've not heard for some time. What is she going to do to him anyway. Jax, I mean. *Does* she know what she's doing? I don't think so, and that man's in a bad way."

"Jax has never been better."

It took Gerry some moments to work this out. "You mean he's always been like that?"

"And always will be. It's his condition. There's no cure."

"But that fit he had! You saw yourself how bad it was. He looked like death."

"Never trust appearances. Trust Maggie instead, she'll look after him. They look after each other. She'll soon have him right."

"How, exactly? By doing what?"

"Give him a few of her pills or something to get him going and raise his temperature. Get him good and hot. Probably give him a bit of a rub. That'll be enough. He'll soon come round."

"It doesn't sound like much to me."

"It's enough and anyway, what more do you expect her to do? It's not as if he's family or anything, even if they are close. And she's got a hungry baby to feed and care for."

"We definitely should have called a doctor for Jax."

"Doctors don't come round here any more, they can't find the place, and even if they could, she can't have anyone like that going in. There'd be complaints."

"No doubt about that. It's a filthy hole. Like a rubbish dump."

"Well, she has so many visitors, sometimes as many as a dozen in a single night. You'd be surprised how difficult it is to get rid of people sometimes and they will leave things about after they've gone. Maggie hasn't got the energy to do anything about it. She's not one for tidying. You've only got to look at her to see she's been overwhelmed by it all. By the life she leads. And that child wears her out. It's very demanding."

"How old is the baby?"

"It's no tiny tot, as you could see."

"It looked as big, if not bigger, than Maggie."

"Yes, well, perhaps. Anyway, as I must have told you, I'm woozy about time. I think we all are here. You get that way. But she must have had it a good few years now. It's amazing how they grow, isn't it?"

"Bloody hell! And it never gets any exercise or goes anywhere?"

"Jax used to take it out in the car when it was smaller."

"For a ride in the country, you mean?"

"Oh, no, nothing like that. He'd put it in a box in the back of the car and sit with it for a while, to give Maggie a break. Jax is not much of a driver nowadays. In fact, he can't go further than the end of the street. He's been here too long. Even if he could drive further, he'd be afraid he'd get lost and end up somewhere even worse. And the baby is too big for him to move now. He's not got the strength. He can't carry it in and out. And of course, Maggie doesn't dare risk showing her face on the street with it."

"Maybe I could help there."

"I don't think so. Years ago I offered to take the poor mite off her hands myself, if ever I found I had time to spare, but Maggie wouldn't hear of it. Said I'd got enough on my hands with my own two, which is right enough."

"That baby—I couldn't make out if it was a boy or a girl."

Mrs. Bendix stopped for a moment in her upward progress on the stairs, frowned, shook her head, then continued on. "Oh, I can't remember things like that and it's such a long time since it was born."

"What's it called, then?"

"I'm not sure Maggie ever got round to making up her mind about that. Anyway, I'm terrible with names."

"But surely, when she wants to get its attention, she must call it something?"

"She's never had any trouble getting its attention, Gerry. That's never been a problem."

They were standing outside the Bendix flat now. Peering across the corridor Mrs. Bendix said, "Did you leave your door open?"

"No; shut, but not locked, in case my friend got back while I was out."

"It's open now."

Mrs. Bendix looked through the gaping door into Gerry's room. It occurred to him that she might have been poking around in there herself, while he had been out looking for Alister's car, and not bothered to shut it on the way out. Deliberately, perhaps, to let him know she'd been there. He realised now, from her conversation about him with Maggie, that there were more sides to her character than he had thought. More than he cared to think about. But her boys could easily have tipped her off that he'd gone away without locking his door before they followed him down. Or *they* could have gone in there, when their mother had sent them up to bed.

"I believe there's someone in there," Mrs. Bendix said as they stood side by side, staring into the obvious emptiness of Gerry's living room. "I'm sure I heard someone moving about as we came up those last stairs."

Inside the room, Gerry's phone started ringing.

He ran into the flat, snatched up the phone and said, "Alister? That you? Where the hell are you?"

"And where the hell have *you* been?" Mary said.

"He's not turned up at your end yet?"

"No. You were going to ring back to let me know if his car was parked outside. Is it?"

"Sorry Mary. I got held up. Got involved in a bit of trouble. An accident. Something like that."

"An accident? To Alister? Oh Christ!"

"No. To somebody else. And the answer is no to your other question too; his car's not there."

"It would only take him an hour or so to get back here."

"Yes. About that. A bit more, perhaps."

"Something must have happened to him on the way."

"It's a possibility."

"Fucking hell, Gerry."

"I know. It doesn't look good. But there was broken glass on the ground where he'd parked, so the car may have been stolen. He might have gone to report the theft to the police."

"He'd have phoned them, Gerry. You can't get him to take a walk anywhere unless there's a pub at the end of it."

Undoubtedly, that was true.

"I'm doing my best to be helpful," Gerry said.

"But you're not succeeding."

Gerry hung onto the cellphone, trying to think of encouraging words to calm Mary down, but failed to come up with any.

During this slight pause in the conversation he heard a noise coming from his bedroom. A chair going over? Something like that. Followed by the sound of someone moving about, presumably up-righting what had fallen.

Still holding the phone near to his ear he stepped across the room and said, "Who's that?"

In his ear Mary, audibly steaming, said, "It's still me, you fool," but he got no other answer to his question.

Gerry walked into his bedroom and found it unoccupied. A number of items of clothing had been flung about on the floor and bed—women's stuff—but, as far as he could tell nothing of his had been moved or removed. But he noticed something extra had been added.

The cheap mirror that he had taken down out of his spare room had been hung on the wall opposite the end of his bed.

There was very little space between bed and wall so it was difficult for him to get at it. A very slender person might have done, just, but Gerry found he had to bend back uncomfortably at the knees to get close up in front of it. Perhaps his awkward position and tense, confused state of mind made him dizzy and blurred his vision because when he looked into the mirror he thought he saw a face there that was not a reflection and certainly nothing like his own. He rubbed his eyes, looked again and found himself staring at something different; a disc of some pale, creamy, pinkish swirling substance.

It was like looking down into a pan of gently simmering flesh, or so it seemed to Gerry.

"I know you're still there, Gerry," Mary said. "I can hear you breathing. Why aren't you talking to me, you bastard? What's your game?"

Gerry was still holding the phone up close to his ear. He had an urge to smash the thing against the mirror but instead said, "Give me a moment, Mary. Something's come up."

While she protested he took the mirror down. He avoiding looking into it but observed as he removed it that it had been hung on the same huge nail, causing similar damage to the wall. He put the mirror face down on the dressing table, crept out of the bedroom and said, "I think we ought to report Alister missing, to the police, Mary."

"What? Why, all of a sudden? What happened just now, when you went silent? Something to do with him?"

"Not at all, as far as I know. But I don't like it here at the moment. Something's not right. It's been a bad day. I can't explain."

"You're making me feel much worse, Gerry."

"I feel worse too, Mary. Let's not fall out about it. Call the police. Tell them what's happened to Alister. See what they say."

"But that's the point. I don't *know* what's happened."

"Nothing much at all, probably. So don't upset yourself. Do what I suggested. Call me back later. I need a break to think things over. I'll let you know if Alister turns up."

"At once? Promise?"

"Definitely."

After turning the cellphone off Gerry stretched out on the bed and shut his eyes. Under his eyelids soft lights and colours spun, reminding him of his recent experience with the mirror and of Alister's 'nightmare', that he now increasingly believed had been no such thing.

He opened his eyes. The sinking sun cast long shadows of the swaying and almost leafless branches of the trees outside his window on the ceiling above him which were much more restful to watch than his own inner visions.

— FOUR —

HE SLEPT FITFULLY through parts of the day, out of nervous exhaustion, but got no rest during the night. As usual there were noises on and off downstairs, of people talking loudly and angrily, of footsteps on the stairs, of doors opening and slamming—some of the noises, he was starting to imagine, came from inside his own flat.

He was certain he'd heard the tap running in the kitchen but, when he forced himself to go and investigate, the thing was turned off and the sink was dry. Occasionally, as he tried to sleep, soft sounds like those made by someone folding and unfolding, or sliding in and out of, clothing, moved in the air around him and he thought, 'She's trying on some of her things' though there was enough light from the window for him to be certain he was alone and that nothing in the room moved except his restless, insomnia smitten self.

He wondered why Mary had not called him back and it was not until four in the morning that he remembered he had switched his phone off. He thought of calling her then, but decided against doing so because he did not want to literally alarm her unnecessarily at that hour and anyway, he had nothing new to say.

He gave up trying to sleep hours before he had to attend his first lecture, at eleven. He was sitting at his work table reading a relevant textbook and munching toast before finally setting out for the University when someone knocked on his door.

The Bendix boys had been rattling about on the corridor for some time. Assuming they must be the cause of the interruption he shouted, "I'm busy. What do you want?"

The knocking came again—quietly, politely even.

Alister? Unlikely. He wasn't a soft knocker. Mary? The police? Maybe.

Gerry went and opened the door.

The man from the flat agency stood there, looking even more downcast and worn out than before. *If he's like this first thing on Monday morning, how does he look on Friday?* Gerry wondered, then recollected he probably didn't appear too merry and bright himself.

The agent ground out half a cigarette with his heel on the carpet outside Gerry's door and stood on the threshold, peering in somewhat anxiously, then seemed to steel himself, reluctantly, to enter.

The Bendix brood must have heard the man knocking at the door because they appeared from somewhere and tried to squeeze past him into the flat, jostling him a little as they did so. The agent pitched forward into the room, shuffled inelegantly along a little way on his bad feet, then twisted round with unexpected speed to face the boys and said, "Get out of here, you little sods."

"You can't say that to us," Andy said.

"This is where we live," Bobby added.

"No it isn't," the agent said. He pointed to Gerry. "It's where he lives."

"Don't tell us where to go."

"I don't *care* where you go as long as you just fuck off. Both of you. *Now.*"

To Gerry's, and maybe to the agent's, surprise the boys, after exchanging looks of outrage, turned on their heels and marched out with the wounded but proud, don't-think-we-won't-be-back air of the general of an army making a tactical retreat. When the agent closed the door behind them they started yelping for their mother, telling her about the man who'd said, 'sods' and 'fuck', taking obvious pleasure in shouting the words aloud.

"Why didn't *I* ever try that," Gerry said, much impressed. "They're only kids, after all."

The agent shrugged noncommittally.

In a hurry to get on with his life Gerry said, "Anyway, what can I do for you?"

"Pay your rent."

Gerry slapped his forehead. "Of course. I forgot. It's due. I've been here a week today."

"You have."

"But listen, hang on a moment, I wanted to talk to someone about that. I'm not completely satisfied with the set-up here."

"You've got some complaints," the agent said, sounding sympathetic.

"Well, there are a few questions I'd like answering."

"What's wrong?"

"A number of things. I was going to make a list but haven't got round to it yet. Some of my dissatisfactions are a bit difficult to put into words."

"You're thinking of withholding your rent?"

"Exactly."

"You've a right to do that. It's in the tenancy agreement."

"It is?"

"Certainly."

"So, if I don't pay, nobody's going to try to throw me out?"

"No chance of that."

"Well, that's very reasonable. Thank you for telling me. In that case, consider me withholding."

The agent drew a small leather-bound note book from his hip pocket and a pen from inside his jacket. He made a brief note. "It'll save me having to call round again," he said. "And it'll give me a chance to get on with more urgent things elsewhere."

"But surely, you'll still have to call in to collect the other rents? One more or less won't make much difference."

"What other rents?"

"The lady opposite, those boy's mother—hers, for instance—and the people downstairs. I know some of the flats are empty, but sometimes the building is teeming with people. It gets like a bloody circus at night. That's one of the things I wanted to talk to someone about."

"I don't bother to call on them."

"But surely they can't all live here rent free?"

"Why do you expect them to pay when you won't?"

Gerry looked at the agent to see if there was any suggestion of humour in his expression. There wasn't.

"But I don't go banging about disturbing and upsetting people," Gerry said.

"Oh, really?"

"I live a more orderly life."

"That's not what I heard," the agent said. "Back at headquarters we've had reports of rowdy drunkenness in here and people from this flat walking about half dressed when they shouldn't, at four and five o'clock in the morning."

"That's wasn't me," Gerry said. "But it could have been a friend of mine."

"Not sub-letting are you? That's not in the agreement."

"No, I'm not. But since you mention it, I seem to be in some kind of room share situation without wanting to be."

The agent looked blank. Said nothing.

"You know what I mean, I think." Gerry opened a drawer and tipped out a couple of pairs of women's shoes and other items not his own.

"I can't get rid of this stuff. I've tried, but it won't go away and nor will the woman who owns it. You didn't tell me about that when you showed me round and I bet that's not in the agreement either."

The agent sniffed and looked thoughtful. "Does she cause you problems? Get in your way?"

Gerry couldn't say she did. Not really.

"I don't expect she likes having you around much, either," the agent said. "As I recall, she never did think much of any member of our sex. A bit of a man-hater, in fact. Had a troubled time of it, like everybody here. Always complaining about the way she'd been treated by the partners in her life, and there had been plenty of them."

Gerry thought, *He's speaking from the heart. He's had a troubled life, too. None more so, by the look of him. I should have realised. He's one of us.*

He said, in a conciliatory tone, "The impression I get is that she keeps her distance, or tries to, I'll say that for her."

"Does she now? She's discreet. I'm glad to hear it. Anyway, it should all sort itself out in time. It's just possible there was a bit of a mix-up, I admit, about letting you in. Things like that happen all the time. Due to administrative problems back at our head office, I expect. The staff there are overworked. We're *all* overworked. Look at me. Sometimes I have to be in a dozen places at once. Mistakes are bound to be made but once they are made, there's not much anyone can do about it except to it give it time."

"You get a lot of people coming and going in these flats, then?"

"Coming, yes, but going, no. Unfortunately. That's why I'm kept so busy. And it's getting worse, of course. It's an endless spiral."

If the agent was trying to engage Gerry's sympathy, he was succeeding. Gerry was also experiencing more than a little fellow feeling for the worn out wreck of a man. He was actually beginning to like him, in spite of his gloomy iteration of his dissatisfactions with his life and work.

But this word work brought Gerry back to a realisation of his own present circumstances. It was half past ten. He had to be in the lecture theatre before eleven.

The agent looked up with surprise and some alarm when Gerry jumped out of his seat, grabbed a shoulder bag full of books, and rushed to the door.

"Got to go," Gerry said. "You're not the only one who's busy. No, don't get up. Take your time for once. Have a coffee on me. Let yourself out when you're ready. But don't forget to lock the door."

For a moment the agent looked vacant, then his face changed as a mixture of emotions pushed against each other behind it to claim expression.

Gerry glanced back once more then slammed the door behind him with a surge of satisfaction that was almost glee, because he was *on his way*. His further education started here and now, and it felt good. He had a sense that if he had not exactly thrown off the past and his misfortunes, he was in a position to build some sort of protective wall between himself and what had gone before. To hell with all that. A new start. He was going to concentrate and make something of the future, or so he told himself. It was the sort of thing he'd been telling himself a lot recently.

But he didn't feel that good for long. His mood quickly changed.

He ran down the first flight of stairs and halfway to the top of the second when something he had seen in the agent's expression just before he'd made his hasty exit slowed him down and, a few paces later, he found he had come to a stop. For more than a minute he stood looking down between his feet at a section of the dirty, dusty carpet in the corridor near Maggie's flat, inside which someone was snivelling and someone else was coughing compulsively, barking like a dog with a bone in its throat.

Gerry overheard these sounds rather than listened to them. His mind was centering in on an idea that was rising painfully up out of its sleep-deprived depths. He could almost feel his brain throbbing with concentration.

At last, a seemingly small but significant insight made itself manifest. Gerry slapped his hip with satisfaction as the revelation unravelled.

Stepping softly and cautiously, he went back up to his room and listened at his own door. Fortunately this time the Bendix boys were not about to comment on his peculiar behaviour.

Inside, he could hear the man from the agency talking quietly but insistently. Whatever he was saying sounded like a recital rather than one side of a conversation.

Gerry pressed his ear to the door and caught the words, "Don't know—loss—forms part—with me—get back—meet."

The man was reading out the few words Gerry had caught from Alister's last, broken up phone call, that he had hastily written down on a scrap of paper and since forgotten about.

The agent's voice was joined by another, a female's—a local woman with the careless, sing-song way of speaking of people born in that part of town, but who nevertheless spoke louder and more clearly, so Gerry was able to understand what she said, which was not much.

The agency man mumbled on again for some time, sounding as though he was reading from another list. The woman just responded with, "Yeah" and "nope" and "okay" every now and then. She sounded bored.

At one point the agent raised his voice and said, "Well, it has to be that way. I've got my instructions."

The woman said something inaudible, this time, that sounded like a mild protest.

"You can put up with it for a while," the man said. "Give it time."

The woman gave an exasperated, on the edge of hysterical and totally humourless, laugh.

Gerry looked at his watch and saw that if he ran off now he still stood a slim chance of getting to his lecture on time. He stood for a moment like a man in a Victorian painting designed to illustrate 'Indecision', then shook his head and took action. He snatched open the door in front of him and swept into the flat with the air of a jealous lover expecting to find his mistress in bed with his worst enemy.

The agency man was standing close to where Gerry had left him. He was facing away from Gerry and holding the mirror, that Gerry had left on the dresser in his bedroom, up in front of his face. His features were not reflected there, however—instead Gerry got his first, very brief, glimpse of the woman who he was sharing the flat with.

Her still young but already lined, gaunt, greyish face, with sunken cheeks, pink rimmed eyes, and slightly open mouth and hanging lower jaw, topped with a tousle of faded blond hair reminded Gerry of many of the women he had found himself standing next to during the previous few days in the cash-desk queue in the nearby supermarket—a local type. In fact, for a moment, he thought she bore some resemblance to Maggie. She was not at all attractive. What distinguished her from others like her, the sight of which Gerry had already become familiar with since he had moved to the city, was the expression on her face, which was of ultimate and utter hopelessness. She looked defeated, doomed, long-gone, lost.

At the point where Gerry must have stepped into her line of vision her head turned, she saw that he had seen her, her face blanked out, and she vanished. The mirror clouded over and became opaque. She'd gone back into hiding.

So far the agent had shown no response to Gerry's premature return to the flat—perhaps he was deaf, and had heard no sound of movement behind him, or he had become rooted to the spot with the shock of it. Eventually, however, after carefully placing the mirror down on the nearby table, he turned and gave Gerry another look at his bleak, careworn face.

Gerry stared back at him in silence. The man gave a tiny, dismissive shrug.

It occurred to Gerry that if he were to explain that he had returned to pick up something important he had forgotten, he could grab any object to support this lie, go out again, get to his lecture and try to forget everything he had seen during the last minute or two.

But no too late for that now. There was too much stacked away in the back-burner of his mind, that he had chosen, or been forced by circumstances to deny to himself—that he had just not been prepared to think about. He knew if he attended the lecture he would learn nothing. For the time being, at least, his ability to concentrate on any kind of study had definitely deserted him and his mind was full of other, less distinct but more compelling matters.

Though still, as ever, ill at ease, the agent seemed to relax a little. Perhaps he could read the confusion on Gerry's face and took that as a good sign. If so, he was wrong.

Gerry felt a surge of choking anger unlike anything he had experienced before, that the agent picked up on at once.

Glowing with fury, his fists clenched, Gerry took a few steps towards him. The man cringed and his face turned a duller shade of grey. He edged back a little way as Gerry advanced until his retreat was blocked by the wall behind him.

He said, "Why are you looking at me like that?" but Gerry didn't need to answer. He could see that the man knew.

"This won't get either of us anywhere," the agent said.

He must be more than a quarter of a century older than I am, Gerry calculated—sickly, and in poor physical condition. He remembered how easily he had dealt with Jax the day before. The agent, though taller and heavier, would be no trouble either. He found walking difficult at the best of times and was already scared, though nothing, so far had been done to him. There had not even been any threatening words to cower him. Just Gerry's stare.

Gerry had a vision of himself tying the man to a chair and torturing him in a variety of ways. Scenes of interrogation from films and newsreels reactivated themselves in his memory and passed through his consciousness in a speedy, jagged procession as he approached the man.

The agent offered no opposition as Gerry reached out to grasp him by the neck with both hands. Instead he took one step back, tripped and tumbled. Gerry tried to catch him as he fell but was unable to stop him from hitting the floor face down. Alarmed by the sound made by the agent's nose hitting the uncarpeted wood, Gerry did what he could to get the man back on his feet again.

The agent's mouth was open wide, as were his tired, frightened eyes. A trickle of blood oozed from his nose, down over his upper lip, and onto his protruding tongue.

At the sight of the blood all Gerry's anger left him. He put an arm round the old man, led him to an armchair and sat him down. Coughing, spitting blood, the agent tugged open the collar of his shirt as though it was trying to strangle him, then massaged his chest above his heart.

The cellphone on the table started ringing. It felt uncomfortably cold when Gerry picked it up, as though it had been left in a refrigerator.

"Who's there?"

Broken words he couldn't understand, but it was Mary's voice.

After a few second he caught, "...the police like you said...—terview you...—missing pers—"

"Mary, this line is terrible. It's getting worse."

"—ust have the wrong address here...—olice say...you because it doesn't exist...phone you either though gave them this numb—"

"If you're saying what I think you are, Mary, how come Alister found his way here? Try to read out the address you have so I can check it's right."

Perhaps Mary understood and did try. She said a whole lot quickly, almost shouting, but the sounds she made were becoming even more fragmented and abstract, increasing Gerry's frustration.

"Mary, listen, please. Because I've got a feeling we might not get the chance to talk again for some time."

A squawk down the line led Gerry to believe that she could hear him considerably more clearly than he could her.

"This place, where I am...it's not easy to find. If Alister is somewhere about, I'll try to let you know but I think we're drifting apart, getting further away. But that's how it is—people go missing all the time you know. Without trace. This place is bad, but it could be worse."

He could no longer recognise the tone of Mary's voice and the phone was getting very cold; too cold to hold.

He said, "I hope you don't think any of this is my fault, Mary. I expect you do. I'm sorry. Can't say any more. Got to go," and he had to put the phone down quickly because it was now like ice in his hand. In fact a thin layer of crystal glistened on its surface, which was covered with tiny cracks. The instrument was starting to disintegrate. Gerry threw it into the waste bin.

«« — »»

After pulling the twin of the chair the agent was in to a position near and opposite him, Gerry sat and watched while the old man, still

spluttering and wheezing, worked his way back to something near normality. As soon as he was able to breath more easily he pulled a pack
of cigarettes from the pocket of his trousers, stuck one in his mouth but
failed to light it because his hands still trembled. Gerry lit a match for
him and held it out. The agent kept a wary eye on him as he inhaled to
ignite the tobacco, then, when the cigarette was burning, he relaxed
somewhat and even signalled thanks to Gerry with a slight nod of the
head.

"I'm sorry," Gerry said. "I could have hurt you. For a moment back
there, I wanted to. Something…came over me." He grimaced, unhappy
with the inane cliche. "I don't lose my temper like that, ever, though
sometimes I've wished I could."

The agent gave him a dour look that contained, nevertheless, a hint
of sympathy, or compassion even and wiped blood from his nose with
the sleeve of his jacket.

"You don't have to tell me about that," he said. "You're not the first
and you won't be the last to try to take it out on me. But I don't have
control over anything. Like you, I found myself here one day, doing
this job, and couldn't find my way out. We're stuck with it. All of us."
The agent lit a second cigarette from the stump of the first without
much trouble now. He was steadying down. "You just have to learn to
accept it."

"Mustn't grumble, eh. That what you mean?"

"Well, we all do a bit. Some more than others."

"You could have warned me," Gerry said.

"No, it was too late for that. Once you've found this place, you're
on the wrong side of the glass, as it were—there's no going back."

"It's a small world," Gerry said.

The agent smiled wearily. "That's a fact," he said. "And as you'll
find out, it's getting smaller." He leaned his head back, blew a cloud of
smoke up towards the ceiling between pursed lips then said, "It
occurred to me a long time ago, soon after I got here, in fact, that in one
way, but in no other, it's a bit like happiness."

"What is?"

"This place."

"Happiness!"

"You know how it is. If you go looking for it, you just can't find it, but if you stop looking, it can come over you sometimes, when you least expect it."

Gerry wasn't sure if he was expected to laugh. He said, "Not here it doesn't. Not that I've noticed."

The agent acknowledged the truth of that.

He stood up. "Well, I'll have to get on. There's work to do."

"You're going to show some new people round?"

"I've a list of appointments as long as your arm. If they turn up, that is. Most of them don't."

"And what happens to them?"

"Nothing," the agent said as he headed for the door. "As far as I know."

««—»»

Gerry was to have gone to another lecture next day, Tuesday, but after some guilty arm-wrestling with his conscience he decided to skip it. He couldn't face the possibility that he might have to give an explanation for his absence the previous day. It was a small point, but it bothered him. He imagined having to present an account of himself in front of the other students in his year, like a troublesome schoolboy called up in front of the class by his teacher. A childish thought, of course, no doubt about it, but one that haunted and immobilised him for days. It wasn't until well into the following week that he was able to pluck up enough courage to put it all behind him, make a new start, and try again. He decided to say he'd been ill and then somehow borrow a fellow student's notes so he could catch up on what he'd missed, before the task got too big for him.

With that in mind he got up and set out early one morning so he could get to the University in plenty of time, but he couldn't find the building. It wasn't where he'd left it last time he'd called there. He followed the same streets but didn't end up at the same place. He wondered about for hours but none of the mystified people he asked for directions had even heard of the establishment. At last, exhausted, when he gave up the search, he was easily able to find his way home, however.

As soon as he was back in his flat he wrapped himself in Alister's 'Polar Explorer' sleeping bag and climbed into bed.

He remained there for a long but indeterminate time.

«« — »»

There was a quiet, insistent droning noise somewhere in the room, a sound that Gerry could not identify the cause of. It was unlike anything he had heard before. It took him some time to come to the conclusion that it must have been coming from his phone, that he had flung into a waste bin next to his work table two or three days before. He listened to its burbling for a while then grabbed the arms of the chair he was sitting in and laboriously pushed himself up and out of it.

The waste bin was only a few steps away but he was feeling dizzy and it seemed to take him a long time to get there. He had to make a serious effort to walk straight because the muscles in his legs would not quite do what was expected of them. He'd stayed in bed most of the day, every day, for how long now?—he wasn't sure—during which time he'd hardly eaten anything and got no exercise. He was weakening. His muscles were seizing up, his limbs atrophying.

Bending down over the bin was uncomfortable too. His permanent dizziness increased and the contents of the bin appeared to be spinning slowly, as though a placid, idling whirlpool had taken hold of his few bits of rubbish. He saw the phone drifting round and reached down for it but each time he tried to take hold of it he was a fraction of a second too late and it eluded him. He observed this phenomenon with interest and even a degree of amusement for a while, dipping his hand in time after time, but always too late, then changed tactics and started to grab with both hands with a similar lack of success. It was not until he had accidentally knocked the bin over and its contents had spilt onto the floor that he was able to get a grip on the phone. As he raised it he could see that it had decayed much further and now parts of it were turning into tiny, tumbling showers of dust in his hand. Nevertheless, he rested the crumbling instrument against his ear, pressed what was left of the answer button and said, "Yeah, Gerry here. Wha'd'y'want."

It was the first time he'd heard his own voice for a long time. He sounded as though he was out in the desert dying of thirst.

"It's me."

"Sorry? Who's that?"

"*Alister*, Gerry. Don't tell me you don't know me."

"Alister? That's not your voice. That really is you? You don't sound right.

"You too."

"For Christ's sake, what happened to you? Where have you been.?"

"I couldn't stand it at your place. What I saw in that mirror—that face—I couldn't get it out of my mind and I couldn't sleep. I needed to talk to you but I didn't want to wake you. Probably couldn't have done, you were so far gone. So I went out on my own."

"To where, at that time of night?"

"To see if I could find that club."

"With the dead girls?"

"That's the one."

"And did you find it?"

"In the end, yes. It's not so far away. Just round a couple of corners. It was still open. And she was there."

"Who?"

"The one I'd seen in the mirror. She works there. She told me she'd been waiting for me. She didn't look too bad in the flesh. Quite acceptable. You know how it is when you're pissed. Sometimes anything will do. Maybe it was that. Well, we talked, or rather, I talked, and we had a few drinks. Well, a lot, it must have been. Anyway, the last one was too much for me. I blacked out. Must have woken up some time some where, but I can't remember anything about that. Since then I've been alone and I must have lost some time, if you know what I mean, or maybe my memory's totally fucked. My watch says it's 17.48 but I don't know what I've been doing all day. I believe I've been wandering round, like I was lost, but I've no recollection where I've been."

"Lost. I'll say you were. How long have you been lost, do you suppose?"

"Must be something like ten hours. More. I'm not sure."

Gerry tried to work out how long ago it was that Alister vanished. More than just a few days. Weeks? Or should that be months? He felt a cold, distant and now familiar panic deep down that made his legs even weaker. He held on to the edge of his work table with his free hand to support himself.

Alister said, "I'm in a bad situation, Gerry. It's very confusing. I've been trying to contact you and Mary all day, and other people too, but no one answered."

"We tried to get through to you, Alister, but gave up a long time ago. I did, anyway."

"Why did you do that?"

Because I thought you were dead? No. Gerry couldn't bring himself to say that. And maybe Mary was still searching. In truth, he'd forgotten about Alister some time ago. Hadn't given him a thought.

When he didn't get an answer to his question Alister said, "You can't know how glad I am to hear you again, Gerry. I've been so lonely. It's empty round here. There's nobody on the streets now. Nobody to ask the way. And I've lost the car, don't know where or what happened to it, so I've had to walk. I tell you, I'm tired out."

"You sound it. Where are you, Al? I'll come and see if I can find you."

"That won't be difficult. I'm standing in the garden outside the main door to your building. I rang the bell a few times but you didn't answer. So I tried the phone. Thank God it worked at last."

"You're that close! Why didn't you say so in the first place?" Gerry said. "I'll come and let you in but it might take a while for me to get there. I'm not feeling too good myself."

"Still got a hangover?" Alister was trying to be cheerful, perhaps, but he didn't sound anything less than miserable and anxious.

"No, that cleared up. I'm on my way down now, Al. Be with you soon."

"Thanks, Gerry. It's snowing again. Hard. Did you know that? And it's as cold as a penguin's arse out here. But take your time. Whatever's wrong, don't make yourself worse."

"I'll try not to."

Gerry put the rotting phone down on the table. The edges of his hand had worn grooves in its sides, he noticed. The casing had split open so it resembled a legless, gutted bug lying on its back.

He gazed round the room and saw through the open door of his wardrobe that all his clothing had been removed from the hangers he had put them on and been replaced by a selection of female garments. He guessed that the pile of neatly packed shopping bags in a corner of the room contained his own stuff. His books had been bagged-up and placed there, too, sometime when he'd been asleep. That sort of thing had been happening more and more often and he'd recently decided not to do anything about it any more. Once or twice he'd taken the trouble to unpack everything but now he couldn't be bothered.

Wishing he had crutches, because his legs were so reluctant to take his weight and he was all the time feeling out of balance and disoriented, Gerry hobbled to the stairs and began easing himself down a step at a time. The banister rail was loose and rattled and jerked back and forth as he clung to it. Nevertheless, he made some slow though unsteady progress. He'd reached the fifth step when the door of the Bendix flat banged open behind him and the boys spilled out onto the corridor. They must have just caught sight of the back of his head as he descended.

"Hey, he's out. Our man's out," Bobby shouted.

"What's he doing there?" Andy said. "Is he stuck?"

"Yes, he is," said Bobby. "Look at him. He can't get down the stairs."

"And he can't get up."

"He can't go up or down."

"He's not going anywhere."

Gerry had come to a halt, partly from tiredness and weakness but also from nervousness about having the pair out of sight behind him. He half turned so he was able to get a look at the boys.

They were standing together at attention at the top of the stairs. They had the bright pink and green plastic guns, that Gerry had seen them slaughtering each other with many times, stuck in their belts. Both were wearing well worn, tattered and dirty combat trousers with many baggy pockets, that might once have belonged to two much bigger people. Gerry thought he could remember seeing a couple of pairs like them on one of the heaps of old clothing on the floor down in Maggie's room. These were topped by shiny black military style jackets, covered with badges and dozens of tiny flashing silver lights, that had a homemade-by-mother look. On their heads were helmets with built-in, goggle-like mirrored shades that hid most of their noses and their ears as well as their eyes. These drew attention to their pug's chins and the tips of their noses—an effect that Gerry might once have found comical.

When their taunting stopped they stared at him and he at them in silence. Seconds ticked by. Nobody moved.

Gerry was expecting their mother to appear at any moment to sort them out. She must have heard something of what they had been saying as the door to the family flat was wide open and the boys had been talking at the tops of their voices, as usual.

Not much more than three or four minutes could have passed since Gerry had put down the phone but he was aware that Alister, alone and at the end of his tether, would be painfully conscious of every passing moment he had to wait to re-establish contact. Nevertheless, Gerry was reluctant to turn his back on the boys and continue down, because of something he detected in their mood and attitude that he had not come across before. Usually, at least some of their belligerence had been aimed by each at the other, but now it all seemed to be coming his way. And, in his weakened state, they might be able to do him harm if they wanted to.

He tried hard to remember Mrs. Bendix's first name. She had told him, when they first met, that she refused to respond to her surname, that of her hated ex-husband. But her Christian name wouldn't come to mind.

The boys must have come to some unspoken mutual agreement because, moving in perfect coordination, they stepped forward and sat down next to each other on the top step, blocking any retreat Gerry's might have wanted to make back to his apartment.

"'Cynthia,' that was it," Gerry recollected aloud. It was not a name that came easily to the tongue, he discovered. Nevertheless he was just about to call it out again when the boys said, squawking in unison, "She won't come. Not this time."

Looking up at the mirrors over their eyes Gerry could see a quartet of his own reflections, clear, no doubt, in every detail in the bright ceiling light, but too tiny and distant for him to be able to see his own expression.

"What did you say?" he said, hearing how hoarse and short of breath he sounded.

"You know. You heard," Bobby said.

"Who won't come?"

"That woman."

"Why won't she come? How can you be so sure she won't."

Andy said, "We won't let her."

"That's right," Bobby confirmed. "You think she's our mom, but she's not."

Not really surprised by this revelation, but not necessarily believing it, either, Gerry said, "Then who is she?"

"She's our prisoner," Andy said. "Always has been. We keep her around to look after us, otherwise we'd get into trouble. And now we've told her she'll have to stay in her room."

"See, she was just part of the es-s-speriment," Bobby's tongue tripped on the word, "but we don't need her now."

"Experiment. What experiment?"

Andy opened the fingers of one podgy hand and waved them round, indicating all directions. "This one." He reached up and pulled thoughtfully at the flesh under his chin. It was the gesture of an old man. "Who do you think we are?" he said.

"Dressed up in those outfits, you mean?" Gerry said irritably. "I've no idea. Why don't you tell me?"

He was thinking, *I've got to get away from them.*

"We're the S. C. K. That's what."

"And that stands for?"

"Star Cluster Kids."

Gerry told himself, *Go.*

He pulled himself as upright as he could and hauled his body round and away from the boys. But he decided it was still advisable not to aggravate them more than he had to so, trying to sound interested, he said, "That's cool. And who and what are they? Characters from cartoons you watch on TV?"

"The TV doesn't work."

"Mine neither. Okay. So the Star Cluster Kids are from a comic book, something like that? And they do experiments." He was walking downstairs now, his back bristling. He expected to get things thrown at him, at least.

"We don't read comic books," Andy said.

"We don't read words written down," Bobby added.

Gerry had reached the bottom of the stairs and soon he would be able to turn a corner and pass out of their sight. Till then, he continued to humour the boys as best he could.

"And why is that?" he said.

"We can't," Bobby said.

"We can't read books, but we can read each other's minds," Andy said.

"Oh, well, *wow,* it must be great to be able to do that," Gerry said as he turned the bend. "Okay boys, I've got to go now. See you again some time, but not too soon…"

He slipped round the corner like an eel, in spite of his infirmities.

"So long Gerry," the boys chorused, in perfect unison. Then they must have decided to end whatever truce they'd called in the perennial hostilities between them because Gerry could hear them going for each other, thumping and kicking, grunting, gouging, probably, and firing their plastic guns and kicking up general hell.

As he descended Gerry became aware of other banging noises ahead of him. More measured than those coming from behind, he thought at first that someone was beating time for a slow march on a drum down in the lobby behind the front door. Then he realised that someone—Alister, most likely—was hitting the door with his fist. Getting impatient.

He hurried on as best he could, reaching out for the wall to support himself and stopping every few paces for seconds to catch his breath.

He called out to Alister to let him know that he was on his way but the banging on the door continued unabated in volume and at the same steady pace.

At last he managed to get to the door and, after struggling with the stiff handle, got it open.

Everything was quiet outside. As Alister had said, it was snowing. Snow had built up inches deep on the steps leading out to the drive. The snow was smooth and unmarked. There were certainly no footprints of any kind on the steps or anywhere else as far as Gerry could see.

He stared out at the white garden with its few bare, black trees and the equally bare, blank concreted wall beyond for some time. He called out Alister's name many times. The blanket of snow softened and stifled the sound of his voice, as though he was shouting into an actual blanket over his mouth.

After a while he was relieved to see someone moving towards him, coming through the gate. But he soon realised that it wasn't Alister. It was the man from the agency, dressed as he always was in his funeral manager's suit, and inadequately for the weather. He came and stood beside Gerry on the top step but gave no sign of recognition or even of awareness that he was not alone. Shivering and coughing he fumbled a cigarette into his mouth, managed, after many attempts, to get it lit in spite of the wind, then screwed his arms up tight against his chest in a futile attempt to keep out the cold.

The person he was waiting for soon showed up. A woman in her late thirties appeared at the gate and trudged uncomfortably through the snow towards the building in inappropriate open high-heeled shoes. Her excessively made-up face looked care worn and worried, but bore a trace of optimism. That faded, however, when she looked up at the building as she approached and clearly did not think much of what she saw. Gerry, remembering his own first impression of the place, could easily read and sympathise with the disappointment that crossed her face.

The agent tossed away his cigarette just before she reached him and, at her instigation, the two of then shook hands. The man urged her inside, out of the weather, with a wave of his arm.

Gerry found he was standing directly in her path. He decided not to step aside to let her pass. The woman wasn't looking at him but side-ways at the agent, who was answering some question she had asked.

"Stop, you can't do this," Gerry said, holding up his hand like a policeman on traffic duty. "Please, both of you, stay here. Don't go inside yet. We need to talk."

Neither of them reacted at all to Gerry's presence or to anything he said. They continued forward.

Gerry stood his ground and the woman walked through him into the building. He didn't feel a thing.

Once the pair of them were inside the hallway the agent, obviously relieved to get out of the cold, turned and carefully closed the door behind him.

LANGTHWAITE ROAD

ROAD

SIMON CLARK

What comes before

When I look out of my room window I see the road I grew up by.

It's a road that runs broad and straight until it reaches Annie Tyndall Wood. There, it makes a sharp left.

I see it in my imagination, too. I can run my mind's eye over it like you can run your tongue over your lover's arm. There's the road: with one lane for traffic into town; the other lane takes the traffic away into the world beyond the wild wood. There's the road sign. Here's the bridge where a river flows to the sea.

Langthwaite Road runs all the way to the city of York. I like to think about that at times likes this. I see myself riding up safe and high in the cab of a truck. The road bridges the muddy fields. A span of firm asphalt that supports the turning wheel. The road has camber. That means it curves so rainwater may escape from it. It is smooth; wheels don't bounce; passengers are not jolted. The line of white dashes along its center guides the driver home.

If you were to rest your eye on the surface you would see its blue-black skin...a skin that feels a thousand tires across its back every day. On hot summer evenings you might smell the tar-rich scent of asphalt.

To press that mind's eye to the surface would take you deeper into the road. Through the cool, crisp shell of asphalt. Into compacted limestone beneath. Below that is a firm, supporting bed of red shale that rests on God's own sweet earth.

I've stood at this window and watched the road ever since I was able to pull myself up from my infant bed. For me the road's always been there. I hear the sound of its pulse at night. Passing cars, trucks, hearses, buses, ice cream vans, ambulances.

Now.

Take it from the top: —

One, two three...

My road is like no other.

My road is unique.

My road devours.

When I was eight I saw a car tearing the length of the road's strong, broad back. The car jumped. I ran out of the house, then down the drive to the road. The car lay belly up on the blacktop. Already it had begun to eat. I saw the driver hanging by the seatbelt. There were bite marks on his face. The road had chewed the meat from his arms. The asphalt had started to drink the life blood that poured from him.

It's happened quite a bit since then. Every few weeks, another car delivers the road yet another meal.

For a while I tried to explain to my mother. She'd smile and pat my head. "My goodness you have an imagination, young man. Now go out and play, Leo. Mummy's meeting a new friend tonight."

So Leo ran and played.

Leo made friends with the road.

But then the road and Leo fell out.

It happens sometimes.

(From **Life Bites**, by Leo)

《《——》》

One

MY NAME'S VIC BLAKE. This is the place to start it as much as anywhere. I've thrown newspaper cuttings onto the bed. You can stick your
hand in and pull them out at random.

Like this one:

ACCIDENT BLACKSPOT CLAIMS ANOTHER LIFE

North Sutton's notorious Langthwaite Road was the
scene of a fatal accident yesterday. A car driven by
Daniel Franks, a local man, was in collision with a stationary tractor.

Or this one:

Police are appealing for witnesses after a hit and run
left a mother of three critically ill in hospital. Kathleen
Wilson, 43, had been cycling toward North Sutton along
Langthwaite Road when...

Or this:

...around thirty local people gathered outside the town
hall to protest about Langthwaite Road, the notorious
accident blackspot which has claimed eighteen lives in
the past five years, and left more than thirty people
seriously injured. Council officials stated that they
would investigate...

Or even this:

Police are appealing for witnesses after a stolen van
was involved in a head-on collision with a car on
Langthwaite Road. All three occupants of the car were
pronounced dead at the scene of the accident. The vic-

tims were named as Mary Douglas (56), her daughter Kate Delgardo (35) and granddaughter, Chloe, aged eighteen months.

More? You better believe there's more. Like this one:

The Coroner, Mr. Stanley Hope, recorded the accidental death of eight-year-old Robin Slater, who was a passenger in the car driven by his grandfather. In closing, Mr. Hope stated that, 'I find it tragic that this, the third inquest I've presided over involving a fatal vehicle accident this year, has yet again occurred on Langthwaite Road. Drivers must remember that speed restrictions are mandatory for a reason. Those who drive too fast endanger not only their own lives, but...'

««——»»

And so it goes on. And so they all go on.

And there are lots of them, I can tell you.

You'll be thinking that people who collect newspaper clipping are obsessed. I agree. It gets you like that.

But first, I should explain something. In the early hours of a Sunday morning five weeks ago my friend Paul Robertson was killed on Langthwaite Road. From tire marks the police concluded that his car swerved to avoid hitting 'some unknown obstruction' and spun off the road. It landed upside down in a field. He was strangled by his own seatbelt.

Dead on arrival, as the saying goes.

I'd known Paul Robertson since nursery school. He was a big softie then. After his mother left him in class he'd wind up on the nursery teacher's knee as we sat cross-legged on the carpet to sing 'The Wheels On The Bus' and 'Wind The Bobbin Up.' He'd soon stop crying (or 'rawping' as we call it round here, an old Viking word our history teacher used to tell us). Every now and again, the nursery schoolteacher would hold a big handkerchief to Paul's face so he could blow his nose.

Paul Robertson was 24—same as me—played in the same pub football team. More or less did the same kind of stuff. But when he left school he went into army while I joined my Dad on the boat.

The army did things to Paul...made him tough. Made him strong. A big, tough artilleryman. He could bend six-inch nails with one hand. No one messed with him. Then he went and ran his car off the road and strangled himself with his own seatbelt.

After the funeral, his mother gave me one of those plastic carrier-bags you get from the supermarket—this one was from Tesco and it was absolutely filled with stuff. 'He would have liked you to have these,' she said. Without looking at what was inside I dropped the lot in one of the big wheelie bins behind the garage.

It's funny. I grew up, like you, thinking that grief made you feel sad. It doesn't, does it? It makes you angry.

Even so, I wanted nothing to do with bloody Langthwaite Road. I certainly wasn't going to collect damn newspaper cuttings about the thing. There was nothing I could do about Paul Robertson, good friend though he was. Like everyone else in his life, once the funeral was over I just had to get on with my own three score and ten.

Then, two weeks after Paul died, a letter came, addressed to me.

> *Vic*
> *Leo Carter thinks you should know.*
> *Paul Robertson saw it happen once.*
> *So Paul Robertson was murdered.*
> *Leo*

So I started collecting newspaper clippings.

"Vic, who are you talking to?"

"No one."

"I heard a voice?"

"I was thinking aloud."

"You know what they do with people who talk to themselves?"

"Yeah, I know...lucky them. Three free meals a day and as much television as they can watch."

"Mr. Grumpy Boots." Faith walked into the bedroom. There were towels round her body and her head. "You'll have to get that shower looked at; it keeps running cold."

"It'll need a new thermostat."

"Oh God, Vic. What's this all over the bed?"

"Just some clippings."

"I need to sit down at that end to dry my hair."

"I'll move th— Don't you do it, your hands are wet. They'll get ruined."

"It's about time they did."

"I'll decide when to throw them out."

"It puts you in a bad mood every time you look at them." Faith pulled the towel free of her head. "Will you plug the hairdryer in for me?" She began to comb her damp hair. "Never mind, I'll do it."

"No, it's okay…just let me shift these off the bed first."

"You haven't done anything with that letter from Leo, have you?"

"No."

"If you take it to the police you'll end up a laughing stock." She reached out to touch my arm. "I don't want people taking you for a fool, Vic."

"They won't."

"So you're not going to take that letter any further?"

"No. Now, what do you want with the chicken—noodles or salad?"

"I thought we were going out for a curry?"

"I don't think I can eat a curry tonight."

She glared. "See? Those bloody newspaper clippings and the bloody letter—"

"I'm just not hungry enough for a curry.

"They're preying on your mind, aren't they?"

"No, Faith, they are not preying on my mind." I put the clippings into the shoebox, then pushed it into the top of the wardrobe. Leo's letter was on top.

Bloody poison, that letter.

"So what do you plan to do after supper?" she asked.

I shrugged. "Nothing much."

"So I take it you won't be going out for another of your walks again?"

"I don't know what I'm doing yet. Or have you written out a damn timetable for me? Supper at seven. Television at eight. Bed at ten—"

"Vic—"

"Lights out ten fifteen."

"Vic!" She pointed the hairdryer like it was a gun. "Stop it. This has gone far enough."

"Damn right."

"Vic. Listen, I'm on your side."

"You've got a funny way of showing it sometimes."

"That's because this has got me worried. Do you think I like to see you lying awake at night raking it all over? Paul had an accident, that's all. It was tragic but it was just another accident out on bloody Langthwaite Road."

"I know. So why keep going on about it?"

"Because you keep going on about it."

"I don't—"

"You might not be talking about Paul, but you're thinking about him. Then you know full well you go walking up the road until you get to…you know. I don't have to paint you a picture, do I?"

The bedroom was hit by one of those silences that can go either way. Into blistering argument—we'd had plenty of those—or to apologies, followed by kisses. And the kisses were sometimes followed by bed.

I heard the traffic going by in the rain outside.

"I'll get a new thermostat tomorrow," I told her.

"It'd be nice to get under without freezing my tits off." She smiled. "See?" She opened the towel. "They get all goosey."

"I'll do salad," I told her.

«« —»»

Downstairs I rolled a tomato backwards and forwards on the table.

Faith came in. She had dressed in jeans and a sweatshirt. She walked through to the lobby and I heard her pull her shoes from the cupboard.

I asked one of those questions that's intended more as a prompt than anything else. "What're you doing, Faith?"

"Going out."

"What about supper?"

She looked at the tomato. "Doesn't look quite ready yet."

"Soon will be. The chicken will microwave."

"How'd the catch go?"

"A couple of lobsters and around a dozen crabs."

"Better than nothing I suppose."

"There'll be more tomorrow. It was running a swell today. Lobsters don't like waves."

"So they stayed at home?"

"It'll be all right next time. The forecast's for light westerlies. Faith?"

"Uhm?"

"Where are you going?"

"Where?" She pulled on her coat, then looped the scarf round her neck. "I'm going out walking with you. We'll do a turn on Langthwaite Road, first."

"Then what?"

"Then we're going up to Leo's."

"Leo's?" This caught me by surprise.

"Leo's," she said firmly.

"But he won't be in?"

"He's always in."

"No, I mean…" I tapped the side of my head with a finger. "He won't be in here."

«« — »»

Two

IT'S FUNNY ISN'T IT? The decision you make in the next ten minutes could result in you dying. Doesn't have to be a big LIFE or DEATH decision. You might choose to take a bath. You slip on the soap: break your neck. You might decide to fix the downspout on the guttering. Only you fall off the bloody ladder.

In our case it was the walk.

I led the way. It was dark. Streetlights burned with that orange light that makes you think the world's gone rusty in the rain.

"I'm not an Olympic athlete, Vic."

"What do you mean?"

"I mean can't we slow down?"

"I'm not walking fast."

"Fast enough," Faith complained. "I'm breaking into a sweat."

"Here." I held out my hand. She took it. Her palm felt hot.

"Cold hands, warm heart?" she smiled at me.

"Yeah...toastie."

She rolled her eyes. "Your mother always said you were a moody bugger."

"You had fair warning then."

She shook her head with one of those long suffering sighs that she did so well. "I know this isn't you, Vic. You are moody at times, but you've never been like this before." Then talking to herself she hissed. "It's that bloody letter."

"Never mind the bloody letter, it's bloody Leo," I said. "Maybe it's time he was locked up."

"I know. I used to feel sorry for him. Not anymore."

We walked hand in hand. When I started walking faster Faith squeezed my hand, then pulled me back with a smile as if to rein me in.

I looked up at the sky. The cloud was thinning nicely, letting a bit of moon peep through.

"It's coming from the south west. The sea'll drop soon."

"Fancy taking a look at it?"

"The sea?" I shook my head. "I'll get enough of it tomorrow."

"So, it's Langthwaite Road after all then?"

"Yep."

"Lovely...a moonlit night; the company of the one you love...and a stroll to a notorious accident-blackspot. You know how to show a girl a good time, Vic, I'll give you that."

"You didn't have to come."

We turned at the junction leaving the houses behind.

She said, "Call me, daft, but even after this long together I still like your company."

"What, a moody bugger like me?" This time I did smile.

"Well, there's nothing on television worth watching."

We walked along the pavement at the side of the road. It was the usual mid-evening in November. Dark. Wet underfoot. In the distance you could make out the sound of surf. If it ran an easterly the surf ripped at the beach. Then you could hear the sea when you were in bed. Tonight the sound was soft. So, maybe we were set for fair fishing tomorrow.

This road was a feeder for the estate so it was mainly cars with the occasional optimistic ice cream truck.

It's only when you reach Langthwaite Road that you get the real speeders. And there are the usual heavyweights: the oil tankers pounding the highway toward the refinery on the far side of North Sutton. When they leave full they're pulling a lot of weight up the slight incline. It slows them down, so that's when you get cars over-taking.

That's what maybe happened to Paul. Maybe he risked passing a slow truck and then spun off. Bastard trucker never stopped if that was the case. A farmer found Paul still strung up by the seatbelt in his car. Poor sod must have been there all night.

I wondered if Paul had been conscious when he'd started to choke. God only knows why he couldn't have reached the seatbelt release—

"Vic...will you answer me?"

"What?"

"You haven't been listening, have you?"

"Course I have."

"What did I say, then?"

"About Christmas." I suddenly realised I'd heard the word.

"What about Christmas?"

"Shopping?" It was a wild guess, and not a very good one.

"Vic." She did the sigh again. "About Christmas Day. Do we go to your mum and dad's for Christmas dinner or to mine."

We left the feeder road. Now we were on Langthwaite Road. Or at least the pavement that runs alongside it. The road runs broad and straight here, with streetlights few and far between. The road surface is black and, in the dark, it always makes me think of deep water.

For some reason, I shivered.

But then, I always shiver when I'm on Langthwaite bloody Road. Imagine...a grown man of twenty-four shivering with— With what? I see that bit of road and the hairs stand up on my arms.

Walking the road alongside Faith, I felt them go up on the back of my neck, too. The muscles quivered in my back.

Faith looked up at me. I couldn't see her face in shadow. Her eyes glinted though. "Cold?"

"No, I'm fine." I curled my toes inside my seaboots. She'd heard the waver in my voice. One of those wavers you get when you're about to cry. Sure, she registered the sound. She had the sense, though, not to pass comment.

I walked, keeping myself between Faith and the road. The oil tankers were roaring by tonight, flinging spray into our faces. Faith leaned into me as she walked, keeping warm, or maybe just wanting to maintain a closeness with me.

"So what's it to be, then Vic?"

"What's what to be?" I asked. Maybe I'd missed another question?

"Your family or mine for Christmas dinner?"

"Neither, we'll have picnic on the beach."

She knew I was joking. "Yeah, right. People already think you're odd so they wouldn't be surprised."

"I must be odd...I'm married to you."

"You swine." She had a smile on her face as she pulled away from me then made as if to thump my arm. I stepped back as she moved forward.

Normally, I'm the clumsy one, but Faith tripped. Her whole body gave a dip as her balance shifted; her trying to recover only made it worse. She sort of boosted herself forward, both arms reaching out.

I remember making a grab for her as she fell, but although my fingers made contact with her coat I couldn't grab the fabric. She tumbled forward onto the road, landing flat on her stomach, arms stretched out. Palms down.

She looked back at me. First, there was surprise on her face at the suddenness of the fall, then an annoyed expression as if she couldn't believe she'd just gone and tripped over own feet.

I looked down at her. One of those split second things where I told myself: It was okay, she would get straight back up onto her feet.

But then the sound came...as a rush at first and then quickly transforming itself into a roar. I looked to my left to see a wall of light rushing towards her.

"Vic!"

The sound of panic did it for me. I pounced, grabbed her arm. Heard her grunt because it hurt her, then yanked her back off the road.

The truck swept by. The slipstream dragged at our hair, clothes, even our faces. Spray blinded us, got in our mouths, road grit scratched against my teeth.

Damn thing didn't even sound its horn. Just tore by us like we didn't even exist...the driver maybe talking on a cellphone or even pouring a coffee.

"Faith, are you all right?"

She brushed her hands down the front of her coat. "Damn it," she said under her breath. When she held her wrist up to what light there was I saw a graze across the heel of her hand.

"Damn," she said again.

"Faith?"

"I'm all right." She looked down at her coat. "I hope that mark isn't oil."

I watched her straightening her clothes, pushing back her hair from her face, checking the graze again. Some blood. Not much.

Like I said. Decisions. Decisions...Make the wrong one and that could be the end of everything for you. If I had decided she could make it to her feet by herself Faith would have gone under the truck's wheels. Another one up for Langthwaite bloody Road.

She started to walk.

"Where are you going?" I asked.

"I'm finishing the walk. Why?"

"Don't you want to go home?"

"Not on your life. Not until we've done what we set out to do."

«« —— »»

Three

FAITH HELD MY HAND TIGHT as we walked after the near accident.

Accident be damned. That old road just wanted to gobble folk up. I could see it in my mind's eye like some Gothic animation. The road, the big black road that looks like deep water. Dozens of swellings appear like tumors...they break open to form mouths that snap. Cats-eyes glinting all greedy and evil. The mouths dart at passing cars. The teeth rip the rubber to shreds. Punctures galore. Cars spin out of control. Crash and burn. The snapping mouths lunge out at pedestrians. There's screaming, there's running—

"Vic?"

"Uh?"

"You're not listening again."

"Oh."

She put her arm around my waist as we walked. "That was quick thinking. Thank you."

"You okay?"

"I am now. But what if you hadn't been fast enough?"

I could feel tremors running through her body.

She gave a nervous sounding laugh. "I'd have been dead, wouldn't I?"

"Best not think about it."

She sighed. "Just be thankful you won't be in the nightmare I have tonight."

I was trying to think of something reassuring when we reached the spot.

"So it was here?" she said.

I nodded. "You can't see much. There's broken branches on the bush over there."

"The car almost went right over the top of it?"

"It must have taken off like a rocket when it left the road. There weren't any marks in the field until about thirty yards out. The car didn't even hit the fence."

Faith looked out into the dark field. "He must have been going fast, Vic."

"You should have seen the state of his car."

Here, the road stood on a causeway a good five feet above the surrounding fields. The ploughed earth looked mushily soft. Even so, when Paul's car hit it must have felt hard as concrete.

Traffic streamed by us, still raising clouds of white spray. Tires hissed like a bunch of mad snakes. Above us, the moon went in and out of cloud. I looked round. There was nothing much here but fields. There were no other pedestrians about. Not many people are stupid enough to stroll along a busy road on a dreary November night.

Faith crouched to look at the bunches of flowers that friends and family had laid on the grass verge. They were bedraggled specimens now, going to mush in the wet. Cellophane wrappers fluttered in the slipstream from trucks. If you had a mind to, you could still make out a few words on the cards tied to the bunches.

> *We love you, Paul...*
> and
> *God bless...*
> and
> *can't believe you were taken from us...*
> and
> *RIP, love Auntie Mary xxx...*
> and
> *From your mates in C platoon...*
> and, of course
> *All my love. Dad.*

Funny thing is, every time I saw the bunches of flowers lying there I felt a real, burning urge to kick the fucking things into the ditch.

I glanced at Faith. She'd turned away from the flowers now. She looked at the only house on this stretch of highway. It was an old stone farmhouse that stood on a piddling bump of a hill. It didn't look much but what it had going for it was that it boasted clear views of Langthwaite Road.

A light shone from an upstairs window.

Faith turned to me then nodded back at the house. "Looks as if Leo's still up."

"You don't have to go if you don't want to."

"Oh, I want to all right. Ready?"

I nearly said to her, *Now take care crossing the road.*

Instead I kept my mouth closed. We had to wait for a while for a break in the traffic, the trucks were coming thick and fast tonight, roaring like monsters. All noise and lights and spray. All motorized aggression in spades.

I gripped my wife's hand as at last we crossed the road to Leo's house.

«« — »»

Four

"YES, OF COURSE LEO'S IN...*Leo? Leo! You've got visitors!*" This last bit was thrown up the stairs. Leo's mother looked pleased. She probably didn't make this kind of announcement often. "Leo. Some of your friends have called to see you."

She shot me a near wolfish grin, her eyes sparking. "It's Vic, isn't it? And—"

"Faith," Faith said.

"Leo?" She called up the stairs again. "It's Vic and Faith...they're here to see you."

She smiled back at us. "He won't be long. He's working."

"That's okay," Faith said. "We should have phoned first."

"Oh, that's no problem." Leo's mother smiled showing lots of eyes and teeth. She was delighted someone had made the effort to see her son at all.

Miss Carter had Leo when she was sixteen. She was the kind of person that towns like North Sutton love to hate. My mother and my friends' mothers weren't slow in filling any gaps in her life down through the years. By the time I was twelve I had the whole case history. Miss Carter had been a wild child. Expelled from school for messing with drugs. A shoplifter ("Brazen as anything," mum told me. "Walked out of Woolworth's with a pile of records that high...") and a teenage runaway ("Left on Christmas Eve with a man twice her age..."). Eventually she returned pregnant with Leo when she was sixteen ("She's nothing but trouble to her parents—well, she's pregnant now. That's her life ruined for good!").

Miss Carter rented a market stall. She sold stuff she got from jumble sales as antiques. By the time Leo started high school she had three antique shops in towns along the coast ("Some people can't but help fall on their feet," grumbled the gossips. "She can't have made all that money herself. A man must be giving it to her.") That'd make men in the pub smile in a knowing way. She bought this big farmhouse and drove a new BMW so she must be doing something right.

Miss Carter was slim, attractive. Her hair was curly, and in a style that wasn't fashionable in North Sutton. To my neighbors she was some combination of tart and snob, but men always took a good long lingering look at her when she glided by.

She may have been unpopular—which she was—but she had style. She had charisma. She made your skin tingle when she looked at you.

Her charisma sparkled as she talked to us, standing there waiting for Leo. "Vic. I haven't seen you for ages. What are you doing with yourself now?"

"I'm on the boats."

"With your father?"

I nodded.

"How's he keeping?"

"Oh, he's all right."

"Faith. I know your mother. She works at the travel agent's in Wood Street."

"She's gone part time now. My Dad had a heart attack last year."

"Oh no, I am sorry to hear that, how awful."

"He's all right now. But he had to give up work." Faith wasn't too sure about the charisma treatment. Miss Carter leaned close to you when she talked. Her eyes searched your face as if you'd mucky marks on your cheeks. For men it sent up their pulse rate. It made women uneasy.

As she talked to Faith I couldn't help but notice the slender shape of the woman's body. She was wearing a black lace top that hugged her figure. Her trousers followed her curves in the right places. On her feet were sandals that seemed to be all criss-crossing straps that left her toe-nails showing. They were painted a vivid red. Her neck was very long and pale. There was something aristocratic about it and I remembered my grandmother used to refer to Miss Carter as 'that little Duchess.' She didn't mean it as a compliment.

I got the feeling that I was beginning to stare. Before Miss Carter and Faith noticed I looked round the hallway. As you'd expect it looked pretty much Victorian with heavy purple curtains. There was lots of dark wood. Pieces of chunky antique furniture. A grandfather clock with a *tick...tock...*loud enough to drive you crazy if you had to sit with it for long.

The stairs with a heavy banister in more of that dark, muscular wood loomed down out of the darkness.

"Leo's taking his time," Miss Carter said with the kind of smile to give you a rush of blood. "He probably wants to make an entrance...oh? I know. I'll make a pot of tea. You can have it in his room. Do you both like chocolate cake?"

Faith smiled. A polite one rather than a warm one. "That would be very nice. Can I give you a hand?"

"Yes please. The kitchen's this way...oh?" She looked upstairs as a light came on. "Leo's opened his door."

I didn't move or say anything. She obviously knew her son's routine by now.

She rested her finger on my arm. "He's ready now, Vic. Go on up. First door on the left."

«« — »»

That's Leo's creation
(let's just leave it at that)

Leo encounters the road.
Smells it.
Scent of tar. Scent of funfairs and ghosts.
Leo gets closer. Sees all the things that make it a road. Its darkness, its cats' eyes, its white lines, its humped back, its coat of many cars and bikes and buses and ambulances and blisters and tears and memories.
Leo remembers the road. He used to dream about it when he was a boy. He'd dream he was trying to cross it. He'd trip. Cars came toward him fast and he'd try and roll across the road away from them.

Trying to get to the other side.

Rolling, rolling...

Rolling across its black hardness as cars power down on him. Leo's going to make it. He's going to be safe before the cars reach him and bite him like the man in the car. In the dream Leo rolls and rolls, over and over, trying to reach the other side. The dream lasts for hours. Leo rolls and rolls.

Leo feels the road.

He's felt it through the soles of his cowboy boots as he crossed it. But never skin on skin. No way: that's how you get the ghost on your back.

Leo steals from the road. He's got all kind of things. He's taken them—POW!—from the road. Leo knows the road doesn't like that.

But what's the road going to do? Leo's got a magic charm, keeps him from harm, keeps him safe as a ghost.

Leo spent a long, long time—nearly six months at least—setting out his road treasure. The arrangement has sophistication. It has aplomb. Everything has its place. And every place has its meaning.

What does it mean, Leo?

Does it have a purpose?

Your road treasure mow—sheene...

All machines got to have a purpose...

What purpose, Leo?

What can it do?

Listen.

The man's considered response is this: 'That's Leo's Creation (let's just leave it at that)'

(From **Life Bites**, by Leo)

《《—》》

Five

The man with the guitar's all right.
The man with the guitar's all right, all right, all right!

CALL ME BARRY CHRIST…the times we'd walked home from the pub at midnight singing that one. It had been a summer hit the year I left school. Like the man said: Catchy enough to do your head in.

Paul Robertson and me used to yell our bloody heads off to it as we walked along the seafront with enough beer inside us to keep our bellies afloat.

"The man with the guitar's all right…"

Only this one wasn't, I can tell you.

I'd gone upstairs just as Miss Carter told me to do. Across the landing carpet to the open door. I'd thought it would be a bedroom but it was done out as a lounge. There were no lights on. Three chunky candles did the best they could to chase away the shadows. A spicy smell took my nostrils by storm. Incense, I guessed. There was a big leather sofa. Sitting on it cross-legged, with a black acoustic guitar like he was just about to play, was Leo.

"Knock, knock, anyone in?"

Leo sat staring into thin air. It looked as if he was trying to remember the chord before he began. Only he didn't start to play anything. He sat there: a white, middle-class Buddha. Staring at the wall. Not noticing me. Not moving.

Knock, knock…Nope, Vic, old son. Nobody's home.

I stood there wondering whether I should go out again. Or maybe I should knock on the door.

Then again, he might be getting his thoughts back together. I waited. I used the time to run my eyes over the room. Even though it was furnished with antiques, with more heavy purple curtains at the window, it had a hippy feel to it. There were paintings on the walls of hippy heads with sunlight bursting out their scalps. I guessed they were Leo's. He hung out with the art set at school.

There were more guitars—Strats and a curvy Les Paul; a Marshall amp stood against the wall like a tombstone. A hi-fi system with a kind of flower design on the speakers. Leo must have decorated it with his own fair hand.

And there was Leo, the man himself. He was thin enough to be gaunt. Long hair, hollow cheekbones. Eyes that stared all the way to outer space. There was something dead about them the way he sat there not even blinking.

I looked at him sitting there, and I felt cold inside. He reminded me of those old paintings of Jesus just before he was crucified…same kind of hair, same kind of wispy moustache and beard. And the same expression on his face.

He wore a T-shirt that had faded to gray with regular washings. His jeans had holes in the knees where you could see hairy skin and he was barefoot.

I thought of his mother's bare feet with pretty, painted nails.

He had long thin toes. The kind that you could use to pick up a dropped hairbrush.

It was then that I wondered why on Earth I had bothered to trek out here to see him. But then I remembered: it was Faith's idea. She wanted to find out why Leo had sent me the letter. The one that claimed that Paul Robertson had been murdered. When everyone knew he'd lost control of the car and wound upside down in a field where he'd been throttled by his own seatbelt. Jesus…

"Leo."

He didn't look up when I spoke.

"Leo. Hey." I wasn't speaking gently. "Leo? What's all this about sending me the letter?"

He gazed at blank wall.

"What the fuck are you playing at?"

Still nothing.

"Paul died because of an accident. No one murdered him." I glared at him willing him to respond or at least to acknowledge that I was there. "You daft bugger…you should be locked up."

He didn't flinch.

What was so interesting about that wall? I glanced at it as, somewhere off in the distance, a truck passed by outside.

Maybe he was watching the road…but watching it through a solid wall. Was there no end to a madman's talents?

Him sitting there like that made me want to smack him in the mouth, the way I'd smacked him a couple of times before. The last time when we were fourteen and Paul had tripped on the stairs at school. He'd gone down half a dozen steps with a pile of exercise books in his hands.

Leo had stood looking down at him, both hands on the stair rail, chuckling away like some kind of devil. He had a mad stare even then. Girls said he'd got eyes like laser beams. They punched straight through you and out the other side.

Just the way he stared down at Paul, lying flat out on his stomach with the books scattered all around him, made me see red...and so I went and smacked Leo in the mouth.

And now he was laser eyes again. Just like school.

"I don't know what you're playing at Leo, but leave it," I told him. "If you send any more of those stupid letters you'll be in trouble. Do you hear? I'm going to come down on you like a ton of bricks."

Nothing.

I shook my head. He was completely out of it. I turned and made to walk out of the room.

That was when he spoke to me.

"Vic. It's true," he said.

"And what makes you think you know what's true or not?" I walked back into the room with my fist clenched.

"Sit down."

"Look, it's probably a game to you but when you send those letters it hurts people."

"Sit down. It's not easy to talk to men up there."

"Leo. Watch my lips. Stop sending letters. No more. Got it?"

"Vic. I haven't spoken to you since I was eighteen." He spoke in a light voice. Like it would easily break if he raised it. "You went fishing."

"Never mind what I did. You just stop the letters."

"Sit down, Vic."

"You know, I've a good mind to stick the things down your fucking throat."

"You've hit me before. I remember."

"Good."

"Tooth got broken."

I saw him run his tongue under his lip. He was finding the chipped tooth.

"Years afterwards I'd lay awake at night and ask myself: 'Why did Vic hit me?'"

What he said cut deep enough into my anger to make me sit down.

"You should know," I told him. "Sometimes you asked for it."

"Did I?" He looked puzzled.

"Not asked asked."

"You still hit hit."

"You know what I mean. It was your manner. How you look at people."

He nodded. "It's wrong in this town to look at people in a certain kind of way."

It's how he said it. He could have spoken in a sarcastic, or in a snobbish way, like he was looking down on North Suttoners as barbarians. But he seemed to speak as though he understood the truth of it.

When Leo spoke again it was still in that fragile sounding voice that had no emotion. "I finished university early, you know?"

"I heard. Didn't you take to it?"

"It was during the second year that I got to understand that I'm different from everyone else."

Yeah, different as in—

"How do you think you're different, Leo?"

"Don't know. Different…just different. Like a fish that's been forced to fly with the birds. You know?"

"So, what now?" I asked, humoring him. "You looking for a job?"

"A job?" He looked surprised by the question. "No. No job. I'm different."

"So you said."

"No…it's like everyone's walking down the road in the same direction. Only I'm taking the backwards way…" He thought for a moment. "Like going in reverse."

"Doesn't sound easy."

"It's not. It's like this. I'm walking back up the road…checking all the things I've passed by earlier in my life. And I know that everyone else is moving in the opposite direction."

"That's why you're different to anyone else?"

"Yes…I think so anyway. Do you catch many?"

"Catch many what?"

"You catch many?" He nodded through the wall. "When you're fishing."

"Not bloody enough."

"What are the fish?"

"Cod, skate, whiting; lobster if we're lucky."

"They look like they should?"

"They've not turned into monsters, if that's what you mean?"

"I wondered, that's all." He gave a tiny nod at the wall and cocked his head to one side. I heard the traffic on the road. A sound that rose and fell. It made the same sound as surf on the beach.

Leo lightly brushed the guitar strings then immediately damped them with his fingers.

"That's where Langthwaite Road goes," he said. "Out into the ocean."

"So I heard."

"A long, long time ago. Instead of making that left turn there it ran straight. No bend. It runs out to…"

"Langthwaite."

We spoke the next words together.

"Langthwaite with a piddle in the middle and a square all around."

It was the first time Leo had smiled since I had entered his room.

Again we both said the same thing at the same time. "Old man, Swinburne."

This time I even cracked a smile. Old Man Swinburne had this poxy hearing-aid that would begin to whistle when he got excited and talked in a high voice. And seeing as he loved local history he'd constantly talk about Langthwaite in a high voice and the hearing-aid would whistle.

I said, "He'd always go on about what it was like round here in Dick's day. Talk about a man obsessed."

"I enjoyed it. When I walked home I could see what it was like. I could stand up here and imagine the road going straight out where the sea is now: to Langthwaite."

"Of course old Man Swinny's dead now. Maybe they should have put it in on his gravestone." I recited again. "Langthwaite with a piddle in the middle and a square all around. Christ. If I had a tenner every time I'd heard him say that." I shook my head.

"Can you remember what it meant, Vic?"

"No…hang on. Wasn't it that the river that ran through the town was called The Piddle? And the square all around part were walls laid in a square shape to keep the pirates out?"

"Langthwaite's where you catch your fish now, Vic."

"I know. More than two miles offshore."

"I imagine fish swimming in and out of windows."

I shook my head. "There's nothing there but sand and weed. Not many fish either."

"In my imagination, there are houses underwater."

"In your imagination maybe. But there's nothing there."

"Coastal erosion. Eating the land away."

"You're not wrong, Leo. North Sutton'll go the same way if they're not careful."

"And the road."

"Might not be a bad thing if the road to get swallowed up. Bloody thing."

"I've been writing it down."

"Huh?"

"I've been taking the backward way. I've written down everything I see."

I noticed he was looking at files on a shelf. Tilting my head, I read what was written on the spines in curly felt tip.

Life Bites by Leo

"It's kind of an adventure story," he said. "About what happens to a man going backwards when everyone else is going forwards."

"Sounds too deep and meaningful for me, Leo."

"You should read it."

"I'm not much of a reader."

"It describes what happened to Paul Robertson."

"You're a bastard. You know that?"

I'd even started to warm to him when we were talking about old Man Swinburne. Then back to this again.

He didn't say anything. He just put down the guitar and walked out of the room. I looked across at the files. If *Life Bites* by Leo was his murder evidence then I didn't see any criminal investigation sprouting wings and flying.

In another part of the house I heard Leo begin to sing. It was a flat, dirge of a sound.

"The man with the guitar's all right. The man with the guitar's all right, all right, all right…"

《《——》》

Six

I DIDN'T KNOW WHERE Leo had gone. I didn't much care come to that. Now that I was alone in the room I wondered what had happened to Miss Carter and Faith.

Kettles take a long time to boil out on Langthwaite Road. That was the sour thought that kept repeating on me.

Outside, the traffic sighed past. The curtains were open and I could see the headlights of the cars, shooting up the slick road. A glint of moonlight on the sea over a mile away. The lights of North Sutton. Nothing much else.

The candles were bright enough for me to see the room. It's impossible, I know, but deep down you have this gut feeling that madness is contagious. So I looked, but didn't touch what Leo touched.

As well as Leo's paintings of heads with light bursting from them, there were also framed photos. These showed scenes of Leo's past. One showed him aged about twelve with a guitar. Another with his arm round a dog's neck. Another looking into the camera lens through the strings of a tennis racket.

He looked strange, even as a boy. His hair was longer than the other kids. There was this certain light in his eye.

And something else: there were photographs with Paul and me, as well. I'd not expected to see them but there we were: the three of us aged around ten, all grinning into the camera like we were the best of friends. I didn't remember the photograph being taken. And I don't remember ever being friends with Loony Leo Carter, as some kids called him. He was always pain-in-the-neck-boy who everyone hated.

On shelves, there were Leo's toys from childhood (farmyard animals and clowns), school reports ('Leo is exceptionally intelligent but tends to lack focus and application'); a letter from a music producer dated three years' ago ('Thank you for your demo disk. Your songs are perhaps the most unusual we've ever heard. However, they are too dark for our tastes. We wish you well in…'). A magazine called *Luddsmill* (its cover boasting: 'Corrosive poetry and incandescent short stories by Leo Carter').

If Leo was following the backward route, as he told me, maybe these old toys and photographs were his service stations on the way.

One object caught my attention. I held a candle to this to get a closer look. It was a little die-cast spaceship with red wings. *Put a rocket in your pocket!* ran the ad. I bought one with my birthday money when I was eight years old. I loved the thing to pieces. Carried it everywhere in my pocket. There was a plastic bubble canopy that contained two seats. In one was the pilot, the other was empty. The times I'd imagine myself into the vacant seat and how we'd go tearing across the universe.

I was so afraid I'd lose it I used a badge pin to scratch my initials in the paintwork on the underside of the wing. It did vanish one day when I left it in my coat pocket in the school cloakroom. More fool me.

I broke my own look-but-don't-touch rule. To hell with contaminating madness. I picked up the spaceship and turned it over. In the candlelight I saw the letters: *VB.*

The thieving bastard!

I kept the spaceship in my balled fist.

Something about the toys being service stations on the road back into the past must have been right. I might not have been dragged kicking and screaming down memory lane, but down it I went. Reluctantly.

«« — »»

The first time my Dad took me out fishing (as work, rather than just a trip on his boat) I was eleven. His brother was laid up with a bad back so I guess Dad figured I should earn my keep.

"Keep in the middle of the boat," he told me as we pulled away from the quay. "She's going to bounce today."

My old man wasn't wrong. The moment the boat left the harbor it lifted clean out of the water as a wave struck.

"The further out we get, the calmer it'll get," he called over the sound of the motor. "Just hang on tight and don't mess with anything."

I watched the green water surge like a million hills. Spray broke over the prow, wetting my face. Salt filled my mouth. I had to spit.

"That'll be a lesson to you, Vic." My dad heaved the tiller over. "Never spit into the wind."

I wiped my eye. "It's not lobster weather, is it, Dad?" I hoped to impress him with my fishing knowledge.

"It's not that, son. They'll stay home on a day like this."

Again I tried to please him with what I knew about the fishing grounds. "We going up to the scaurs?" These were broken fingers of rock that reached out to sea from under the cliffs.

He shook his head. "With a sea like this? Don't be daft, Vic."

So much for my fishing knowledge.

I guessed again. "Tory Banks?"

"You'll get nothing much this time of year. Besides the price you get for skate wouldn't pay for the diesel." He nodded out to sea where water turned black. "Old Langthwaite. We'll shoot for cod."

I looked out across the swell that had grown nasty white heads.

"Looks rough out there, Dad."

"Frightened?"

"No."

"It'll calm down once we're over the steeple."

I learned later that was a joke. Local fishermen talked about fishing over the steeple. Or shooting for crab in the graveyard. But the drowned church would be long gone.

Again I tried to sound interested but the bucking boat was making me feel sick. "Dad?"

"What is it?"

"How'd you know where Langthwaite is?"

"You put your ear to the water. When you can hear children singing in the streets then you know you're there." He shook his head, his eyes on the mud cliff. "Just pulling your leg, son."

"How then?"

"See the cliffs? See how flat they are at the top?"

"Yeah."

"When you see the little dip, like a V-shaped cut. See it?"

"Over there?"

"No, to your left. Where the bushes are."

"I can see it!" I shouted out, excited. Normally, I never could see anything he'd point out which exasperated him no end. *"It's got bushes at both sides."*

"Good lad. That's where the Langthwaite road used to run."

"Right over the cliff?"

"There was no cliff in those days." He swung his arm like a pendulum, pointing with his finger. *"It ran straight out, due east."*

He swung the tiller, turning the boat's prow out to sea. *"If I keep the cut in the cliff square at my back and run out straight for a couple of miles I'm following the line of the old road. When I've got Tracey Beacon directly off starboard then I know I'm right over Langthwaite."*

I crept to the gunwale and looked down into the water.

"You won't see anything, Vic. The road's long gone." He pointed to a box. *"You can start laying out the lines in the bottom of the boat. And watch those hooks, they're fucking sharp."*

It was the first time I'd heard Dad say 'fuck' in a conversational way. He'd said it often enough stubbing his toe on a table leg. But then to him I wasn't a kid anymore when I worked the boat. I was another fisherman there to earn his keep.

A few minutes later he seemed satisfied we'd arrived. He killed the motor, letting the boat coast.

"You can't hang around in this game, Vic," he told me as he clambered forward into the boat's middle. *"Come on, get those lines out…and for fucksakes don't tangle them."*

I handed him the buoy without been asked. I'd ridden along with him and my uncle enough as a passenger to know the routine. Now I was part of the team.

"Don't let the anchor foul the lines," he said.

I picked up the small anchor and passed it to him. Taking the buoy and anchor from me he twisted the top half of his body and threw them overboard.

Next came the lines. Handling them came automatic to him after all these years. *"When you fish Langthwaite your lines have to be four hundred fathoms, it's bloody deep out here. You put your hook at every second fathom. See how they're baited? Mussels are best but fish guts'll do at a pinch. Push the bait right past the barb so the fish has to swallow the hook to get at it. Got that?"*

I nodded. It was heavy work but my dad handled the line incredibly fast, and with a fine delicacy that made me think of how a surgeon works.

He threw the line over the edge of the boat in such a way it unravelled in the air, so it sank through the water straight out, rather than in a tangle. Weights would carry the end of the line to the seabed while the other end remained connected to the buoy. A line would be left to 'fish' by itself. We'd come the next morning to haul it in and find out what had hooked overnight.

I took the chance to kneel at the edge of the boat and look down into the water. Dad was right. The sea was calm here. I saw it was clear enough for my eyes to be able to follow the pale lines stretching downward into the bones of old Langthwaite town. Of course, being a kid I imagined it would look like a town, only underwater with fish swimming along the streets and crabs scuttling in and out of doorways. There'd be skeletons too still sitting in chairs in drowned living rooms. I thought I heard the tolling of the church bell twenty fathoms down.

"Vic. You're here to work, not to watch...pass me the first aid box...No, lad. It's there right under the seat."

I passed him the box. He held up his finger. Blood painted it a juicy strawberry red.

He said, "Told you those bloody hooks were sharp."

When we returned the next day there was plenty of cod on the line. There was the corpse of a man, too. I remember shouting at my dad that we'd brought up one of the people from Langthwaite.

Dad snapped at me not to be silly and radioed the coastguard.

He told me to look away as he covered it with the tarpaulin. But you know what young kids are like. I couldn't take my eyes off it.

It didn't frighten me because it didn't look like a person. There were no arms or legs. The thing didn't even own a face. When I think back it looked more like a big, soggy lump of yellow foam rubber with shellfish and kelp clinging to it.

Not much more was said. Someone told me at school that the police thought it was the body of a tourist who disappeared when they went swimming from North Sutton beach more than a year before. The corpse must have become water-logged and rolled about the sea bottom at Langthwaite fishing grounds for months.

It's just come back to me who told me about the corpse. Leo Carter.

«« — »»

Seven

LEO SHOWED NO SIGN of making a re-appearance—and it was getting on for a half-hour since Faith and Leo's mum had gone to make a pot of tea.

Keeping the spaceship that Leo stole from me fifteen years ago, I went downstairs. For a moment I stood looking at he doors leading off from the hallway. Which one was the kitchen?

Miss Carter had led Faith off down the passageway to the left. I headed down the corridor with all that dark wood panelling hemming me in.

Through the door at the end, I found the farmhouse kitchen but no Faith and no Miss Carter. The teapot was on the tray. The cups empty. I touched the kettle. It was hot but the gas ring had been switched off.

I was beginning to feel that someone was making a fool of me. I shoved open another door and discovered steps leading down to a basement.

Yet another door opened up onto an anteroom with a washing machine and butcher's slab, and knives hanging down from the steel rail suspended above it. Switching off the light, I returned to the dingy hall at the foot of the stairs. There, I looked up, half expecting to see Leo come looming across the landing. But it was dark up there.

I crossed the hall to another door. This was partly open and lights were on inside the room beyond.

I heard Miss Carter say in soft voice, "How does that feel?"

Then Faith's response: "All right..." She was panting.

"I don't want to hurt you."

"No...no...that's okay. As long as you don't press too hard inside."

"How's that?"

Faith breathed in sharply. I thought I heard her moan, too.

"Don't worry, Faith. I'll be as gentle as I can. Trust me."

"There…that's better. Oh. Hold it there…yes, just there." I heard my wife give a deep sigh.

I pushed open the door and walked into the lounge. Miss Carter and Faith sat side by side on the couch. Faith was breathing deeply and I could see perspiration on her forehead.

"I'm sorry about this, Vic," Miss Carter said evenly. "What must you think of me?"

"What's going on?"

"I asked Faith to cut the cake. Like an idiot I didn't warn her about the knife. You see, I always keep them brutally sharp…there, hold that against your finger. And best keep your hand in the air."

I crossed the room to Faith. "How bad is it?"

"Not that bad," she said. She was trembling.

"It's a deep one, Faith," Miss Carter told her. Then she turned to me. "She'll need to get it looked at."

Faith leaned back against the sofa. She looked faint. The bandage around her forefinger turned red.

"Wait here," I said. "I'll go back and get the car."

"No." Faith tried to sit up straight. "I'll walk back with you."

"I'm sorry, Faith. You aren't in a fit state to do that." Miss Carter stood up. "I'll get the car and run you to the hospital. It'll be quicker."

"I'm sure I'll be all right."

"Believe me, that's going to need a couple of stitches."

I could see that Faith didn't want Miss Carter to drive her to the hospital.

"If you drove me home, Miss Carter, I could pick up—"

"No, Vic. I won't hear of it. This is my fault." She smiled. "And don't worry, I'll have her back to you in less than an hour."

"I'll come with you. We can get a taxi home from the hospital."

Miss Carter screwed her face as if she had to ask a painful favor. "Ah, there's a bit of a problem. I don't leave Leo alone in the house when it's dark. Ever since he was ill…well, I don't leave him."

"Leo can come with us."

"He won't use the road at night. It upsets him. Sorry."

"Upsets him?" I was about to say I didn't give a damn about Leo being upset by the road. I wanted to go with my wife to hospital and make sure she was all right. But even as I opened my mouth to tell Leo's mum, Faith spoke over me.

"Vic. It's alright. I'll go with Miss Carter."

"But you might not—"

"Vic. Miss Carter will be with me. Don't worry."

"I'll look after Faith, Vic. We'll be back before you know it."

I felt beaten.

"I'll stay here with Leo, then." I saw Faith recognize the sullen note in my voice. She gave me one of her little Behave Yourself, Vic glares.

"Help yourself to whatever you want to eat or drink. There's beer in the fridge and spirits in the cupboard over there." Miss Carter smiled, her eyes giving me that twinkle. "But stay away from the knives."

I forced a smile. "Don't worry, I will."

I didn't like it. Faith was shaky on her feet. I could feel her trembling through the sleeve of her coat. But there wasn't a lot I could do. I helped Faith into the passenger seat of Miss Carter's crisp new BMW, then stood back and watched them go.

The red taillights swept down the drive to Langthwaite Road, paused for a while as a pair of trucks thundered past, then with a squeal of tires the car was away, heading in the direction of North Sutton. The car's lights lit up a huge chunk of the road like a fireball. A second later it was gone.

It seemed odd to be standing there on the driveway of someone else's house as if it was my own. The breeze stiffened from the sea. The trees surrounding the house started to shiver and groan.

"Christ, I wouldn't live in this place," I muttered as I walked back across the drive to the front door. I remembered my cousins when they were little kids. They always called it the Witch House when we drove by. I began to see their way of thinking.

Miss Carter's house was miles from anywhere with no neighbors, it stood all on its lonesome on a hill. It always looked cold and empty as if its owner had just gone and died. All that was needed to complete the whole bleak picture was a hearse standing outside the front door.

That, and a white face at the window.

I looked up at all that dark stone. There in the candlelit window was Leo...white faced, hair like Jesus; mad, staring eyes. He wasn't looking at me, he was watching Langthwaite Road.

My hand tightened around the toy spaceship. I'd searched for it for weeks afterwards. Looked everywhere.

I went inside, closed the front door.

«« —— »»

The night light song (something for the road)

When I look out of my room window I see the road. I grew up here not that far from it.

I'm writing this as Vic Blake waits for me downstairs. My mother's left the house. I don't know why. The road's got her now, out there in the dark.

My night light's burning bright.

The sound the road makes is surf on the beach. Whispering, whispering. In and out: soft as ice cream in a park.

A little while ago I touched the strings of my guitar. It sounded so sweet. The notes made you think of honey on fresh bread. I thought of the little sweet strawberries you pick from the plant; they're warm from the sun in your hand. The words of my Night Light Song are very gentle. I sing them in a whisper. A pleasant lullaby. I sing them when I'm warm and relaxed in my room. When scented candles illuminate. When I've pieces of chocolate in the rose bowl. When it's dark outside. Inside it's so very warm and cozy; my clothes are soft; my cushions gently support me.

After I sang my song I began to write.

And when I've finished this in a few minutes I'll go down and take Vic to the Road Treasure Machine. He's an old friend from school. A years' old friend. Together we'll make the Road Machine Work.

First, I'll talk to him in the lounge where the log fire burns. My friend will be warm and relaxed and safe from harm in a room full of soft rugs. The road will be far from his thoughts. I'll remind him of the old days when we were at school.

School lunches, tennis matches, carol concerts, the last bell before holidays. I'll give him cake with cream. There is wine, too. Then I'll put on my jacket and scarf and I'll take him outside to show him the Road Treasure Machine. With his help I can make it work tonight.

You see, I was friends with the road.
When we were friends, me it could not eat.
Not like the people I've seen it eat before.
Like Paul Robertson and the man in the cauliflower hat.
But the road fell out with Leo.
It will harm Leo the first chance; the first chance it gets.
With the Road Treasure Machine revolving, generating, multiplying...
It will gift the strength of the road to Leo.
With its power...almighty power...everlasting power
I can leave the house and go out into the world again.
Safe from road harm.
Safe from road teeth...
Safe...safe...safe...
(The Night Light Song—Friday evening demo, tape 3, pedal drum and bass)

Okay, Leo? Are you ready to talk to Vic? Because:
It's time to put down the pen...time to close the file...

(From **Life Bites**, by Leo)

«« — »»

Eight

I WAITED IN THE LIVING ROOM for them to return. The clock ticked loudly in the hallway. As I sat there it came back to me about Uncle Ray, Dad's brother, the same one who partnered him on the boat.

He used to take long walks along Langthwaite Road, just like me. He never cared for the sea and like plenty of sailors never learned to swim.

«« —»»

Uncle Ray would always walk a mile along the road, past the Carter house, as far as the bridge where the river flowed (years ago that would have been the River Piddle that ran through Langthwaite; now it was The Calder). When he got back to town he'd have a couple of pints at the Duke of Danby then go home.

It must have been ten years ago when The Langthwaite Road did it again. My parents had gone out for their wedding anniversary; that means it must have been the end of October. I stayed in, watching a video that my Dad had rented for me. I'd nagged him into getting *The Evil Dead*. I was thirteen or so. Horror films wouldn't have any affect on me.

"Are you sure you'll be all right watching that thing?" my mother asked for the tenth time just as she was going out.

"It'll be a laugh," I told her.

"Are you certain?"

"Horror films don't scare me."

"We can drive down and get you another one. Your Dad won't mind."

"Dad will mind," he said as he pulled on his shoes. "I booked that table for eight. It's ten to now."

So they left me to the horror film.

After watching the first twenty minutes I thought it seemed darker than usual outside. Also, there were clicks and thumps coming from the bedrooms. I was alone in the house. And suddenly going upstairs to take a look round didn't seem such a good idea.

I switched off the central heating. At least that changed it from a thumping sound to a tapping.

Hot metal expands. Cold metal contracts. The bit of science I knew still didn't give me the courage to go upstairs. What's more, even turning round to look back over the armchair now seemed dangerous. What if a face was there just inches from mine? I told myself everything would be okay if I kept looking forward at the screen: I reasoned that the face could only attack me if I didn't see it.

Not that there was a face there, of course. But then again, how could I be sure there wasn't a leering face if I didn't check?

But if I looked back it would attack.

This seemed to be a problem without a solution. Well, the best solution, I figured, was to keep watching the screen. Worse was to come. I'd been wrong about *The Evil Dead*. It was frightening. Blood terrifying might be a better description.

Then the telephone rang.

My whole body lifted a foot out of the chair I was so startled. I stared at the telephone on the coffee table as it screamed at me.

Then I answered it.

"Hello."

For some reason I knew that there would be something terrible about the call. My dad had been driving fast. They were late. Langthwaite Road was a real bitch. In winter it could turn from being wet to treacherous ice in minutes. Fogs rolled in from the sea killing visibility to near zero. Still cars would go to fast. They always went too fast.

"Hello?"

No reply. Maybe them not saying anything was the worst part. I listened harder. I could hear breathing, only it didn't sound right. Then a man began to speak. The voice was deep and whispery. He began to say something but then broke off as if he'd made a false start.

"Ber—ber—"

"Hello." By this time I felt sick. It was one of those zombie voices.

"Mur—"

More labored breathing like the caller was painfully out of breath. Next time they spoke more clearly. "There's something wrong."

"Dad?"

"I've got a bad taste in my mouth."

After that, a click followed by the dialling tone.

I put the phone back quick like it had turned into a dead animal in my hand. Who the hell was that? It sounded a bit like Dad, but my dad didn't speak in such a slow, deliberate way. He didn't slur either.

The best thing I decided was to watch the video. Just pretend it hadn't happened.

I fastened my eyes on *The Evil Dead* for another ten minutes then the telephone rang again. I knew I had to pick it up, and I knew it would be the same slurred voice. I went cold inside.

I didn't speak. Just listened.

"Uhh." A deep groan. "I can't find a way out."

"Dad, is that you?"

"It's just dark—"

"Dad?"

"I think something's gone wrong—"

"Is that you, Dad?"

"I've been thinking about it…I don't know what to do."

"Where are you, Dad?"

"I was on Langthwaite Road. I know that."

"Is Mum there?"

"But I don't know where I am now." The voice was more than slurred. It sounded like someone falling asleep. "You know…I can't find my way home." The breathing came in long rasps into my ear. I was thinking about putting the phone down when he said. "It's dark in here…it's dark…will you come and find me?"

"Dad—"

"Bring me home, Vic."

Hearing my own name spoken by that voice did it for me. I slammed the phone down.

Then I sat still without moving a finger. I went hot and cold. I felt sick. I wondered if I should phone someone. A relative? That seemed best, but who? Most were elderly by then. The obvious one seemed to be Uncle Ray. He lived just a couple of streets away.

I dialled his number. Got ringing tones. No answer. I telephoned his mobile, ready to tell him something happened to Mum and Dad.

He answered. I heard a long, drawn-out breath in my ear then: "Hmm-uh?"

"Uncle Ray?"

I heard him groan. "Vic. I've got a bad taste in my mouth—" Then he started murmuring. I couldn't make out the words.

I got the credit for doing something right. I called Paul Robertson's dad who knew Uncle Ray's habits. He took a torch then went out to look for him on Langthwaite Road. He found him sitting on a grass bank with his feet in the gutter. Uncle Ray had gone for his walk as usual. A truck had run by too close. The nearside mirror high on the cab had clipped the back of his head. The blow had been hard enough to fracture his skull. That's why Uncle Ray slurred when he spoke on the phone. He couldn't walk and was too dazed to ask for help properly. All he could do was phone and mumble. Ten years on he's recovered enough to walk with a stick.

«« — »»

I sat in Miss Carter's lounge waiting for Faith to get back from the hospital.

It's funny how you can think of different things when you're in a different environment. I'd forgotten about where Uncle Ray had the accident—out there on Langthwaite Road just a few minutes walk from where I was sitting now. I suppose I must have blotted out the calls, too. I had nightmares about those for months afterwards.

"Vic, I've got a bad taste in my mouth."

My head snapped up. Leo stood in the doorway, staring at me. "What did you say?"

"There's blood in the kitchen, Vic. It's all over the chair. Well, the back of the chair."

"You said something else."

"No… I wondered about the blood. Someone must have got hurt."

"That's Faith."

He looked right through me.

"Faith," I snapped "I married Faith Escrow."

"She was in the year below us."

I nodded. I didn't want to get into an elaborate conversation with the idiot. Instead I said. "She cut herself in the kitchen. Your mother's driven her to hospital."

"Oh…there was all this blood. I began to get a little bit…worried." That same fragile voice, like it was tricky for him to get the words through his lips without damaging them.

I got to my feet. "I best clean it up."

He stood back to let me through. I felt his breath on my face I passed that close. I held my breath and entered the dark tunnel the passageway again.

His voice followed me. "Do you want to know what happened to Paul Robertson?"

"No." I opened the kitchen door "Do you want to tell me why you stole my property?" Without turning, I held up the rocket so he could see it.

«« —»»

Nine

"LEO. I ASKED YOU why you stole it?" I nodded at the spaceship toy that I'd put on the kitchen table. I was scrubbing Faith's blood with kitchen towel.

Leo stood framed by the doorway. "I wanted to talk to you in the lounge. I've poured you a glass of wine."

"Bugger the wine. You knew that toy belonged to me."

"I was going to bring you cake as well. There's a nice fire burning."

I shook my head as I scrubbed the chair back. "I should have known better than to try and get any sense out of you."

"I'm taking the backward way."

"You can say that again, mate. Pass me that sponge...no, wet it first."

"I wanted to talk to you, Vic. It's important."

"You can see I'm busy, Leo. Why don't you go play with yourself or something."

"I can play my guitar if you like?"

"Fine."

"I've written lots of songs."

"You're a bloody genius, Leo, did you know that?"

"Mainly about the old days. School and holidays."

"Leo. Make yourself useful. Pass me the detergent. There...that's it in the bottle by the sink."

"This?"

"No. The green bottle...good grief."

"This one?"

"Yes."

"I'm sorry, Vic."

"You must be a right little mother's helper, aren't you?"

"I play my guitar when she cooks."

"Yeah, you're worth your weight in fucking gold to her, aren't you?" I finished wiping the stains and pushed the chair back to the table. "Bet you can't even tie your own shoe laces anymore." I looked down at his bare feet. "Or even put your own shoes on, come to that."

"I guess lots of things became a hassle for me when I came home from university."

He still talked in that fragile way. As if he had to think about each word before he spoke it, in case he chose the wrong one. Mutton head. His mother must be working her way into an early grave looking after him. But then she must have had a completely different idea about his future.

«« — »»

Leo Carter had been one of the brightest hopes North Sutton High School had ever seen. To the other kids he was the weirdest, no doubting that. He was artistic, he played guitar, wrote songs, he painted weirdo portraits with light beams shooting out of heads. He also whipped up the Leo Crack Ups. This happened at least once a year. Boys at the school would for one of those mysterious reasons gather in this huge gang. There might have been a fight the day before or someone had been expelled; anyway something got their juices flowing, then the pack instinct kicked in. You'd get a hundred or more third formers charging through the school with the girls running behind all excited and ready to see what happened next. I think it was Paul who called this the Leo Crack Up.

The pack of boys would tear round the place, shouting their heads off, their faces blazing. When they found Leo in the library or walking by himself they'd attack. They'd kick the living crap out of him. They'd be shouting and laughing and pushing each other out of the way so they could get their boot in his mouth.

Once they cracked three of his ribs. Leo was in hospital for a week.

Something happening like that must contribute to the way you turn out.

For Paul Robertson and me our future was at sea, fishing with our uncles and fathers. Although to my surprise Paul sidestepped that one

*and went and joined the KOYLA—the King's Own Yorkshire Light
Artillery. I left school at sixteen and (as the saying goes) went fishing.*

*Leo headed off to university. I don't know what he studied there.
Something arty I expect. But halfway through the course he had a breakdown and walked all the way home. Paul and I worked out that the walk
back to North Sutton from London would have taken at least four days.*

*After that, Leo never left the house. Of course that was meat and
gravy to the gossips. Drug addiction. Homosexuality. Agoraphobia.
Schizophrenia. Leukemia. AIDS. Debt. Homesickness. Pathological
indolence. Gossips worked overtime on every kind of rumor.*

Now we'd reached today. An evening in cold November.

《《——》》

I was washing my hands after scrubbing my wife's bloodstains. Leo
Carter was watching me from the doorway; his brains scrambled beyond
the point of no return. While across town Paul Robertson's ashes were
taking a well-earned rest in the crem's garden of remembrance.

"Well, fuck you all," I said aloud as I dried my hands on kitchen roll.

Leo had said nothing for a while. He just did the eyeball laser beam
thing, staring at me. He watched me push the tissue into the swing bin.

"I took the rocket," he said.

"I know you did, Leo."

"I took it out of Paul Robertson's bag."

"You're a twat, you know that?" I looked in the fridge. I was ready
for a beer. They had lager. I hate fucking lager. Behind bags of lettuce
I saw bottles of *Old Peculiar*...which seemed apt. I pulled one out,
twisted the cap, took a long cold drink.

I looked at Leo. "If you took the rocket from Paul, why didn't you
give it back to me?"

"I wondered what to do for the best."

"Bet you did."

"I decided I could keep it safe for you. I knew how much you
valued it."

"Thieving bastard." I wasn't angry; this was all matter of fact.

"The road takes so much from people."

"You thought it would take my spaceship." I picked up the toy and held it up. The red wings glinted. I loved doing that, just tilting it slightly from side to side, watching the wings shine. For a young boy that was true beauty. And the seat next to the pilot was still empty. One more for a trip around the Milky Way. Yeah, I think I'd grown too big for even my imagination to fit into that little seat anymore.

I took a swallow of beer. "Well, thanks, Leo—for keeping it safe all these years." Sarcastic as hell, I know, but I gave him a salute with the beer bottle. "Cheers. I'll take it home now."

For the first time he seemed concerned. "No."

"Oh, but I will, mate."

"Look it's still not safe to take it away."

"Oh, I think I can manage it now."

"But the road's still out there."

"Langthwaite Road?"

He stepped forward, nodding quickly. "The police say it's a blackspot."

"I know that, Leo."

"I've lived here all my life. I've seen the road take people. It-it keeps things that don't belong to it."

"Oh, for God's sake, Leo."

"Th-that's why I should keep the spaceship for now."

"No can do. Mine." I trousered it. *Put a rocket in your pocket.* The jingle came back as I took another swallow of beer. "Now, that's good beer. Nice and cold, too."

"Listen, Vic…" Leo's hands trembled. "I wanted to tell you something important."

"Okay, tell me, then." I glanced at the clock. Miss Carter should be back with Faith soon. Good. Was I ready for home.

"It's not easy."

"Well, don't tell me then. Your call, mate."

"It's complicated."

"And it's about the road? Langthwaite Road?"

"Yes."

"That it steals people and possessions."

"In a way…it's a blackspot."

"You're getting it confused with a *black hole*." The beer was giving me a buzz.

"No, Vic. It gets hold of people and it doesn't let go."

"Look, it's a nasty stretch of road. That's all."

"All those deaths…you should have seen what happened to the people. The way they looked after the road got them, you know?"

"You shouldn't go nosing at accidents. I'm going to have another of these." I binned the empty *Old Peculiar* bottle and pulled another from the back of the fridge. It was strong beer and, drinking on an empty stomach, it was hitting the spot a treat.

Leo talked: "The road pulls people in. It keeps their possessions. Listen, I've been taking things back from the road. But I've made it angry, Vic. It's not my fault. But it's angry and it won't let me leave."

"Wait a minute, Leo. Do you take medication?"

"It won't let you leave now, Vic, that's why we—"

"You've gone and missed a dose, haven't you, you soft bugger?"

Leo took a deep breath and said: "I've made a machine, Vic. Tonight I'm going to use it."

"Use it for what?"

"You and me are going to use my machine to save everyone the road's taken." His eyes glittered. "Listen to me, Vic. We're going to bring Paul back."

《《—》》

Ten

"BRING PAUL ROBERTSON BACK? Now, how are you going to do that, Leo?" This stupid talk of his was doing my head in. I could have smacked him in the mouth.

"I've built this machine. It's taken me months. There's things I took from the road…" Leo stood there in the middle of the kitchen venting delusions. "I haven't been able to make it work yet. Now I know why. I needed help."

"Never a truer word said, old son." Still taking deep swallows of beer, I searched kitchen cupboards.

"It has things from the road. My song's on the green tape."

"Green tape's the best." I wasn't humoring him. I was taking the piss. "Go on."

"And I've connected all the components, you know? Like a circuit.

It's got what the road values. What it worked so hard to get all these years. But I've found some. I brought them back, but I had to be careful not to get too close to the road, then I laid them out in—"

"Okay, Leo. Where does your mother keep the pills and stuff?"

"I don't need medicine any more. I'm all done with it."

"Like hell you are."

"You swallow it…you're like drowsy…tired all the time. Makes you put on weight."

"How awful." More piss-take.

"You bloat."

"Well, well, what a dilemma. Fat and sane, or thin and barmy?" I found a packet. "What are these?"

"My mother's."

"Are you sure?"

"There's her name on the label. They help her relax."

"Wow…and she'll need them with you." I drained the bottle. *Noinkkk.* Opened another. It tasted sweeter by the mouthful. Warms the inner man. I drained half a bottle in one go.

"Leo."

"Yes?"

"Your doctors will have prescribed you medication. Where is it?"

"Vic." Still the softly fragile voice. He didn't raise it even when I turned nasty. "Vic. I've done with it. They're making me ill. My hands shake; I can't play the—"

"Leo, Leo. You're not listening. You need that stuff to stop your brains from boiling. Do you understand?"

"They make me nauseous."

"Ah. I get it. You've been *pretending* to take the pills for your mother's benefit. Then what? Spit them out the window? Hide them up your backside?"

He touched his forehead. "This isn't what I'd planned," he said, his voice whining now. "You were going to come here and we were going to make the machine work together."

"Are they in the bathroom?"

"We're friends…you'd help me."

"When were we ever friends?" I gave up on the medication being in the kitchen. "Where's the stuff you take, Leo? You need it."

"Don't."

"Remember? It'll keep the monsters away."

I walked back into the passageway to look in the other rooms. Leo followed but instead of following me into the lounge he turned and walked out of the house.

"Fine," I called after him. "You get some fresh air. It'll do you good."

I was all ready to sit and drink beer until Faith and Miss Fancy Pants Carter came back from the hospital…until I remembered Leo's mum had made me responsible for him. I would have to bring him back.

Finishing the beer off in a couple of gulps I followed him outside.

««——»»

I closed the door behind me. The wind had picked up from the sea. It was bitingly cold. Clouds flew across the sky, sometimes blocking the moon. Leo stood in darkness. I could see his silhouette against the car lights on Langthwaite Road.

"Leo," I said. "It's not warm enough to go arsing about in the dark."

"Vic?"

There was something about his voice.

"Vic?"

"What?"

"The road's closer tonight."

"If you like."

"It's closer to the house. We've got to make the machine work, or it's…"

"Leo. Get yourself back here."

"Please…you've got to help me work the machine. If we don't do anything, the road's going to be up here at our throats…"

"God's teeth. Leo, you've got nothing on your feet."

"Come on, we've got to make it work tonight."

Now he did sound agitated. I looked at him, then at the road, and finally back at him…all of it without speaking.

"Vic. Don't you see it? The road's getting closer all the time. We can't leave it any longer."

"Come here."

"Vic, help me please."

"Come here, you little bastard."

As I moved toward him, he ran back toward the house. You could see his bare feet flicking in the dark. The soft skin on the soles would be crunching down on sharp stones.

I followed, ready to slam the door behind us. Then I would show him.

Only he went and did it again. He veered away from the house, running across the grass. Worrying that he might just decide to leg it into the hills, I chased after him. He didn't run far. At the side of the house was a garage with an up and over door. Grabbing the handle he swung it open and disappeared inside.

I stood in the doorway trying to see into the darkness. Now it struck me he might have gone to find a weapon.

"Okay, Leo. It's time to stop this now."

I listened. There was some kind of movement. But I could see nothing in the dark other than my white breath bursting out like something from a steam engine.

"Come back to the house," I told him. "I'll make us a hot drink."

A bright light flickered on. I squinted into the garage. No wonder I couldn't see far. At arm's length from my face was a wall of amplifiers. They nearly touched the garage roof. A white electric guitar leaned against the center amp.

I squeezed between the amp stack and garage wall. Behind the amps there was a leather armchair, more guitars, one of those old reel-to-reel tape machines. I noticed the tape on the spool was green.

Leo stood with his back to me. He moved his hands across a blackboard that hung on the end wall; the thing was big enough to pretty much fill it.

He didn't look back but he knew I was there. "You sit in the chair. You'll have to work the tape machine…"

"Leo…"

"We need to make it work now. We're running out of time."

"Take it easy, mate. Come back indoors."

He touched objects that were nailed to the blackboard. The way his hands moved reminded you of a technician operating a control panel.

A touch there. A twist here, followed by presses with his thumb. I moved closer.

He'd drawn white chalk lines so the objects were linked. He'd made himself a circuit board.

"When I say 'go' switch on the tape. Then you have to keep switching between fast and slow play. You've got to do it quickly while I work this. That's why I need two people to operate it."

"This is the machine?"

He glanced back over his shoulder. "Sit by the tape player. You've got to be ready when I tell you. Fast-slow-fast-slow. Got that?"

"Jesus Christ, Leo. What on earth have you got there?"

"Sit down, Vic. We're nearly out of time. The road must be halfway up the hill."

"Is that blood?"

"Can't you hear how close it is?"

I shoved him aside.

"Vic. The road's going to destroy us if we don't do it now."

"Where did you find this stuff?" I couldn't believe my eyes.

"I told you. I took it from the road."

I looked at the pieces nailed there. "These are surgical dressings, aren't they?"

"They were at accident sites. I managed to get them away from the road."

"You're sick, mate. Do you know that?"

"They are its power; it feeds—"

"First aid dressings soaked with blood. Someone's watch. A wallet. A doll. Cigarette lighter. Maps…is that blood on them, too?" I shook my head, a bad taste rising. "Plastic water bottle. CDs. Windscreen cloths. Rear view mirror. A hubcap. Registration plate. Mobile phone. You've been a busy boy, haven't you?"

"It took lots of work."

"It must have." I looked at him. "So you've been down to where cars have crashed and stolen all this stuff."

"But stolen from the road. So it couldn't keep it."

"Bollocks." Then the penny dropped. "When you took this stuff, Leo. Was it just after the accidents?"

"You've got to move fast."

"So there were passengers still in the cars? People who were hurt? And you robbed them?"

"No, saving it for them, before the road took—"

"Jesus, man, you take the prize." Now I did want to strike out. "Before the police and ambulances got there, you robbed injured people?"

"No."

"Dead people?"

"You don't understand. It's not like—"

"You sick fuck." I looked back at the blackboard. The way the white lines ran out from the bloody dressings and crumpled wallets. "All these white chalk marks...where do they lead?" I followed the lines with my finger. They converged on one point in the center. When I reached where the lines imploded into one chalked disk I pulled my finger back fast.

"You really should have swallowed those pills," I said. "They're going to put you away for this."

It looked a bit like a piece of banana skin that had been left in the sun. Nailed in the center of the board was a shred of brown material nearly the size of my hand. It was wrinkled; the edges were raw. Uneven. From one corner bulged a rounded lump.

"I take it that's an earlobe," I told him. "So all this brown skin must be someone's cheek."

I stepped back from it. Written in green chalk on the wall above the blackboard were the words: *ROAD TREASURE MACHINE*.

"I'll work it here. You sit by the tape recorder."

He started to walk forward. I shoved him in the chest.

"Don't go anywhere near it," I said.

"Vic, we've got to activate it now."

"You're not touching it." I shoved him again so hard he went back against the amplifiers. "And what's more your mother's going to have to explain all this to the police."

"Vic. We're going to be too late. The road's up to—"

"Yeah, yeah, the roads going to come and eat us all up."

"Please, Vic...please let me use the machine. It will bring back Paul and the others."

"Get back to the house. Now."

"It won't take long. You'll see Paul."

I shook my head.

Turning, he reached out to a powerpoint on the wall. He flicked the switch. The amps behind him began to hum.

"I'm not playing along with you any more," I told him.

"I really believed you'd help me." His eyes had that martyred look.

"You're ill, Leo. What you've done, stealing from injured people, isn't right."

"I had to. It's the only way to stop the road."

"You're not well in the head. But you don't know that, do you? You think all this is normal." I nodded at the blackboard with its bloody trophy display. "All this is going to get you—"

Without any fuss he stepped forward and moved a lever on the tape machine. The moment the spools turned a sound like thunder rocked the garage.

"Shit!" I pushed my hands against my ears as hard as I could. *"Turn the fucking thing off!"*

It was so loud it actually hurt the inside of my head. I lunged forward, tried to find the lever to turn it off—I found one and twisted it but all it did was change the tape speed. The sound groaned downward, deep bass notes punched into my stomach. Giving up on finding the off switch, I grabbed the spools and ripped the tape from the machine. Those sounds, amplified to God knows what, were painful enough, but they only lasted a second. Once the tape was out the sound stopped.

My nose began to run. When I wiped the back of my hand across it I was surprised to see blood smearing the skin. It had been so loud it made my nose bleed.

Squeezing through the gap between the amps and the brick wall I ran out onto the driveway. Halfway down the drive, and walking toward Langthwaite Road, was Leo.

The moonlight was bright enough to show his bare feet moving quickly. Hanging by the strap from one shoulder was the white guitar. He wore it like a soldier would carry a rifle.

When I followed him this time my fists were clenched.

"Leo?" I called after him. *"Leo!"*

«« — »»

Eleven

IT WAS HARD ENOUGH TO make him stagger back.

Leo touched his cheek where my open hand had cracked against his face.

"Next time it's this." I showed him my balled fist.

"Why are you hitting me? I'm trying to stop you from being harmed."

"Look, before I get really nasty, let's just go back up to the house."

He stood at the edge of the driveway. The moon shone down on him and he was giving me the martyred Christ look again. We were only a few yards from the road now. The sound of the trucks was loud enough to nag the headache that had started since Leo's tape had all but sliced my brain in half.

Instead of looking miserable Leo suddenly opened his eyes wide. "You know, we can still do it."

"Leo."

"We can do it right here."

He slipped the guitar strap from his shoulder and held the instrument in its playing position.

By this time I was half-resigned to his madness. "You can't play your guitar here. It won't work."

He showed me the body of the electric guitar. A wire hung down almost as far as his knees.

"It's got a radio pick-up. The receiver's plugged into the amps."

"So you want to stand out here in the dark, in a freezing cold wind, and play your guitar? God help me."

Even so, I'd had a belly-full of being the idiot's keeper. I was half-inclined to let him play bare foot in the dark if it kept him occupied until his mother—his soft as butter over-indulgent mother—returned home to tuck darling genius into bed.

He turned the volume control. Then he picked a string with the nail of his forefinger. From up in the garage the guitar note came buzzing back at us. A real missile of a sound. It whistled over our heads, over the road, over the fields and out to sea.

"If I can hit the right sequence of notes…"

Leo worked the strings. He picked out a sequence of notes at something like funeral pace. The transmitter plugged into the guitar jack channelled radio signals through the stack of amps in the garage a hundred yards away. Every touch of the steel strings sent a barrage of sound down the hillside.

It was weird music. There was an alien kind of rhythm but not a lot in the way of melody. The guitar's voice ranged from buzzing thumps to a howling roar. You heard that sound and it made you think of dinosaurs calling to each other across a swamp. When his left hand moved up the frets the notes rose to a jet engine screech before mutating into a human-sounding scream.

Leo's face in the moonlight had altered. A look of ecstasy, as if beautiful things were happening inside of him. His eyes blazed. In his mind he was a Messiah. A Messiah working miracles that were bigger, brighter and more beautiful than all the rest.

He rolled his eyes from the road upwards. The sky fascinated him. Maybe he was seeing angels blazing overhead. I glanced up. What I saw were fists of cloud punching the moon, driven by that biting wind from the sea.

In an excited voice he called to me, "It's working...*it's working.*" Leo began to walk toward the road. "It's moving back!"

His hand went at the strings in a rapid stabbing movement. The thing now sounded like a machine gun, driving back invaders.

"It's working, Vic. We're doing it."

By this time he was twenty paces from the road. A bus rumbled by. I saw passengers' faces looking at us.

What the hell's with those two lunatics?

A car went by, sounding its horn. The driver and passenger were pointing and laughing. Leo was playing like our lives—maybe *many* lives—depended on it, shaking his head, long hair flying out, mouth chomping air-pie the way idiots do.

"Leo, it's worked," I told him. "Time to go home now. Show's over."

He didn't answer; he was busy making the guitar howl.

A couple of cars slowed down. People shouted abuse through the windows. One car actually pulled up. A kid of around seventeen stood up with the top half of this body through the passenger side window. He lobbed a beer can in Leo's direction. It struck him in the face.

Leo never noticed. He played like he was trying to set the air alight. Guitar sounds roared down from the garage.

The kid in the car shouted, "You mad wanker…" He did the mime with his hand. *"Mad wanker!"*

The driver was enjoying the scene, too. He pulled slowly away, jabbing forked fingers in the air, shouting some abuse at Leo that I couldn't hear above the sound of the guitar. A truck tried to pass as the car driver accelerated away without looking. The trucker braked hard. I saw brake lights blaze in a mass of red, then the rig jack-knifed.

"Christ Almighty!" I shouted as I ran forward along the side of the road. The truck skidded sideward, the whole rear end swinging round to straddle the road. I saw the car with the shouting kids miss it by a hairsbreadth; they tore off like they'd a better place to be.

The truck skidded on, the trailer whipped out, its back wheels dropping into the ditch at the side of the road. Then the whole rig stopped dead with a terrific bang. Smoke that stank of rubber filled the air. The back doors of the trailer had been flung open, dumping the load out onto the road. Broken boxes lay scattered a hundred yards or more.

And Leo played on.

From the boxes objects began to creep. Little dwarf men with dirty yellow legs and bulbous bodies.

One ran toward me. The thing seemed to have springs for legs the way it jerked up and down as it ran.

"Nice one, Leo." I spoke to myself more than to him. "Battery hens…there's hundreds of the buggers."

The battery hens swarmed over the road. They ran through the fence into the fields. Some fell into the ditch where they flapped their skinny wings in the water.

"I'll check the driver." I might as well have talked to the hens rather than to Leo. He played faster now, the notes running into one.

I jogged down the road toward the truck.

The runty-looking battery hens were everywhere. Some were injured. I found myself stepping on them. More than once I slipped on bloody poultry. Then swearing I'd have to pull myself up and run again.

The truck had stopped part way off the highway, the rear end overhanging the ditch, but the cab had jacked to the right, blocking the road.

I reached the cab; the door had opened part way. I pulled it full open and looked in.

"Are you okay?"

The driver looked dazed. He turned his head from left to right as if trying to focus his eyes.

"Can you get out of the cab by yourself?"

He looked down at me. The eyes focussed. "You stupid cunt."

He raised his foot then stamped down into my face. I fell back. I heard the sound my skull made as it cracked against the asphalt.

As I rolled over onto my stomach, struggling to get on all fours I heard him swearing. "What the fuck were you doing with the guitar…you must have known you'd cause an accident?"

"It wasn't me. I was—"

He kicked me in the side. Red lightning tore the inside of my head.

"You stupid cunts. Look what you've done. You'll never get all those chickens back in a month of fucking Sundays."

I knelt up, raising my arm just in case he kicked again.

But the trucker had made it as far as the grass verge. He was holding his own arm at the elbow. It swung the wrong way when he moved. Groaning, he sat down.

"Thanks to you I've gone and busted it." He cradled the arm in his lap. "That's my fucking overtime gone and just before Christmas."

He was going to rant but he wasn't going to do any more kicking.

To hell with the trucker, to hell with Leo, to hell with the sound of the guitar shrieking like crazy.

I knew one thing. It was down to me to stop cars from ploughing into the jack-knifed truck.

«« —»»

What Vic sees,
What Vic does
(live improv with guitar solo)

This is what I see all around me.
My house on the hill.

The moon all round, bright like a ghost.

Hard road, black road.

My bone guitar with strings and things to make it sound good.

Vic.

My music brought angels to the ground. They're small. They're dancing in the road with Vic. My songs for the road are working. It's returned to the bottom of the hill again. No more creeping. No more killing.

No more weeping. No more pilfering...

I make my guitar sing. Vic is dancing with angels on the road. The world has turned aluminum. The moon shines; the fields bright.

It's starting to happen, just like I said.

Vic's with the road angels. He's waving his arms as bright lights approach.

The word that fits the action is: SUMMONING.

Vic is summoning all the people the road has taken. The song of my guitar and Vic's SUMMONING is bringing them back.

I feel the road under my feet grow warm and loving.

I'm running to angels.

Vic...mother...God. I'm running!

*(From **Life Bites**, by Leo)*

《《—》》

Twelve

THAT FALL HIT ME HARDER than I realized. I walked through those godawful battery hens (they cried like babies...didn't 'cluck' at all), my head was spinning, blood streamed down from a gash in my scalp, my legs were soft as mush. Half a dozen times I fell flat on my face.

When I stumbled the squealing hens swarmed all over me—alien things with eyes that stared right into you. They pecked at my hair, face and neck.

And all the time, Leo played the guitar. It was shrieking and howling. The road vibrated under me the thing was that loud. I wiped my eyes over and over. They watered so much I could hardly see.

If a car were to come now, or another truck…there'd be carnage.

"Leo. Switch that thing off!"

It was stupid to even make the effort to say it. Leo was in his own world, playing his mad little heart out. I wiped my eyes, then strained to focus. The truck blocked the road. I made my way round it. There were lights ahead, bearing down on me. I waved both hands shouting for them to stop.

The car pulled up short of the truck. Then he backed away hazard lights flashing orange. The driver had sense. They'd warn traffic heading along the road toward North Sutton. Now for traffic coming in the other direction.

I turned around.

Walking toward me, following the white lines in the middle of the road, came Leo. He held the guitar high in front of him like some cock-eyed pilgrim holding up a cross. The neck gripped in one hand while he still played with the other. The notes went rocketing over the fields like the sounds of bloody warfare. And he had this holy expression on his face, his eyes were fixed forward and slightly raised like God himself loomed over the horizon.

I slipped on a carcass. Went down to chin the pavement. I heard a tooth break.

When I stood up again the world was really starting to turn around me. I swayed. Then staggered forward.

Sometimes the moon was at my feet as if I dribbled a football. The music was going right through my head.

"Get off the road, you idiot."

I thought someone else had spoken then I realized it was me. I stumbled off the road, fell to my knees, let my face sink into cold grass. There were other things, too. Bunches of flowers. Cards fluttered in the breeze.

To Paul, we can't believe you're gone.
Dave and Marion

To our mate Robbo'. Rest in Peace.
From everyone at the Marquis.

To a much loved son…

The sea gale blew harder, stripping petals from the flowers.

Jobs to do, Vic. Got to stop cars…Langthwaite Road's a mincing machine. You know that…only needs one jack-knifed truck.

I pushed myself up by my hands into a kneeling position. Out there in the field was where my friend Paul Robertson had flown his car…garrotted himself with his own seatbelt. The times I've walked out here to imagine him hanging there upside down in the car. The black strap's crushing into his throat and he's making this sound…like a deep moan that comes out through his throat because it can't escape his mouth. He's conscious, his eyes are open. They're huge and terrified because he knows what's happening but the seatbelt lock's jammed.

I wiped my eyes.

There, in the middle of the plowed field, was a car. It lay upside down. One wheel still turned, steam whistled from the engine. I hadn't even heard it come off the road. But then, who would? With Leo's guitar screaming like a bag of ghosts.

I pushed myself forward to surf down the grass bank on my stomach. Then I was on my feet, rolling over the fence. When my feet touched the ground at the other side I started to run. Soft muck sucked at my boots. The harder I ran the slower I got. My legs ached like damnation.

Someone was at the car first. They had pulled open the door. Now they were trying to help the driver.

I got closer. I saw the figure in the moonlight, pulling at the driver by the arm. Only they weren't helping.

"Hey!" I shouted.

They were pulling a watch off the man's wrist.

Jesus Christ. So that's what Leo had been doing. He had got down here before me. The bastard was robbing the injured man in the car. I lunged at the figure but he dodged away, running easily across the mud.

The figure was dark. I had an impression of short hair. So it wasn't Leo after all.

Not that it mattered. What mattered was—

I froze as I crouched beside the car.

Hanging upside down…his face swollen, purple…his mouth open in a frozen yawn…was Paul Robertson. There had been a mistake. He wasn't really dead after all…but now he'd had an accident in the same place that…

I shook my head; the world was revolving at a speed that turned me sick to the stomach. How could this be? How could anyone mistake identifying a body?

"Don't worry, mate." I told him. "I'll soon have you out." I lunged into the upside-down car, Paul's arms hanging down around me like a pair of thick vines as I reached for the seatbelt lock. When I had my thumb on the button I pressed. Nothing happened. I kept pressing. I felt Paul's body twitch. Then it convulsed against mine.

"Stay with me, Paul! I'll get you out!"

I pushed hard with my thumb. The seatbelt buckle snapped from the lock. Suddenly Paul came down on me, his weight crushing me against the car roof. His face pressed against mine.

His eyes were now open. They stared into mine from just inches away.

"Paul. Don't worry…I'm going to get you out…you'll be okay…"

I wormed my way from under him. He tracked me with his eyes. The shock of the accident had clearly dazed him. He didn't recognize me.

Then he opened his mouth and slammed his face against mine. I felt his teeth crunch into the skin of my cheek.

I screamed at him to stop. He didn't. He didn't move. He just lay on top of me, biting.

I wrenched back; something gave way on my face.

It hurt like hell but I'd got away from his mouth. This time I kept backing out. I didn't stop until the car's roof had vanished from under me and I was on all fours on the mud. I backed away further. The car lay there in the field; a dark mound; a steel tumulus.

A pale arm flopped through the window. Paul's head followed it. Slowly, without fuss or effort, he squirmed from the car. He rolled over onto his stomach. Then like some over-sized maggot he began to worm on his belly toward me, leaving a furrow in the soil.

I looked back to the road.

Lit by moonlight, Leo still stood there, playing a sequence of cascading notes.

I stood up only to fall flat again. Dizziness came at me in waves. The moon rolled. Sometimes it was above me. Sometimes below.

With a deep breath I pushed myself to my feet again. I plodded through the mud toward the road. My skull felt like it was in pieces. There was a deep hole in my cheek that poured blood.

I've got a bad taste in my mouth...that was the only thought that was clear in my head at that moment. I've got a bad taste in my mouth.

I only looked back once. Paul still followed. He dragged himself along using his arms, with his legs trailing dead behind him.

At the fence I started to climb over, then realized that my own legs were going. I slumped forward with my arms over the top rail. Everything blanked for a few seconds. The sound of the guitar receded. For a spell I felt nothing. Heard nothing. I can't tell how long it lasted...probably no more than a minute.

When the sound of the guitar came rolling back and my head began to ache again I realized someone was pulling my jacket open. I opened my eyes. A boy of around ten stood in front of me. He'd unzipped my jacket. Now he had his hand inside it groping at my breast pocket.

Boy?

I thought: boy.

Only his face was shrivelled. Lines radiated from the mouth, etching deep gullies that reached his hairline. The nose lumped from the center of the face. The eyes were creased hollows.

This boy is dead, I thought dizzily. He's been dead a long time. The boy drew my wallet from my jacket.

Still only half conscious, I looked at my left arm as it hung over the fence. A little girl with blond hair was tugging my wristwatch over my knuckles. Her entire face had been torn off. It hung inside-out from her throat.

Effective mask, I told myself. Then I threw up.

When I looked up again the pair were climbing the grass bank to the road. They ran past Leo. He noticed them. Played harder, sending howling guitar sounds higher and higher.

A hand closed over my ankle. I looked down. Paul stared up at me; his mouth hung open; his jaw must have been broken. I kicked free of the hand, climbed over the fence. Then, panting, heart laboring, I made it up the bank to the road.

Leo jerked the neck of the guitar. Now the instrument emulated falling bombs...feedback plunging down into an explosion of sound.

Shrapnel echoes. Screams of feedback. Murdered orphan notes that decayed in the night air.

The moon burned hard now. I could see the full stretch of Langthwaite Road from the crossroads to where it kinked a sharp left at Annie Tyndall wood. It was littered with broken cars.

Leo's face blazed. "They're back. I've brought them back!"

He didn't stop playing. At the side of the road I saw a pair of pulpy gray hands appear on the grass verge. Paul was making his comeback, too. I ran in the direction of the truck. Battery hens cleared a path for me. They revealed a motorbike on the road, a '50s BSA. A man in leathers with flying goggles lay on the ground. He sat up when I got close. His forehead was caved in exposing brain.

I saw that the cars belonged to every decade. From roofless things that looked like carts with wooden wheels and open-top engines to a '20s Bentley, to a WW2 Jeep, to a '60s holiday coach. There were trucks, bikes, vans, cars. They lay on their sides, or on their backs. Some were blackened shells. Some torn to pieces by the collision, leaving scrap metal and individual seats scattered across road-tar.

This was the battlefield between road and humanity. All the war's casualties were there. The schoolboy walking home who'd been hit by a car. The farmer whose tractor had turned over in the ditch. The party girl who'd had too much champagne before running her car into a tree.

Leo's guitar called them all back. They crawled from wrecked vehicles. They emerged from the ditch. Climbed over fences. Came down from the trees.

Leo's music drew them like the Pied Piper drew the children...or the rats. They were all coming this way.

I heard a scream.

The girl and boy who had stolen my watch and wallet were feeding on the truck driver with the broken arm. He writhed under them. He tried to scramble free but his face was already gone. Only when they got to work on his throat did the screams fade.

With so many figures blocking my way I turned and ran back.

Ahead was Leo. But beyond Leo more of the things were closing in. Above me the moon had become a monstrous yellow eye. Looking down to see what happened next.

Thirteen

THIS IS WHAT HAPPENED NEXT.

There was a ball of light. It roared out of the darkness from the direction of town. Leo played the guitar in the center of the road. He gazed into the sky, the image of one those paintings of Christ on the Cross gazing up toward heaven.

Guitar notes swooped down across the fields, weaving power chords with sweeter notes that rose then fell to die over the ocean.

I was around thirty paces from Leo. The things that walked still came slowly forward.

I looked at the ball of light. These were powerful headlights on a big executive car. It raced toward us. Eighty? Ninety?

The driver was going for broke. He was stopping for nothing.

Leo didn't move. I saw the car glide from the side of the road until it followed the center line. I glanced at Leo's bare feet. One foot was to the right of the painted line, the other to the left.

That was a time for mad thoughts. Maybe Leo's insanity was contagious after all. Because the thought that hit me was: The road's fighting back.

"Leo...Leo! Get off the road!"

I shouted the words but it was too late. The car was only yards from him now. Its lights were blinding. The motor screamed.

"Leo!"

He turned to face the car just as it closed in. It went for him like a panther.

I froze ready for the impact, already seeing in my mind's eye Leo being smashed apart. But the car bucked, just as if some invisible force had struck it sideward on. How it missed Leo, I don't know: the door mirror brushed his T-shirt, ripping a vent in the side, his hair fluttered in the slipstream.

Then it was past him.

It veered and I put my hand up, expecting it to slam into me.

Only it kept going. I turned as it screamed by inches from me. I saw the passengers in the old Mercedes. They were all dead. Long dead. Rotting.

The car plowed into the grass verge in an explosion of soil then it flipped end over end into the field in a mist of rust and mud.

In the moonlight it became nothing more than a mound of dead metal.

Leo still played. As he played, the walking things approached. But they could only get so close. They stopped in a line thirty paces from him. They weren't coming any nearer.

I walked up to him. He lowered his eyes from the sky to look at me. Those laser-beam eyes shooting eerie lights.

I asked him straight: "How'd you do it, Leo?"

He smiled at me, a faint one, but a smile.

"Do what, Vic?"

"How are you making me see all this stuff?"

He didn't reply.

"You've made me hallucinate. I want to know how you did it." I looked back at the roadkill lured by the guitar music. "Zombies goofing on rock music is old fashioned, Leo. That's ancient pop video stuff."

He shrugged one shoulder; carried on playing. They were discordant sounds now—random chords, squealing sustains that made my headache.

"I didn't eat anything. I only drank out of sealed bottles. But you managed to slip me something didn't you? One of your pills…something that makes you hallucinate."

He shook his head.

"It's time to stop this, Leo."

He shook his head again.

"Stop playing."

"Can't."

"I said—" I grabbed hold of the guitar, wrenched it out of his hand, then swung the wood body back into his mouth. His head snapped back. He steadied himself. Blood formed a near-black outline around his lips.

"Give me back the guitar." He sprayed blood when he spoke. "Give it back, Vic. I've got to keep playing, or—"

"Or the road's going to eat us. Yeah." I threw the guitar aside. It bounced on the asphalt where it settled on its back. The strings still rang a metallic jangle from the speaker stack in the garage.

"It's time to stop this now, Leo."

"You have stopped it, Vic." His eyes focussed on mine. "You should be very proud. You got what you wanted."

He turned away from me. Unsteadily, he walked across the road to the grass verge. There he sat down with one knee raised so he could rest his head forward on his arm, blood dripping from the gash in his mouth. He was beaten now. Exhaustion dragged at him like a dead weight.

I glanced back along the road. In the moonlight I saw the black strip of tar run out across the fields. The truck blocked the road. A few battery hens still bobbed their heads on the grass verge. The driver sat cradling his arm. Nothing had bitten him after all; even so, he only looked half-conscious.

Leo's walking road dead had gone. There were no corpse boys and girls to steal watches and wallets and cell phones.

I went across to Leo. He didn't raise his head fully but I saw his eyes roll up so he could see me through his fringe. As much as hurt there was disgust. As if I'd stolen his most treasured possession.

Payback time, eh?

I patted my pocket, feeling the hard winged shape of the spaceship.

"I nearly did it." Leo's voice was tired. "I nearly stopped the road for good…"

"Shut up."

"The road couldn't have harmed anyone else, if you'd let me—"

"Leo, shut up."

I walked back to where the guitar lay in the road. All I needed now was for a motorbike to hit it and throw the rider. I decided to move the guitar, maybe lob it into the ditch. Then telephone the police from the house.

The wind blew hard as I walked. It caught the guitar strings. The amp stack picked up the signal and the instrument moaned like a ghost. How did Leo slip me the mickey that triggered the hallucination? Come to think of it, did the bottled beer have screw tops? What better way to hide your illegal stash then dissolve the substance in beer and stick it at the back of the fridge. The beer did seem to affect me faster than usual…it was all simpler than I thought. I'd gulped down the madman's drug of choice.

Ho, ho, ho…

The cold winds were biting. I looked down Langthwaite Road. It was deserted now. Along with the zombies, the usual traffic had gone…maybe it was getting late. I had lost track of time.

I might even have been laid unconscious as the drug fooled around with my brain cells. Pulling up my jacket sleeve, I looked at my watch. Well, that wasn't the case. I looked at the back of my wrist where the watch should have been. The strap must have broken when I was tussling with Leo. It wasn't an expensive watch...no, make it a very expensive watch. Send the bill for a replacement to Miss. Carter. She can afford it.

The guitar lay like a lump of white bone on the black road. I bent down, gripped it by the neck. Pulled.

Do roads melt in winter?

The tar stuck the instrument tighter than glue. I looked down at the road surface. It was black. Glossy. More like glass than asphalt.

Maybe that's why this was a blackspot? The road-surface had worn smooth. Tires slipped off like the stuff was Teflon.

I put both hands round the guitar neck, then bracing my foot against the road I pulled harder. Damn it, if it wasn't stuck solid. Must be something spilt on the road.

I found myself trying to see if a resin or chemical had been splashed there, something to cement the instrument down. It was certainly slick. It had a wet look. I could see my reflection.

Only it wasn't my reflection. It was the face of the dead boy who'd stolen my wallet. With puckered dimples where the eyes should be. With creases in the skin radiating out from the lump of a nose. There were more faces swimming there. Paul Robertson with his jaw open wide; eyes staring. The little blond girl without a face. A jostling crowd of faces calling up at me like they were on the farside of a glass screen. I heard muffled voices.

Calling for help, Vic. They're calling for help...

The stuff in the beer was kicking in again...the drug clearly hadn't left my blood yet...

I raised my head. The world tilted. The moon ballooned hugely above me. Leo watched from the roadside.

What do you see, Leo? Do you see light beams shooting from my head? Just like the portraits in your room?

I stood up. Dark shapes flitted along the road. They looked like shadows...the kind formed by clouds. There was no real shape to them but they were large, very dark, and moved quickly.

They flowed by me. Heading toward town. Dazed, I thought of migrating birds, or of shoals of fish. But what they really reminded me of was sharks. Big, evil sharks swimming just beneath the surface of the road.

These were road demons. They had prowled this river of tar for a century or more. Tracking cars, trucks, even pedestrians. Following them. Then, when the time was right, closing in for the kill. Closing my eyes, I could imagine them keeping pace with Paul's car that night five weeks ago. All it took was for them to reach up through the highway and give the front wheels a nudge. The car spins out of control. In less then ten seconds Paul is hanging upside down, choking his life out on the seatbelt. Then scavengers follow the predators. Hungrily picking what they need from the dead and dying and...

It's the drug, Vic. That's what's making you see these things shooting through the blackness of the road. That's what's making you believe this stuff.

I looked at Leo. He had lights shining from his head. A sunburst of purples, reds, golds—ghost lights.

And the light in the road was black. A river of black light through which the things that were dead—and the things that made them dead—swim. This was black light; this was the color of death.

The white BMW sped by me. Without slowing it rammed into the side of the jackknifed lorry. Its massive trailer tires took the force of the car's impact. They burst, allowing the car to impale itself on the axles.

I ran to the car to find the bodies of Faith and Leo's mother. Something vicious had chewed mouthfuls of skin from their faces.

"Leo...Leo!" I scrambled across the grass to him where he sat. "Why didn't you warn me! I never even saw them!"

Dazed he tried to look at me and failed. His head slumped down.

He spoke in a murmur. "Saw who?"

"Faith and your mother. They've hit the truck."

He looked. "There's nothing there, Vic."

I twisted back. There was the truck. A few battery hens. But nothing else.

"I saw the car go right into the side."

"It's not happened yet."

I had imagined it. The fucking drug...

Then Leo spoke again. "It will happen though…soon…next few minutes."

"Liar."

He shook his head, defeated. "Wait and see…" He tilted his head. "Can't you hear it now?"

I listened. I could hear the sound of a car heading this way out of town.

But Leo's mother would slow down before making a left turn onto the driveway to the house. Only the car was accelerating. I could hear the note of the engine rising.

Cold winds blew into my face, taking the sound away from me. Then it was back louder than ever. I saw headlights a quarter of a mile away. The car coming faster and faster.

Once more I saw them in my mind's eye. Black shapes pouring out through the road. They would slide up the tires. They would slip into the engine. They would run their sensors across whatever they found there…over brake pads, clutch cables, accelerator linkage.

Dark tentacles would coil round the carb, exerting pressure. Soon the pedal would depress all by itself. The engine would race hard. The car would accelerate. Nothing the driver could do would slow the car. The driver would lose control at the bend. Either that…or they would slam into the first obstacle they reached.

I looked back at the hulking mass of the truck blocking the road. In my mind's eye, I saw Leo's mother pumping at the pedals…getting no response. Now she would be watching the needle rise. Leaving seventy, crossing the eighty line, nudging ninety.

Faith shouting, What's wrong?

I don't know. It's the car. I can't—

For Godsakes. Slow down!

But the only thing that would stop the car was the side of the truck. The impact would rip their beautiful bodies to pieces.

But Leo had succeeded until I prevented him…he was stopping the road…

I lunged at the guitar where it lay. Reached down, knocking the strings. The barrage of notes roared down the hillside. Immediately, the guitar came free in my hand.

I lifted it. Feedback rose into howl, calling to the moon.

I could see the car now. It hadn't slowed...it was stopped. As simple as that.

Leo was barely conscious but he lifted his face to look at me. Then his head sagged down again. He rolled on his back, arms out by his sides.

I couldn't play the guitar. But I knew how to make the sounds. I held the guitar by the neck but kept my fingers clear of the strings so it wouldn't dampen them. With my free hand I slashed the strings. One snapped with a crack like thunder. The others carried the note, sheer volume sustaining it. The car, I saw, was still at a standstill. I dampened the strings.

The moment silence descended the car roared. It became a pulsating ball of light that hurtled toward me. I hit the strings again.

Once more the car was still.

Fucking drugs, eh? See what they've done to you, mate. See what they're doing to your mind...

I could put the guitar down. Surely Miss Carter and Faith could come to no harm...only there was a stronger voice saying, *Don't you believe it.*

I kept the sound of the guitar rolling; discordant thrashing noises that shattered the night air. From the car came the shadows. They swam back along the road surface. The road was dark. Only *they* were darker. *They* sped toward me. The road demons knew what had spoilt their plan. They were coming back for me now.

Were they attacking?

Or had I Pied Pipered them?

I knew one way to find out.

My eyes flicked across to Leo. He watched me steadily. There was no expression on his face.

Reaching into my pocket, I pulled out the toy spaceship. I threw it under-arm. It landed beside him on the grass.

"Keep that safe for me, Leo. Until I get back, okay?"

He blinked. Then reaching out he grasped it.

Black shadows swarmed along the road, joining with one another, splitting away, pooling again...liquid darkness running through road-tar.

The guitar sang in my hands as I turned and ran. The jolting of my body shook the strings, making them vibrate. The radio pick-up transmitted the signal to the amp stack in the garage. The amps gave it voice. And what a voice. A cosmic voice that filled the night sky.

I ran hard along Langthwaite Road.

I had Pipe Pipered them.

They were following.

They'd go where I go.

《《——》》

Fourteen

THE ROAD MAKES A SHARP LEFT at Annie Tyndall wood but I ran straight on, down through a gap in the fence where yet another car had plunged through a few days ago. I kept moving. Following the narrow dirt track flanked by trees.

I was following the old route of Langthwaite Road, from the days when it ran out to Langthwaite. The way was almost overgrown now. But I could see enough in the moonlight not to lose it. I ran with the guitar. I could still hear its beautiful sounds calling to the shadows. They followed me in a pulsating mass.

Dark light.

Black light.

The color of death.

They were closer now. I saw fingers of darkness reaching out to me. They could trip me just like they tripped the young boy as he crossed the road last July. They could reach out to nudge a steering wheel. They could probe and pick at a weak tire wall.

Grass snagged my ankles. Brambles tried to stop me from running but I was pushing hard. I'd got the adrenaline flowing. I was going for it hard. I wasn't going to stop yet.

The wood ended. I was running over grass, heading for the V-shaped dent in the ground ahead. A moment later I was over the lip of soil, running down the incline in a cascading mass of dirt and pebbles. I slipped when I reached the bottom of the cliff. I looked back to see the flood of shadow pour over the top then come sliding down the slope after me.

I was on the beach now, still running.

I remembered what my father told me. About keeping the cleft that marked the position of the old Langthwaite Road directly at my back. I crossed the sands to the sea. The tide had turned.

The shadows followed. Getting closer and closer.

I never even noticed how cold it was. I plunged into the surf with the guitar held high over my head to keep it dry. The waves seemed to do their best to push me back but I drove forward through the flow. When I couldn't wade any more, I swam, using my free arm, still holding the guitar free of the waves.

Behind me, shadows moved across the water. A blade-shaped stain that followed me hungrily.

Ahead, were the fishing grounds where Langthwaite lay on the ocean bed. Moonlight shone on the water. Seemingly far away, the voice of the guitar was calling. Distorted by distance now, it became the tolling bells of the submerged cathedral.

My arm ached. I knew I was tiring. But I wasn't going to give up swimming.

Not for a long time yet.

«« — »»

The man with the guitar

Leo Carter got well again. He's working on a fishing boat now. The bad dreams have gone; he's doing all right. Rumor has it that he's seeing a girl down Bridlington way. And, don't you know it, if the rumors are true, then there might even be a wedding come Spring.

Miss Lynne Carter never did know why her car ran out of control on that November evening. Mechanics could find nothing wrong. It's just one of those apparently random peculiarities of life. The throttle stuck wide open for a dozen seconds, then as quickly the pedal freed itself. She stopped six feet short of the jack-knifed poultry truck. It didn't stop her and Faith Blake, however, from having the shakes when they climbed out of the car.

And one thing's for sure, the scare didn't do Faith any lasting harm. She's expecting a baby now. And if the timing's right young Miss or Master Blake might be putting in their first public appearance at that Spring wedding I've just been talking about.

Writing about events has a certain therapeutic quality. Why...even if life does turn out badly we can couch it in hopeful terms...with a splash or two of optimistic light. You know...the kind of light that well-meaning people tell you waits at the end of that dark and lonely tunnel.

So...I write down what I see. What happens to me. What I hear. What I do...which is a definition of autobiography, I guess. Right now, I'm sitting in the bows of the boat, writing in this exercise book with a pencil I found a long, long time ago in Paul Robertson's locker at school.

The sea's calm, and as fabulously blue as a swallow's egg. We're anchored out at Langthwaite fishing ground. In the bad old days, when I wasn't well (or especially happy), I'd imagine the town still existed down there with houses and streets, and a church bell that would toll with the turn of the tide. Not anymore. I write only what I see with these two eyes and hear with these two ears.

Right now, the skipper of the fishing boat is tying the coastguard vessel alongside. He's helping the coastguard officer from the bigger boat to our small craft. The man has to step over lobster pots. He's looking at an object laid on a plastic sheet.

The two men are talking. I'll record their speech just how it comes: —

"When did you find it?" asks the coastguard officer.

"About an hour ago. I radioed it in as soon as we'd got it out of the water."

"Good work. We'll have the helicopter come out and pick it up."

"Don't bother about that," the skipper says. "I'll bring the body in."

"You don't have to, you know?"

"I'll do it all the same, Jack."

"Can you bring it in now? We'll need to start the process of iden-
tification."

"There's no need," the skipper tells him. "My name's Blake. That's
the body of Victor Blake, my son."

At this moment, I pause. And all of a sudden wonder if I should
put my ear to the sea, would I hear the sound of my guitar, weeping
undying melodies on what remains of Langthwaite Road in an inun-
dated town?

*(From **Life Bites**, by Leo)*

In The Valley Where Belladonna Grows

Tim Lebbon

MARY HAD NOT SEEN ANOTHER HUMAN BEING for sixteen years when one wandered into her valley. It was on a day when the water in the well tasted sour, the family of foxes on the slopes barked at nothing, and Belladonna bushes danced to no breeze. She supposed they could have been omens of what was to come. She should have taken heed, although by then it was too late. But her heart had always been so trusting.

In her valley, Mary believed that everything would be all right.

She was sitting on a rocking chair in her garden. There was a clay pitcher of cold tea and a plate of cookies on the table by her side. It was a hot day so she wasn't wearing much—a loose, thin skirt, a baggy vest that had seen better days—but when she saw the man she felt no need to rush in and change. She was almost seventy now, a big woman, long hair in its usual ponytail, the flesh of her face heading further south every passing year. It was a man, true, but she felt no fear. She was not worried that he was here to harm her.

Her suspicion, her fear of these things, had ended years ago.

Mary took a sip of tea and closed her eyes, relishing the coolness on her throat. It spread through her body, giving her a precious few seconds' respite from the heat. She kept her eyes closed until the sensation had totally faded away.

She'd spotted him almost half an hour before. A smudge on the ridge surrounding the valley, an imperfection to the skyline that she'd noticed instantly, so familiar was she with the horizon. He disappeared for a while, and she hoped that he'd turned around and gone back. But then, heading down the dusty yellow road that still connected her with the outside—a useless vein, an artery carrying nothing that could give life—she saw movement.

The binoculars had brought the shape closer and defined it in her mind. Not only human; a *man*.

So Mary sat and awaited his arrival, wondering what he had come to do or say. Perhaps there was something important to tell her. Maybe Sherlock was dead and an apology had been left to her in his estate, an abstract apology that could never be known or experienced, useless because regret from the grave was like a kiss from a mile away. Pointless. Unfelt.

Every few minutes she lifted the binoculars to track his progress. And every few minutes he was closer, and closer. She hoped that one time she'd look and there would be nothing there, just the long empty road she was used to seeing, a yellow slash in the land that refused to be swallowed by undergrowth and trees, unwanted and unwalked. But he *was* there, always there.

And when it became possible to make out his features, she decided to look no more.

Mary wouldn't admit to the fear, but she picked at her grubby nails and bit her thumb until she drew blood. She thought of painting bloody red lines across the bridge of her nose to make herself look fearsome, but then she realised how foolish that would seem and laughed out loud.

Someone laughed back. She looked up. There he was, standing at the edge of her garden, a tall man in knee-length shorts, topless, muscled and sweating and staring right at her. He was smiling. Mary thought he looked nervous, but her own smile probably seemed the same to him.

"You're the first person I've seen in sixteen years," she said.

He didn't move. He seemed jittery, even though he was the one invading *her* space, trespassing in *her* valley. The rucksack over his shoulder looked heavy, but it may simply have been the way he was standing in the strength-draining heat. Mary noticed the pistol and bullet pouches on his belt.

"I have cold tea," she said. As if that would finally coax him in after he'd walked so many miles to meet her, talk with her.

Talk…or something else.

Maybe he was here for something else.

The pistol.

"I won't bite," Mary said, "and I'm too old and wise to make a pass at you."

The man showed his teeth as he laughed and that pleased Mary, it made her trust him, however foolish that was.

"The tea sounds very good," he said as he walked out of the wild and into her garden. "And I'd kill for one of those cookies."

«« — »»

Mary had not fetched another chair for him to sit on. Flustered, embarrassed at her rudeness, she'd gone to stand and go into the house when the man touched her hand and sat on the ground.

"Please," he said, "I don't mind, really." He crossed his legs and sipped from the jug of tea—she hadn't brought a cup for him, either—and when he bit into the cookie his expression was gratitude enough.

"You haven't come to kill me?" Mary asked at last. She'd lived a long time, and she wanted to live a long time more. Curiously, she felt sad rather than afraid.

The man smiled. "Only if you don't promise me a bag of these cookies to take back."

Mary smiled and nodded, setting herself moving in the rocking chair. He looked nice, *kind*, and even though the pistol on his belt was a heavy draw for her senses, she felt no real threat from him. The weapon's simple wooden stock was smooth and dark with sweat. It had been used a lot.

"You sure you haven't come to kill me?"

The man set the jug down slowly and looked at her. Mary waited for his hands to stray to the weapon on his belt. There'd be no escape—she hadn't run in a decade, and her old rifle was way behind her in the house. Besides, she really didn't think she could shoot another human being…whatever the threat. But when his hand moved it was to pick up another cookie. There were only a couple left now, and she'd have to bake some more tomorrow. But it was good seeing how much he liked them.

"You've been here a long time, haven't you?" he said.

Mary nodded. She shifted in the rocking chair, joints protesting, vest stuck to her back and breasts with sweat. The man's stare was making her uncomfortable.

"Sixteen years, give or take," she said. "That's why I'm…well, you'll have to excuse me if I seem a little rusty when it comes to social niceties."

"These cookies are the best social niceties I've had in ages," he said.

"So you won't kill me?" She was joking this time, almost convinced of his benevolence, but that gun still weighed heavily, a weight begging her awareness. It hung on his belt like the python she'd killed three summers ago on the east slopes, coiled and filled with murderous potential.

"No," he said, "I won't kill you. In fact, I rather hope I've come to help."

Mary looked away from him for the first time. She glanced around her valley, taking in the sights that were so familiar to her now and feeling their wonders as richly and as personally as she had the first time. The eastern slopes, home to a range of fruit trees and bushes, split by ravines in several places where the stream sprang from the ground and headed down into the heart of the valley. She could hear it now; only fifty paces from where she sat, its sound was as familiar and ignored as her own breathing, her heartbeat, the life of the valley and her life also. To the north, slopes were yellowed with rape and golden with barley and hops. Around her sat her homestead, the one part of the valley she had adjusted to her own tastes, forming an acre of gardens, paths, ponds and beautiful sand-sculptures that she had not wanted to change since their creation. She maintained, repaired and weeded, but she never altered.

South, the wild woods, filled with caves and animals and other untamed things. West, more wilds, places where she would find a slope of strawberries one year, a field of potatoes the next. It was as if the birds and animals kept this part of the valley to themselves, seeding it to suit their tastes year by year. On this western slope was the cave into which the stream disappeared. Perhaps it emerged again on the other side, perhaps not. Mary had once lived beyond that hill, but she had long forgotten.

Her horizon was a matter of miles in any direction. This was her world.

"What help could I possibly need?" Mary said. She'd never dreamed of somewhere more beautiful.

"If you want," the man said, "I can set you free."

Mary looked at him again. He seemed kind and honest.

"*Free?*" she hissed. And for the first time in sixteen long years, she knew herself capable of violence.

««—»»

Her crime had been faith in a love gone wrong.

In the city, Sherlock was her life. He was a great money-trader then, a lender and an advisor, someone used by businessmen and dukes, criminals and kings. He didn't mind who he dealt with—most of the time he pretended not to know—so long as they paid their way. And they all did. Sherlock and Mary lived in a huge mansion by the river, and she wanted for little. Money, jewels, fine clothes and finer food, they were all hers. Sherlock was hers as well, totally. He was a fine husband and a good lover.

He never raised a hand to her.

Not a *hand*…not to begin with.

But he welcomed a party of drug traders to the mansion one fine summer evening. There was eating and drinking on the balcony, beautiful escorts wearing slinky summer dresses, free bedrooms if they were required, anything else that was needed or asked for. Mary was Sherlock's constant hostess. He told her to be there but not there, a presence to prove his manliness yet unobtrusive, quiet. A beautiful shadow, that's what he wanted her to be that evening. And when she started talking with the drug men, laughing and joking and nodding as they complained of import taxes and infiltration by the smuggling gangs…Sherlock steered her away. And he shouted at her, a vicious scream that bruised her as much as a punch would have, more. It bruised her heart and dented their love.

Later he told her how sorry he was, that it was all a matter of face.

But Mary—already middle-aged, and numbed until now by happiness—had seen perfection shatter in the spittle-spray of his shout.

Things were never the same again.

««—»»

Mary watched the man leave her valley. She sat in the same rocking chair drinking from the same cup, but the cookies were all gone now, and she couldn't bother herself to go and make more. She'd given the man—she'd never even asked his name, and he had not volunteered it—the last cookie from the plate. He'd smiled, frowned, asked her again, and left when she shouted at him.

She hadn't raised her voice in years, because she never had cause. It had hurt her throat and made her cry, startling her that she could make such a sound. At night she awoke sometimes from dark dreams, panting and wondering whether the scream was real. But this shout was *obviously* real, and intentional.

She picked up her binoculars and watched him struggle up the western slope above the treeline. He hadn't paused since he'd set out, pushing at his legs as if climbing himself. He hadn't glanced back either, and this almost made Mary feel sorry for him.

She downed the remnants of the cool tea and shook her head. Damn, he'd been sent to do this errand, he'd walked dozens of miles through the heat and the swarms of insects and who knew what else, and she'd sent him away with a cookie. Hadn't even invited him to stay for a proper meal. And the least she could have done—whatever he said, whatever he offered, he couldn't know, couldn't understand how he was offering to steal from her by giving her freedom—the *very least,* was to give him a bed for the night. She'd shot the messenger. Damn.

He was almost at the ridge now, blurring with the heat-haze. Mary watched as the stranger grew from the hilltop, stayed there for a moment, and then shrank back down the other side.

Gone.

She stood from her rocking chair. It creaked forward and almost spilled her to the ground, but she clasped its arms and grimaced as pins and needles attacked her left foot. Teeth gritted, she pounded her foot at the ground, stamping in anger to kick-start her bad circulation.

Sherlock sent me, the man had said. *His message is this: 'Too long has passed. Too much is changing. Retribution is no longer my aim, but neither is forgiveness. Your exile is over, you can leave the valley, but never enter the city. That is still, and always will be out of bounds'.*

Mary walked a few steps and glanced around the valley. The ghost of the man's presence was still there; the tang of sweat, the echo of his voice in her memory, imagined but strong. The sun was glinting from the stream like a thousand diamonds juggling themselves together. The crops on the northern slopes undulated with the slight breeze that evening, shadows snaking east to west as if the great hills were shrugging their shoulders, shedding the day's events in readiness for tomorrow. The sun was diving for the wild western hills, perhaps to follow the man. A pair of buzzards circled high above, spotting rodents for supper, wings flapping every minute to drift them into another thermal. Mary wondered how far they could see from up there. After so long here, anything beyond the valley was forever.

And that's forgiveness? she'd said to the man. *Look around you, look at what I have. Do you think release from here is any kind of release at all?*

Mary smiled when she recalled the man's confusion. Because he *had* looked around, and he'd seen that she was right.

"I've got all the freedom I need," she whispered again. It was the last thing she'd said to him as he reached the edge of her garden. He'd looked back to her, like a scared boy standing at the extremes of order and facing the wilds for the first time.

Mary went and stood where the man had been, looked back at her empty rocking chair, wondered whether he'd actually heard those final words. The chair was a way away, and her earlier shout had shocked her into a whisper. She tried to put herself in his shoes. He must have known that she was right. The valley was Heaven.

She'd built a fence around the garden years ago, complete but for the wide gap where the unused dust road passed through. Perhaps that had been a subconscious admittance that she'd be seeing people again someday, would be entertaining visitors, but it also prevented her from feeling totally enclosed within the garden. The fence was built from thick trunk uprights with twisted willow branches pinned between them, curled in, out and in again, tied off with shredded willow bark. It had taken her two years to build.

It kept the Belladonna out, at least.

The plant grew in profusion all around her garden. It pressed against the fence, never intruding but always there. She'd tried killing it at first, cutting it down, hacking, burning, but it always came back. It hadn't taken long for her to give in and accept its presence…and soon she even came to like it. It felt as though it belonged there. As if she needed it. It was holding Mary and the garden under siege, but a benevolent one, because she never fought anymore.

The plants flowed and shifted in the breeze, and as Mary watched a stronger wind came down from the slopes as if to blow away her concern.

"Time for tea," she said. She'd been speaking to herself for the past few years. She enjoyed the sound of her own voice, but sometimes she argued. She supposed most people would consider her mad. "A nice pasta tonight, with parsnips and whole garlic cloves. Kills my stomach. I'll be up all night. But I like the night. I do."

She stared up at the western slopes one more time, wondering whether the man had camped just over the hill's crest. If he had perhaps she'd smell the smoke, see the glow of his camp fire as the sun went down.

Mary wondered just why that should excite her so.

«« — »»

She always cooked fresh. Pulling or cutting her dinner was a huge part of her day, a reward for the hours spent toiling in the fields or garden. She only killed on rare occasions. After sixteen years the ammunition for her rifle was too precious to waste. The opportunity rarely presented itself anyway, and when it did more often than not she would miss. Her eyesight was fading with age.

She had once read that ladies used to press Belladonna leaves to their eyes to dilate the pupils. She wondered whether, after years spent surrounded by the plant, its toxicity had permeated her skin or stroked her eyes through the air. She and the valley were so close.

Today there were parsnips to dig up and garlic to pull. She had made the pasta that morning. She supposed it was an innocent pasta, created before she'd seen the man walking down into her valley with purpose in his stride. Before, yes, but to be eaten after, an ongoing act that spanned between her times of utter contentment…and doubt.

Because doubt was there now. It was the shadow of a memory at the back of her mind, a smell long forgotten, a message in birdsong, something so nebulous that she was almost unaware of its presence. But as she pulled the parsnips and saw worms crawling in the soil, feathery roots struggling to retain contact with the ground, the rich green leaves on the vegetables' heads, she thought of the man, and what he had said. *Freedom* was the word he'd used, and it was something she had. Something she'd possessed *more* of since being sent here than before.

But still…

"Got to slice you and fry you first," she said, trying to talk the feeling into submission. "Mix in some herbs, mashed and whole garlic, diced tomato…fit for a king. Mix you with the cooked pasta…" The pasta she'd made before meeting the man. An innocent meal, to be swallowed past her doubt.

Is freedom really real if it's imposed? she thought and immediately shook her head.

She picked her herbs. "Basil, oregano, some thyme." Her herb garden was a wonder, a square of subtle smells and bright greens, rich earth and a stone path trodden into smoothness over the past sixteen years. The herbs kept her alive, she thought. They mixed and merged and spiced her blood, gave her breath, eased her lungs and built muscle.

How free do I feel?

"I feel free!" she said, and her voice rose again, startling her. A bird took flight from the roof of her house, and she felt bad for frightening it. She whispered, again: "I feel free."

She picked the last of the herbs and loved the smells ground into her hands and released to the air. The breeze was picking up even more now as the sun touch the western hills, and the smells were stolen away. She wondered if the foxes would catch the aroma, or the wild things in the woods, or the goats that stalked the hillsides. Sometimes the animals came close to her garden the morning after she had cooked, knowing that she always left scraps for them. She hoped they'd come tomorrow. She craved their company, their comfort.

Armed with the ingredients for her meal she went indoors.

It was a simple house, built a hundred years before by the first people to farm this valley, see its potential, relish its privacy. Its walls were of stone, thick enough to ensure coolness in summer and warmth in winter, the open wood fire venting through the massive chimney. Its roof was timber and slate. There were leaks, but not many, and once each year Mary would venture up and try to plug the cracks and gaps with a mixture of stream mud, whipped egg and the guts of crushed rats. The repairs seemed to hold well enough, so long as she spent the day following her labour throwing stones at birds as they tried to peck them away.

There were three rooms. The main room was where she lived, cooked, ate and relaxed. There was a small bedroom off to one side and a bathroom next to that, the water supply an intermittent flow from an underground stream. Upon arrival she had installed her own toilet system, draining waste into an underground chamber outside and using it, eventually, to enrich the soil of her garden. She liked the idea that together she, her house and garden formed a self-perpetuating, self-sufficient partnership. And she also loved the surprise she felt at what she could do…a lady of the *city,* at that!

Really she had little other choice. She was a prisoner here, after all.

The pasta was in the cool-hole under her oaken table. She set about making dinner, slicing and dicing and mixing and tasting, taking her time because time was all she had. She would rather spend three hours making a meal than one, four hours to plant a row of cabbages instead of two. Keeping busy kept her alive.

Mary glanced from the window at the twilight flaming the valley. The gardens were dark already, but the slopes still caught the last rays of the sun, giving the impression that the whole valley was sinking slowly into the earth.

"Sing up," she said quietly, "sing up." And the songbirds sang. The sounds came in from the south, each song twisting with curious echoes as the birds sang deep in their caves. For the first few months here Mary had thought that she was listening to the mournful wailing of ghosts or angels, or the deadly promise of demons. She had cowered in the house every evening at twilight, trying to find sense in the tunes and, eventually, lending them her own fears to carry and swell. They had almost driven her mad. It was only a brave daytime exploration that had assuaged her fears and saved her sanity. The birds had been upset at her intrusion, and their objections were voiced in long, high songs, the sunlit cousins of the night-time warblings Mary had come to fear so much.

Now, she loved to hear the birds sing. It wasn't fear she attached to the sound any more, but contentment. It gave her peace of mind.

So the birds sang, and Mary cooked, and all the while she was thinking of Sherlock and the pretence of freedom he'd sent the man to offer.

«« —— »»

There was a storm that night. Mary heard it oozing into the valley long before she'd finished eating. It set the fire in the grate hissing and dancing, sent its rich smell of potential violence into the air, scratched at the door and windows with insidious cool claws.

Protected as it was by the hills, huddled in the bosom of the land, storms would usually pass by the valley, or merely stroke it with the fringes of their fury. Sometimes Mary could sit and watch as the world seemed to end in the west, nearer the city. Thunderheads would rise a dozen miles into the sky, boiling and rolling into each other, stirring themselves with pent powers, momentous explosions flashing in their depths. On occasion she would even hear the thunder many seconds after the flash, but it was a whisper rather than a shout. She liked to sit and watch. It made her feel safe, secure in her own little valley, whilst elsewhere people were being assaulted by the rain and wind and lightning.

Tonight the valley would not have such a quiet ride.

Perhaps Sherlock could even control the weather now. Maybe her shunning of his unexpected, petty offer of freedom had angered him too much.

So the storm rolled in, and Mary made sure the door was securely bolted and the windows covered with their little-used storm shutters.

The first slew of rain hit the house like a hail of stones. Mary screamed out loud, wide-eyed, bathed in cold sweat. She *knew* there was nothing awful out there, she *knew* it was only rain…but the noise was so loud, so intrusive, that it terrified her. The wind screeched at the eaves like demons being exorcised. The fire hissed out puffs of steam as water trickled down the chimney. Shutters rattled in their frames, and there was a sudden *crack* as a pane of glass broke. The impacts on the slate roof sounded like hammer blows, and Mary expected to look up and see the roiling undersides of clouds at any second.

But it was only rain.

She'd lived through storms like this before. Not often, but they had happened.

So why was she so scared?

She could hear her animals crying and squawking and snorting in the enclosures behind the house, the chickens calling stupidly into the dark, pigs panicking, goats tugging at their leashes and scraping their horns against the stonework as they danced mad dances to the lightning. She almost wished she'd brought them in—she'd done that six years before, spent four weeks of that dreadful winter living as one with her own livestock so that they didn't freeze to death—but nothing had warned her that the storm would be so fierce.

She wondered how the valley would fare. What would she do if the crops were ruined, the animals killed, the well fouled or poisoned by ripped-up Belladonna blown into it?

And again, she had the crazy idea that Sherlock had orchestrated this to make her reconsider his offer.

Is freedom really real if it's imposed, she thought yet again, and the house and valley suddenly felt more claustrophobic than they ever had in the past.

She sat by the internal wall that split the house in two, listening to the storm, unable to sleep, stoking the fire when wind-blown gushes of water tried to smother it. And although it was only an hour before it passed, it felt like sixteen years.

«« — »»

Leaving the house the next morning, reluctant to inspect the damage and fearing the silence from the animals' compound, the last thing Mary expected to see was a man coming down from the hills.

She walked through her garden to the gap in the fence, watching him all the while. He looked as if he'd been walking all night. The storm had soaked his clothes, and they hung heavy and stretched. A rifle was draped casually over one shoulder. His hair was a wild mess, his eyes fearful and wide, and there were several scratches on his cheeks and nose, weeping blood. It was diluted by the water dripping down from his hair, staining his grubby shirt pink.

"You're still here," he said.

Mary wondered whether this man had passed her visitor from yesterday, and what they had discussed.

He stopped several paces away, glancing over her shoulder at the house and garden then back into her eyes. Mary's gaze was strong, even though she was scared. This was her *home*.

"I'm Nathan," the man said, looking down at his feet, then up again. "You're still here!"

"Why shouldn't I be?"

"I thought you might have left. After yesterday, after your freedom, I thought—"

"I *am* free," Mary said, and she stepped through the gap in the fence as if to prove the fact.

"Don't blame you for staying," he said. "Way things are. Way the city's running down. Don't blame you at all. Last night, the storm, that was just the first of it, there'll be a lot more like that…lot more…" Nathan trailed off but his mouth still worked. Mary guessed that inside he was still talking to her.

She waited until he was still.

"Who do you think I am?" she asked.

"You're Mary. Sherlock's wife. He sent me to make sure you were on your way, asked me—"

"I'm not leaving."

Nathan looked up sharply. "What?"

"How many more did he send?" she asked. Yesterday's visitor couldn't have made it back to the city before this one was dispatched. It was a two day walk. They must have passed each other on the road.

"None. Me. That's it."

"And that man yesterday."

Nathan nodded. "Yeah, him too."

A few seconds ago she hadn't feared this man, only the personal contact. Now, her fear was changing emphasis. She was pleased that after so long she could still converse, and perhaps the long absence of conversation had sharpened her senses rather than dulled them. Unhindered by social conventions, manners of speech or self consciousness, she could see that this man was someone to be afraid of.

She stepped back.

"Stay out of my garden," she said. The Belladonna bushes huddled along the fence shifted in an invisible breeze, snickering.

Nathan raised his hands innocently, palms out.

"I'm not here to harm you," he said. "I can see that after so long this may be a shock, maybe you've been...alone for too long, but—"

"I'm not afraid of you," she said, but her voice betrayed her.

From behind the house she heard a snort as one of the pigs overturned its food trough. The chickens clucked and the goats butted the fence, and Mary breathed a sigh of relief. At least they hadn't been killed or set free by the storm.

She wondered if she could say the same for herself.

"You here to kill me?" she asked.

Nathan shook his head. Water droplets caught the morning sun as they sprayed from his hair and speckled the plants beside him.

"No, I told you, I'm just here to see if you've left."

"I haven't."

"That's obvious."

"I like it here," Mary said

"It's very nice." He looked around the garden again, raised his eyebrows. "A bit windswept, but nice."

"What did you say about the city, about things running down?"

Nathan did not answer, would not meet her gaze. He seemed more tired than she had thought at first, almost as if his senses were fading in and out, attacked by the storm perhaps, dulled with fatigue.

"Whatever," Mary said, "I've no interest in it anymore. I'm old. I'm happy here."

Nathan blinked and looked back at her, startled and vacant for a second as if he'd forgotten where and who he was.

Mary glanced at the rifle. It looked awkward on his shoulder. And he had a nice face, friendly eyes. He didn't look like an assassin.

"You want something to eat?" she asked, stepping aside to allow him symbolic access to her garden. Nathan didn't answer so she turned around and started walking back to the house. "Milk the goat for me and we'll have scrambled eggs." His footsteps, shuffling and heavy, were his reply.

Walking to the house, Mary took the opportunity to give her garden a quick check-over. A couple of small trees were down, the stream was running fit to burst, and there were twigs, leaves and branches scattered across the lawns. Other than that, there seemed to be little damage. The house didn't look too bad either, although a few slates hung askew and one of the storm-shutters on the front window had buckled its hinges.

She had weathered these storms before. This one was no different. Strange timing, for sure...but no different.

Trying to convince herself of this, struggling to combat the doubt and confusion that had been conjured to her world—a world where simplicity had always been the calming force—she turned and stared into the rifle's throat.

«« —— »»

Sherlock had always been an experimental lover. He despised the constraints of inexperience, craving originality, adventure and sometimes pain.

Mary was not. Rightly or wrongly sex was a chore, and on the odd occasions when she had submitted to some of Sherlock's more outrageous requests, she hated it and herself all the while. He was aware of this and usually held back, but sometimes his desires got the better of him. He never actually hurt her, not really, but there were times when the atmosphere after sex was distant and charged. Loaded silences. Glances avoided. Sleeping apart, not touching, in case the truth of what they had done could be felt in the sweat of their tacky skins.

Mary loved her husband. She never, ever thought badly of him, and she accepted that in some ways they were very different from each other. He had to accept that too.

And he did to begin with...but his acceptance did not last.

Perhaps his infidelity was tied in with the time he first raised his voice to her in public. It was possible that the later abuse was a twisted manifestation of guilt. And for a time, Mary pitied him.

The defining moment of her life—the instant when the change in things edged beyond redemption—was when she walked in to find him with three naked women.

The things they were doing.

The *things.*

Even with all the terrible events that followed, that day was still the worst of her life.

«« — »»

Mary knew that she was not going to die.

The rifle was pointing at her face, shaking as Nathan gripped its rest and stock, its barrel black and menacing. It was a battered old thing that had obviously seen a lot of use. The bullet belt around Nathan's waist—funny, she noticed it only now—was less than half full. Both his eyes were open, he had leaned forward into a shooter's stance, the stock was hard into his shoulder…and yet she knew that he would not fire.

He was too frightened.

Nathan shook, sweat ran into his eyes, a vein throbbed at his temple.

The chickens launched into an intense squabble behind the house, startling Nathan. Then, that one moment, Mary closed her eyes. She was *certain* that he could never pull the trigger, but how ironic if he was surprised into doing so.

She opened her eyes again and looked into Nathan's eyes.

"Why have you come?" she said. "You look pleasant enough. You have a wife, I guess. Children? Yes, children, I can tell. Before I came here I could always see the joy in a parent's eyes, and I guess I never lost the knack. So…why have you come to kill an old woman? What will you tell your wife, your children, when you go home with my blood on your hands?"

"I'm not going to kill you!" he hissed, angry at his own fear.

"You're pointing a gun at me."

"Sherlock told me to make sure you'd left."

"By shooting me?"

Nathan frowned, the gun wavered, and Mary could have moved quickly and knocked it to one side. After that she didn't know; she certainly couldn't fight him, however weak and tired he appeared. But she did not move. She waited as he lowered the gun himself, and that was a greater victory. Mary was in control now. He'd walked all this way with a gun and an order to see her away, and she was in control.

"Can we eat now?" she asked.

"I have to make sure—"

"I'm not leaving, plain and simple. Look, over there!" Mary pointed across to the stream. A heron stood like a freakish garden ornament, dipping its head at the rapidly moving water, flipping a fish into the air and catching it in its huge beak. It gulped its feast, shook itself and tucked its wings back in, motionless again apart from the shiny olive glint of its eyes.

"And there," she said, pointing back over Nathan's shoulders. He turned to see a flock of siskins dancing from branch to branch in a big old oak tree, moving ever-closer to the garden and its gourmet delights.

"It's all very nice," he said. "Really, it is. Beats the city." He turned back to Mary. He looked wretched. "But Sherlock really expects you to leave."

"Because he's allowed it?"

"Well…yes."

Mary snorted. "He always was a pompous prick!"

Nathan obviously wasn't used to hearing Sherlock referred to in such terms—his eyes went wide and his skin actually paled—and Mary laughed out loud at the reaction she had caused.

"Nathan, boy, you're so young. You may think you've lived, but you haven't. I'm not so young, and let me tell you: once a lady like *me* makes up her mind, there's not much someone like *you* can do to change it." She glanced down at the rifle still cradled in his hands. "Short of shooting me."

Nathan looked down, embarrassed, and slung the rifle back over his shoulder.

"Goats, back of the house. Milk them for me, would you?"

Nathan could only stare.

"You *do* know how to milk a goat?"

"I…I live in the city."

Mary shook her head and turned her back on the young city-boy, who moments before had seemed ready to shoot her.

"Think you can collect eggs?"

"From where?"

"From underneath chickens." Mary heard him following her, heard his little snort of embarrassment. *Humour.* That was good. Humour could tackle just about anything.

TIM LEBBON —

The gun hadn't been what had scared her the most. It was Nathan's obvious nervousness that had presented the real danger.

"And while we're eating," she said, "you can tell me about the city. Haven't been there for sixteen years. Don't want to go back, never will, and really I'm not that concerned. But..." She paused, looked up into the morning sky where the dregs of storm clouds were fighting a losing battle with the sun. "Well, there are a few places, a few people, I'd like to hear about." She turned back to Nathan. "Will you do that? Tell me some things?"

He smiled, a small twitch of the lips that changed his face completely.

"Good," Mary said. "Now then. Eggs. Break any of them, and I'll break you."

«« — »»

They sat in the garden and ate their breakfast. Mary's nervousness had hidden itself behind the brief flush of victory, but it soon crept back as she watched Nathan eating: she'd been alone for so long that none of this felt right. She had never let herself forget the city and its people, but over the years it had become far more distant and insignificant, a billion miles away from her little gaol oasis. Now, watching and listening to someone else eat, she couldn't help but feel skittish.

She craved her privacy. And there was plenty of work to be done following the storm.

The storm...

"You said the storm was just the start of it," Mary said. Nathan looked up. Scrambled egg speckled the skin around his mouth. She raised her eyebrows, demanding an answer.

"It's only what people say," he said. He dug his fork back into the pile of eggs, seemingly unwilling to expand on that.

"You're not faithful to your wife." Nathan did not glance up, which was enough of an answer for Mary. "I can see it in the sheen of your hair."

He did raise his head then, running a hand through the tangled mop.

"She doesn't know," Mary went on. She leaned to one side, pretending to take a look at his fingers where they clasped the fork. "Ahh. And you're on the verge of leaving her."

— 176 —

Nathan looked away across the garden. "How can you..." He trailed off.

"The pinkness of your nail beds," she said, smiling. She took a mouthful of scrambled egg to try to stifle the laughter threatening.

"So tell me about the storm, and the city. And tell me how the library is faring. And the concert house? Have they finished building the damn thing yet?"

Nathan put down his fork, still looking at the garden. He stayed that way for a while, rubbing his head, sighing, saying nothing.

"I can tell you when and how you'll die, if you like," Mary said quietly. She did not avert her gaze when he looked at her. She kept her eyes on his. *How powerful is my stare,* she thought, *after sixteen years with no one to receive it?*

Nathan wiped his hands down over his face, closed his eyes.

"Sherlock's lost control," he said.

"Control?"

He looked at Mary and she could almost hear his thoughts. *She's been away for so long. I was a kid when she was exiled. She doesn't know anything.*

"He's very powerful," Nathan said, glancing around as if expecting Sherlock to pop up from behind a bush. "After you...left, his business empire grew quickly. There are lots of tales about how he got there—they're told in the dark corners of pubs at midnight, and even then some who tell them disappear soon after—but the truth is, he simply had all the money. Bought his way up, and money buys power. He's not a king or a duke; he's more powerful than that. He goes far beyond crime now. He rules lives."

"From his wheelchair?"

Nathan nodded. "From his wheelchair." He took a mouthful of tea and sighed. "That's lovely."

"It is, isn't it? Now...the city. The storm. Is there a connection?"

"They say that because Sherlock is losing control—there have been riots, there's a disease, and I've heard rumours of someone trying to take over—the elements are in turmoil as well. The city is so vast, so *major*, that it's the beating heart of the land. It has problems, so does everywhere else. Those passing through spread the blight, just like bad blood."

"That's crazy."

"Sixteen years is a long time," Nathan said, as if that were an answer.

"But it *is* just crazy. Look around you; I know the power of the land as well as anyone."

"I was a little boy when you were exiled here," Nathan said. "I didn't really know much about it; my mother and father were too busy trying to feed us to take notice of society gossip. What I do know is that the city today is a very different place from how it was back then. It's more…nebulous."

"How do you mean?"

Nathan sipped more tea. "Well, I used to think it was because I was growing up. The weirdness, the way reality seemed to slip through my fingers every time I tried to grab it. But it was happening all around me as well, to my parents, my friends. The nature of things was changing. You missed it. That's why I can accept—I *know*—that the elements are tied into the health of the city, and you can't."

"Magic?" Mary asked ready to scoff, but at the same time too afraid. She had known only too well of Sherlock's predilections. His dabblings.

"Magic's only the truth as we don't yet understand it."

"You sound like Sherlock," she said, immediately wishing she hadn't raised his name. Nathan turned away and stared sadly at the rushing stream, the heron waiting patiently for another easy meal.

"I don't know what's going to happen," he said at last. He sounded so scared, so lost, that Mary couldn't help but shiver. He was still watching the stream and heron, and at that moment the fox family started barking and yelping, their voices like those of young children being beaten or stolen away. They'd always been company for Mary, their presence comforting and pleasing, but now they only sounded like a bad omen. They seemed to be crying out from promised pain, enough to scare her badly.

"Just what's happening?" she said.

"Are you leaving?" he asked, his voice a monotone. He'd changed suddenly.

"I told you, no, never."

Nathan stood. He seemed confused for a while, not knowing which way to look or turn.

"Then I'd better go," he said at last. "As you said, I have a wife. Children. They need me. They *will* need me." There was pain behind his words, perhaps the pain of being discovered as unfaithful...but Mary thought not. She thought that this was much more deep-set; a psychological agony borne of the inevitability of things.

Things he had barely started to mention.

"You can stay for a while if you like," she said.

"There's no more I can tell you."

"I didn't mean..." But she trailed off, because that's exactly what she had meant. *You can stay awhile, because I'm curious now and I hope you can tell me more.*

"Mary, thank you for the breakfast. And I hope that you remain...happy here."

There was nothing Mary could do but watch him leave, this second man to depart her valley in as many days. He walked through the gap in the fence and past the Belladonna bushes, along the road turned to mud by the storm, heading for the hills and whatever might now lay beyond.

"What will you tell Sherlock?" Mary called, but although Nathan wasn't far away he didn't seem to hear. She watched for half an hour until he disappeared into the forest at the base of the western hills.

Nathan didn't once turn around.

Later, she stood wearily from her chair—she had hardly slept at all the previous night because of the storm—and gathered their plates and mugs. The sun had won its battle against the shredded storm clouds, and Mary began to sweat as she worked. There were animals to feed, storm damage to fix, and she'd been thinking of checking out her crops on the northern slopes as well. Without grain, without bread, her diet would be reduced drastically. A woman couldn't live on carrots and eggs alone.

She ached, she was tired, her legs were paining her again. She guessed that even if she did desire to walk to the top of the surrounding hills, she may not get there. Old age had done as much to trap her here as Sherlock.

Beyond everything, she was disturbed. Two visitors in as many days, offering the freedom she had convinced herself she already had. Sherlock's change of heart must have been drastic. Nathan's mutterings of things fading in the city, things running down, hadn't really hit Mary at first. The city was a foreign land now, so far away in time and memory that distance no longer mattered, and anything that happened there may as well have been between the pages of a book. But the look in Nathan's eyes as he left had brought the city's strange troubles closer.

Mary didn't care. But she *was* interested.

And more than anything, she hated that Sherlock was at the forefront of her mind for the first time in years.

Once she'd cleaned up around the house, washed and changed, fed and watered the animals and repaired their enclosures, she stood in the garden next to the stream and looked to the west. If Nathan was still climbing the hill she couldn't see him. She closed her eyes and breathed in deeply…and believed herself to be alone in the valley.

Yes, he'd gone. Home to his children and his wife. Back to the city that was changing, where there was a disease, riots, someone attempting a *coup d'etat*.

Why, for a single instant, would Sherlock believe that she would ever?

The shocking idea came that he believed her to have been suffering for the last sixteen years. Perhaps he imagined her scraping food from the dust, sleeping under bushes, running like a naked mad-woman when the moon was full, slaughtering the valley creatures with her bare hands and eating them raw. And Mary laughed. Whether that was the truth or not, she was pleased to have proven it wrong.

《《——》》

It was almost midday by the time she set out for the northern slopes. She carried some bread in a small goatskin bag, a canteen of water, and her rifle. She didn't expect to encounter anything dangerous—there *were* things in the southern caves, though she rarely saw them—but the visits had shaken her, and the uncommon ferocity of the storm had upset the sense of balance she normally maintained.

She passed the livestock on her way to the garden boundary. The pigs snorted, the chickens clucked and pecked at their seed, and the goats stared balefully as if in disbelief that she was leaving them.

"I'll be back soon," she said. One of the goats blinked. "Hold the fort!" The second goat sneezed and rubbed its horns against the wooden fence. "Eat grass," she said, "make milk! I'll be hungry and thirsty when I get back. It's only a couple of miles there and back, but I'm an old lady."

She was talking to herself by now, the animals having recommenced their rituals, Mary no longer a part of their day.

"Maybe I've missed conversation more than I thought," she said, glancing left at the hills rising to the ridged edge of her world. Nathan would be over there and gone now, for sure. But in the short time he'd been with her he'd made an impression: his long, messy hair; his nervousness, evident in the way his eyes couldn't hold her gaze for more than a second or two; his shame and even pain at the disloyalty to his wife.

Mary had lied to him, made him believe that she could see things, tell things about him which she had actually only guessed at.

But then she closed her eyes again and knew for sure that Nathan had gone. And she wondered.

She came to the wooden fence bordering the garden. Her vegetable patch ended a few steps behind her—nothing planted where she stood would live for long, the Belladonna's influence would seep into the soil and distort it, bleed it of life—and the ground here was bare and sticky from the recent rains.

Mary climbed the fence and shoved her way through the Belladonna, feeling it kissing the bare skin of her hands and arms. Soon she was out of the copse and heading across a wide plain of grass and wild flowers, their colours stark and fresh after the recent downpour. The ground was soft—her goatskin shoes sank down and her feet soon became soaked—but it actually made walking easier. Her back was aching, her knees stiff, her shoulders seeming to grind as she walked, all a result of the tension of the previous night, waiting for the storm to abate.

She took her usual path out to the fields of crops. Over the past sixteen years she'd worn it into the land, walking this route so often during the summer and autumn that it was little more than a hard-packed path of mud, slick and wet now after the storm but still solid. Each winter she returned this way one last time, and when spring urged life from the land once again she came back.

The path wound its way across the plain of grass, skirting familiar tumbles of stone and mounds of detritus deposited by the glacier long ago, and cut eventually into a small wood. On the other side lay the first of her fields, forming a patchwork on the gentle hillside to within a few hundred feet of the summit. She had never ventured all the way up. Her own stubbornness and pride maintained her exile. If Sherlock *had* posted guards around the great valley, their employ was wasted.

The woods showed the scars of the previous night's storm. Bright fresh wounds stood out on the trunks, and branches and boughs lay scattered across the ground. A few trees had tumbled, one of them a massive old oak that had stood at the woodland's edge for hundreds of years. Its sad demise had revealed its great secret—it was hollow, harbouring a huge void inside that seemed to have been used for decades by some bird of prey. Nest had been built upon nest in the tree's trunk, filling it with old twigs and the spittle and crap of long-dead hunters. There were bones in there, too many to count, and the shells of old eggs, all mixed and merged down into a grey-brown filling. There was no sign of any present occupant, but Mary clicked the rifle's safety just in case. She had seen buzzards circling many times, and they were larger than most.

As she passed through the wood and reached its far edge, and the haze of yellow rape caught the sun beyond, she heard a noise.

A growl.

She paused and held her breath, the thumping of blood in her ears and the thud of her heart louder than ever.

Again, the growl. Low and meaty, like moss-covered stones rolling in a barrel.

She stepped back but the sound came again, louder and more urgent, warning her to keep still. There were no other sounds around her, and it was only in its absence that she noticed the buzz of nature that always accompanied her. No birds chattering in the trees, no rustling of foraging mammals, no scraping of tiny lizard claws on tree trunks.

The growl came again, nearer and sharper, as if the thing making the noise was moving at the same time.

Mary glanced back the way she had come, to her left, her right, but she could not pinpoint the direction. Damn her old lady's ears! She faced left and stepped forward, hoping to provoke another response.

She needn't have worried. It didn't growl again because it didn't need to. Merely stepping onto the path, standing exactly at the natural division between forest and field, announced the grandiose threat that this thing presented.

It's a dog, Mary thought, but she may as well have called a sabre-toothed tiger a pussy-cat.

She'd seen feral dogs before. She'd tracked down and killed a pack in her valley a decade ago, spending three days sleeping rough, stalking them as they stalked her. She had been younger then and more mobile…but none of them had looked like this. Wild yes, but not mad. Mean maybe, but not wicked-looking like this thing.

It stood chest-high to Mary. It certainly wasn't a breed she recognised, but it was the biggest, meanest-looking dog she'd ever seen. Head as big as a bucket, paws like slabs of meat, eyes intelligent and focussed, jaws parted and dribbling. And it stank. It exuded a peculiarly familiar smell, a wet-dog stench that brought a brief flurry of flashbacks from days long-gone.

Mary lifted the gun and aimed.

The dog crouched and slid forward. Its paws pushed mounds of loose dirt before them. Its head hunkered down and rolls of fur and fat formed a collar around its neck. It growled and farted, and Mary almost snickered. Almost. She thought that anything from her now—a sound, a movement, a loose thought—would make the thing leap.

She held onto the rifle, trying to keep it still. She hadn't fired it for a good while, hadn't bothered cleaning it.

And for the life of her—oh for the stupid, forgetful stupid-bitch life of her—she couldn't remember whether she had even loaded it.

"Get out!" Mary screamed. Her voice frightened even her, along with the fact that she'd screamed at all. *What am I doing?* But the dog stood and actually backed away, edging into the field. Mary aimed the gun and pressed her finger to the trigger. *Don't come at me, don't, don't, I really don't need to know whether it's loaded, and whether I can still shoot…*

The dog whined and tilted its head, as if begging for a treat.

"Go!" she shouted again, putting everything into it. Her throat stung and her neck twinged. Something ran away through the forest, and a flock of birds took noisy flight from the trees above her head.

The dog glanced up, back down at Mary, growled, turned around and ran quickly across the field, heading up.

Mary slumped to her knees and watched it go.

She'd never seen anything like it. It was an oddity in this week of oddities, and as it pounded up the slope towards freedom Mary couldn't help associating it with the two human visitors she had had. She took a drink and watched the creature until it was a spot high on the hillside, used her binoculars to make sure it mounted the summit and disappeared to the other side. It had paused a few times but never looked back. It hadn't attacked her. It was almost as if it had expected something of her, some action or word that she couldn't possibly know to give.

Its eyes had reminded her of Nathan's and the first visitor's. Questioning. Confused. As if she had answers to things of which she could not possibly know. She didn't feel that way, she didn't think of herself as an Oracle or someone with knowledge beyond her boundaries, but she closed her eyes and knew that the dog was out of the valley. The birds were singing again, nature was back to its usual self...the dog had gone.

She wondered if it would return with a pack.

With that image in mind, she walked up into the field.

The storm hadn't done too much damage. There were a few areas where the crop had been flattened, spaced across the fields like a giant's footsteps; mini-whirlwinds, she supposed. At one point, where the field dipped into a shallow gully, the subsoil had been scoured away by a flash-flood. Lines of drying muck lined the rocky banks at the water's highest level. The stream was a trickle again now, innocent and ignorant of what it had done. Other than that, the crop was fine.

Mary looked uphill at the other fields, but suddenly she didn't want to go that far. She felt very tired. The walk had drained her, and the confrontation with the dog had killed any remaining enthusiasm. So she turned and walked back through the woods, rifle at the ready, enjoying the birdsong and the sound of small things living their secret lives beneath the trees, hidden away by bracken and tangled shrubs. A busy woodland meant that there was nothing there to scare it into silence.

Three things from outside. Two frightened men with news of change, and a dog gone bad.

Mary looked up through the tree canopy at the blue sky, hoping that no more storms were brewing. But she had a feeling that they were.

Beyond her sight, beyond her life of the last sixteen years, newer, more powerful storms were gathering strength, boiling with the potential of things still untold.

Soon, Mary knew, she would have another visitor.

She took the path back to her house, and it was harder than going up.

《《——》》

There was no storm that night, but Mary dreamed.

She was standing on the western ridge of the valley, staring out towards the city in the dim distance. Everything looked peaceful, tranquil, undisturbed, but the whole landscape had the uneasy appearance of a painting rather than reality. It was as if someone had tried to copy perfection when there was none there in the first place. The solitude was false. The order was a sham.

She suddenly began to feel dizzy and sick, sweating and cold at the same time. Her arm twitched for a few long, terrifying seconds, and then became still again. The whole world swam before her eyes. And as she turned to look back into the valley she saw, distorted as through water, her house ablaze. In the gardens where she used to sit and eat and take pleasure from life, something was squirming and thrashing on the ground, aflame. Its limbs pounded.

Mary's head thumped, her heart raced…

The heat must have been intense because the grass around the struggling figure turned brown, then black. And then that blighted patch suddenly spread, heat shrivelling leaves and burning stems, rippling out from the homestead and passing across meadows and fields, swallowing the house, exploding copses of trees, turning the stream into a haze of steam, washing against the hillsides and then climbing, never slowing. Reaching out burnt black fingers for Mary, where she dared to stand beyond the valley…

…weak, tired, hallucinating even as she slept.

《《——》》

"The city's burning," her next visitor said.

Nathan had been gone for several weeks, and Mary had begun to believe that the interruption of her solitude had been a brief affair, something never to be repeated. Sherlock had his answer and that was that. No need for any more envoys of hope.

"I don't mean on fire," he said, "not really, not literally. Although that may not be long in coming."

He was an old man, and Mary was amazed that he had walked so far. He looked at least a century old, though he claimed only eighty-five years. He'd introduced himself as Ahmed Din. He had an hypnotic manner, a way of moving his hands in time with his voice when he spoke, and Mary found herself wanting to hear more. Even though most of what he had to say was not good, she wanted to hear.

"There *have* been flames," he continued, "more fires than normal, unexplained conflagrations, but all in secret. Does a fire burn when there's nobody there to see it?" He closed his eyes as if composing, then began again. "The city wakes to find another house gutted, more bodies carbonised. They blame the gangs, the Usurper, the gods. I just blame time. Nothing is forever, and change is always opposed."

"Who is the Usurper?"

"Nobody knows, but he *will* remove Sherlock."

They were sitting on the grass outside Mary's house. The old man had come down from the western hills, taking so long to walk the dusty road that Mary had food and drink ready by the time he arrived. She had seen him on the horizon, just as she had the first visitor, and by the time he reached her she'd baked dinner.

They broke bread together and talked.

Did Sherlock send you to me? she'd asked.

No.

Then why are you here?

A break from the city. To speak to someone without the city on their mind. I used to be a thinker, an intellect, a lover of the city, and it's so ingrained in the byways of my mind that its downfall is mine. My thoughts are no longer my own. I believed that maybe out here, I'd find some of myself again.

Mary had shaken her head and smiled. While her mind could not accept that he was not from Sherlock, her heart told her that he spoke the truth.

"Maybe it won't be so bad," Mary said. "Change is good."

"I agree," Ahmed Din said, as if surprised that he could think so too. "But the people don't seem to believe it. The *city* doesn't. Change is ruin. The people are losing their spirit, their love, their sense of belonging. Their faith is fleeing too." He looked at the ground and frowned, running a thick blade of grass between his fingers. "The Usurper is destroying their faith. Perhaps that's his greatest crime."

While his attention was elsewhere Mary took the opportunity to look closer at Ahmed Din. The skin of his hands was wrinkled and pale, his neck gnarled like that of an old tortoise, sparse white strands of hair pasted across his scalp by sweat. And while age could be held responsible for much of his appearance, there were some things about him which must have been caused by something else. The boils on his forearms, for instance. They bled and oozed. And across his top lip, scabs marked where he'd been picking at sores. He was old, yes. But he was ill as well.

"Can't you fight back?" Mary asked. "Can't Sherlock do something?"

"Nobody knows where he is." The old man shook his head sadly and ate some more red berries. "These are very good. I haven't eaten anything this good for a long time." He moved his hands as he spoke, as if his whole life were a dance.

"Do you know who I am?" Mary asked. "Why I'm here?"

"Of course. Most people do." Ahmed Din seemed uninterested. Perhaps he was telling the truth and he really had come here only to talk, communicate with someone outside the city. Mary only wished that she could help him more; she felt useless, a placebo to his mental ills when he needed a true cure.

She tried to engage him in more serious talk—as fast as her interest in the city had waned after Nathan's departure, it had returned the instant Ahmed Din appeared on the hillside. She asked more about the disease Nathan had mentioned, the Usurper, what Sherlock had been doing these past years. But her visitor merely ate, drank, stroked his bare feet through the grass, and looked around more and more as his hunger was sated.

"You live in a lovely place," he said, not answering Mary at all. "Be glad it's not aflame."

Mary thought of her dream from the previous night. There had been fire, she was sure, and something dying in flames. But the dream was like her life before this place; she could not remember any detail.

"Why did you come here?"

"I've told you," Ahmed Din said.

"And?"

He looked suddenly more tired and ill than before, although his eyes sparkled with intelligence.

"Can I stay for a few hours?" he asked. "Go about your day, please, but I'd love to wander your garden. The city parks are in a bad state now. And besides…parks are so sterile. I can see your influence in this place."

Mary didn't want a stranger walking around her garden, prying into what had become an expression of her life within the boundaries of the wild valley. Ahmed Din could pollute it, pull a rose by the stem, eat the wrong berries, deadhead a living flower. But he also seemed genuine, and his voice held her entranced.

"I used to love the parks," he said, "the living organs of the city. We people would flow like blood between them. I'd spend a lot of time there, talking and teaching. I was a street-side philosopher, or so I was told, and then things began to change and people became too worried to visit the parks. And they're too busy now trying to survive to listen to me. Philosophy is a luxury of a balanced populace, it seems, but here…"

"You can think and do what you want," Mary said. She'd intended it as a question, but it sounded like a statement. Yes, he could stay. In fact…she'd quite like that. Just for a time.

So Ahmed Din stood and wandered off towards the stream, his gait pained but never awkward.

Mary watched him go, then went about her chores. Animals to feed and water. Some shrubs to trim and prune in the garden. The well rope needed rethreading and retying, and there were still those slates disturbed by the storm several weeks before. She was old, she didn't want to climb onto the roof, but somehow Ahmed Din's presence made her more inclined to get up there and do it. More *proud*. Either that, or…but she shook her head and snorted. Ridiculous! She was an old woman. Nothing like that bothered her anymore.

Still, there was that way he moved, like an aging ballet dancer reliving times gone by.

She bumped into Ahmed Din now and then as she went about her business, always aware that he was there. Once she found him sitting by the stream, staring into the water as it gurgled by. Mary wondered what the river became by the time it passed through the mountains, across the plains and into the city…and maybe Ahmed Din was dwelling on this as well.

Another time she was behind the house feeding the animals when she heard a commotion in the garden. She hurried around and saw her visitor chasing a wounded bird across the lawns. Its wing seemed to be broken—Mary never knew whether he had done it himself, or found it in such a state—and it cried out as it fluttered towards the Belladonna bushes pressing against the fence. It never reached them. And Ahmed Din seemed somehow to know what would happen. He stopped and looked up as the shadow of a buzzard swooped from the sky and plucked the injured bird to its doom.

He caught Mary's eye. "Mercy killing," he said.

It took Ahmed Din until late afternoon to ask Mary if he could stay for the night. She had already assumed he would—it was a long way back to the city, and it was pointless starting out any time after midday. But still he seemed embarrassed to ask. Almost troubled by the prospect.

Mary showed him into the house and he sat on the old wooden chair in front of the unlit fire. Mary went about preparing some more food, but within a couple of minutes she heard gentle snoring from the old man. His jaw was open, his head tilted back, and if it wasn't for his breathing Mary could have believed that he'd died there. She fetched a blanket to cover him up…and then looked at his arms.

It was the first time she'd had a good look at his sores and boils.

And she realised straight away that they weren't all natural.

There was a burn on his arm, too regular to be accidental, its edge firm and melted into his flesh. He had been tortured or branded, or perhaps something had been scorched from his skin. It was quite recent. The wound was still moist, and the flesh at its edge was puffy with infection.

Mary stood back, covered Ahmed Din with a blanket and sat in the chair opposite.

From outside she heard strange barking and a prolonged scream of animal pain. Again, something new in her valley.

«« — »»

Ahmed Din left the next morning. He accepted Mary's offer of breakfast, thanked her for her hospitality and went on his way. She walked him as far as the garden boundary.

"These are poisonous," he said, pointing to the Belladonna bushes.

"Yes," Mary agreed.

Ahmed Din smiled. "The potential of danger is far different from danger itself."

She didn't know what to say, but again his voice danced over her, and she realised with a jolt that she was going to miss him.

Ahmed Din left and Mary stood there for fifteen minutes, leaning on the fence, watching him walk slowly along the dusty road. The bushes hissed quietly beside her in a breeze she could not feel. One of the big buzzards circled high overhead. Mary wondered where its mate had gone. And as Ahmed Din paused for the first of many times on his way out of the valley, she heard the call of something wild and unseen from the southern slopes. The sound rose into the morning air and silenced the whole valley for a few long seconds. It was a bad sound, something that promised danger in a far more threatening way than the Belladonna bushes.

The cry faded, Ahmed Din continued on his way, and Mary went back to the house.

«« — »»

She had never thought that Sherlock would strike her. Even as things started to turn bad, as his attitude towards her changed from love to ownership, as he took on lovers without even attempting to hide them from her, still he never offered physical harm. He wasn't that sort of man. He had *honour.*

But even that has its failings. Especially an honour skewed and perverted by the fear of failure.

The first slap was a whiplash backhander at dinner one night. They were alone, and Mary had seen fit to question one of his business decisions. She hated his work anyway, despised the sheen of respectability with which he and his associates coated their seedy, crime-ridden world, but she had never actually said so. He guessed, she knew, otherwise their love would never have suffered as it had. But while she kept up the pretence, so did he. Until that night.

Do you really have to steal—

That was as far as she got.

The slap was so shocking that it didn't hurt, not for the first few seconds. It froze the moment, changing everything in the room into a mute witness to the atrocity. Mary's heart pummelled in her chest, her vision misted as blood rushed to her cheek, and then she sat back in her chair and gasped.

To begin with, Sherlock did not speak. And then he smothered whatever regret he felt, the sorrow and the sadness, and told her to never, ever question him again.

Ever.

The threat was implicit. A boundary had been broken and new walls erected. Mary was to become a silent wife.

«« — »»

Mary fetched her binoculars from the house and watched Ahmed Din start up the western hills. It seemed as if he had been walking forever, and she was becoming concerned. Once he made it out of the valley he would be far removed, out of her world, but if something happened to him now—if he stopped, slumped down and became a still lump on the road—it was still her domain. She would have to help. She liked him, after all.

And though he was old, he was being worn down by something other than age. The wounds and boils were physical manifestations of this. There was a malady of the mind, a sickness of the soul, a conviction that things were failing and hope was slipping from his grasp. He had reminded Mary of a teenager, so pumped up with the promise of adulthood that the harsh reality—that childhood's end promises nothing but mounting problems, widening responsibilities, complexities in a life used to simplicity—hit him hard. For some, truth is unbearable.

She'd never imagined old age to be like that. Her own advancing years were buffered by her strange circumstances, but Ahmed Din had seemed content, even happy that he was entering the twilight years of his life.

The city, and whatever strange things were happening to and in it, was polluting him.

Another wild animal cry came from the south, echoing through the caves and exhaled from the earth as an amplified call, filling the valley. It may have been a bark lengthened by the echoes, or a growl made louder.

Mary lifted the binoculars again and saw Ahmed Din pause, glancing to his left. Then he turned and stared back. The distance was too great for her to make out his expression, but his whole bearing told her that he was tired and afraid.

The call came again and the man continued on his way.

Mary stood the binoculars on a stone bench, went inside and lifted the rifle from its wall mounting. This time she made sure it was clean and oiled and loaded before venturing back outside. The small bag of ammunition—all she had left from the supply she'd been given sixteen years before—barely added weight to her dungaree pocket. A dozen bullets maybe. And probably a couple of duds amongst them.

The sound came again…and it had moved. Mary turned left and right as it echoed from the hills, trying to place its source. South, yes, it came from the woods or the caves honeycombing the hills there, but it was more to the west than it had been before. She searched for Ahmed Din and located him at the base of the hills, maybe half a mile away from the cover of the treeline.

Whatever it was making that noise—and Mary could only think of the dog, made monstrous by whatever blight had struck the land beyond the valley—seemed to be aiming to meet Ahmed Din.

Probably in the woods, Mary thought. *It'll wait until he enters and come at him from behind the trees. Like it did with me…*

An old man, a frail man, someone who was rotting away physically and mentally and yet could light her up inside when he spoke, his voice a song because of the words, she realised now, because of the words he used. It was as if anything he said could be an ode to a dying world, and for some reason he'd chosen to come here to speak it.

To speak to someone without the city in their mind, he had said.

The thing called again and its tone had changed. It had something to shout about now—a target—and it was hunting. Not stalking, Mary realised as she stood and aimed the binoculars southwest, but *hunting*. It didn't need to stalk someone as weak as Ahmed Din. It could see him across the valley, smell his weakness, sense his confusion, and it was going for him.

Mary's heart was beating faster. She was sweating and cold. The southern slopes were a maze of forest, gulleys, caves systems, old ravines cut in by streams long-since dried up, and she didn't have a hope of spotting the hunting thing. Still she scanned, panning from left to right until she saw Ahmed Din again. He had stopped, leaning forward with his hands on his knees, looking left across the fields that led eventually to the wilds woods.

"Shit!" Mary said, even though she did not like swearing. After sixteen years here on her own there was no need, but now she was thinking beyond the valley, worrying about the safety of this intruder. Like it or not her past was thrusting unwelcome, sticky fingers into her present.

She had to help. He had been sad, weary and brave, and above all honest. Mary _had_ to help.

The Belladonna bushes rustled as she passed by. *These are poisonous*, he had said, and she had always known that. They felt almost like friends.

With the rifle slung over one shoulder, binoculars over the other, Mary strode briskly along the road. She was seventy but she lived off the land, worked it to its full potential. Maybe one day in twenty she would spend sitting in the garden, rereading one of the few books she had been allowed to bring for the tenth time, but most of her time she spent working. To begin with it had been her release, her way of burying the fact that she was not here by choice. But she had quickly grown to love it. And it kept her fit.

He was a mile away, maybe a little more. The thing in the woods was calling almost incessantly now, its voice rising and falling with each impact of its feet on the ground. It sounded angry, enraged, vicious, unlike anything Mary had ever heard before. The call had come from the caves to begin with, but it was definitely out in the woods now, and all the more terrifying for that.

She paused and looked at the old man. He was walking again but slowly, glancing to his left every few seconds. Mary panned the binoculars that way and saw nothing, only swaying grasses and a buzzard dipping down and up, breakfast twitching in its claws.

She walked on, panting, kicking up puffs of dust. She hardly ever came this way, and she tried to follow in Ahmed Din's footsteps.

The thing cried out again, and Mary thought she could hear the crashing of undergrowth as it bounded through the woods far to her left. She used the binoculars again and saw a flock of birds startled from the tree canopy, rising as one and heading further south. *There.* That's where the thing was now, maybe the dog she'd seen, perhaps something else, something worse. She panned right. Two miles from there to Ahmed Din. And less than a mile before she caught up with him.

No chance, she thought, but she started again, breaking into a clumsy trot with rifle and binoculars bumping her hips.

More birds took off from the woods and spiralled skyward, calling out in surprise. The buzzard circled over the road, drifting higher on warm currents and watching the startled birds with interest.

Two minutes passed, three, without any more calls from the wild thing in the woods. Ahmed Din was advancing slowly towards the edge of the western woods and the bare hilltop higher up. However desperate he was to escape, his old man's legs would not allow it.

It all happened very quickly in the end.

Mary saw the shape burst from the tree-line to her left and streak across the meadow. It barked a long, throaty call, and she knew that this was their monster. It may have been the same mutated dog she'd faced; it was moving so quickly that she could not tell.

She was close enough to be able to see without the binoculars, so she placed them gently beside the track before moving on, rifle clasped in both hands.

Ahmed Din stopped and looked, unable to do anything to protect himself. He saw Mary, but she was too far away to hear anything he may have said.

Three more shapes burst from the cover of the trees.

Mary slowed, slowed, stopped. There were four of the things now. The front one cried out again, another one answered it.

She glanced back at her homestead, almost a mile behind her now, and for the first time she thought of her own safety.

The lead dog was halfway across the meadow. It would reach Ahmed Din in a minute.

"Oh no," Mary said, "not in my valley, no, not here." She wished that they had waited for him to reach the woods so that she couldn't see…but they did not appear to be creatures of compassion.

She raised the rifle to her shoulder and sighted on the lead dog.

She was too far away. The rifle probably had the range—though she was not *certain* of that—but her eyes were old, and she was nowhere near a markswoman.

Squeezing the trigger, breathing out slowly, sighting just ahead of the loping beast, Mary offered a quiet prayer for the first time in years.

The rifle kicked her shoulder and nothing changed.

Missed.

She reloaded quickly, shouldered the rifle again and aimed in one movement. *One more shot,* she thought, *maybe two. Then they'll be on him.*

Ahmed Din looked her way. She could see his terrified face lit by the sun high up behind her. She fired again.

Nothing changed.

The lead creature glanced her way, perhaps, or maybe that was her imagination. The other three bore down on the old man.

He's dead, Mary thought, *stop wasting ammunition.*

She reloaded, shouldered, aimed and fired. And she realised just how close she had come to shooting Ahmed Din as the first creature barrelled into him.

He screamed as it tore at him with tooth and claw. The three other dogs hit him as well, and his screaming stopped very quickly.

"No!" Mary shouted, knowing that it couldn't have ended any other way. She loaded again, shouldered and fired without aiming. One of the dogs squealed and jumped, hopping onto its hind legs and whining. It looked back at her briefly, and then buried its head back into what was left of the old man.

Mary fired twice more before realising she was down to her last half-dozen bullets. Both shots found their target, she was sure, but none seemed to have any effect.

And it was only minutes until the dogs started raising their heads to look her way.

«« —— »»

Mary hurried back to her house. By the time she passed the fence she was exhausted. Going out towards the hills she'd been on a mission of mercy, but now her exertion was driven by fear. Her muscles and joints had almost seized up, and her shoulder screamed from the repeated kicks from the rifle.

She'd looked back every fifty steps to see if the dogs were following. There came a time when she thought she would reach safety before they reached her, though even then she dreaded seeing them give chase. But they were feeding, fighting over the dregs of their meal, and they seemed to have forgotten Mary as soon as she turned her back and fled.

She collapsed through the front door and slammed it shut behind her, gasping in lungfuls of air with rasping sobs. They had killed the old man, slaughtered him like a wounded deer, and now they were eating him and she could never be alone in the valley again. He had been killed in her own private place, and there was no escaping that. His ghost, his memory, the echo of his musical voice would be here always.

It must have hurt, Mary thought, but she drove that from her mind.

What she couldn't shake was the fact that the dogs were here to stay. Wherever they had come from—and her three visitors had told her of the declining city, the changes to the landscape, the polluted river and the disease and unease—they had found food here. And like any wild animal, they'd continue eating until their source of food was exhausted.

And Mary was exhausted.

Not as if she could run very far anymore.

She wedged a chair under the door handle and checked that the rifle was loaded, leaning it against the table in the centre of the room. She didn't know what to do. She had hunted and killed a whole pack of dogs years ago, but she had been younger then, she'd had plenty more ammunition…and though feral, they had been normal hounds. Not like these things, twisted into unnatural, monstrous forms. She was sure she had put at least two bullets in one of them, and it had flinched as if stung by a bee.

Trying to calm herself, Mary poured some water from the cold-hole under the table…and spilled it down her dungarees. *He was dead.* An hour ago she had spoken with Ahmed Din and now he was spread across the road, already being digested inside those creatures' guts, his ideas and his philosophies open to the air, dried by the sun, bleached from memory. He could never have communicated everything he thought and knew, and his great mind had died with him.

What a waste, Mary thought, and she began to cry. Not really from sadness—she hadn't known him at all—but from shock. Things like this never happened in her valley. One of the foxes had taken some chickens a couple of years ago, and she had caught it in a snare and thrashed it with a willow stick. It had not visited her homestead again. She hadn't needed to kill it. Things like this never happened...

But beyond the valley the city was plunging into ruin, and who knew how its influence could spread?

'Beyond' was not somewhere she cared to think about.

She glanced from the window at a view so familiar to her. It still *looked* the same out there, but now things unseen were a danger instead of merely a mystery. She had never been threatened in her valley until now, not really. For the first couple of years she'd frequently felt uneasy, but her exile had also brought an ironic sense of protection. Things, she had thought, couldn't get in.

But now *things* had.

She could look southwest at the wooded hillsides, but now they presented more than just a beautiful landscape. Beneath that lush green canopy, monsters stirred. Maybe they were sleeping off their recent meal. Or perhaps they were working their way around the valley, using whatever wily, wild instincts they possessed to plan the best approach to her house, her homestead, her. They hadn't needed much teamwork to bring the old man down, but for all Mary knew they could be intelligent, scheming as she stared fearfully from her window.

Her hands smelled of old grease from the gun. Sweat tickled her sides, her forehead, her cheeks. Her heart was still thudding fast, and she wondered just how fit she was. Death did not frighten her—it hadn't for a long time—but pain did. Many times she had considered what may happen if she were to injure herself or fall ill, stuck here with no one to help her, no one to pinch shut a slashed leg or nurse her past a heart attack. Dying slowly, alone, *did* frighten her.

Not a concern if those dogs forced their way in.

So Mary watched from the window as her heart calmed and her sweat dried, glancing back at the rifle every now and then to make sure it was still there. She would have time to reach it and get back to the window if the dogs appeared at the gate or pushed through the Belladonna bushes. Time to defend herself. Time...

And time did its work. An hour later she was thirsty, an hour after that she had to urinate, another hour and the sun was kissing the western ridge, casting its dying rays over the stain that Ahmed Din had left in the dust. Mary was hungry and tired; she couldn't stay like this forever. And strangely when she closed her eyes she thought of Sherlock, how he had loved her in the beginning, how he had not really become the totally evil man she had feared at the end.

She hadn't given him the chance.

Mary leaned against the rough wood of the window frame, her forehead slipped slowly down the glass, and with the moon shining down and making a ghost of her pale face, she slept.

«« — »»

She was standing atop the hills again, staring back at her valley where things were going wrong, and forward out into the wilderness of forgotten life, where reality seemed to be imitating art in a sham of its good self. It was a fine sham, one that would have been believable to anyone other than Mary. But Mary hadn't seen this view for a long, long time. Her vision had been purified by its absence.

She knew that looking right didn't necessarily mean that things *were* right.

And now she could barely see at all, because the vomiting was blinding her with her own splashed stomach acids, her limbs were shaking, her brain could not decide which way was up, down, sideways...

Behind her the valley was a wreck and a burning shape writhed in the herb garden as she writhed on the hill, sending puffs of aromatic, greasy smoke into the air.

Before her, the world outside offered memories at every turn. False and sugar-coated though they may be.

Through the fear and sickness, Mary felt a decision looming. And although it seemed clear-cut, she had no idea which way to go.

《《—》》

She must have woken during the night, because when morning came she was in her bed. Fully dressed, the gun by her side, but refreshed from a full, comfortable night's sleep. There were dregs of a dream, but Mary gladly let them flit away. They didn't feel right.

It was a warm, beautiful day, and before she realised what she was doing she'd opened the front door and stepped out into the garden. Maybe night had diluted yesterday's fears, the darkness bleeding away terror and instilling an unreasonable calm.

She paused, held her breath, looked around. There was nothing unusual about her surroundings. The stream flowed by, a brief visitor in the valley. A few birds hopped around in the long grass. The Belladonna bushes hugged the garden fence, and high overhead some crows were chasing a single buzzard across the sky. There were no signs to indicate that the dogs were anywhere near.

Mary closed her eyes. She was certain that they had left the valley. Things here were as they always had been. No danger. No threat. Just Mary, her home, her animals and gardens and fields. Her life in a nutshell, and while there had been intruders of late, the shell itself was all but solid.

She only wished that she could plug the hole.

《《—》》

In the end, Mary thought it was weakness that drove Sherlock insane. One time she burst in on him and one of the servant girls. The girl glanced up, then defiantly carried on sucking, but Sherlock had started to cry, held out his hands, offering regret or trying to grasp mercy even as Mary turned to leave.

That same day he hit her and cried again.

Mary never knew where the dividing line was. She could remember his anger and dismissiveness, and then his sorrowful, violent self-loathing, but nothing in between. If there was ever a chance to save him—save *them*—it must have been that time lost to her. Given time they could have worked things out, perhaps, found that missing moment when thought had translated into violence. But things were becoming more and more difficult. The violence was increasing. Contrite though Sherlock seemed at times, his rage was building, his strange madness starting to consume him.

Mary knew that, were she to survive, something had to be done.

The irony was, it was Sherlock's abuse making her strong.

«« — »»

Time passed, no more visitors came. Routine calmed Mary's recent upsets and made placid the upheaval that had struck the valley. There were no signs of the dogs, and as each day went by they shed more of their monstrous representation in Mary's memory. Three weeks after Ahmed Din's horrible death they were simply a pack of wild hounds. He'd been an old man, after all. Weak. Slow. Easy prey.

Mary put the rifle away, hiding with it the fact that it had twice emptied itself into one of those creatures.

She went about her days and nights as she had for sixteen years. Very occasionally the thought would cross her mind—whilst feeding the chickens, weeding fields or pulling water from the well—that she was hiding or ignoring some terrible truths about her recent visitors. But behind each of these thoughts there reared something altogether darker and much, much more terrifying: the idea that she had been ignoring such truths ever since she had been brought to the valley. Her only defence was to forget. So she would spread seed, pluck weed, haul on the rope.

But she would never, ever forget her next visitor.

«« — »»

She hadn't seen movement on the dust road since Ahmed Din's death. She was in the chicken coop behind the house when she caught sight of something from the corner of her eye. She stood and shielded her eyes from the sun, staring west and feeling a terrible sense of dread. The fact that everything was still made it worse. It convinced her that something was stalking closer, twitching bushes and flitting from tree to rock to dip in the ground.

She looked down at her feet, then up again quickly.

No movement.

Mary closed her eyes, and although she thought that she was no longer alone in the valley, she felt safe. Something was here, some*one*, but they were very weak, difficult to sense at all. She tried to keep the sun from her eyes as she scanned the hillsides around her. To the north the fields were calm and still, bathing in the sunlight. West, following the rough road up the foothills and into the woods on the lower slopes, she saw something by the side of the road. It was too distant to make out properly—she would have to go inside to fetch her binoculars—but she knew at once that it was her new visitor.

Someone from the city.

And they had come this far, only to fall still and silent in the dust.

As Mary dashed inside she thought of everything her visitors had told her. The ideas came full and rich out of the fog of memory she'd tried to bury them in, concerns of outside that had intrigued her at first, and then had a chilling effect with Ahmed Din's death. By the time she'd fetched the binoculars she realised what the three visitors had actually brought her: not a semblance of forgiveness from Sherlock; not a desire to interact; not news of things she thought she'd forgotten.

A warning.

The shape by the road side was moving slightly, lifting its limbs and trying to drag itself across the ground, but it seemed very weak. It wore a black cloak, even in this hot weather. From this far away it resembled a giant spider.

Mary breathed deeply a few times, trying to calm herself and steady her thumping heart. She turned around and glanced up at her crops growing on the hillside to her left. They would need tending soon, watering if this unseasonable dry weather persisted, more weeding. And the well needed cleaning out. The water was tasting stale again, and she was terrified that something had fallen down there and died.

She actually took a step back towards her tool rack before she acknowledged what she must do. There was no way she could ignore this, whatever fate her new visitor may have brought. More efforts at forgiveness from Sherlock, a knife in the gut, a plea from the city to help, *help* it…

He looks almost dead, she thought, but that could never be an excuse. *By the time I get there…so I could just forget…*

She took one more look around at the garden that had grown and matured along with her, so much so that it was almost a part of her now. And even though things still *looked* the same, she knew that they never could be again. The weeks since Ahmed Din's death felt foolish now, lived by someone old and confused and on the verge of crazy. She should have known better. Solitude had changed her so much, yes, but her mind had kept fresh and strong, unpolluted by media, clear of outside influences, unsullied by the foolishness of others.

She should have known better.

With the rifle slung over one shoulder, binoculars over the other, Mary set out along the road. She passed the Belladonna bushes and they rustled against her arm. *These are poisonous,* Ahmed Din had said, and she was reliving her frantic chase to save him from the dogs.

The shape was lying still in the road…the rifle hit her hip as she hurried along…the binoculars brought her future closer…and an awful foreboding settled over her.

The dogs were not here, she was certain. But that didn't mean they weren't on their way.

What are you going to tell me? she thought. *What more is there to tell of the city three weeks on? Has the disease spread? Has the Usurper succeeded? Is Sherlock dead?* And none of it should matter. She had been away for so long that it was someone else's life back then, a stranger. None of what this exhausted, dying visitor had to say should matter to Mary. But as she walked, the realisation that she was more concerned with what they had to say than actually saving them pressed in. She didn't like the idea, hated herself for even thinking it, but Mary had not lied for decades.

She didn't like the truth.

Don't die before I reach you, she thought, *or I'll wonder forever.*

Several minutes after setting out she took a look through her binoculars. The shape was still now, the only movement a slight breeze tugging at its cloak. The rifle strap was chaffing one shoulder, the binoculars the other, and Mary considered turning back and going home. Dead, her new visitor was dead, and all she could do now was burn the corpse to prevent the wild animals from eating it.

But the wild animals, mostly, were her friends. Why deny them a good meal?

Then she thought of those mutated hounds; definitely *not* her friends. And as if conjured by the memory their presence smashed at her senses. Her hackles rose, danger pressed in like stifling heat, birds stopped singing. Mary looked past the prone visitor, lifted the binoculars over the woods and up at the distant western hillside, the track leading up to and over the ridge. There was nothing there, no sign of the visitor being pursued.

She walked on, nerves still tingling with a sense of danger. Over the years Mary had grown to trust her feelings; she had little else to communicate with. She paused again and looked south, scanning the meadows, the edges of the wild woods, and higher to where the southern slopes rose into craggy peaks. And there, little more than smudges on her eyes, she saw several black shapes working their way down from the ridge. They must have just entered the valley, perhaps on a hunting trip where they knew there to be food.

And the fact they they'd chosen the very day when a new visitor came into the valley...coincidence?

Mary thought not. It was possible that the dogs were patrolling beyond the valley, picking off potential visitors as and when they approached, and that this one, the person a mile away from her now who may already be dead, was merely a mistake. Someone they had missed. A late meal, soon to be ingested if she didn't hurry up.

Mary thought that the dogs would reach her in half an hour. She looked along the road again, willing the person not to move, *don't show a sign, don't let me know you're still alive.* But a hand rose as if clasping at the warmth of the sun, and now Mary had to go on. She checked her rifle. She had seven bullets left.

Another chase was on. She could only pray that this one did not end in a death.

Mary ran as best she could, careful not to expend too much energy, knowing that she'd needed to get the person back to her house. *If he's still alive when I get there*, she thought. But wishing him dead was evil and selfish...and besides, she needed to know what he had come here to say.

The dogs had already disappeared down into the tree-line. They would be off the dangerous slopes soon and then there would only be the thick, wild forest to slow them down. Then, soon after that, a couple of miles of open meadow between them and fresh, warm food.

The shape drew closer, and Mary was pleased with her progress. Adrenalin brought her alive, expanded her old woman's senses, and when she heard a groan from the crumpled visitor she put on a spurt of speed.

She drew close, slowed, scanned the southern treeline, saw no dogs as yet. They were still working their way through the woods. She looked back the way she had come, then down at the shape. She may have time. *May.* If she could get the visitor to walk.

"Mary," a voice said. Mary gasped and stepped back, not only because the visitor had uttered her name. *It was a girl's voice.*

The cloak drew back and a little girl looked up at her, eyes sunken with more than exhaustion, face drawn and pale with more than the fear she must feel, the terror at her encroaching death.

"Oh, dear. . ." Mary said.

"Help me, Mary," the girl said. "Please…"

"What's your name, girl?"

"Alice."

"Alice. Alice. Such a pretty name. Welcome to Wonderland."

The girl coughed, and the trickle of sputum hanging from her mouth was pink.

"Listen to me, Alice. Can you walk?"

"Don't think so." Weak, so weak.

"You've come from the city, made it this far?"

Alice nodded. "Dying all the way."

"I can get you to my house, help you, treat you—"

"Didn't come here for that. Came to die. Came to…find peace. Away from that fucking *hell*." The curse coming from the little girl's mouth was as shocking as the blood.

"Alice!" Mary didn't know what to say. The girl had been pretty once. The disease had not stolen that fact, but it *had* done its best to strip away what may have given her that beauty. Her hair was bland and bled of life, her eyes, though large in her shrunken face, were dull and distant.

"Alice…I don't want to die. And there are things coming that will kill me if they reach us before I can get you to my home. You understand? Alice?"

"The dogs. . .?" Alice said. It may have been a statement, not a question, but Mary answered anyway.

"Yes, dogs."

"How strange," Alice said, and she pushed herself up, standing slowly like a rotting scarecrow coming to painful life.

"What do you mean?"

Alice gasped and reached out. Mary stepped forward and caught her, shocked by how hot and light the girl was, like a log burned in the fire, ready to crumble

"Strange…strange that the dogs…"

And then they were coming. The hounds burst from the treeline to the south with an explosion of barking and pounding paws. Birds scattered skyward and smaller mammals fled through the tall grasses, setting the meadow shimmering in complex patterns of flight.

"Come on!" Mary hissed. But it was already too late.

She should have left the girl. Ignored the shape in the road. Stayed with her chickens. At least then she would have only heard the dogs, growling and running and, eventually, fighting over another meal.

But again, she knew that she could have never done that.

The dogs were a mile away. They would be on them within minutes. There was no hope at all of getting back to the house, and nowhere nearer to hide. The hounds had smelled them, seen them, sensed them, and now they were coming again.

Mary looked back along the road to where Ahmed Din had been killed, slightly nearer to her house. She hadn't even acknowledged that placed when she had passed it moments before.

"Oh damn," she said.

"I'm sorry," Alice said, "I'm dying. Leave me, run, get away. They'd never attack you anyway, would they?"

"*Why* wouldn't they?"

"Well…" Alice said, but she was coughing again, spitting more blood, burning up in Mary's arms.

"I can't leave you," Mary said.

"Why?"

She did not answer, could not. Because there *was* no logical answer at all, other than to say that she was human and she cared. Whatever this girl had seen and lived through in the city—whatever it had started turning her into—Mary still had her morals, her sense of humanity, what was right and wrong. They had survived what Sherlock had done to her; sixteen years in the wilderness could certainly *never* have taken them away.

"I've got a gun," Mary said. "If I can stop the first one the others may be frightened off. Long enough for us to get back to my house, at least."

Alice nodded, pushed herself away and slumped to the road.

Mary unslung the rifle and checked the breech. It was loaded. She had the spare bullets in her pocket, a half-dozen slivers of hope.

She could see the lead dog's teeth shimmering in the sun, spittle flying around its head each time its feet hit the ground.

She took aim.

If she fired early, it may startle the dogs into halting for a few seconds, presenting her with a stationary target. But that would waste a bullet. Alternatively, the shot—which would almost certainly miss—may not faze them at all, and they'd be upon her before she'd even had a chance to reload.

So, she should wait until she could smell the lead dog's breath. If she missed, there'd be no second chance. And if it needed more than one good shot to kill one of the bastard things...

"Screwed either way," Mary said.

She leaned into the rifle, took in a deep breath and let it out slowly.

The lead dog came on, and how could she even call it a dog with eyes like that, mad eyes, eyes that told of pain and rage that only a human could really feel, surely?

Mary waited, waited. The dog would soon be a single bound from the road. It was all she could see along the rifle, the aiming nib cut its head in half, she couldn't possibly miss, but her eyes were old, and her hands were shaking with fear.

"Now!" Alice croaked. "Now! *Now!*"

Mary waited another second. The monster dog leaped the shallow ditch by the side of the track—it was not slowing, that was certain, and its mouth was a grillwork of huge, bad, yellow teeth—and that was when she fired. Mid-leap. When the dog seemed to hang suspended in mid air, split by the rifle sight, frozen for an instant in time.

It squealed as the bullet smashed home into its skull. The air misted with blood and bone and the big animal completed its leap, crashing down into the dust and sliding the last few feet at Alice.

It was still growling, its jaws gnashing, even as a thick pink jelly oozed from its head-wound. Paws as big as Mary's hands dragged the deadweight of the thing towards the girl, who struggled away, flailing in the dust.

Mary glanced up at the other dogs. They had paused in the meadow, sniffing the ground and contemplating the scene before them. One of them was whining. She reloaded quickly, aimed at the back of the wounded creature's neck…and then turned the rifle around. These things would get the message better if they could see what was happening. A bullet they could not understand. Brute force, savagery, violence was their language.

She bashed the dog's brains out with the stock of the rifle, only stopping when the thing was totally still and its head was no more.

The dogs whined, all of them, and Mary breathlessly lifted the gun and tucked it into her shoulder. The stock was warm and wet, but it felt good. It felt like victory.

One of the dogs moved forward—only one step—and Mary shot it. It was a long way off, but still the bullet struck its shoulder and knocked it onto its side. It stood quickly, snapping its head sideways as if to bite at a bee worrying its hide, spinning in circles. The other two hounds watched and Mary took the pause to reload, panting with fear, exertion and excitement.

"How many bullets have you got?" Alice asked.

"Enough," Mary said. But that was a lie. Even now, if the dogs charged they were finished. She'd been luckier than she could have ever hoped.

She aimed at the panicked hound and almost fired. But from this distance the kill was not assured, and to wound it again could drive it into an attacking frenzy. So she fired at one of the other dogs instead. The bullet kicked up a spit of sod by its feet and the thing turned tail and fled.

As if at a signal the other dogs followed, the wounded one zig-zagging across the meadow like a ricocheting bullet.

Mary let out her held breath and slumped to the road, exhausted. Her legs were shaking, her back soaked with sweat, and she started to cry.

"You should go," Alice said. "Before they decide to come back."

"I don't think they will," Mary said. But she wasn't sure.

"Go anyway."

Mary slung the rifle over her shoulder and stepped around the dead dog, trying not to look at the mess she'd made of its head. When she helped Alice to stand the girl protested, saying that she should be left to die in the open, in the sun. But that only made Mary angry.

"You came to see me, yes? Did you see what I just did for you? Did you see? You're coming with me, like it or not." The girl smiled, nodded and let Mary help her.

Together they staggered down the road towards Mary's home. The dogs did not return.

Halfway there the birds started to sing once more, and a family of rabbits played in the meadow, and the valley was Mary's again.

«« —»»

"What's wrong with you?" Mary asked.

"Blight. That's what my mummy called it. Before she died."

"How old are you?"

"Thirteen."

"I'm sorry to hear about your mother."

Alice smiled at Mary but there was nothing there, no warmth or gratitude. Any expression, any true *emotion* had been stolen by the disease that twisted her face.

"So what is the blight? Where did it start?"

"Don't know," Alice shrugged. "Why ask me? I'm just a kid. I'm more worried about whether Peter Ashworth fancies me, who the next big band will be, the rumours that Maria did it with Billy Jenkins. What do I care about disease and revolution?"

"You sound much older than your thirteen years now." *And more cynical*, Mary thought.

"I'm going to die. I feel all grown up."

Mary sighed sadly and felt tears burning behind her eyes. She shouldn't cry, not now, not here. There was hot food to be made for this poor weak Alice, she needed fluids, she had open sores that were weeping infection. How self indulgent would it be of Mary to vent her own sorrow? How selfish?

"You're not going to die if I can help it," Mary said to the girl. "I'm seventy years old, I ran a mile and fought monsters to save you. Last thing I'll do is watch you die."

Alice said nothing, but her eyes spoke volumes. *Hopeless,* they said.

Mary stood and winced as her old joints cricked, her muscles screaming in protest at being used *again* after such a trial. "Damn it!" she muttered.

"You live in a lovely place," Alice said. "I wanted to live somewhere like this, when I was younger and not dying. I like the idea of being alone, thinking my own thoughts. Not having my head polluted by what's going on around me."

"And what is going on? What's happening in the city?"

"Bad things," Alice said. "Everything changed very quickly. People stopped smiling, and suddenly they were all frowning. Revolution, war in the streets, fighting everywhere. Even Mum and Dad, fighting, in the end. Then there was just me and I had no one I wanted to fight, so I left."

"Why did you come here?"

"I heard you were someone to see."

Mary didn't know what to make of that. She asked Alice what she meant but the girl had closed her eyes, seemed to be asleep. Mary stood, went to the front door and stared out at her garden. Things seemed quiet, but changed. Nothing had moved places or altered colour, but this was the garden *after* she had killed to survive, *after* she had saved a life. She closed her eyes and tried to feel safe and at home, but she realised that she had changed as well. After all these years, she had changed. Her perception had been thrust wide open, hauled up and out of the valley to probe at the world beyond, the world she had given up.

But perhaps now, after so long, Sherlock was getting his own way at last.

Mary didn't want to feel trapped here, but with the world outside falling to pieces she had never felt so closed in.

She watched Alice for the rest of the day. The girl was asleep or unconscious, sweating and shivering and moaning. Mary stripped and washed her, tried to treat some of the vicious weals on her skin with homemade herbal remedies. She would not drink, so Mary had to force a pellet of herbs into her mouth, working Alice's throat with her fingers to make her swallow. It calmed her to a small extent, turning a troubled sleep into a deeper slumber.

But Mary wanted her awake. She wanted to know more of the city and Sherlock, why Alice had *really* come here, what she had hoped to find, why she had risked so much to flee the only place where she could have treatment for the blight…but all the while, Alice's words taunted her with their mystery.

I heard you were someone to see.

Mary had nothing to offer. She was a lover cast out, a wife abused and discarded. She'd married power because, as a younger woman, she believed that was what she wanted. Sixteen years of exile had shown just how foolish that was.

Power was on the inside. And she was strong.

She sat opposite Alice that evening, picking at some bread and fruit, wondering whether she would catch the blight that was slowly, surely taking this girl away.

Outside, foxes barked at the dusk. They sounded like the ghosts of children she had never had. Alice grumbled in her sleep, and Mary went to her and wiped her hot brow. Here was someone else's daughter, orphaned and dying in the home of a stranger.

"Just what the hell are you doing here?" Mary asked.

Belladonna bushes rustled in the breeze and stroked the fence around the garden, dropping berries onto the lawns and vegetable patch, leaning in closer and closer as if seeking warmth and shelter inside the house.

Mary went to them, stroked their leaves, squeezed berries, sniffed her fingers. They smelled like freedom.

Those are poisonous, Ahmed Din had said. Mary had always known that.

Freedom to choose was freedom defined. That's what Mary had always thought. For those first few years alone in the valley the option to take herself away from here had been a precious thing to her, like a favourite dream remembered forever, stronger than true memory. Slowly the option had faded into the background, victim of her increasing confidence and contentment.

Still there, though. Buried, but still there.

And the Belladonna bushes grew and grew at the periphery of her life.

When Mary went back inside, Alice was dead.

《《—》》

Both buzzards were hovering high above her as she laid out the corpse on a bed of sticks and lumber. Mary wanted them to go, but they had more right to be here than her. At least they would not have any part of Alice.

She lit a torch from the fire she kept burning indoors, came out and set light to Alice's pyre. Then she turned and walked away, not knowing where she was going, aimless, not wishing to see and smell this little girl burn away to nothing.

《《—》》

The violence grew, and the abuse grew, and the bitterness inside Sherlock fed his madness. He would be sorry for every impact of his fist, but each slap or punch merely drove him into a deeper frenzy.

Nobody seemed to know. The people who surrounded Sherlock—his 'workers', he called them, but they were hired thugs and criminals and mercenaries—either turned a blind eye or, more hurtful, smiled when they looked at Mary. She saw mockery in their gaze, though perhaps it was nervousness. Sherlock was not one to cross or question, Mary knew that from experience, and he *loved* her.

That final time in the penthouse suite…even then it wasn't the violence, though it was worse than it had ever been. And it wasn't the way he dishonoured their love. It wasn't even pity for Sherlock, the man she had once loved gone insane.

It was fear, pure and simple. It was the threat he gave, the promise he made.

"You'll never be away from me!" he said. "Never be free, *never*! Your life is mine! You'll always be here, I'm your prison cell, Mary!" And even in that short speech which doomed him, his insecurity came out.

"Don't think you can get away. Don't even try!"

"You're not a man anymore," Mary said through swollen lips. *You're a monster*, she thought. His eyes widened, his rage seemingly smothered beneath disbelief, but then he saw her defiance—the fact that she would *always* be defiant—and he struck out again.

But Mary kicked, pushed, punched back. The fear guided her hands and legs like a marionette. It must have taken Sherlock by surprise because he stumbled back towards the glass doors, balance snapped away by Mary's rebellion. He tried to hit her but missed, and she kicked him.

She should stop.

And if she stopped, what would he do?

She'd loved him once.

Once.

One last push sent him into the glass doors. And through them.

Seven stories below a shrubbery broke his fall, and the ground snapped his spine.

《《——》》

Perhaps Mary had always expected to know one of her visitors. If Sherlock had granted her freedom all those weeks ago, and she still hadn't gone running to him, it was likely that he'd have sent someone she knew to finally grant that freedom forcefully.

Or maybe they were all dead.

She watched the last person come into her valley two days after the funeral pyre had finally cooled. The smell still hung over the garden, the tang of a fire long-gone but here to stay. The scar was there as well, a blackened boil on the land, a sign of rot. The speck of a person passed over the ridge to the west—Mary could just make out the movement through the binoculars, though she had no idea why she had known to look just at that moment—and she followed it down to the treeline.

"Someone else who's heard I'm someone to see?" she asked, but she was talking to ghosts. Even before she'd spotted the new visitor, when she closed her eyes she no longer felt alone. Ahmed Din and Alice were here in her valley forever, their memories little more than a breath on the breeze. But every breath she took could have been theirs as well. They had come here to die, and now they were trapped as much as she.

It took a very long time for the shape to emerge from the trees and start down the road. So long, in fact, that Mary had begun to doubt her own eyes. Maybe there had been a fly on the binoculars instead of a shape on the distant hills. She was old, after all, her eyesight faded by time and stung by the flames of Alice's death. She had started going about her day's business, glancing up only occasionally, when she saw the person staggering towards her homestead.

He looked very tall. He was too far away for her to make out properly, but Mary was sure he was looking her way when he went to his knees, knelt there for a few long, loaded seconds, and then fell forward onto his face.

His skin had looked as red as blood. Sunburn or sores.

He didn't move for hours.

"He was coming to see me," Mary said, looking around her garden and trying to feel at home. She sat down and ate lunch, purposely not glancing up at the road snaking into the hills. Afterwards she closed her eyes and the sun comforted her into a shallow sleep, one where she heard the birds and the stream but falsely distant, seen from a—

«« —»»

—hillside that her valley was attacking. Burnt black, its rot spreading like a cancer through the land, putrefying trees in seconds, melting rocks, making new ravines that squirted magma into the air in thick sheets of fire. And her puking felt aflame, her head swimming with pain, and she wondered if she saw what was actually there, or only what she expected.

Out towards the city safety was a sham made of false dreams, its colours too garish and its promise so false. Here you can live free and untouched, it said, lying through the mockery of the landscape she saw. She could hardly breathe through its untruths. Her lungs burned. It was a monstrous lie that she told herself, as bad as the teenaged conviction that everything gets better with time.

Mary squatted on the ridge, looking back at certain death and forwards at a land of lies, and she did not know which way to turn.

«« —»»

When she woke up the man was still dead in the road. She left her garden again with the intention of burying him, yes, that's why she was going, that's why she took a shovel and her rifle. She was going as far as the man and no further.

But for once her vision went higher than the ridge surrounding her valley. Up there, reflected from the underside of the heavy clouds drifting down from the north, she saw a shepherd's-warning redness in the middle of the day. It was as if the whole world beyond the valley— the world she had denied for so long—was aflame, and she could see only the destruction's mirror image.

She passed the stream where it came closest to the road and saw that it was running full and heavy. There must have been a storm somewhere outside. The stream carried bits of the valley with it: broken sticks; leaves shed too early; a tangle of roots; a colourful bird, neck broken, wings spread like a pinned butterfly as it span slowly on the water's sur-face. All these things would leave, dive into the western hills with the stream and emerge wherever it came out, eventually to turn into a river. They would become a part of outside. Which made them alien already.

There was not a breath of breeze to stir the grasses and bushes. That made the atmosphere more eerie. There was a storm beyond the high ridge, Mary was sure of that, but in this sheltered place where she'd spent a quarter of her life there were no signs of anything being wrong.

Other than the dead man.

And the greasy smell of dead Alice in her hair and clothes.

Mary shook her head, watched her feet kick up dust as she walked, and wondered if she had really been deluding herself for so long with that blessed sense of freedom. It was easy to miss the obvious if it was too painful to bear.

There was no sign of the mutated dogs. If they wanted a free meal the man was lying in the road, still warm, his blood still fluid. Perhaps they were afraid of Mary. Either that or they had found richer pickings elsewhere.

The birds sang cheerfully all the way across the valley, keeping up the pretence.

By the time she reached the man, she knew that this time it was different. First, she checked that he was dead. There was no real doubt even from a distance, because the red mask she'd seen was fresh blood, and his eyes seemed to have flooded with it. The weals and lesions on his body had virtually grown into one; there was barely a patch of unblemished skin left. He'd fallen to the road and rolled onto his back, one arm draped across his chest, blood-filled eyes staring skyward as if reflecting the red-smeared clouds.

"So what was your name?" Mary said. "And why were you here? Heard I was someone to come and see?" She knelt down next to him and reached out, touched his neck, felt the tackiness of drying blood. He was much warmer than he should have been, even alive. "Burning up," Mary said. "The whole world's burning up." She thought she'd dreamed that once, but it was distant and obscure.

She looked further along the rough road towards the trees. Through there, up the hillside and back into the sun, then up to the ridge and...she would see.

Outside.

A place beyond her home, a place that for sixteen years had only been there on those rare occasions when she allowed it in memory.

"Wonder who else is left," Mary said quietly. When she looked back down a fat bluebottle had landed on one of the man's open eyes.

She stood and backed away a few steps. He stank, not just of death but of fire as well, stale food, vomit, smoke, the city. She should drag him to the side of the road at least, cover him with pulled grass or dust, but she didn't have the strength or will. The memory of sweet dead Alice still lingered strong in her mind, and this man was nothing to her. She didn't know his name, for a start. She'd never spoken to him. He was a *stranger,* and although there was a lot more to knowing someone than a name, she could no longer think of Alice as such.

She looked right, back down the slope at her house sitting on the valley floor. She could see movement as her livestock worried over food. The neck of the garden was cut in two by the silver necklace of the stream, while its body was the organised wilderness of roses, clematis and honeysuckle bulging out towards the south.

There was home. There was the place Sherlock had sent her, where she had defied and defeated him with happiness and acceptance of her lot.

And left, through the trees and up the hill, was the truth.

Mary dropped the shovel, turned left and began walking.

It took her an hour to pass through the woods. She heard all the normal sounds of nature, nothing unusual. The foxes barked occasionally, but the mutant dogs did not show, and she almost forgot that she was carrying the rifle.

There was a strong sense of disquiet about what she was doing, a feeling of betrayal. But the only person she could truly betray anymore was herself.

She needed to see. Needed to realise what was happening, why Sherlock had experienced this sudden change of heart. Freedom, he'd offered her, not realising that his own supposed liberty was the true prison. He must have had a reason after so long, and as the visitors to Mary's valley had became sicker and more desperate, the truth seemed to grow.

She didn't have to stay here anymore, after all.

I can go, she thought, and the realisation struck straight home for the first time. *I don't have to stay. I can go. I don't have to remain. I can leave. Go...stay...leave...remain...*

Eventually the words blended together, a mantra that guided her up the hillside she had not set foot on since travelling the opposite way sixteen years before. She'd had many people with her then, bringing the animals and equipment and food and grain and seeds that were intended to keep her alive, her life a living hell. Now, going up instead of down, she carried only the clothes she wore, the gun and binoculars. Yet still the going was hard.

«« — »»

She reached the ridge without realising where she was. She had been looking at her feet for the last hour, counting her steps, losing count and starting again. Pain thrummed through her bones, settling throughout her body, not simply in her legs. But it was a strange sensation; a memory of pain, unlikely and rich, unfeasible yet keen.

The gun and binoculars had vanished. Maybe she'd put them down somewhere, although she could not recall where. The going suddenly became easier; she looked up, the ground flattened out and—

—she opened her eyes.

Straight ahead, out across the endless plains towards the impossibly distant city, she saw the truth. And it was white.

«——»

Mary wanted to go back to the valley. She tried to turn around, to *move*, but something was holding her in place. She felt as if she were cast into a white block, and whiteness had solidified around her and frozen her motionless. She could still breathe, though it hurt to do so, but she could not move.

I want to go back, she thought.

Somebody was crying.

Her hand was hot. She tried to look down to see what was wrong with it—it felt as though a dog had taken it into its warm wet mouth and was resting it there, waiting to bite—but she could not move her head. Her eyes felt sticky and sore. There was something in the white, some shape struggling to make itself known, but she could not focus, the truth was obscured.

Mary tried to close her eyes and turn around, walk quickly back into the valley and safety and comfort she knew so well. But she realised with a shock, a terrible sense of dislocation, that even Mary was an enigma here, distant and intangible as a character from a favourite book. Mary who had planted crops and fixed fences, cooked cookies and milked goats…*that* Mary did not feel real here.

She could not close her eyes. There was a squeal, and it could have come from her own throat.

"Mary," someone said, a voice replacing the crying. The dog bit down on her hand and she felt the bones being crushed, the skin pierced and muscles mashed. She tried to call out but she could not, there was something in her mouth, something reaching in and down. Perhaps it was a Belladonna stem. Had she brought some with her on her trip, picked and packed dismissively as a final, terrible solution? There was no pain any more, only a sense of weight all across her body. It should be crushing her but she breathed, she could feel her chest rising and falling. Shapes struggled to form from the white, it may have been fields but the squares were too regular, the grid too even. Lines, black lines. She could not see where they led.

"Mary!" the voice said again, and it sounded like a dog barking. Her hand was dropped and footsteps receded away from her. A voice shouted in the distance, and she struggled to close her eyes again to see where it was coming from. Another visitor perhaps, down the road towards the city, calling her name as they fell to their knees so close to death?

"She's awake!" someone said, and it was no longer someone, it was Sherlock.

Mary closed her eyes at last and drifted away, but she could not find her way back to her valley. Instead there was only darkness.

«« — »»

And she rose again from nothing into something. Opening her eyes she saw the shapes set against the harsh whiteness: tiles, square tiles above her, hanging there to form a ceiling.

Mary wondered who was looking after her livestock.

And suddenly she had a new visitor, the one she had been expecting ever since the first man had wondered down into her place of safety and hope. A face blanked out the white ceiling, the black lines, filling her field of vision and bringing such a flood of emotions that, for a time, she could not breathe.

Sherlock.

He had tears in his eyes. The smile could not be false. He looked as if he loved her, and although he was far older and more weathered than she could have thought, it was not madness that hung there above her.

"Oh my God, Mary. Mary. Mary." It was all he could say, her name. And with each reiteration, she felt the Mary of the valley becoming even more vague, wraithlike in memory and possibility.

Somebody spoke in the background, a voice that held authority. Sherlock turned aside and listened, nodded, his expression earnest. Then he looked back down at Mary and smiled again. A tear dropped from his nose but she could not feel it hit her skin. She wondered why.

"I can't stay long, the doctor says you need rest. How strange. Rest, after so long. Oh Mary, I'm so…so glad…" More tears fell, Mary could not feel them. But her eyes seemed to blur and something inside her broke, some vestige of a bad dream flittering away in a valley tempest, and Sherlock smiled and touched her face.

"Don't cry," he said. "I've done enough of that for both of us."

Mary closed her eyes as exhaustion hugged her close. She heard the mumble of voices again, several people talking quietly, but Sherlock was the only one she could understand.

"…time to live again…" he said.

«« — »»

She could see more the next time she came out of the dark. They must have propped her torso so that she could see the walls, the equipment lining them, the tubes in her arms and the backs of her hands, the monitors and wires and leads that all seemed to connect to her. She had the conviction that she was running everything in the room instead of the other way around. Sherlock's footfalls must have wakened her, because he came through the door just as her vision cleared. He used a walking stick. The limp was not that bad.

"Hello darling. The doctor says you've been mumbling a lot in your sleep," he said when he sat down. "Lots of strange stuff. He wanted me to chat to you about it. And some of it worries me, because…Mary, I really don't know where you've been. I've talked to people about this, professionals, and they all say the same thing. After sixteen years in a coma, perceptions can change." He held her hand as he spoke, stroking and squeezing. It no longer felt like a dog preparing to bite.

"Things are strange," Mary whispered, and her throat hurt. Speaking felt like living someone else's thoughts.

Sherlock nodded. "I know, but some of what the doctor told me you were saying…Mary, I never hurt you. *Ever.* We had a row, but who doesn't row, and the crash was my fault if it was anyone's. Maybe you saw that; perhaps you knew I wasn't paying enough attention to the road."

Mary searched her memories, but she could only find the dust track in her valley.

"Maybe you *blamed* me," Sherlock said.

She would have shaken her head if she could, but her muscles would not allow it.

"There's more you need to know," Sherlock said. He looked down at her hand—she could see parts of herself now, and her hand was wasted, wizened, more like a claw than anything else—and kissed it. "We can live again, Mary, we can know each other again, there's so much I want to tell you and show you…but you have to fight. You have to be brave, Mary. You're ill."

You're ill. The words followed her down as she drifted once again into darkness. There were other voices, activity, hands touching and turning her, but Sherlock's words were the only thing that made any sense.

You're ill.

«« —— »»

Later, after periods of white and dark, times when she could sit up and listen, talk to Sherlock or simply enjoy his company, times when all she could do was lie there and scream inside at all the pain, Mary found her way back to her valley.

It appeared out of nowhere, and it had changed almost beyond recognition. She had obviously been away for a very long time.

Cancer, Sherlock had said. *They tried a treatment, said it was experimental for people in such a state, and the first dose seemed to work well, it reached the cancer and attacked it and you showed real signs of acceptance. But then each successive dose worked less and less. Even seemed to be aggravating the illness, the doctor said.*

No more visitors now, and no more dogs. She stood on the hillside and closed her eyes, enjoying the fresh breeze that brought the smells of green growth, even though beneath it all there was the definite taint of decay. Things had died down there and were rotting.

He said you were dying. Said he'd tried to reach you, help you, but then it always was experimental. He said sorry. And then he walked away.

Sherlock had never hurt her. Only her own, final memory before the crash, aggravated and emphasised in her deep, deep sleep. Tears squeezed from her eyes as she realised how much she had betrayed his love, creating a monster out of the man who adored her so much. The tears pattered onto the grass at her feet, and she prayed that he would never really know.

You've got to fight it, Mary! They can use normal treatment now, soon, when you're well and strong again. The doctor says there's hope, but you've got to be willing, you've got to be strong! I've been waiting for sixteen years, Mary. You've got to be strong for both of us.

She looked down into the valley. There were no more mad mutated dogs, no more visitors trying to bring hope, no buzzards or fields of crops. The Belladonna had grown wild and clogged the valley totally, infesting the woods, smothering the fields, pushing finally through her fence and invading the garden, the house. There was only one way that she could remain here now, and that was to accept death.

The world she knew so well, the valley, had changed so much; the world outside…she could not even begin to guess.

She heard a growl, or perhaps it was the scraping of chair legs on a hospital floor.

Mary took several steps down the grassy slope until she came to the outer extent of the Belladonna growth. She reached out and touched a leaf, squeezed a berry.

She had a lot of thinking to do.

STUMPS

MARK MORRIS

1

"Hey, Mum, look at this!"

Bridget Morgan looked up at her daughter's shout. Ellie was standing in the waist-high grass of their new, untamed garden, waving her sickle in the air. Both the blade of the sickle and Ellie's golden hair caught the sun in fleeting, brilliant flashes. There were moments, of which this was one, when Bridget was struck by her daughter's vital, perfect beauty, by how her youth made her seem both invincible and achingly vulnerable.

"What is it?" Bridget asked, trudging across. Though she couldn't see them for the moment, she knew that somewhere nearby Colin and Miles were also engaged in hacking their way through their newly-acquired jungle.

The four of them had moved into the house three days ago. It had been unoccupied for some time and there were a million and one things to do. Bridget's pessimistic parents had had nothing but negative things to say when they'd seen the place, but Bridget was relishing the challenge, not least because it would give her and Colin a common goal, something they could work to achieve together. It would be a symbol of their re-discovered unity after the awfulness of much of the past eighteen months when their twenty-year relationship had almost fallen apart.

"Look at this," Ellie said again, and reached down to part the grass as Bridget approached.

Bridget gasped, felt her entire body clench, pulling her up short. Ellie, noticing her reaction, gave her the kind of pitying look that only self-assured sixteen year-olds are capable of.

"It's only a piece of wood, Mum."

Bridget laughed. "I can see that now. For a moment, though, I thought…well, I don't know what I thought. It seemed to move. Must have been the sunlight sliding across it."

Ellie placed her hand on the object, stroked it as if it were a dog. "It is very shiny, isn't it? What do you think it's meant to be?"

Bridget pursed her lips. To her, the object jutting from the ground looked like the tip of a giant finger, made of dark, burnished wood. The pattern of the grain even mirrored the concentric whorls of a fingerprint.

"I'm not sure it's meant to be anything," she said, oddly reluctant to voice her true thoughts. "It's just a tree stump that someone's decided to sand and polish."

"I think it's a sculpture of some kind," said Ellie, still dabbling her fingers lightly over the surface of the object as if it were water. "If you look at it from certain angles, you can see…shapes in it."

"How do you mean—shapes?"

"Well…just try it. Walk round it slowly. Watch how the shadows and sunlight move on its surface."

Bridget did as her daughter suggested, and sure enough, from different angles, the polished, rounded stump did seem to assume a number of subtle shapes, each of which became elusive almost as quickly as Bridget glimpsed them. The overall effect was of a shifting collage of images contained within a shimmering, semi-transparent sac. Here, for example, was a rudimentary face, the mouth gaping open as if struggling for air; here was a foetus in a womb; here a squatting, simian figure.

"I don't think they're *really* shapes," Bridget said, as if trying to convince herself. "I think it's just the cloud principle at work."

Ellie wrinkled her nose. "The cloud principle?"

"Yes. We have a tendency, as human beings, to look up at the clouds and see shapes in them."

"Oh." Ellie waggled a finger. "I know about this. It's like seeing the face of the man in the moon, isn't it? Or like religious people who see Jesus's face in a…a potato, or in the stains on a wall or something."

At that moment, Miles, red-faced and dishevelled, appeared around the side of the house. "Oi, you two, come and see what me and dad have found." Then he saw what his mum and elder sister were standing beside and his eyes widened behind his spectacles. "Oh, wow. You've found one as well," he said.

2

By the end of the first weekend, the grass had been hacked down to a level able to be handled by a lawnmower, and seven of the strange, polished stumps had been discovered. They were arranged in no particular pattern. There were two at the back of the house, where Bridget and Ellie had been working, three at the front, and one at each side. Each of the stumps stood two to three feet tall, were made of the same dark, highly polished wood, and were similar—though not identical—in shape.

The stump closest to the house stood maybe eight feet from the wall on the east side, whereas the one furthest away stood at the far end of the back garden, perhaps fifty feet from the house, shadowed by a horse chestnut tree and close to the stone wall of the dirt track that ran along the rear of the property. Several times in those first few days, especially at dusk, Bridget glimpsed the two stumps in the back garden out of the corner of her eye when she was passing the kitchen window, and each time would give a start, thinking that they resembled small, crouching figures. On one occasion she made herself march out of the house and pat the nearest stump on the head, before scolding herself for thinking of the object's rounded tip as a head at all. When she was washing up, she couldn't prevent her gaze from flickering upwards every few seconds to ensure that the things were still there, still motionless. The stumps unsettled her, but she supposed she would get used to them in time.

3

"What do you think they're meant to be?" Ellie asked, echoing—whether consciously or not—her own question of a few days before.

It was late on Monday evening, the long August day having finally, reluctantly succumbed to darkness. Though the nights were short at this time of year, the absence of street lights made them seem far blacker than any the Morgans had experienced in their previous home near Leeds. Furthermore, this particular night had brought with it a chill that had sent them scurrying from the kitchen table to the 'snug', as they had already christened the cosiest of their two high-ceilinged sitting rooms. Colin had cleared out the grate and laid the fire, and the four of them were now clustered around it on their squashy three-piece suite. Miles was engrossed in Harry Potter as usual, Bridget was making a 'goals' list for tomorrow (*1. Buy paint, new rollers, stepladder etc 2. Speak to Ruth about curtains 3. Ring up man about boiler*), and Colin, shattered after a third consecutive day in the garden, was staring at the burning logs as if mesmerised.

Ellie had been flicking disdainfully through *Hello!* magazine before asking her question. Miles tore himself from his book and looked at his sister. "I don't think they're meant to *be* anything," he said. "They're just sort of…shiny blobs."

Ellie's contempt for the magazine was now diverted to her brother. "Of course they're meant to *be* something," she said. "All art has meaning. Isn't that right, Mum?"

Bridget shrugged. "To the artist, certainly, I would think."

"See," Ellie said to Miles with a supercilious sneer.

"All right, clever clogs," said Miles. "What *are* they meant to be, then?"

Ellie gazed into the middle distance for a moment, her face becoming composed as she thought. Finally she said, "I think they're watchers."

Colin blinked as though roused from a trance and looked at his daughter. "Watchers?"

"Yes," Ellie said. "I think they were put there to watch the house."

Bridget shuddered. "What a creepy idea."

"No, I mean *friendly* watchers," said Ellie. "They look after the house while we're asleep, make sure no harm comes to us."

Colin, who had been sitting at one end of the settee with his stretched-out wife's feet resting in his lap, leaned forward as if to demonstrate to the fire that his eyes could imitate its capering flames. "You mean like guardians," he murmured.

"Guardians, yes. Like little soldiers who guard the house."

Something burst in the fire and a shower of sparks flew up the chimney, making them all jump.

Miles raised his eyebrows and made a point of turning his attention back to his book. "You're all a bunch of nutters," he said.

4

Something woke Bridget with a jolt. A dream, maybe. Or perhaps a sound. She was lying with her back to Colin, knees drawn up. The room was still and silent and very, very dark. She tried to slow her breathing, flaring her nostrils to inhale deeply, pursing her lips to blow out a thin column of air.

Then, from over by the window, came a creak which Bridget immediately recognised as the sound that had woken her. Slowly she turned her head in that direction, and saw a hulking shape that was marginally darker than the window in which it was framed. A gasp escaped her, which caused the shape to twist what she assumed was its head in her direction. To prevent it crossing the room and seizing her in the dark, she sat bolt upright and scrabbled for the switch of her bedside lamp.

The hulking shape, illuminated by apricot light, resolved itself into Colin, half-rising from the chair which he'd dragged over to the window.

"What-are-you-doing?" The words came out of her unplugged throat in a rush.

Colin blinked, his stubble heavy as smeared soot, his black hair tousled. He looked exhausted, but he said, "I couldn't sleep. Sorry, Bridge. Did I wake you?"

Bridget drew up her knees and wrapped her arms around them as though to muffle the sound of her rapidly-beating heart. "Why can't you sleep?"

He shrugged. "Too much on my mind, I suppose."

"Like what?"

He gave her a calculating look, and immediately she thought, *Oh please, God, not all this again. I haven't got the strength for it right now.*

However he said, "Did we do the right thing coming here, Bridge?"

"Of course we did!" she exclaimed, getting out of bed and padding across the wooden floor to join him by the window. "How can you doubt it?"

He looked out through the glass, though the moonless night concealed almost everything. The only way Bridget could be certain there wasn't a void out there was because some sections of darkness were blacker than others.

When it seemed he wasn't going to answer, or at least not straight away, she went on, "It's a beautiful place, and the kids love it. It'll take a lot of doing up, but that doesn't matter. We've got all the time in the world. I love you, Col."

He turned from contemplating the darkness, and gave her a forced smile, which he evidently thought needed the reinforcement of his hand taking and squeezing hers.

"I love you too," he said. "More than anything. It scares me to think I nearly lost you."

"Shh." She pressed his face into her stomach so he couldn't see her stricken expression, her terror of the responsibility he was imposing upon her. "Nobody's going to lose anybody."

"We *can* afford to live here, can't we?" he said, like a child craving reassurance.

She knelt in front of him, cupped his face in her hands, looked directly into his eyes. "Colin, listen to me. You have just sold your new book for fifty thousand pounds. You have just sold it to the Americans for a hundred thousand dollars. You have just sold film rights for quarter of a million dollars. Your agent has foreign publishers snapping her hand off. You're on the up and up, Colin. The past is behind you. Behind both of us. It's a bright new future from now on."

"But what if I can't follow it up?" he said. "What if this is it? What if I lose it again?"

"You won't. I have faith. Now, come to bed."

They tried to make love, but it was dry and uncomfortable, without issue. Eventually Colin rolled away from his wife. "Sorry," he said, "I'm...I'm too tired."

"That's okay," said Bridget, hiding her disappointment. She reached out to the dark hump of his body. "Just hold me."

They clung to each other in the darkness. Bridget was on the verge of slipping away when Colin said, "They weren't there before."

Bridget felt as if she'd been drifting down a long corridor. Now she came part way back. "Hmm? What?"

"The…the stumps. They weren't here the first time we came to look at the house."

"Don't be silly," murmured Bridget, drunk with sleepiness. "They must've been."

"They weren't. We walked all the way round the house, through the long grass, all four of us. We didn't find a single one."

"They were hidden, that's all," said Bridget, now not even sure whether she was speaking the words or merely thinking them. "Hidden in…in…"

The sentence came apart as the oily warmth of sleep crept over her. If Colin said anything else, she didn't hear it.

5

Bridget was attempting to tease white gloss from under her fingernails the next day when there was a knock on the door. "Can someone get that?" she shouted, though as far as she was aware, Colin and Miles were still clearing out the attic which they were planning to convert into a study for Colin (a job which she had foregone because of the likelihood of spec-tacularly large spiders leaping out of every nook and cranny), and Ellie was unpacking boxes in her room with her Walkman clamped to her head.

Sure enough, there was no answering call, no thundering of willing feet descending the stairs. "Shit," Bridget muttered, and reached for a wad of kitchen roll, which she used to dry her turpentine-smelling hands as she crossed the quarry-tiled hallway to the front door.

The couple standing outside were about the same age as her and Colin. The man, who was tall with an amiable, broken-nosed face, was wearing a short-sleeved shirt, baggy shorts and sandals. The woman, hovering somewhere between voluptuous and dumpy, was wearing a yellow summer dress and large sunglasses. They both sported the grins of little-seen relatives springing a surprise visit. The woman had a huge punnet of strawberries draped over one arm.

"Hello," said Bridget, thinking that she was about to be told how much the strawberries were.

"Hi, we're your new next door neighbours," the woman said chirpily.

The man pointed off to the left, over his wife's head. "We live about five minutes in that direction, in the white house at the bottom of the sloping drive, surrounded by trees. Maybe you've seen it?"

"Er, yes, I think I have. Isn't there a basketball hoop above your garage door?"

The woman looked both amused and puzzled, evidently thinking this a strange detail to pick up on. "Ye-es," she said slowly.

Bridget smiled. "Sorry, the reason I remember is because my son spotted it as we drove past, and has been pestering me ever since to get one for him."

The couple laughed, then the woman said, "I'm Claire and this is Shaun. We just thought we'd pop by and see how you were settling in— oh, and bring you a little housewarming present."

She held out the punnet. Bridget exclaimed, "Oh, that's really lovely, thank you! Won't you come in for a cup of tea?"

Claire looked at Bridget's paint-spattered overalls and the wad of kitchen roll in her hand. "We don't want to impose. You're obviously very busy."

"You're not imposing at all. I was just knocking off for lunch. Why don't you stay too? We've got plenty. I'll give the others a shout."

Less than an hour later, the four adults, plus Ellie and Miles, were sitting in the garden, eating bowls of strawberries and cream. Colin had opened a bottle of Chardonnay, and then another, and now Bridget was floating on a gentle sea of contentment, her spirits buoyed by sunshine and alcohol and the *bonhomie* of new-found friends.

Shaun and Claire's surname was Woodall, they had two children, a daughter of fifteen and a son of eleven, and they had lived in the area for nine years. Shaun was a partner in an accountancy firm and originally hailed from Doncaster; Claire, of Welsh farming stock, worked part-time as a nurse at the local health centre.

"What about you, Colin?" Shaun asked. "What do you do?"

Bridget saw Colin wince slightly, as he always did when asked this question. "I'm a writer," he mumbled.

"Really?" cried Claire, the wine making her shrill. "What do you write?"

Colin half-shrugged. Ever since Bridget had known him, he had felt uncomfortable talking about his work. And for him, it was something that had become harder rather than easier over the years, simply because people always asked the same questions.

"Crime mostly," he said. "Psychological thrillers, whodunnits, stuff like that."

The inevitable questions followed: *Have you had anything published? Do you write under your own name? Don't you have to have a devious mind to write what you do? Has anything you've written been made into a film?* And that eternal bugbear: *Where do you get your ideas from?*

"Just…from anywhere and everywhere," Colin muttered, Bridget acutely aware that his answer would sound as lame to him as he believed it always did. "They just come to me."

Bridget decided to wade in and rescue him. "You've recently had some good news, haven't you, Col?"

"Mmm," he said non-committaly.

"Oh, do tell," said Claire.

"Yes, don't leave us in suspenders," said Shaun with a grin.

Once again Colin winced, and Bridget said, "He's too modest to tell you, so I will. He's recently sold his new book for oodles of cash in America. And he's also sold the film rights to Steven Spielberg!"

"Not Spielberg," Colin said, trying to make himself heard above Claire's shrieks of excitement. "Dreamworks."

"Yes, but that's Spielberg's company, isn't it?" Bridget said.

"Well, yeah, but it doesn't mean he'd have anything to do with the film if it got made."

Despite Colin's embarrassed attempts to play down his recent success, their new neighbours still reacted as if the four of them had just scooped the lottery on a shared ticket. Toasts were made and backs slapped; Shaun made jokes about needing to borrow a fiver. Ellie and Miles gave each other raised-eyebrow, oh-god-not-this-again expressions, though Bridget knew that secretly they were enjoying Colin's success as much as she was (and as much as he himself was too, she suspected, even though he often gave the impression that he thought himself unworthy of it).

It was certainly an incredible contrast to eighteen months ago when

Colin's chronic bout of depression after being dumped by his previous publisher had resulted in her seeking solace in the arms of another man. Her brief affair with Jason MacNeill at the Leisure Centre where both she and he worked as fitness instructors had almost blown her and Colin's marriage apart.

It had been a horrible, horrible time. For a while they had teetered on the edge of the abyss, peering long and hard into its depths. Even now things were fragile—Colin was certainly a lot more subdued than he used to be. But their long-term future, Bridget believed, was rosy, and not only because of Colin's new-found success. They had begun to claw their way back from the brink even before his good news. They had done it with the aid of a fantastic marriage counsellor called Shelley, and by re-discovering what they had somehow lost in the preceding couple of years—the art of communication. True, their conversations during this time had been interminable, tearful, gruelling. They had disassembled their relationship, analyzed each tiny, individual component, and then reassembled it with excruciatingly infinite care. They had bared their souls, revealed their secrets, admitted their most personal desires and fantasies. Bridget (and she suspected Colin too) had felt embarrassed, ashamed, angry, distressed, occasionally even suicidal, during the course of this appalling but necessary process. Yet ultimately it had been worth it. Despite Colin's introspective nature, Bridget believed that she and he were mentally closer now than they had ever been. Sex was still a problem between them—Bridget knew from their sessions with Shelley that Colin found it hard to make love to her without imagining Jason doing the same—but, upsetting though it was, Bridget felt sure that time and patience and their new-found love for each other would eventually win through.

One of the hardest things of all had been to convey an air of normality to the majority of their friends and colleagues, and more specifically to protect the children as much as possible from the emotional maelstrom. She liked to think that although Ellie and Miles had known that their parents were having 'a few problems', they had not at any time known the true depth and extent, had not seen or heard anything that would pierce them deeply enough to leave memory-scars that they would carry into later life.

Looking around at her family now, relaxed and happy in the sun-drenched garden of their new home, Bridget again felt a surge of contentment, and also of renewal. Moving two hundred miles south at an age when friendships were strong and established must have been tough for the kids, but they had taken to their new life with a selfless enthusiasm and maturity that made her proud. And she was proud of Colin too, proud of how he had risen, phoenix-like, from the ashes. She walked across to him and linked arms with him just as he was saying, in an obvious attempt to deflect attention away from his recent triumphs, "Have you any idea what these things are?"

He had asked the question of Shaun, but all six of them turned to look at the closest of the stumps Colin had been referring to, as if it had just shifted in the earth. Shaun pulled an elaborately perplexed face and said, "I have absolutely no idea. Odd little buggers, aren't they?"

"I thought at first it had a face," Claire said, "but I can't see one now."

"Sometimes it looks like a face," Ellie said, "and sometimes other things. It depends where you're standing."

Colin looked impatient. "Have you any idea how long these things have been here?" he asked.

"Or who made them?" Bridget added.

Their new neighbours shook their heads.

"Can't say I've ever noticed them before," Shaun said.

"Not even the ones at the front when you were driving past?"

When Shaun again shook his head, Colin looked at Bridget with a told-you-so expression.

"That doesn't mean they weren't here, Col," Bridget said. "The hedge is high at the front, remember. You probably wouldn't have seen them from a car."

Colin scowled as if he had been out-maneuvered, and Bridget wondered what he was hoping to prove by having his insistence confirmed that the stumps had not been here when they had viewed the house.

"Did you know the Lanchesters very well?" Bridget asked.

"Not very," said Claire. "I'd pass the time of day with Jean sometimes. I've actually got to know her better since she's moved into the village. I pop in now and again to see how she is."

"Harry, her husband, was a bit of a bugger," Shaun said pointedly.

"In what way?" asked Bridget.

Shaun and Claire exchanged a glance, and Bridget got the impression that the Woodalls were silently debating how much she and Colin should be told.

Then Shaun said, "I don't like to speak ill of the dead, but Harry was a bullish, opinionated man. He did lots of work for the local community, but not many people liked him."

Claire leaned forward and lowered her voice, as if they were in a crowded room and she didn't want to be overheard. "He used to beat Jean black and blue, not that she'd ever admit it, of course. Sometimes I'd see her with bruises on her face. When I asked her about them, she'd say she was a clumsy old woman, always bumping into things." She glanced at Ellie and Miles, who had finished their strawberries and were both now out of earshot. "Then there were all the rumours about him leching after young girls. I didn't believe them until I started coming over to the house a couple of years ago after Jean had moved out, to check things were okay and to pick up any post. I came one day and there was a grey plastic envelope addressed to Harry. As soon as you saw it, you thought there was something dubious about it, didn't you, Shaun?"

Shaun nodded. "I just put two and two together. I know I shouldn't have opened it, but I didn't want Jean to be sent something that might upset her. She's a sweet old lady. I didn't know how much she knew of her husband's reputation for being a dirty old sod."

"She must have known," said Claire.

Shaun's expression was akin to a facial shrug. "You'd be surprised at the secrets people keep from one another, even in a marriage."

Claire raised her eyebrow archly, swaying a little. She was the most drunk of the four of them. "Oh yes, and what secrets are you keeping from me?"

Shaun looked comically alarmed. "I wouldn't dare keep anything from you, my sweet," he said.

"So what *was* in the envelope?" asked Bridget.

"Pornography," said Shaun. "Real hard-core stuff. I mean, *real* hard-core."

"Opened my eyes, I can tell you," said Claire, her eyes widening behind her sunglasses as if to demonstrate.

Bridget grimaced. "I hope we don't get sent any of it. I'd hate it to fall into the kids' hands."

"Warp 'em for life, it would," said Claire.

"Give them a head-start over their classmates, at any rate," said Shaun with a chuckle.

Colin had been quiet for a few minutes. Now he said, "I wonder if it was Harry Lanchester who had these things made."

"I suppose they do look a bit rude if you think of it like that," said Claire. "All sort of…"

"Tumescent?" suggested Bridget.

The two women giggled.

"Steady on, you two," said Shaun. "There are children present."

Colin was the only one who didn't seem to find their banter funny. "Yes," he said quietly. "Maybe that's what they are. Fertility symbols of some kind." He seemed pleased with the idea. "Maybe it's nothing to do with…"

"With what?" said Bridget, and thought she saw a look of guilt pass fleetingly across her husband's face.

"Oh, nothing," said Colin airily. "I was just going to say, maybe they're not guardians at all, or watchers, or whatever you want to call them. I'm just pontificating."

"You don't want to do too much of that, it makes you go blind," said Shaun.

They all laughed, and though Bridget joined in, she didn't feel as content as she had earlier. Maybe she was just being silly, but she couldn't shake off the feeling that there was something Colin wasn't telling her.

6

After the Woodalls had gone, Bridget got back to work. She was determined to finish glossing the snug before tea-time. She had done the skirting boards and window sills before lunch, and spent the afternoon concentrating on the window frames. Though she had carefully masked the edges of the panes to prevent paint getting onto the glass, it was still a fiddly job. The combination of wine and sunshine had made her woozy, and she had to concentrate extra hard to prevent her eyes from blurring and her hands from shaking. Her concentration was not helped by the fact that in the back garden, twenty feet away but directly in front of the window, was one of the stumps. A constant lurking presence in her peripheral vision, it resembled a dark, hunched figure, silently and motionlessly watching her work.

All this, plus the high, sharp stink of the paint, meant that by five she had a splitting headache. She tried to ignore it for as long as possible, but eventually it got so bad that she thought if she didn't lie down soon she'd pass out.

She washed her brushes with her eyes half-closed, the pulses of pain in her head so intense that it felt as if someone were repeatedly cleaving her skull with an axe. The house was so silent as she trudged upstairs with a cold, damp flannel pressed to her temples that she could almost believe she was alone in it. She stumbled into the bedroom, blundering into unpacked cardboard boxes like a blind woman, before collapsing with a groan on to the bed. There she lay, her head awash with pain. She tried to sleep, but her headache was so acute that all she managed to do was drift into a state of semi-delirium.

Though she had no memory of getting out of bed, Bridget was all at once aware that she was standing at the window, looking into the garden below. Then she glanced up, her attention snagged by a flicker of movement in her peripheral vision. Beyond the dirt track at the back of the house was a corn field, and bordering that, separating the field from the sky, was a sizeable splotch of deep-sea green which was all she could see of the densely-packed trees of the yet-to-be-explored wood. The movement that had alerted Bridget had been caused by what appeared to be a clump of green detaching itself from the main mass.

Instantly Bridget realised that what she had initially, and ludicrously, thought was a clump of foliage was in fact a figure. It was moving away from the trees, moving through the field towards the lane that ran behind the house, leaving a wake of trampled corn behind it. It must have been an effect of the sun that made the figure, which was enveloped in a heat-haze that blurred its silhouetted outline, appear scrawnier and more ragged than it seemed possible to be. Perhaps it was the same effect that made the figure appear lopsided, as if one of its legs were considerably longer than the other, and that made it move with a remorseless, lurching gait that for some reason she couldn't fathom struck a chord of fear in Bridget's heart.

She tried to tear herself away from the sight of the figure, but something—some force—rooted her to the spot. She had the irrational notion that it was her mind that had conjured the creature into being, and that it existed only because she believed in it. The figure was over half-way across the field, and no more defined than when it had first emerged from the woods, when Bridget became aware that, below her, Colin had entered the back garden.

At once she felt panic rushing through her, and clenched her right hand into a fist to bang on the window. She told herself that it was only the amplified thud of her own accelerated pulse that made the sound seem as muffled as if she'd been thumping a mattress, but if that was the case, why didn't Colin look up? Abandoning her assault on the window, she tried shouting a warning down to him, but even her own voice sounded to her as if she was trying to make herself heard underwater.

As if sensing Colin's presence, the figure in the field suddenly began to move with greater urgency. Its rolling, crab-like advance now seemed horribly eager; it moved in a way that made Bridget terrified of seeing it at close quarters.

Colin, meanwhile, continued to be oblivious to the advancing presence. He strolled across the garden, his languidity an unsettling contrast to the other's frantic energy. Bridget saw him approach the closest of the stumps and raise his arms, palms outspread, as though he was warming himself at the fireside. At the same time she saw the thin, ravaged figure, its features still indefinable, reach the fence at the bottom of the field, and then—despite its apparent disability—scale it with hideous, monkey-like ease.

"*Colin!*" The scream tore itself out of her lungs and tasted coppery as blood, but again there was no response from below. Bridget could only watch in horror as Colin stepped forward and placed his hands on the glossy surface of the stump. As soon as he did so, the hobbling figure became a dark smear of purposeful, terrifying movement. In an instant, it had crossed the lane, entered the garden and was rushing in a blur towards her husband.

It was Colin's screams that caused Bridget's tightly clenched eyelids to fly apart. She only realised she was still lying on the bed when she sat up, the damp flannel sliding from her forehead into her lap. During the few seconds it took for her husband's cries to rise into a piercing crescendo, Bridget leaped to her feet, ran down the stairs and dashed out into the garden.

She found Colin lying on the grass at the base of the stump she had seen (or dreamed she had seen) him place his hands upon. She ran over and dropped to her knees beside him, her gaze darting over his body, looking for evidence of injury. Yet although she could see nothing physically wrong with him—no cuts or bruises, no sign that he had suffered a stroke or heart-attack—Colin's eyes were wide and wild, and although he was no longer screaming, he was whimpering now, like an animal caught in a trap, which in some ways was worse.

"Colin!" she shouted. "Colin!"

He didn't respond, didn't even seem to recognise her.

Ellie ran out of the house, closely followed by Miles. "What's happening, Mum? What's wrong with Dad?"

"I don't know," Bridget said. "I can't see anything."

Colin was lying on his left side, knees drawn up to his belly. Bridget placed a hand on his right shoulder. Beneath his t-shirt, his muscles were rigid.

"Colin," Bridget said again. "Colin, can you hear me?"

Still he did not respond, except with breathy, panicked whimpers, like an injured dog.

"Miles, go inside, dial 999 and ask for an ambulance," said Bridget. "You'll have to give the address. You can remember it, can't you?"

Miles, his eyes wide and scared behind his spectacles, nodded and ran into the house. Bridget asked Ellie to fetch Colin a blanket, then— the first aid training she had received as a fitness instructor clicking into gear—attempted to put her husband in the recovery position.

When the ambulance arrived, there wasn't room inside for all of them, so Bridget followed it with Ellie and Miles in the car. The nearest hospital was ten miles away through mostly country lanes, a fact which they'd been briefly concerned about, then glibly dismissed, when they had been debating whether to buy the house. The journey was undertaken in grim silence, Bridget gear-changing jerkily. She stared at the white metal doors in front of her and wondered what was happening behind them. Worst-case scenarios raced through her head, in all of which she was the chief villain. She imagined hospital staff angrily demanding why she hadn't administered first aid at the scene; Colin laid out cold and white on a mortuary slab; her children shooting her accusing looks at their father's funeral.

Was it possible she had mis-read the symptoms, failed to see what to a trained eye may have been obvious? At the same time she was thinking this, she continued to relive what she kept telling herself must have been a dream, but which even now seemed far more than that. She had *seen* Colin attacked by…by what? An animal? A man? A creature more shadow than substance?

"Dad *will* be all right, Mum, won't he?" Miles asked as they swept in through the hospital gates.

Ignoring the car park signs on their left, Bridget followed the ambulance round to the main entrance. Miles looked so anxious that Bridget was desperate to reassure him, but what if she told him Colin would be fine and then he wasn't?

"Let's hope so," she said, trying to make her voice bright. She opened her car door as the back of the ambulance yawned and the burlier of the two ambulance men jumped out and pulled down the ramp. The other man, the gleam of light on his bald head flashing blue then white as the roof-light of the ambulance strobed, pushed out the wheelchair into which Colin had been strapped, leaning backwards in order to keep the chair vertical on the slight slope.

Colin's eyes were closed, his head lolling on his right shoulder. The thick, rust-coloured blanket swaddled around his tethered body made him seem frail, child-like. The ambulance men had asked Bridget all sorts of questions as they had calmly administered to Colin back at the house. They had proferred several possible explanations for his condition—an adverse reaction to an insect bite; an allergic response to something he had eaten or drunk; a panic attack; epilepsy; diabetes. But it had been clear to Bridget that they didn't really have a clue what was wrong with her husband, which was why, in the end, they had decided to take him into hospital for tests.

"How's he been?" she asked now, hurrying forward with the children in tow. And then, noting her husband's closed eyes, "Why is he unconscious? Did you have to sedate him?"

The burly ambulance man's smile exuded calmness, confidence, capability. "Don't worry, he's fine. He had a comfortable journey and all his vital signs are normal. He came round a little bit on the way here, though he's still pretty confused. I tried to get him talking, but he was pretty out of it. He said he was tired, then he drifted off to sleep."

They wheeled Colin through a pair of double glass doors, into a world of bright lights and activity. This hospital was smaller than most of the big city ones Bridget had been in, but that was the only difference. There was the usual confusing array of signs pointing off in myriad directions; there were people waiting for appointments, looking anxious or bored or forlorn; there were patients shuffling about in shapeless hospital gowns as if lost; there was the familiar smell that Bridget hated, like the faint odour of vomit overlaid with the ammoniac sting of disinfectant.

Though she was loath to let Colin out of her sight, Bridget knew she and the children would be nothing but a hindrance to the doctors as they set about their quest to find out what was wrong with him. For over two hours they waited, perched on seats with covers so threadbare that in places the weave had parted to expose the crumbling orange foam beneath. Ellie and Miles gulped lukewarm Coke whilst Bridget sipped sludgy coffee from a plastic cup that was almost too hot to hold. For want of something to occupy themselves rather than because they were hungry, they all three filled up on empty calories from the food dispenser—Kit Kats, crisps, mini-packs of chocolate chip cookies. Bridget read every poster on the walls and leafed through every tatty, out-of-date magazine she could find, and after a while, when the kids inevitably fell to bickering, she took a walk up the corridor to prevent her anxiety exploding into anger.

At nine o' clock Ellie and Miles, despite the junk they had been eating, started to complain about being hungry. Bridget gave them more money for the machine and then closed her eyes briefly to ease her headache, the dredges of which were still sluicing through her mind like a sluggish and polluted tidal swell. Footsteps came and went in the darkness like anxieties patrolling the corridors of her mind. Eventually one set of footsteps stopped beside her.

"Mrs Morgan?"

Bridget opened her eyes. The world seemed bleached of colour, but momentarily more sharply defined than she'd been expecting. The white-coated man looking down at her was short, with a handsome, boyish face and hair that reminded her of Shaggy in Scooby Doo. Bridget pushed herself into a more upright position.

"Yes."

"I'm Doctor Urwin. We've carried out every test we can think of on your husband, and I'm pleased to report we can find absolutely nothing wrong with him. His heart's fine, his blood pressure's normal, there's nothing in his system that shouldn't be there. We've monitored brain activity and that's fine too. In fact, for a man of his age he's in very good shape."

"He looks after himself," Bridget heard herself saying. "He goes running, and we have a healthy diet."

Dr Urwin smiled indulgently. "We're still waiting for the results of a few tests, but there's no reason why Colin can't go back home with you now."

"Is he conscious?" Bridget asked.

"Oh yes. He's been chatting away nineteen to the dozen for the past hour."

Bridget found that hard to believe. Colin was a fairly taciturn man even at the best of times. "Did you ask him what happened?"

Dr Urwin shrugged as if it were of no consequence. "He says he can't remember. All he can recall is being out in the garden and then coming to in the ambulance."

"He doesn't remember screaming?"

"He says not."

"What do *you* think happened to him, doctor?" Bridget asked.

"It's hard to say. We're still looking at the possibility of epilepsy or some form of panic attack, but as I say there's no evidence to support either of those theories at the moment. What we do know is that it's not heart-related, it's not an insect bite, it's not drugs, it's not diabetes. There *was* a small amount of alcohol in your husband's system, but he would have to have an unusually low tolerance level for it to have affected him so badly."

Bridget waved her hand dismissively. "We had a few glasses of wine in the garden at lunchtime, but Colin's had far more than that before without it having this effect on him."

Dr Urwin spread his hands. "Okay, well that's about all I can tell you at this juncture. I'm sorry we've been unable to get to the bottom of your husband's little episode."

"That's okay," said Bridget. "At least you haven't found anything bad."

Urwin smiled. "No, we haven't. Hopefully this'll just be a one-off. One of life's little mysteries. The best thing to do is go home and forget it ever happened."

"And if it happens again?"

Urwin's smile widened. "Let's cross that bridge if and when we come to it, shall we?"

7

Concentrating on curtains was hard, but Bridget did her best the next day to pretend that everything was normal. Her best friend, Ruth, an interior designer, had driven all the way down from Chester to measure up, and Bridget was desperate to give the impression that all her problems were way, way behind her, that moving down here was the best thing she and Colin had ever done.

She only wanted to give that impression, she told herself, because it was true. In no way was she trying to pull the wool over her oldest friend's eyes. She simply didn't want Ruth to go home with the false impression that things were still not right between her and Colin. Yesterday's episode had nothing to do with what had happened this past year, but Colin's behaviour since had been so odd that the truth actually sounded unconvincing. That was why Bridget had felt compelled to tell Ruth a little white lie about Colin's condition, even though Ruth was the only other person apart from Shelley who knew the whole story. Bridget wondered over lunch whether Ruth had believed her when she had told her that Colin was in bed with a 'bit of a bug,' wondered too whether her forced cheerfulness was too obvious. If so, Ruth wasn't letting on.

Any other time Bridget would have been delighted to have seen the friend she had known since they were both six, and to whom she had remained close even though they had gone to different universities and had lived in different towns ever since. In fact, she had been looking forward to Ruth's overnight stay since they had arranged it almost two weeks ago. Now, though, she found herself wishing that Ruth had been due to arrive tomorrow or the next day. Ideally, she would have liked to have devoted her time today to finding out exactly what was wrong with Colin.

Even though Dr Urwin had assured her that nothing was *physically* wrong, it was obvious to Bridget that yesterday's events had left Colin with scars of some kind. Since his 'attack', he had been surly and uncommunicative. When, in the car on the way home from the hospital, Bridget had tried to get to the bottom of what had happened, he had muttered only that he couldn't remember. Bridget had felt upset and frustrated at his unwillingness to talk to her, but hadn't wanted to make a scene in front of the children, particularly after the stress they had already suffered that day.

She had been hoping to have some time alone with Colin back at the house, but as soon as they stepped inside, he announced that he was tired and was going to bed. By the time Bridget managed to follow him upstairs, having fed the kids, put the pots to soak, locked up the house and switched off the lights, Colin was fast asleep, the covers pulled up to his chin.

Frustrated, Bridget had banged about whilst getting ready, hoping he would wake up, but he had slept on as though he'd been sedated. At one point, however, he had turned over with a murmur that seemed almost to be a word, to reveal hands that he had heavily, though inexpertly, bandaged. Intrigued and disturbed by this, Bridget had prodded him gently whilst speaking his name, but he had stubbornly refused to respond. Eventually she had given up and turned out the light, only to lie sleepless for several hours, obsessed by the image of Colin placing his hands on the smooth, rounded surface of the stump, and of the scrawny, lopsided creature that had emerged from the woods flowing with terrifying purpose towards him.

Finally she had slipped into a light sleep laden with fitful dreams, only to jerk awake once again at first light. Her eyeballs felt poached, her limbs almost feverishly hollow, and her stomach ached with tiredness. Colin, beside her, was lying on his back, his mouth wide open as though something had forced his lips apart to gain either ingress or egress during the night. In the pearly dawn light, his skin looked waxy. Bridget watched him for a while, willing him to wake up, but eventually had to resort to prodding him in the ribs until he stirred.

"We need to talk," she said when he groaned and turned away from her.

He growled something incomprehensible, his eyes remaining defiantly shut.

Cuddling up close to his back, she kissed his bare shoulder and murmured into his ear, "Please talk to me, Colin. I couldn't sleep last night for worrying about you."

"I'm fine," he muttered.

"No, you're not. You weren't yesterday. Something happened. I want to know what it was."

He was silent for a while, and, thinking he had drifted back to sleep, she was about to prod him again, when he muttered, "Already told you. Can't remember."

"You must be able to remember *something*," she said.

"Can't," he growled.

"You don't remember feeling any pain? You don't remember anyone…attacking you?"

"No."

"Why have you bandaged your hands?"

"They hurt."

"Why do they hurt?"

"Don't know."

"Do you remember putting your hands on one of the stumps?"

He went very still and Bridget held her breath. She was aware of her heart pumping against his back, like the pulse of her anxiety, urging him to remember.

Eventually he muttered, "No."

"Are you sure?"

"Yes. Leave me alone."

"I won't leave you alone, Colin, because I love you and I want to find out what's wrong with you."

"Nothing's wrong. I'm just tired."

"What's wrong with your hands?"

"Told you. They hurt."

"But *how* do they hurt? Describe the pain."

"Hot. Stinging. Burning." Then he hunched his shoulders as if trying to shuck her off and growled, "I don't know."

"Can I get you anything?"

"No. Just want sleep."

She sighed. "All right. Go back to sleep for a bit. But we'll talk later. If there's something wrong, I want to know about it. No secrets, remember."

Ruth didn't arrive until noon, but Colin still hadn't emerged even by then. Bridget had been up to him a couple of times in the meantime, but on each occasion had been met with a similar response. Even when she had told him that Ruth would be arriving soon, he had simply grunted and pulled the covers tighter around him. Now that Ruth was here, Bridget had been forced to push her frustration and anxiety aside, and to try to match her friend's superlative-laden enthusiasm for the house—a task which she would have found easy only twenty-four hours earlier.

"Everything's not all right, is it?" Ruth said.

The question only shocked Bridget because it didn't come until mid-way through the afternoon. By this time the two old friends had had a gossipy lunch, had gone through the house room by room (excluding hers and Colin's bedroom, of course), discussing colours and fabrics, and had done all the measuring-up downstairs. Now they had stopped for a well-earned coffee, which they had taken out into the back garden. Though she had found remaining cheerful something of an ordeal, Bridget was beginning to think that she must be carrying it off pretty well.

"What do you mean?" she said, attempting to hide behind an insouciant smile.

"Oh come on, Bridge. I thought we'd known each other long enough to be honest."

"We have. It's just…" Bridget looked out across the garden and the cornfield beyond, her eyes drawn to the spot where she'd dreamed she had seen the figure emerge from the woods yesterday. "I didn't want you to get the wrong impression, that's all."

"What impression's that?" Ruth asked. She was small and dark and elegant. Like Bridget, she would be forty in less than a year, and, although Bridget worried about her sometimes, Ruth was forever insistent that she was perfectly content to be childless and intermittently single.

"I didn't want you to think that Colin and I weren't getting on, because we are, we're getting on really well. We love the house, and we've had a great first week here, and we both know that this is the best thing we've ever done."

"So?" said Ruth. "Where's the problem?"

Bridget sank on to the wooden bench on the small patio area directly outside the back door, her mug clasped in both hands. "It's just…something happened yesterday. Something odd. I didn't tell you before because…it just sounds too weird."

"I'm intrigued. Go on."

Bridget told Ruth everything, and though at first she spoke haltingly, reluctantly, she soon realised that she was finding the experience so cathartic that she almost wished she had told her friend the truth from the outset. On the other hand, the events she now felt grateful to relate were not exactly something you could hit someone with the minute they stepped through the door. She had kept the story from Ruth not only because of its strangeness, but because she had not wanted Ruth's initial impression of the house to be a negative one, had not wanted her to think that the four of them were anything but happy here. Bridget was determined to believe that what had happened yesterday was not their first week's defining moment, but simply a glitch, an abberation. It had been alarming, yes, but would ultimately, Bridget hoped, become nothing more than a half-forgotten oddity.

"You see now why I didn't tell you?" she said when she had finished, and offered a rueful smile. "I didn't want you to think that I'd lost my marbles, that all this fresh air and wide open spaces were getting to me."

Ruth placed a supportive hand on Bridget's forearm. "I wouldn't think that," she said. Then she glanced at the woods beyond the cornfield and shuddered. "Do you really think there's something up there?"

"No I don't," said Bridget firmly.

"So what do you think happened then?"

Bridget had forgotten how much more willing than herself Ruth was to accept the existence of the supernatural. "I don't know, but I was half-cut, I had a headache and I'd been breathing in paint fumes all day. It all seems a bit of a blur now when I look back on it."

Ruth had turned her attention to the closest of the stumps, and was regarding it with a kind of wary respect. "All the same, it's obvious that something pretty drastic *did* happen to Colin. Have *you* touched one of these things before?"

"Course I have," Bridget snapped, disliking the direction in which the conversation was going.

"Do you dare me to?"

"Oh, now you're getting ridiculous!" All the same, Bridget couldn't prevent herself from glancing uneasily at the spot where she had seen the figure emerge from the woods yesterday.

Ruth crossed to the stump. She raised her hands as if about to attempt to push it over, but then hesitated. She glanced back at Bridget, who raised her eyebrows to express her indifference, though her body felt tense. Abruptly Ruth tilted forward at the waist, pressing the palms of both hands to the stump.

Nothing happened. Bridget lowered the shoulders she'd involuntarily hunched. "Satisfied?" she said.

"Disappointed," said Ruth. "I was hoping I'd feel something at least."

"What happened to Colin isn't a joke, Ruth," said Bridget.

Ruth looked shocked. "I know it isn't. I never thought it was. I just thought…I don't know, maybe there was an electrical charge or something running through this thing."

"Come on," Bridget said, "let's go and measure some more windows."

She picked up their coffee mugs and the two women went back into the house. Turning right into the kitchen, Bridget said, "I'll just check up on Colin before we—" Then she stopped dead.

Colin was standing in the middle of the floor, swaying from side to side as if drunk. He looked ill and unshaven, his mouth hanging slackly open, his eyes dull, glazed. He had pulled on his dressing gown, but it was hanging open and he was naked beneath it. His slight paunch bulged above a nest of greying pubic hair, within which his penis curled like a shrivelled sea creature.

Bridget heard Ruth gasp behind her.

"Jesus Christ, Colin!" Bridget said, taking a step towards her husband.

At the sight of her, Colin's face twisted into a dopey but savage expression of anger. "Was it him?" he snarled thickly. "It fucking was, wasn't it? You're all conspiring against me, you cunts."

He raised his bandaged hands, fingers hooked into claws, and lunged towards her. Shocked, Bridget jumped back, banging heads with Ruth. The pain caused her to drop the mugs she was holding, which smashed on the floor.

"*Fuck!*" Bridget yelled, clutching the back of her head.

Colin's bare foot came down on a jagged chunk of broken mug, and his face changed again, his demented anger becoming an almost clown-like moue of agony. He stumbled, seemed somehow to get his legs entangled in his flapping dressing gown, then fell forward and banged his chin on the floor, his jaws closing with a clack that made Bridget wince despite her own pain.

He lay there, groaning, eyelids fluttering wildly. His arms were still outstretched towards Bridget, though the gesture now seemed more like a plea for help than a threat of violence.

"Oh God, Colin," Bridget said, and still rubbing the back of her skull, crouched down beside him. He was lying on top of the broken bits of mug. She tugged at his arm, but he was a dead weight. "Help me with him, will you?" she said, turning to Ruth, but then she saw that her friend was sitting on the floor outside the kitchen door, clutching her face. "Are you all right?"

"Fantastic," said Ruth weakly. She moved her hands slowly away from her face as though afraid part of it might fall off, and Bridget saw a lump, already empurpling as the blood rushed to it, above her friend's left eyebrow.

"Oh shit, Ruth, I'm so sorry."

"Wasn't your fault," muttered Ruth.

"Here, let me get you a cold flannel to put on it." She got to her feet, sidestepped Colin's prone figure and hurried to the sink. Unable to find a flannel, she unwound a long strip of kitchen roll, ran it under the cold tap, squeezed out the excess water and hurried back across to Ruth.

"There, that'll keep the swelling down," she said, handing the wad of wet paper to her friend.

"Thanks," Ruth said. She pressed the makeshift compress to the lump, puffed out a long breath as if it contained all her dizziness, then got to her knees and shuffled forward. "How's Colin?"

"Not good," said Bridget. "He's lying on all those broken bits of mug, but I can't shift him."

"Try pouring some water on his head. That might bring him round."

It seemed like adding insult to injury, but Bridget couldn't think of an alternative. She rose to her feet, but as she made to move back across to the sink, Ruth stayed her with a hand on the leg.

"Hang on, what if he wakes up and he's like…what he was like a minute ago?"

For a moment Bridget didn't answer, then she said stubbornly, "He won't be."

"But how do you know? You saw him. He looked crazy. He looked *possessed*."

Bridget scowled. "So what do you expect me to do? Just leave him lying on all those bits of broken pot? God knows what damage it's doing to him."

"I thought maybe we could…I don't know…call the emergency services or something." Before Bridget could reply, Ruth raised a hand. "No, that's a stupid suggestion. Forget I said it."

Bridget crossed back to the sink, grabbed a mug off the draining board and filled it with cold water. She crouched over Colin and tilted the mug slowly. Water spattered on the side of his forehead and trickled down his face. His eyes jammed tight shut, then his face crumpled like a man recovering consciousness only to discover he is in a great deal of pain.

Ruth, still on her knees, shuffled back from him, looking anxious.

"Colin," Bridget cooed softly. "Come on, Colin, wake up."

Colin's eyes flickered, then snapped open. His mouth opened too and released an inarticulate cry of pain and shock.

"Oh, fuck," muttered Ruth, and shuffled back a few more inches.

Bridget, however, stayed close, gently stroking her husband's tousled head. "It's okay," she breathed. "Take it easy, Colin. I'm here. I just want to help."

Colin's left eye, the only one they could see for the moment as the right side of his face was still pressed to the kitchen floor, glared wildly about, then focused on Bridget.

"Bridge?" he breathed.

"Yes."

"Wass…wass happ'nin?"

"It's okay," she said soothingly. "You've had a little accident, but you're okay. Can you move?"

"Dunno," he said, "I…aww, it hurts."

"What hurts?"

"All over." He closed his eyes briefly, then opened them again. "My front. Oowww."

"You need to get up, Colin. You need to push yourself up on your arms. Can you do that, if I help you?"

"I'll try," he breathed.

Using his arms for leverage, helped by both Bridget and Ruth, Colin raised himself off the floor. His naked flesh disengaged from the quarry tiles with a slight sucking sound. Bits of broken mug, like shards of multi-coloured bone, fell from his stomach and chest in a light, tinking rain. There was some blood, but not as much as Bridget had feared.

With the two women supporting him, Colin managed to clamber to his feet. He seemed dazed, completely unaware of his nakedness. He was fine until he put his weight on the foot that had stamped down on the broken mug. His scream was shrill, almost girlish, and the agonised jerk of his body caused him to lose his balance, almost dragging Bridget and Ruth back down to the floor with him.

The two women hung on grimly and, though they staggered and swayed with Colin between them, managed to remain upright.

"Sit him down here," Bridget gasped, nodding at a chair a few feet away. Puffing and panting, the two women manhandled Colin into it. He slumped there, moaning, his eyes half-closed, his skin pasty and damp with sweat. His arms hung limply by his sides; his chest, covered with trickles and smears of blood, heaved with each stertorous breath.

Bridget palmed sweat from her brow, then crossed to her husband and tugged the two sides of his dressing gown together over his groin.

"How are you doing?" she asked Ruth.

Ruth squinted at her beneath the rapidly swelling lump on her right temple. "Oh, I'm fine, apart from a splitting headache and a couple of slipped discs."

"Why don't you sit down too? I'll see to Colin."

"I will once you've pointed me in the direction of the paracetamol."

Bridget spent the next few minutes tending to her husband's wounds and clearing up the mess of broken crockery and spilled blood on the floor.

Throughout all this, Colin sat half-dazed, his head lolling from side to side, his face expressionless apart from the occasional wince as she applied TCP to his cuts and punctures. A few pottery splinters had embedded themselves so deeply into his flesh that Bridget had to pry them free with tweezers. The gash in Colin's foot was the deepest cut and had shed the greatest amount of blood. Bridget cleaned the wound, applied antiseptic cream and bandaged it tightly.

When all that was done, she and Ruth helped Colin up to bed, where he sank into the pillows with a groan. It wasn't until she was back downstairs, half-way through making a pot of tea, that Bridget started to shake. It began in her stomach and quickly spread outwards, until her hands were trembling so badly that she couldn't do a thing with them. Ruth made her sit down and finished making the tea. Then, hunched forward and clasping their mugs in both hands like exhausted climbers rescued from a freezing mountain, the two women drank together in silence—silence, that is, apart from Bridget's teeth chattering against the rim of the mug.

At last, quietly, the tea drunk and re-filled and drunk again, Ruth said, "Well, what was all *that* about?"

Bridget raised her head. Suddenly she felt as tired as Colin had been claiming to be all day. "I don't know," she said dully. "He must have been having a nightmare."

"He had his eyes open," said Ruth. She spoke calmly, reasonably, but Bridget felt a spark of anger.

"So? People often sleepwalk with their eyes open. My brother used to do it all the time when he was a kid."

Ruth looked at her for several long seconds, her right eye half-closed because of the lump that had ballooned above it. Eventually Bridget became irritated by her composed scrutiny. "What?" she snapped.

Ruth sighed. "Bridge, I don't want to fall out with you over this, but because you're my best friend, I feel as though I should say what I think."

"Which is?"

Ruth paused again, as though choosing her words carefully. "What do you think would have happened just now if I hadn't been here?"

"What do you mean?"

"What I mean is, if we hadn't banged heads together and you hadn't dropped the mugs, then Colin would have attacked you."

"Don't be ridiculous," said Bridget, but she averted her eyes.

"Bridge, you've got to face facts. You were just lucky that I was around. The way I see it, and from what you've told me, Colin is ill. Who knows what might have happened if it'd just been you and him. Think what the kids might have come downstairs to."

Bridget was silent for a moment; then, almost as silently, she began to weep.

Ruth went across and put her arms around her. "Hey, Bridge, come on, please don't cry. Look, maybe I shouldn't have said what I did. Maybe I'm just over-reacting."

Bridget clung to Ruth as if it was the only thing she could find that was real and solid. "No," she sobbed. "No, you're right. Something *is* wrong with Colin. Something happened to him yesterday. I don't know what, but it did. Something changed him and I don't know what to do about it. I'm frightened, Ruth."

"Hey, come on. Nothing to be frightened of. We'll get it sorted out, don't worry."

Bridget knew that Ruth's words were hollow, but she found them comforting nonetheless. "How?"

"Well…first, you'll have to take him back to the hospital. There must have been something they missed yesterday."

"Then what?"

"Then…I don't know. We'll just have to see what they say." She paused as if weighing up her words and then added, "But you've got to tell them everything, Bridge. You've got to tell them what happened just now. You've got to make them realise how serious things really are."

"But what if they take Colin away from us, lock him up somewhere?"

Bridget felt as though she'd been reduced to a child, voicing child-like fears, needing the reassurance of an adult.

"They won't," Ruth said soothingly. "They'll see that he's ill and they'll try to help him."

"How?"

"I don't *know* how, Bridge. I'm not a doctor, I don't know what's wrong with him."

Bridget thought again of the scrawny, hobbling figure, of the way it had become a streak of dark and terrible energy when Colin had placed his hands on the stump.

Could that…that *thing* somehow have got inside her husband? But she had only imagined that, hadn't she? Dreamed it? And what was she really talking about here, for God's sake? Demonic possession?

"What do you think he meant, Bridge?" Ruth murmured.

Bridget thought that Ruth was referring to the emaciated figure that she could see clearly in her mind's eye, and felt momentarily confused and embarrassed. Were her thoughts so transparent that Ruth could see them?

"What?" she said.

"What do you think Colin meant by what he said before he attacked us?"

"Er…" Bridget's mind felt like mush. She could remember Colin saying something, but his actual words eluded her.

"'Was it him?' he said," Ruth reminded her. "And then he accused us of conspiring against him. Who's 'him', do you think?"

Again Bridget saw the crippled figure suddenly transform into a terrifying, unstoppable force. "I don't know," she said.

8

When Bridget woke in the night she felt more than drunk, she felt pickled. After a dinner throughout which she and Ruth had tried to maintain an air of chatty normality for the sake of the children, the two women had retreated to the snug and worked their way through several bottles of wine. This was not unusual in itself; alcohol always tended to feature heavily whenever they got together. However, after what had happened in the past couple of days, Bridget had drunk tonight not in a mood of celebration, but with a grimly determined hope that the alcohol would deaden the gut-churning anxiety inside her.

It had worked only because she had eventually slipped into a drunken stupor. Thinking back now, she could recall the evening merely as a series of fragments. She remembered kissing Ellie and Miles goodnight with such an uninhibited display of affection that they had raised their eyebrows in embarrassment; remembered staggering upstairs to try to persuade Colin to eat some food, though succeeding only in getting him—through sheer drunken persistence—to sip a little water; remembered hugging Ruth fiercely and telling her she didn't know what she'd have done without her; remembered feeling sick and sleepy, and slumping sideways on the settee, and the sensation of her head and the cushion she had laid it on melting into one another like warm butter.

She supposed Ruth must have put her to bed, assumed that at some point her friend had persuaded her to haul herself off the settee and stagger upstairs. Certainly it seemed inconceivable to Bridget that she had performed the operation herself. In fact, from when she had allowed her head to sink into the cushion up until a few seconds ago, she had the impression that she had been profoundly, druggedly asleep, and so wondered now what had woken her. Perhaps it had been nothing but her still-spinning head or her increasingly sour guts, though she couldn't help thinking it was more than that.

She sat up slowly, feeling as though the contents of her body were shifting like wet cement, and put out a hand not merely for balance but to feel Colin's reassuring presence in the darkness. However, there was nothing to touch but at first air and then the warm hollow where he had lain.

Bridget's brain seemed to spasm in protest as she turned her head to confirm by sight what she already knew. The darkness, which seemed to prickle her eyes like smoke as she strained them to penetrate it, was not quite thick enough to conceal the fact that Colin was gone. Of course, he may simply have gone to the toilet, or downstairs for a drink or some food, or—having slept most of the day—had risen early, no longer tired. However, in her present state of mind, beset by anxieties which the darkness and her drunken nausea only exacerbated, Bridget found it impossible to remain calm. Ignoring her body's desire to slump back on to the mattress and curl in on itself, she pawed aside the duvet, rolled groaning from the bed, and padded out on to the landing in her bare feet.

The house was silent and dark; not a single light was glowing. Retaining just enough presence of mind not to make so much noise that she woke the children, Bridget stood at the head of the stairs and hissed, "Colin, are you there?"

When no answer came back, she descended as quickly as her drunkenness allowed. At the bottom, she registered for the first time that she was wearing not the clothes she'd passed out on the settee in, but a white nightshirt, though she might not have noticed this at all if it hadn't been for the fact that the garment was billowing around her knees. The breeze causing this was colder and stronger than it should have been indoors, and seemed to be coming from the back of the house. Ruth hurried in the direction of its source, adrenaline and alcohol creating an odd sense of heightened reality inside her, a state of mind and body that seemed to be simultaneously dreamlike and intensely vivid. She ran past the kitchen and saw that the door leading out into the back garden was yawning open. Pausing only to drag on a pair of grass-stained trainers she'd been wearing for gardening and had left by the door, she plunged out into the night.

The fresh air seemed to bypass her lungs and rush straight into her brain, where it chased the alcohol round and round like a dog pursuing a cat in a cartoon. Bridget staggered, then all at once felt horribly sick. She turned and vomited into the grass, and was initially horrified at what she produced, only to realise almost at once that it was not blood, but red wine.

She giggled, out of relief rather than humour, and wiped her mouth with the back of her hand. When she felt able, she took a few steps away from the house and called, "Colin, are you out here?"

At once her vision was snagged by the suggestion of movement from somewhere ahead of her. She craned her neck and narrowed her eyes as if that might enable her to better focus upon it. Sure enough, someone or something was moving in the corn field across the road. Bridget could make out a dark shape floundering through the thigh-high corn, which glimmered palely in the moonlight. She felt a jolt of fear at the base of her throat before she realised that the shape was moving away from, not towards, her. She hurried down the garden, past the stumps which crouched like bald-pated trolls, to the old iron gate in the stone wall. Rust scraped her fingers as she tugged the gate open.

"Colin!" she called again, but the shape did not pause or falter. It was quite a way ahead of her, almost at the boundary of the woods, in fact, but its progress was slow enough for her to feel certain that she could catch up with it if only she could keep it in sight.

She hurried across the lane and clambered over the wooden fence that bordered the cornfield, scratching her arms and legs on the brambles that entwined its weathered posts. The route that the dark shape up ahead had taken was visible as a shadowed hollow of trampled corn stalks, some of which were now struggling upright again.

A warm breeze pawed at Bridget as she struggled along, causing her white night shirt to flap around her. She supposed that to anyone looking out of a back window of the house at that moment, she would resemble some kind of phantom. The shape up ahead (too hunched to be confidently called a figure) could only now be seen as a patch of feebly moving darkness against the greater and deeper blackness of the wood. The trees, still too far away at this point to resemble anything other than a solidly black wall, seemed to rise out of the ground as she approached.

"*Colin!*" Bridget yelled again, though felt the word plucked from her mouth by the wind. "*Colin, hang on!*"

Did the shape turn briefly to look at her, or was it merely changing direction to enter the wood? If the former, it certainly didn't wait for her to catch up, or even acknowledge her. Instead it moved closer to the greater darkness beside it, and an instant later had been swallowed by the trees.

"Shit," Bridget muttered, and put on a final burst of speed. Her legs itched as if the corn stalks that scraped constantly against them contained some irritant. As she drew level with the boundary of the woods, the outermost trees that had appeared to be a solid wall of black now became separate entities, giant threads picked apart delicately by the moonlight.

Bridget approached the closest of the trees and placed her hand on its bark. She leaned forward to peer between this tree and its neighbour, but saw only a tangle of blackness beyond…a blackness whose suggestion of restless movement must have been caused by the wind. It must have been the wind, too, that was responsible for the furtive rustling she could hear; either that or the foraging of some nocturnal creature. Wishing that she had had the presence of mind to grab a torch back at the house, Bridget leaned forward and once again called, "Colin! Colin, are you there?"

A burst of rustling answered her, causing Bridget to jerk upright. After a moment the rustling subsided, and she smiled wryly, though her heart was beating fast. When she went out running, small creatures—

mostly birds, and occasionally rabbits—often darted away through the undergrowth at her approach. The commotion they made always made them seem much larger than they invariably were. Bridget knew that the sound only seemed more alarming now because it was dark, and because she couldn't see what was making it. *There's nothing to be afraid of*, she told herself silently but firmly, and, as she stepped into the woods, she tried once again not to think of the scrawny, lopsided figure that in her mind had emerged from these very trees.

Though throwing up had made her feel better, Bridget still had enough alcohol in her system for the darkness to make her progress through the wood a nightmare. The unseen, uneven terrain required a steady step and a clear head, but as Bridget had neither she spent much of her time thrashing and flailing, bumping her head, tripping over roots and tangles of undergrowth, or planting her feet only to have them skid away from her. She felt like a blind woman in a fairground funhouse, felt as if the ground was undulating, as if tree branches were writhing like snakes around her, and small bushes were uprooting and re-planting themselves in her path.

Within ten minutes she was filthy, hopelessly lost and on the verge of panic. She shouted Colin's name dozens of times, her voice growing increasingly more ragged. How the hell had she hoped to find him once he had slipped between the trees? Even hampered by his bad foot, there were numerous directions in which he could have gone. She would have been better off waiting on the wood's periphery. For all she knew, Colin might have emerged from the woods minutes after entering them, sleepwalked home none the wiser, and was at this moment tucked up back in bed, warm and snug. The thing was, she wouldn't know that until she had found her way out of here and back home, by which time it might be too late.

Immediately she admonished herself. Too late? Too late for what? What did she think Colin was going to do, for God's sake? Just because he had almost attacked her this afternoon didn't mean he was a danger to himself. Even in his presently unstable state of mind, there was no way he would jeopardise the wonderful new life they had only just started to build for themselves here.

With an effort she forced herself to stand still. For the last few minutes she had been blundering around in a blind panic, achieving nothing but the accumulation of more cuts and bruises. She stood and listened, but heard nothing except the ever-present rustling of the undergrowth. The wind, she thought. Just the wind. She could feel it, sidling past her ankles, and tried hard not to entertain the notion that the wood was alive around her, and that what she could feel was its breath on her bare skin.

She looked up, trying to pinpoint the moon, trying to work out which direction she was facing. She saw it almost immediately, but it was directly overhead, and seemed smaller than she remembered. A spiny, upreaching branch bisected it, making her think of a marsh-mallow skewered by a stick. She looked around, but the trees and bushes and the tangled blackness between them seemed to crowd just as thickly in all directions. Unlike Colin (and Ellie, who had inherited the skill from her father), Bridget had no sense of direction, no homing pigeon in her head. However, she knew that the wood wasn't that big, and so reasoned that if she walked in a straight line, she would be bound to emerge from it eventually.

Feeling more purposeful, she set off. The fresh air, her concern for Colin, and her very real, though primitive, fear of what might be lurking in the stealthily shifting darkness, were all combining to sober her up more quickly than might otherwise have been the case. Forget hangover cures containing raw eggs and Worcester sauce, she thought. The thing to do when you're pissed out of your skull is to go for a walk in a pitch-black wood in the dead of night. If that doesn't sort you out, nothing will.

Yet, despite her renewed sense of purpose, she was still unable to prevent her mind from conjuring all manner of demons in the dark. Here was a wild dog, lips curled back, fangs bared in readiness to attack, prowling through the undergrowth beside her; there, in that patch of shadow just ahead, waited a man with dead eyes and a blood-crusted cleaver; above her, scuttling along the branches of the trees, was a swarm of rats, about to drop and tear at her flesh with razor-sharp incisors...

There's nothing there, there's nothing there, there's nothing there. She repeated the phrase over and over in her mind, a silent mantra that attempted, but didn't quite manage, to stifle the unwanted contrivances of her imagination. It did, however, succeed in keeping the worst of her panic at bay. Scared though Bridget was, she kept walking, forcing herself to move slowly and steadily, in what she hoped was a straight line.

She had been going for perhaps ten minutes when a new sound made her halt. Adrenaline and exertion had quickened her heart-rate, and she placed a hand on her chest, trying to slow her rapid breathing. When she had managed to do so, she moved her head from side to side like a radar, listening again. Yes, there it was, the sound she hadn't been sure she had actually heard or simply imagined—a faint but unmistakable scraping.

An image rose instantly to her mind: someone hunched over a spade, digging. The sound was coming from somewhere over to her left. Bridget hesitated, wondering whether she should move towards it or carry on ahead. She peered in the direction she'd been walking, saw only the usual black stripes of trees connected by twisted, equally black masses of foliage. Though she felt reluctant to deviate from her route, if only because she'd been determined to let nothing distract her, she told herself that she'd be cutting off her nose to spite her face if she ignored the sound. And it wasn't as if her plan was foolproof. How did she know that she wasn't about to encounter some obstacle she couldn't get round or over? How could she be sure she was even moving in a straight line? For all she knew, she may have been wandering round in circles for the last ten minutes.

Her mind made up, she began to move to her left. A part of her wanted to call out Colin's name. She even imagined hearing his bewildered answering cry: "Bridge? Is that you?" The greater part of her, however, advised caution. What if it wasn't Colin making the scraping sounds? There was only one reason she could think of for someone to be digging a hole in the woods in the dead of night. But then again, if it *was* Colin, what was *he* digging a hole for? She tried to visualise the black shape she had followed through the corn field, tried to remember whether it could possibly have been carrying a spade. All she could recall was how slowly the figure had been moving, which she supposed could have been because it was encumbered not only by an injured foot, but also by some awkward or heavy implement.

As she drew closer, she realised that the scraping sound was now accompanied by an occasional hacking, which she imagined was the spade's blade being thrust into the stony, weedy earth. She was moving with extreme caution now, probing the ground at each step with the toes of an outstretched foot before planting her weight. Even so, the dry detritus of earth and stone and leaf and twig was not crushed nor displaced silently; the faint snap and crackle of each of her footsteps made her grit her teeth so tightly that her jaws ached.

Eventually she reached the point at which she felt sure she was almost on top of the sound, yet try as she might, she still could not see who or what was making it. She could only suppose that the lattice of trees within its thick soup of darkness was conspiring to distort the acoustics of the place, and thus mislead her senses. She took another hesitant, probing step, clenching her jaw once again as if she could contain the minute sounds of destruction beneath her feet within the tautness of her own body. Her eyes throbbed from the glare she was subjecting the darkness to. Still unable to see anything, she raised her leg to take another step forward—and the sound of digging abruptly stopped.

Bridget froze, instantly certain that the reason the digger had ceased was because she had somehow given herself away. Maybe she was close enough to him for the tiny snap of a twig to have finally reached his ears; maybe he could see the glimmer of her white night shirt through the trees. She imagined him rising slowly, turning his head in her direction. In her mind he was huge, ape-like, long-armed, shaggy-haired. He stood in silhouette, back-lit by tree-filtered moonlight, wreathed in mist.

She saw herself from his point of view—weak and skinny, poised like a deer sensing a predator. But unlike a deer, she was blind whereas he had night-vision, she was slow and stumbling whereas he was fleet of foot. She was clothed in white—white like a lamb, like a lamb to the slaughter—whereas he was almost certainly swathed in black. Perhaps he was creeping towards her even now, a wolf in the darkness, all teeth and claws and hunger.

She retracted the foot she had extended forward and slowly began to back away. After six or eight steps, she turned to forge her way through the unseen obstacles of bushes and trees, arms outstretched, hands waving in front of her. Because the darkness prevented her from moving as quickly as she would have liked, the latest surge of adrenaline in her system once again overspilled swiftly into panic. As before, Bridget was soon stumbling and slithering, adding yet more cuts and bruises to those she had already collected, her breath lurching and rasping out of her in a series of gasps and whimpers.

Inevitably, she fell. Her foot slipped on a patch of wetness and her forward momentum sent her belly-flopping to the ground. Her breath *oofed* out of her and both her elbows and her left knee collided painfully with the earth. It had been a day of falling—first Colin, now her. It was like being reduced to childhood again, when falling over was an everyday occurrence. Of course, back then bones were made of rubber—a few tears, a few consoling words, and the shock and pain were forgotten. Things were different now, though. Despite her better than average level of fitness, a crack on the bone meant stiffness and bruising, a few days of wincing, careful movement.

For maybe half a minute Bridget could only lie there, incapacitated by her struggling lungs. Sparks danced in front of her eyes as she toiled to gulp in air. And yet, despite her fear and discomfort, the ground she was spread-eagled upon was almost comforting in a way. She wanted to melt into it, wanted it to absorb her, to conceal her until daylight made the world safe again. She listened, but could hear nothing except the inner struggles of her own body. Perhaps she had been mistaken, perhaps the digging had not stopped because the digger had sensed her proximity, perhaps she was not being pursued at all. She began to feel foolish, despite the fact that no one except herself need ever know of this. She hugged the ground for a few more seconds until her lungs had recovered and she was able to breathe in the mulchy verdancy with relative ease, then she pushed herself gingerly to her feet.

As expected, her joints throbbed where she had whacked them on the ground. She bent them experimentally, and was rewarded with a glassy pain that was sharp but manageable. She wondered how long she had been blundering around in here. It seemed like hours. If she didn't get back before everyone got up, she wondered whether they'd worry or whether they'd just assume she'd gone out for an early run. What if neither she nor Colin were there? Would it set the alarm bells ringing in Ruth's head, or would she just think that Bridget had taken Colin to the hospital early to avoid any awkward questions from the kids?

Bridget had no idea in which direction she should go, so she simply started walking. It was pot luck now. Her only reasoning was that she couldn't see a way out from where she was, so she had to go somewhere else. She moved steadily and carefully, neither hurrying nor moving with her earlier caution. After ten or fifteen minutes she fell into a rhythm, every step the same, her probing hands performing a pattern of movements so consistent they seemed almost ritualistic. She pushed aside springy tree branches and facefuls of leaves as if warding off evil spirits. She was so enclosed within her own thoughts that when her left hand skimmed across rough tree bark and touched human hair she didn't register it at first.

It was only when the owner of the hair began to move that she snapped from her trance. She jumped back with a cry, her eyes widening to take in the man-shaped block of darkness sliding across the path in front of her. All at once she was aware of breathing other than her own. The hoarse respiration of the figure sounded eager, triumphant. She saw the oily glint of its eyeballs in the almost-darkness, but could not make out any of its other features. She clenched her fists to defend herself, was about to scream at the figure to keep away from her, when a voice said, "Bridge?"

Because it was so unexpected, and because it was too dark to see the figure's mouth move, Bridget had the momentary, unearthly notion that the voice was disembodied, that her own name, softly-spoken, had drifted down from the trees. She even glanced upwards before realisation made her jerk her head back down to the figure standing in front of her.

"Colin?" she said in a kind of wonder.

The figure moved its head in what she supposed must be a nod. "What are you doing here?" he asked softly.

He sounded so calm, so reasonable, so concerned, that she was unable to suppress a sob, which immediately made her feel as though she had unplugged herself. What meagre energy she had been retaining to hold heart and soul together now rushed out of her, and she fell forward, her legs buckling, into Colin's arms. All the aches and pains, all the cuts and scratches she had sustained since entering the wood an eternity ago, leapt instantly into singing, stinging life. She felt feverish and faint, as though her blood was boiling through her veins and burning her up. She was Dorian Grey, suffering a lifetime's postponed agonies in a single tumultuous moment.

"What is it?" Colin said. "What's the matter, Bridge?"

Bridget sagged against him. His bandaged hands were the only things stopping her from crumpling to the ground. "I was...so scared," she gasped between sobs.

Colin gathered her to him, enclosed her in a hug. "It's okay," he said softly. "There's nothing to be scared of."

He seemed back to his normal self again, back to the Colin she had known before they had all been consumed by the madness of the past two days. That in itself was disorientating. She stared at his face in the darkness, but could see only a vague suggestion of his features. She touched his cheek with a trembling hand as if afraid he was an imposter, that she was somehow being duped.

"Can we sit down a minute?" she said.

"Er…yes, okay."

He lowered her carefully to the ground, then sat cross-legged beside her. Bridget allowed her head to slump forward, took long, deep breaths until a little of the fog had cleared from her mind. Finally she raised her head and said, "What the hell's going on, Colin?"

"What do you mean?"

"*What do I mean?* How can you even ask that?" She waved her hand wildly. "All this, for a start. What the hell are we both doing out in the woods in the dead of night?"

He was silent for a moment, then he said, "What are *you* doing out here?"

"I followed you," she said. She told him how she had woken up to find herself alone, and everything that had happened since. When she had finished there was a silence. She wished she could see the expression on his face. "Well?"

"Well what?"

"What's your story?"

She saw him shrug, heard him sigh. In a low voice he said, "I don't know why I'm here. The last two days have been…" He paused, struggling for words, and eventually said, "It's like I've been sleepwalking, trying to wake up."

"You seem all right now," said Bridget.

"I banged my head on a branch or something. It must have knocked some sense in to me. I woke up, flat on my back, with my foot hurting like hell. I didn't know what was going on or where I was. I wandered round for a bit, and then by chance I saw a glimmer of something white through the trees. I followed it, but it kept moving away from me. Turns out it was you."

"So when you woke up, you had no idea where you were?" Bridget said.

"I worked out pretty quickly that I must have been up in the wood behind the house, but I have no recollection of how I got here, no."

"And that doesn't frighten you?"

"Of course it frightens me."

"You don't *seem* very frightened."

Colin gave a mirthless bark of laughter. "You know me, Bridge. I'm not very good at showing my emotions. I keep things bottled up." Another pause, then he said, "I'm just trying to deal with my problems as they come up. One at a time."

"What *do* you remember?" she asked. "Since yesterday, I mean."

"I remember my hands burning. I remember being in hospital. I remember being very tired. I remember falling and banging my head. I remember the pain of sharp things sticking in me, remember the bottom of my foot feeling like it had been cut open. I know some of what I can remember is real because the bits of me I remember hurting still hurt. But…but the whole thing is like a nightmare, like I was drugged and watching it all from a long way away. Some bits are just blank."

"Do you remember attacking me?" Bridget asked.

"Attacking you? God, no. Did I attack you? I didn't hurt you, did I?"

"No, that's when you fell and hurt yourself."

"Oh, Jesus. I don't remember any of that." He raised his hand again and rubbed the top of his head as if trying to massage his memory back into life.

"How do you feel now?"

"Confused, but…but like I've woken up after a long sleep." She saw his head move, his eyeballs glint as he looked at her. "I feel a lot better for finding you."

"How do your hands feel?"

"They're aching. Tingling. What did I do to them?"

"You tell me."

He was silent for a moment, then she saw him shake his head. "I don't remember."

"Do you remember touching the stump nearest the house in the back garden?"

She wished she could see the expression on his face before he answered. "The stump? No."

"Do you remember what you came up here for?"

He sighed. "Again, no. Sorry, Bridge, I'm not being very helpful, am I?"

"No, you're not." She touched his face gently, like a blind woman trying to form a mental picture of what someone looked like. "Do you remember digging?"

Was it her imagination or did he stiffen slightly? "Digging? What do you mean?"

"I mean digging. Digging with a spade."

He laughed hollowly. "Why would I be doing that?"

"I don't know. I heard someone digging, that's all."

"Well, it wasn't me."

"How do you know?"

"What?" he said, a little sharply as if he thought she was trying to catch him out.

"How do you know you weren't doing it in your sleep? Sleep-digging."

"It seems a bit far-fetched."

"But it's possible, isn't it? If you can walk in your sleep, you can dig in your sleep, can't you?"

"I don't know. Digging requires…effort. Strength."

"So does walking when you've got a bad foot. Besides, if it wasn't you digging, then it means there's someone else in the wood."

"Maybe you imagined it."

"Give me credit, Colin."

"All right," Colin said, and she saw him raise his hands in a placatory gesture. "Maybe you didn't imagine it, but maybe you were mistaken. Maybe it wasn't digging you heard."

"What then?"

"I don't know. An animal perhaps. An animal burrowing."

"I don't think so."

"Well, I don't know," he said, suddenly exasperated. "Does it matter?"

"It seemed a bit suspicious, that's all."

"Well, suspicious or not, there's not much we can do about it now, is there?"

"No, I suppose not."

"I think we should just concentrate on getting ourselves home. Are you strong enough to stand?"

He held out a hand and she grasped it. "Yes, I think so."

"Then let's get out of here," he said.

9

"Listen, are you sure you'll be all right?"

Bridget squeezed Ruth's hands to signal that her friend could relax her grip, but Ruth seemed reluctant to let go.

"Of course I will," Bridget said. "I've told you, Colin's a lot better this morning. We've had a long talk."

"But you will get him checked over, won't you?"

Bridget laughed. "He's not a dog."

"It's not a joking matter, Bridge. After what happened yester—"

"It won't happen again," Bridget interrupted firmly.

"But how can you say that, when you don't really know what was wrong with him in the first place?"

"I've told you, he had some sort of fever, which has broken now. He was delirious. He can't even remember half of what happened."

"But if a fever is all it was, why didn't they detect it at the hospital?"

Bridget shrugged, looking evasive, and at last slid her hands free from Ruth's grip. "Maybe it hadn't properly shown itself back then."

"That's bullshit, Bridge, and you know it. Look, I'm sorry to go on, but it's only because I care about you. I don't want to see you getting hurt."

"I'm not *going* to get hurt," Bridget said, laughing.

"But you look so tired, so worn down by it all."

"Most of it's hangover. As for the rest, well, it's been a tough couple of days, but I'll get over it. I've got plenty of time to chill out if I want to; I'm a lady of leisure now, remember—at least until I start looking for a new job once the kids have gone back to school."

Bridget wondered what Ruth would say if she told her the real reason she looked so tired. Hand in hand, she and Colin had managed to find their way out of the wood and back home just as dawn was breaking. Bridget had no idea how much time had elapsed between waking up to find herself alone in the dark and crawling beneath the rumpled duvet again in a room steeped in soft tangerine light, but she guessed it must have been two or three hours, maybe longer. After soaking in a hot bath and dumping her night shirt in the laundry basket, she had fallen into an exhausted sleep, spooned by Colin's naked body, his right hand gently cupping her left breast.

Ruth looked as though she had more to say on the subject, but just then Colin came out of the house, accompanied by Ellie and Miles. Colin was limping and his hands were still bandaged, but he looked better this morning, albeit tired. He had apologised to Ruth over breakfast, despite having no memory of exactly what he had done the previous day, and although she had accepted his apology and told him that what had happened was not his fault, the atmosphere had remained frosty between them.

"You just off?" Colin said now. Bridget hoped that Ruth was as aware as she was of how eager Colin was to make up for his behaviour yesterday.

"Yes," Ruth said with an iciness that dismayed and annoyed Bridget.

"Well, goodbye. Have a safe journey home. Hopefully we'll see you again soon."

The perfunctory hugs that the children gave to Ruth made Bridget remember a time when they were little and had adored Ruth to such an extent that they had hated to see her go. At five, Ellie had gone through a stage of clinging to Ruth's leg whenever Ruth was about to leave the house after one of her visits, of wailing in utter despair and pleading with her to stay.

In some ways that seemed like a lifetime ago now, yet in others like only yesterday. As Bridget watched Ellie give Ruth a dutiful kiss on the cheek, she felt a sense not exactly of panic, but of the grim magnitude of time passing, of life slipping away almost unnoticed. It made her want to gather around her all that was precious, to cling tightly to it, protect it from whatever the future might hold. Knowing that she couldn't, that nothing she did would halt the rush towards the inevitable, made her feel suddenly and unutterably sad. Just as Ruth was about to get into her car, Bridget stepped forward and hugged her again, hugged her as if it was the last time she would ever do so, as if she were trying to retain some essence of her friend merely by the fierceness of her grip.

Ruth seemed instinctively to understand and hugged Bridget back with equal fervour. "You look after yourself," she said.

"I will."

"And if you need to talk about anything, anything at all, you ring me, okay? If I'm not at home I'll be on my mobile."

The four of them waved at Ruth's car until it disappeared from view, then, scowling at the stumps jutting from the front lawn, Colin said, "Right, I'm going to get on to someone about getting rid of those bloody things. After that I might do a bit of writing, if that's okay with you, Bridge."

"That's fine," Bridget said. "I'm delighted that you feel up to it."

"Are you better now, Dad?" Ellie asked cautiously.

"Much," said Colin.

"What was wrong with you, Dad?" asked Miles, looking at his father as if he expected him to have a relapse at any moment.

"I think maybe I was poisoned by something leaking from one of these disgusting things."

"Really?" said Ellie, voicing Bridget's own surprise.

"Really. Which is why I don't want either of you to go near them, okay?"

"Okay, Dad," Ellie and Miles chorused dutifully.

Bridget spent the rest of the morning in an odd mood. Most of the time that Ruth had been staying with them, Bridget had wished that she and Colin could be left alone to talk things through. Now that Ruth had gone, however, Bridget found that she was missing her far more than she normally did. She chipped away at the hideous tiles in the bathroom, readying the walls for the plasterer who was coming next Monday, with a sense of nervous apprehension. She felt as if she were waiting for a piece of news that was more likely to be bad than good. What made it worse was the fact that she couldn't pinpoint the cause of it. She supposed it was a delayed reaction to the emotional demands of the past couple of days, a kind of hangover from the cocktail of fear and anxiety that her system had been forced to cope with. Or maybe it was simply that many of the strange events that had caused her so much stress remained unexplained. She tried to tell herself to put it all out of her head, to simply rejoice in the fact that Colin was seemingly back to normal, and that therefore things were looking up again, but she couldn't shake the notion that there was a cloud hanging over her.

She worked grimly until lunchtime, whereupon she decided to make the four of them a plate of sandwiches, which she envisaged them eating together, out in the garden. She trudged downstairs, wincing at the ache in her knee, hoping that the company of her family coupled with the beneficial effects of the summer sunshine would help to eradicate her gloom. She was about to enter the kitchen when the telephone rang. It was Claire Woodall, who wondered whether Bridget wanted to pop round for coffee that afternoon. Bridget's first response was to say that she had too much work to do on the house, then she thought, *What the hell*, and was about to say yes when inspiration struck her.

"I've got a better idea. Why don't you all come round for a barbecue later? Say around five o'clock? It'd give the kids a chance to meet each other."

"That would be lovely!" Claire exclaimed. "But are you sure? You must have oodles to do."

"I think we all deserve a break," said Bridget. "And it would be something to look forward to."

She went into the kitchen a few minutes later, feeling infinitely more cheerful. What better way to get things back on an even keel than a warm, sunny evening with good company, good food, and a few bottles of wine?

I must be turning into an alkie, she thought, recalling how plastered she had been last night. She took the bread out of the bread bin, thinking that if she wanted to find work as a fitness instructor down here she was going to have to get herself back into shape. She was reaching an age where the level of fitness she'd been used to for the past twenty years was becoming harder to maintain. She put the unsliced granary loaf down on the bread board and crossed to the knife block, reaching out automatically for the bread knife.

Then she stopped in surprise. The knife block was empty.

It was a professional chef's knife block, which normally contained twelve knives, each of which had a different purpose. Bridget had bought it a couple of years ago when she'd gone through her foody phase, inspired by *Masterchef* and Jamie Oliver. For a while she had produced gourmet meals for the family on a regular basis, her enthusiasm only waning after a remark made by Ruth one weekend when Bridget was visiting her in Chester. The two of them were in the steam room of a Turkish bath, having decided to pamper themselves before going out to dinner that evening. They had been sitting side by side, sweaty and naked, when Ruth—who had always been slightly intimidated by Bridget's toned physique—had exclaimed, "I don't believe it! You've got love handles!"

"I have not," Bridget had said, looking down at herself.

"Yes, you have—look." And Ruth had reached out and pinched an inch or so of flesh just above Bridget's right hip.

"Shit," Bridget had said. "You're right. They'll have to go."

"Oh no, please don't get rid of them," Ruth had said. "I like them. They make you *normal*."

It was largely thanks to that remark that Bridget had started doing extra work-outs at the gym, which in turn had led to her working out with Jason. She wondered what would have happened if Ruth had kept her mouth shut. The affair had been a mistake, yes, and had almost done irreparable damage to her marriage, and yet in some ways its long-term effects had been undoubtedly beneficial. Her fling with Jason had shaken Colin out of the complacent, self-pitying torpor that had enveloped him since he had been dumped by his previous publisher. Without that kick up the backside he might never have written the novel that was currently creating such a buzz, which in turn meant that they might never have been able to afford this place.

Bridget was not naive enough to think that she and Colin could negate whatever problems might still exist between them simply by the implementation of physical distance, which led to her wondering, not for the first time, whether what they frequently and optimistically referred to as their 'fresh, new start' was, in fact, simply a way of avoiding admitting that they had run away. However many times she told herself that they had had nothing to run away *from*, in her heart of hearts she remained unconvinced. It was true that few of their friends or neighbours had known of Bridget's affair and its subsequent fall-out (in fact, she and Jason had been so discreet that Bridget even believed that the vast majority of her work colleagues had had no inkling of what was going on). It was also true that as soon as Colin had found out about the affair, Jason had performed an impressive vanishing act by sending a letter of resignation in to work, effective immediately, and making no subsequent attempt to contact Bridget.

At the time Bridget had been rather non-plussed to think that she had meant so little to him, though in hindsight she was glad that he had quit the scene as quickly and as thoroughly as he had. She liked to imagine he had done so at least partly for her benefit, though realistically she doubted that was the case. For him, the whole thing had evidently been nothing but a bit of fun, which, as soon as it had started getting even the teeniest bit complicated, he had walked away from.

It was funny really, she supposed, to think of Jason fleeing in panic, to think of this fitter, younger, stronger man being so afraid of a confrontation with Colin that he hadn't even bothered to say goodbye. Perhaps his intentions *had* been noble, perhaps he hadn't wanted to be forced into a position where he would have had to have physically humiliated Colin. That would have been awful, especially if it had taken place in front of her work colleagues, or her neighbours, or even worse, in front of Ellie and Miles.

She closed her eyes briefly, and shuddered, and almost jumped out of her skin when a voice said, "What are you doing, Mum?"

Bridget swung round. Miles was watching her quizzically from the doorway. She suddenly realised how odd she must have looked, one hand still stretched towards the empty knife block, a vacant expression on her face. Struggling to recover her composure, she said briskly, "I was going to make us some sandwiches, but as you can see, I've got nothing to cut the bread with. Have you any idea where my knives have gone, Miles?"

Miles raised his eyebrows in a facial shrug. "No idea. Maybe they're in the dishwasher."

"What, *all* of them? Some of these knives I've never even used."

"Well, I don't know. Don't blame me. I haven't had them."

"I'm not blaming you, it's just…frustrating, that's all." Bridget had been about to say 'weird', but she didn't want Miles to think there was anything sinister in the knives' disappearance.

"See if you can find something to cut that bread with," she said, "but don't try doing it yourself until I get back. I just want to check something."

Leaving Miles looking through drawers, Bridget went out of the kitchen and into the back garden. There was a rickety shed where she and Colin had been storing their gardening tools, tucked between the left-hand fence and a gnarled old pear tree. The shed was full of packets of ancient seeds and boxes of rusty nails, not to mention an impressive menagerie of over-sized bugs. Bridget raised her face briefly to the sun as she walked across to it before stepping into the tree's twisted shadow. She tugged on the shed's ill-fitting wooden door, keeping her sandalled feet away from the line of rust-red ants scurrying hither and thither across the threshold. Dust sifted down from the ceiling as she stepped inside. As well as the creaking of the warped floor, she fancied she could hear the sound of many-legged activity.

It took only a single turn of the head to confirm what she had been dreading. She felt her chest tighten, felt her mind attempt to offer excuses, explanations. Just because the spade was gone didn't mean that Colin had taken it into the wood last night. And even if he *had* been digging, it didn't mean that he had deliberately lied to her.

She marched back into the house. Miles greeted her by holding up a small hacksaw. "This was on top of the toolbox in the corner cupboard," he said.

"Well done, Miles," said Bridget, trying not to show the concern she was feeling. "I'll just go up and ask your dad what he wants in his sandwiches."

She ascended the stairs to the top of the house and knocked on the door of the attic room. The tapping of Colin's keyboard stopped, but before he could say anything, she pushed the door open.

Colin was sitting at his desk, surrounded by unpacked boxes of books. He had opened the single skylight in the sloping ceiling, but the band of sunlight that illuminated every frayed fibre of the balding carpet and transformed at least a portion of the yellowing wallpaper to a warm, buttery gold could not conceal the fact that the room was anything but gloomy. The light from the anglepoise lamp craning over Colin's desk gave his face a stark, shadow-etched simplicity as he turned to face her. When he smiled, shadows made his mouth look as though it was caving in. "Hi," he said.

All at once Bridget felt reluctant to confront him with the disappearance of the knives. After the last few days she craved a return to normality, and seeing him sitting here working at his desk, watching him turn with relaxed amiability towards her, was as close as it was going to get. She didn't want to spoil that by putting him on the defensive, creating an atmosphere of distrust between them. If she accused him of taking the knives, she felt sure he would deny it, and then she would be left wondering whether he was lying, whether he honestly believed he was telling the truth, or whether she had been mistaken.

But if Colin hadn't taken the knives, even if unwittingly, then who had? One of the children? Ruth? Or was it conceivable that someone else had got into the house, taken her knives and nothing else, and then left as silently as they had come?

"How are things going?" she asked.

"Oh, fine. I'm just trying to ease myself back into it. It'll probably be a week or so before I'm up to speed again."

She looked around as though seeing the space for the first time. "Are you happy with your room?"

"I will be when it's done. I can't wait to get some shelves up and unpack some of these books."

"We'll have to strip this wallpaper off first and decorate. We might even have to get the plasterer in."

"I'll do some stripping tonight," said Colin. "Perhaps you can help me."

"Now there's an offer," Bridget said. "The thing is, I've invited the Woodalls and their kids round for a barbecue at five. I hope that's okay."

Colin stretched. He looked relaxed enough to doze off in his chair. "No, that's fine. It'll be fun. I'm sure stripping can wait until tomorrow."

There was a pause. Bridget wondered how best to bring up the subject of the knives, but then found herself asking, "How's your foot?"

"A bit sore. Not too bad if I keep the weight off it. How about you?"

"Oh, I'm okay. A few bumps and bruises, but I'll survive." In fact, both of Bridget's elbows and her right knee were stiff and painful. She had scratches on her arms and legs that made her look as if she had been wrestling with a wild cat.

A shadow darted across the band of sunlight on the carpet. Bridget looked up in time to glimpse the tail feathers of a passing bird. "I came to see what you'd like in your sandwiches," she said.

Colin waved a hand airily. "I don't mind. Cheese, tuna, turkey...whatever."

"Okay." There was a moment when she thought she was going to retreat without saying anything more, then she said casually, "The only thing is, I can't find the bread knife. You haven't seen it, have you?"

If Colin had something to hide, he concealed it well. Shrugging, he said, "Dishwasher, maybe? Or perhaps Ruth put it away somewhere."

Bridget wondered whether she ought to take this opportunity to tell him that *all* the knives were missing, but decided it would make her suspicion too obvious. Instead she nodded. "Yeah, you're probably right. Sandwiches in ten minutes, okay?"

"Okay."

10

"I really like these, Mum," Ellie said, holding a pair of hipsters and a pink, skinny-fit t-shirt up against herself. "Could I have an advance on my allowance so that I can get them now? They might be gone by next week."

Bridget pursed her lips. "Are you sure about that top? There's not much of it, is there?"

"Mu-um!" Ellie rolled her eyes. "It's how everyone's wearing them these days."

"I know, but...well, it's a bit revealing."

"You can only see my stomach. And anyway, I'll need some shorter tops to show off my piercing."

"*Your what?*"

Ellie winced and looked around, but the muzak, the clatter of trolleys and the general hubbub of conversation had instantly dampened and absorbed the shrillness of her mother's exclamation.

"I'm going to get my belly button pierced," she said firmly, and then quickly added, "When I'm old enough." She looked at Bridget with an expression that fell somewhere between rebel-without-a-cause and little-girl-pleading-for-sweeties.

Bridget sighed. Her instinct was to say *no way*, but not for the first time she had the odd sensation that her own mother was trying to speak through her, that she was feeling compelled to trot out all the tried and trusted phrases that she herself had hated as a teenager: *What-do-you-look-like, You-can't-go-out-looking-like-that, You'll-give-people-the-wrong-idea.* She remembered how, when she was sixteen, her mother's two-fold mission in life was, a) to stop her having a good time, and b) to show her up in front of her friends.

Of course, it all looked a lot different from the other side of the fence. Ellie wouldn't understand a parent's protective urges until she herself had children, couldn't be expected to fathom that their killjoy tactics were in fact motivated by nothing more than an overwhelming, soul-wrenching love. Bridget wondered how aware Ellie already was of her sexuality, whether she had noticed how many men—many of whom were old enough to be her father—turned their hungry, lustful eyes towards her. Were kids really more aware, less innocent, than they had been even twenty years ago? Certainly Bridget remembered her own sexual awakening as a time of confused naiveté, concealed beneath a cloak of haughty bravado. Had she been aware of the lupine stares of older men when she had been sixteen? Not that she could remember. Bridget's one consolation was that the generation gap was no longer as wide as it once was, and that she could talk to Ellie about things that her own mother would never have dreamed of discussing with her.

All of this flashed through her mind in little more than the length of time it took Bridget to sigh. She reached out and tenderly cupped Ellie's cheek in her right hand. "You're growing up so fast," she said wistfully. "It frightens me sometimes."

Ellie looked almost offended. "Why does it frighten you?"

"Because you'll always be my little girl. Because it seems like only yesterday when you were crying in the night to be fed, crawling around in nappies, starting school…"

"I feel like I've been at school for *ever*," Ellie said.

Bridget smiled. "Your perception of time changes as you get older. You start thinking about something—some good time you had, some place you once went to—and then suddenly you think, 'God, that was twenty years ago', and you wonder where all the time has gone."

It was clear from Ellie's expression that she only had a vague inkling of what her mother was talking about. "Mum, you're not *that* ancient."

"Well, thanks, I'll take that as a compliment," Bridget said. "Come on, I'll buy those clothes for you for everything you've done around the house this past week. You've worked really hard. You deserve it."

"Aw, thanks, Mum," Ellie said, "you're the best." She put the clothes in the trolley, on top of all the stuff they'd got for the barbecue, then gave Bridget a sidelong glance. "And what about my piercing?"

"We'll cross that bridge when we come to it."

The supermarket trip with Ellie had succeeded in lifting the oppressive fug that had settled on Bridget like a hangover of the previous day's events, and long before they got back to the house she was brimming with renewed energy and optimism. Almost immediately after leaving behind the endless grey car parks and vast, drab warehouses that comprised the retail estate, the landscape became a sun-drenched green blaze of trees and hedges and fields.

"Little darling," Bridget bawled suddenly out of the open window of the car, "it's been a long, cold, lonely winter."

"Mum!" Ellie looked stricken with embarrassment, though they hadn't seen another vehicle on the road for several minutes. "What are you doing?"

Bridget broke off from yelling, "Here comes the sun, dutton-doo-doo," to grin at her daughter. "I'm singing."

"I can see that," Ellie said scathingly, "but why?"

"Because I'm happy," Bridget said. "Look around you, El. We're surrounded by all this beautiful countryside. We've got a fantastic house, we're healthy, we've got money in the bank, there's not a cloud on the horizon."

"What about Dad?" Ellie said.

Bridget's smile faded just a touch. "What do you mean?"

"Well, in case you've forgotten, we had to rush him to hospital the other day."

Bridget flapped a hand dismissively. "Aw, he's fine now. The doctors couldn't find anything wrong with him. And he seems a lot better, doesn't he?"

Ellie shrugged. "I guess."

"Don't worry," Bridget said confidently. "I promise you, El, from now on, things are going to get nothing but better for us."

11

"The kids are getting on well, aren't they?"

Claire, in her wide-brimmed straw hat, large sunglasses and flowery shorts looked every inch the colonial Englishwoman. She was sitting in her deckchair, sipping a Pimms, occasionally using her straw to swirl around the chunks of ice and pieces of chopped fruit in her glass.

"Yes they are," said Bridget, glancing down to the bottom of the garden where the four of them were playing badminton amidst much giggling and banter. "Your two are lovely. I'm sure they'll all be great friends."

"Why, thank you," said Claire. "Will and Fliss were really excited when they found out that you were moving in. I can't tell you how big a favour you've done us by coming here. Usually by this stage of the summer holidays our two are so bored they're climbing the walls."

"And so are we," said Shaun from over by the barbecue, one hand curled around a cold bottle of Beck's, the other wafting at smoke. "Climbing the walls, I mean."

"I think he means the kids would be driving us mad," said Claire, *sotto voce*, to Bridget. "But what does he know? He's usually at work."

"Actually that was one of our main reservations about coming here," said Bridget. "The isolation. Not for us so much—we love the peace and quiet, and we've always got the car if we find ourselves craving a bit of hustle and bustle—but the kids are used to having friends close by, everything on their doorstep. We did wonder how selfish we were being in buying this place."

"Oh, it's not really as bad as all that. If the truth be told, our two love it here. There are all sorts of places to explore, and I'm quite happy to act as a taxi service if they want to venture further afield. And we find that if you go away for a couple of weeks in the middle of the summer holidays then it doesn't leave a lot of time either side for boredom to set in."

"Have you been away this year?" asked Bridget.

"Yes, we spent a couple of weeks in Brittany." Claire held out her arm to display her tan and said mock-offendedly, "Can't you tell?"

Bridget felt at ease. Colin had taken over barbecue duties and was now standing over the sizzling meat with Shaun, drinking beer and chatting happily away; the children, after an initial bout of shyness, were getting along as if they'd known one another all their lives; and she herself was finding that the more time she spent in Claire's company the more she liked her.

Much later, Bridget would remember this afternoon as the last occasion on which she felt truly happy. She would cling to the memory like driftwood, and the bright, optimistic innocence of it would both comfort her and cause bitter, regretful, disbelieving tears to come tearing, wrenching out of her.

The food—chicken marinaded in coconut and lime, six types of sausage, salad, coleslaw and fresh baguettes—was delicious, and devoured with gusto. Afterwards, when the leftovers had been scraped into the empty salad bowl and the plates had been stacked in readiness for the dishwasher, Miles suggested taking up the badminton racquets again. Apart from Will (who at eleven was two years younger than Miles and evidently enjoying the kudos of having such a mature, grown-up friend), everyone groaned.

"I'm too full," moaned Ellie.

"Me too," said Fliss.

"How can you even *think* of running around after such a huge meal?" said Bridget.

Miles shrugged, as if such feats were commonplace to him. "Do you like football, Will?"

Will nodded eagerly.

"Come on then."

The two boys trudged down to the shed. Miles pulled the door open, went inside, and emerged a moment later with a plastic football.

"Can I show Fliss my cds, Mum?" Ellie asked as the two boys began to kick the ball back and forth with more enthusiasm than skill at the bottom of the garden.

"Course you can, sweetheart. But don't play them too loud. We don't want our peace shattered by Limp Bizkit."

Ellie gave her mother a look of scathing pity, and the two girls trooped into the house.

With the kids occupied, the four adults re-filled their wine glasses and sank back in their deckchairs, the conversation, punctuated by the occasional exclamation mark of laughter, ebbing and flowing between them. After a while, her belly warmed by food, her head fuddled by alcohol and the warmth of the evening sun and last night's lack of sleep, Bridget felt her eyelids beginning to droop.

"Are we boring you?" Claire said.

Bridget snapped awake. "Sorry, I…no, no, of course not. I'm just very tired. I hardly slept last night."

"Leave the poor girl alone, Claire," said Shaun, his face threatening to turn as red as the wine he was drinking. "Let her snooze if she wants to."

Bridget attempted to pull herself more upright in her chair. "I'm sorry, it's very rude of me."

Claire reached across and touched Bridget's arm, her expression indicating that she hadn't meant her previous comment to be taken as a slight. "Of course it isn't. I always think it's a compliment if the person you're with feels relaxed enough in your company to nod off."

That was when it happened. Bridget was opening her mouth to reply to Claire when Colin leaped out of his deckchair and screamed, *"What do you think you're doing? Get your fucking hands off that!"*

For an instant every living thing in the immediate vicinity seemed shocked into immobility. Birds stopped singing; bees ceased buzzing; even the air seemed suddenly, unnaturally still. Bridget, Claire and Shaun gaped at Colin, Bridget appalled at the expression on her husband's face. Colin did not look merely angry, he looked apoplectic. His face was crimson, his teeth bared in an almost feral snarl, his eyes bulging madly from their sockets. His body was rigid as if poised to spring, his arms like ramrods by his sides, his hands balled into fists. Bridget took all of this in in an instant, and then—her neck muscles crackling as if they had been locked into position for hours—she turned her head to focus on the object of his fury.

Miles and Will were as motionless as the adults. Their horrified expressions reminded Bridget of reaction shots in a movie. They couldn't have looked more stunned if Colin had transformed into a werewolf in front of them. Bridget saw that Will, slight for his age and blonder than either of his parents, was standing beside the stump at the bottom of the garden—was standing, in fact, with his palms pressed against the stump's smooth surface, and his right foot on top of the football which had come to rest in the slight hollow at its base.

At once Bridget saw what had happened. A wayward kick had evidently caused the ball to become lodged in the dip. Will had run over to retrieve it and had put his palms flat on the stump to steady himself in order to roll the ball backwards with the sole of his foot.

Colin began to stride towards Will, arms swinging like pendulums. *"Did you fucking hear me?"* he bellowed. *"I said get your hands off that!"*

Will was frozen like a rabbit in head lights, too terrified to respond. His expression crumpled from shock to utter terror as Colin advanced on him. A despairing sickness washed over Bridget, which was caused not only by the awfulness of the situation but also by the realisation that whatever had afflicted Colin had not disappeared after all, but had merely been lurking in the shadows, like a crab under a rock. This despair as much as alcohol and tiredness dulled her reactions, weighed down her limbs. Even so, she was first up out of her deck-chair after her husband, first to find her voice after he had dumbfounded the day with the sheer force of his rage.

"Colin, no!" she shouted as she pursued his striding figure in a stumbling run, stretching out an arm as if to cast a spell that might immobilize him.

It was only as Colin reached him that Will snatched his hands from the stump, though only in order to hold them in front of his face. Colin reached down, grabbed the cowering boy's bare arm in a grip fierce enough to make him howl with pain, and wrenched him sideways. For a moment Will swung in an arc through the air, then hit the ground with enough impact to make his legs buckle beneath him. He lay on the ground, wailing in terror. Before Colin could do anything more to the boy, Bridget reached out and grabbed his arm as fiercely as he had grabbed Will's, and yanked him round to face her.

"What do you think you're doing? What the hell's wrong with you…you…*stupid man!*"

Colin's face was still twisted with anger, but beneath the anger was a kind of glazed-eyed slackness, as if he was drugged, or as if the real Colin was being kept subdued within his own body, in thrall to this deranged interloper.

When Colin spoke a buckshot of spit flew from his mouth, speckling Bridget's face. His words too were like bullets. "You saw what he did. He touched that thing. That fucking abomination."

Before Bridget could respond, Shaun was suddenly beside her, a big, sweaty, angry presence, thrusting his face into Colin's. "What the bloody hell was that all about? How dare you touch my son like that! I ought to knock your bloody block off!"

Colin stepped back, his bulging eyes flickering from Bridget to Shaun. He looked confrontational rather than contrite. Bridget imagined the two men coming to blows and felt sick. She thrust her arms between them, palms splayed, in an attempt to placate them.

Colin, however, seemed incapable of seeing sense. He was shaking his head, saying, "Didn't you see what he did? Don't you people care?"

"I care about my son, not your bloody…" Shaun waved a hand at the stump, his anger rendering him temporarily powerless to speak.

"Think what you're saying, Colin," Bridget urged, her own anger now diverted into an attempt to prevent the situation escalating even further out of control. "Think what you're *doing*. So what if Will touched the stump? It's just a lump of wood. Nothing more."

Colin looked incredulous. "Nothing more? *Nothing more?* Don't you people understand anything?" Then all at once his eyes narrowed slyly and he began to back away. "No, that's not it, is it? You're all in it together, aren't you? You've planned this all along."

Shaun was still fuming, but he looked wary now too. "You're crazy," he said.

Bridget felt like sobbing, felt like throwing herself despairingly at her husband and shaking whatever kept taking him over and making him insane out of him. "Listen to yourself, Colin," she said. "Just listen to yourself for a minute. You don't know what you're saying. You're making no sense."

She reached out to him, but he jumped back as though her touch was poison. All at once she was aware of a blur of movement beside her, of someone smaller than she was rushing between her and Shaun. For an instant she recalled the stick-thin figure flowing across the garden towards Colin, and then she realised it was Miles who had now stopped in front of her to confront Colin. Her thirteen year-old son looked almost as furious as his father had done moments before. There were high spots of colour on his cheeks and the anger in his eyes was magnified by his spectacles.

"Look what you did to Will, Dad," Miles shouted, pointing behind him. "Look what you did. You made him cry."

Instinctively Bridget glanced behind her, and saw Will still crumpled on the ground, weeping, Claire cradling him in her arms, kissing his forehead, murmuring words of comfort.

Colin looked to where Miles was pointing, but he seemed unmoved, his eyes dead.

"Look what *I* did?" he said. "Look what *he* did. He touched that filthy…that evil…" His face puckered as if he had something unutterably foul in his mouth, a taste he couldn't get rid of.

"So what?" Miles shouted. "Like Mum says, it's just a stupid piece of wood. It's not poisoned like you told us, at all." Suddenly he ran over to the stump, and before Bridget could say or do anything to stop him, not only put his hands on it, but embraced it, pressed his cheek against it. "See!" he shouted, looking momentarily as crazed as his father. "See!"

Colin released a roar like an animal protecting its young and lunged at Miles.

"*Nooo!*" screamed Bridget, and took a flying leap on to Colin's back, wrapping an arm around his throat. Her action slowed Colin enough for Shaun to get in front of him. The bigger man thrust out both arms, his hands locking on to Colin's shoulders.

"Oh no, you don't," he said. "You're not hurting anyone else today."

Miles had darted away from the stump the instant Colin had gone for him, but now he took a couple of tentative steps back towards the trio of struggling adults.

"Why do you have to spoil everything, Dad?" he wailed, and Bridget saw that tears were now running down his face. "Why can't you just be *normal?*"

Bridget herself might have asked the same questions if her first priority hadn't been to try to calm Colin down. Still clinging to Colin's back, she gasped, "Just shush will you, Miles? You're not helping the situation."

"He needs to see a doctor," Miles wept. "He needs his head examined."

"Miles!" snapped Bridget. "What did I just say!"

Miles's chin trembled, then he blurted out a volley of sobs that tore at Bridget's heart, turned and ran towards the house. As he did so, Colin twisted his head to watch him go, and called after his son, "Don't think you can hide behind the boy. Don't think I don't know who you really are."

12

Despite her lack of sleep the previous night, Bridget was still wide awake at four o'clock the following morning. She was sitting in the snug in semi-darkness, nursing her umpteenth cup of tea, going through the day's events again and again in her head and wondering whether she had done the right thing.

She was alone in the house. The children were sleeping at the Woodalls' and Colin was in hospital, his welfare once again in what she hoped were the capable hands of Doctor Urwin. Officially her husband was in for 'observation and assessment', though exactly what that involved, or how long it might take, Bridget wasn't sure.

She supposed she could have found out, could have stayed and talked all the ins and outs of it through with the doctor, but she had been in no fit state to do so, and Urwin, to his credit, had recognised that. Placing a reassuring hand on her upper arm, he had said, "No disrespect, Mrs Morgan, but it's obvious you've had a tough day. Why don't you come back tomorrow when you've had a chance to collect your thoughts and get some sleep, and we'll talk then."

Sleep. That was a good one. Shattered though she was, at the moment Bridget couldn't imagine ever sleeping again. Her head ached with monumental thoughts, each of which seemed to fragment into numerous avenues of mostly dire possibility. Whenever Colin was asked where he got his ideas from, he often waffled on rather self-consciously about employing the *what if* principle. *What if* someone you thought was dead suddenly rang you up? *What if* you witnessed what you thought was a murder from a passing train? *What if* you picked up a young girl in a nightclub and slept with her, only for her to tell you the next morning that she was the daughter you never knew you had?

Now it was Bridget's turn to employ the *what if* principle, though the answers to the questions she was asking were mostly out of her hands, and would lead not to excitement, adventure and intrigue, but more likely to anguish and uncertainty.

What if there was something seriously wrong with Colin? *What if* they decided he was dangerous? *What if* they wanted to section him? *What if* he just got worse and worse instead of better, to such an extent that he no longer recognised his own family?

Don't think I don't know who you really are. What had he meant by that? Or was there even any point of trying to make sense of his ravings?

Claire had used the word, 'schizophrenic'. "Has Colin ever displayed any schizophrenic symptoms before?" she had asked. Bridget had looked at her fearfully, as if merely by mentioning the word, Claire had magically inflicted the condition on Colin. At the time, Bridget had been too distraught to ask whether she was just using the word carelessly, or whether she was implementing her medical knowledge, identifying incontrovertible symptoms. Certainly Dr Urwin had said nothing about schizophrenia, but maybe he hadn't wanted to jump the gun, or was deliberately keeping her in the dark so as to spare her more anguish. Perhaps she ought to ring Claire, find out how sure she had been about Colin. She had actually crossed the room and picked up the phone before she remembered what time it was.

With a sigh that was more like a groan, Bridget replaced the receiver. She was torturing herself here. She should have taken up the Woodalls' offer to stay with them tonight. They had done their best to try and persuade her, but she had been adamant that she wanted time alone, to think. The last thing Claire had said to her was, "If you change your mind, you just call us, all right? Any time." But even so, Bridget doubted that Claire would appreciate being woken at four in the morning to discuss the finer points of her husband's sanity.

Her mind constantly trying to assess and analyse, to find answers to unanswerable questions, she thought back again to the way Colin had suddenly slumped beneath her not thirty seconds after Miles had fled across the lawn and into the house as if trying to outrun his own tears.

Her husband's legs had buckled, his eyes had rolled up as if he had a sudden urge to gaze at his own brain from the inside, and his head had lolled sideways on to his shoulder. Bridget, still clamped to his back, would have collapsed on top of him if Shaun had not been holding him up. Even so, the three of them staggered and almost fell. Then Shaun, recovering his balance, had laid Colin on the grass with a carefulness that Bridget—both considering and despite the circumstances—found touching.

Claire, still comforting Will, who had been recovering a little by then, said, "What's wrong with him?"

"I don't know," said Shaun, peering into Colin's face. "He just fainted."

"Let me see." Claire gave him a perfunctory examination. "You'd better take him to the hospital."

"Why, what's wrong with him?" asked Bridget, alarmed.

"Hopefully nothing serious. His breathing's normal and his colour's fine. He's probably just fainted, as Shaun said. But there's always the possibility that he could have had some sort of seizure. It's best to get these things checked out."

"A seizure?" Bridget had sunk to her knees, too wobbly to stand. Her voice sounded as if it was echoing up through a long tunnel. "What do you mean?"

Claire raised her hands as if to abdicate responsibility for her diagnosis and attempted a smile. "It's just a catch-all term, Bridget. I don't mean anything by it. It just seems to me that there may be some…abnormal brain activity. They'll have equipment at the hospital that will be able to tell if anything's wrong."

Shaun drove, claiming that he felt sober enough to do so, whilst Bridget sat in the back with her recumbent husband, his head resting in her lap, a blanket laid over him. With his eyes closed and his face composed, Colin looked so innocent, so vulnerable. Bridget stroked his hair.

"Has anything like this happened before?" Shaun asked.

"Only in the last few days," Bridget said.

"What do you mean?"

Haltingly Bridget told Shaun everything that had happened since hearing Colin scream in the garden and rushing out to find him collapsed at the base of the stump. Shaun listened, lips pursed, a slight frown creasing his forehead. When she had finished he said, "Why do you think these stumps, as you call them, are affecting him so badly?"

"I don't know," said Bridget. She hesitated, then decided not to tell him about the dream she had had immediately before Colin's first 'attack'; she didn't want him to think she was crazy too. "Maybe the stumps are just an excuse, something for his mind to fixate on. If it wasn't the stumps, maybe it'd be something else."

"You ought to get rid of them," said Shaun. "See if that helps."

"We're going to. Though before we do, I'd like to find out why they were put in the garden in the first place."

"Why don't you go over and see Jean? I'm sure Claire would go with you if you wanted to."

"I might just do that." Bridget paused, then said, "I'm really sorry about all this, Shaun. You must be wondering what kind of loonies have moved in next to you. Colin's not usually like this, I promise."

"Hey, no need to apologise," Shaun said. "He can't help being sick."

"Yes, well, thanks for being so understanding. Especially after what Colin did to Will—"

"Forget it, there was no real harm done." He half-smiled and said almost apologetically, "Though I must admit I was on the verge of knocking his block off for a while there."

"I don't blame you." Bridget looked down at Colin's face. "He looks so peaceful now. It's weird how this thing comes and goes. And it always seems to take so much out of him, physically I mean. It's like he's possessed."

"By old Harry," said Shaun with a chuckle.

"Why do you say that?"

Shaun shrugged. "No reason really. It's just that…well, Harry owned this place before you did, and he was a bit of a dubious character, to say the least. Maybe *he* put those things in the garden. Maybe they're…oh, I don't know…evil totems or something." He glanced in the rear-view mirror and saw the expression on Bridget's face. "Hey, come on, I'm only joking. Just making up a lot of silly horror film mumbo-jumbo." Suddenly he grimaced. "Claire's always telling me what a tactless bugger I am."

By the time they got back from the hospital it was dark, and Bridget was feeling like the defeated opponent in a boxing match. Her tiredness made the cuts and bruises she'd picked up in the wood last night throb with renewed pain. The inside of her head felt pummelled by the thoughts that were fighting for room in her skull. Her throat was sore and her limbs felt feverish, as though her immune system was straining under the weight of too much pressure. Even her heart ached, a physical sensation that she nevertheless felt sure had an emotional basis.

Not for the first time, she sat in her new kitchen with her trembling hands clasped around a hot mug of tea and her head drooping in defeat. It was here where she had agreed to let the kids stay at the Woodalls', but stubbornly refused to go herself; here too where Claire had asked whether Colin had ever displayed any schizophrenic symptoms.

And now it was late—or early, depending on your point of view— and she was alone. She stretched out on the settee where she had fallen drunkenly asleep in Ruth's company yesterday (was it *really* only yesterday?) and closed her eyes.

At first, when she heard the scratching, she groaned and pressed a hand across her eyes, thinking it was inside her head. It was only when she heard the clunk of what sounded like a door opening and felt a cool breeze sliding across her prone body that she realised the sounds were coming from outside herself.

Her eyelids jerked up over eyes that felt hot and raw, their movement only a part of the spasm of reaction that made her body jolt into a sitting position. Turning her head into the breeze whose unexpected chill made her cheeks feel as though they were damp, Bridget saw that the door to the snug was ajar. Had she left it like that? She thought she had closed it, but she might have been wrong. The trivial little instances of day-to-day living were as uncertain as her family's future currently appeared to be.

"Hello," she called out, and though her own voice suddenly frightened her because it seemed to do no more than emphasise how isolated she was, she forced herself to add, "Is anyone there?"

Her body tensed in anticipation of an answer, but none came. Bridget thought of the darkness all around her, of the black fields and even blacker woods surrounding the house, and of how the glow of her little lamp, diffused though it would be by the thick, red, moth-eaten drapes left behind by the previous owner, would shine like a beacon in the night, advertising her whereabouts to who—or *what*—might decide to pay her a visit.

She wasn't sure whether it was the settee or her knees which creaked when she stood up. Certainly her bones, hollowed by tiredness and aching from last night's exertions, seemed more than capable of protesting that loudly. Walking as if on a tightrope, trying to contain her weight by keeping her body balanced, she circled the settee. At the door she stood and listened, annoyed by her own breathlessness. She told herself again that she needed to get back into shape, even whilst a small part of her wondered why she didn't want to admit that her heart was beating so fast because she was scared.

Pulling the door open felt like dragging the darkness beyond it towards her. Before her nerve could fail her, she stepped quickly out, clawing at the wall to her left to locate the light switch. The click of plastic was like her body switching on its relief. She tried not to think that by surrounding herself with light she was in fact making herself a more visible target, and that whatever might have entered the house would be just as dangerous in the light, and have just as much time to do whatever it intended with her.

She crossed the hall quickly and peered up the stairs. The shadows up there had absorbed some of the light into them, giving the upper landing a brownish cast. All seemed still, though the door to Miles's room was ajar, releasing a strip of black too solid for her eyes to penetrate. Before her mind could stifle the thought, she imagined something staring back at her, with unblinking eyes.

She turned with a disdain she didn't really feel, and which made her wonder who she was trying to fool. The breeze she had felt on her skin was coming from the back of the house, and as she approached it she felt as though she was trapped in a loop of events, forced to repeat her actions of last night. She hoped she would have the presence of mind not to follow any figure she might see up into the woods this time. At least on this occasion she would know it couldn't be Colin, though she doubted whether she could possibly find anything comforting in that knowledge.

She couldn't see the door that led into the garden until she had bypassed the staircase, whose jutting banister obscured it, but as soon as she could she stopped. The door was closed, which meant that the breeze, and whatever might have come in with it, had found some other point of entry. Bridget moved cautiously forward, feeling compelled to test the door, though she had no idea what that might achieve. However, when she came parallel with the kitchen she halted again. A breeze strong enough to make the door widen slightly had rushed out at her as if it had been building itself up for that moment.

The light from the hallway was not as strong back here, and preceded Bridget only feebly into the kitchen as she pushed the door open. Her own shadow, framed by the light behind her, was hunch-shouldered. Taking a breath that smelt of corn and warm earth, she stepped smartly forward and once again used her left hand to locate the light switch. As soon as the overhead fluorescents—which she hated and was planning to change for something more ambient—had flickered on with a series of soft popping sounds, they illuminated frantically flapping movement at the periphery of Bridget's vision, which she jolted round to face as though tugged by her heart which had leaped like a startled cat inside her chest.

She saw an open window above the sink, a curtain animated by the breeze that was attempting to fill the house. Her relief was tempered by the knowledge that she hadn't touched this window since they had moved in, so it couldn't have been her who had left it open. Perhaps Colin had opened it earlier that afternoon and she hadn't noticed, though that still didn't explain why the catch had become dislodged and why the window was now yawning. It would surely take more than this gentle summer breeze to lift a bar from the stub of metal that would ordinarily anchor it to the sill.

As she leaned over the sink and stretched forward into the night to drag the window back towards its frame, she tried to make herself believe that she was spooking herself unnecessarily. What did she hope to achieve by reaching a point where she was convinced there was an intruder in the house? The window frame was old, that was all, and almost certainly warped; the catch had probably not fitted snugly for years. She tugged the window shut without bothering to check her theory, refusing to be undermined by any more doubt, and was in the process of turning away when she saw movement in the garden.

Because it was so dark, she was not entirely sure that she *had* seen it. It had been barely an impression, so nebulous that it seemed almost to have bypassed her senses and registered as nothing more than a tiny glitch in her brain. She turned back towards the window, leaned forward until her forehead was almost touching the glass, and peered out. The movement she thought she had glimpsed had been close to the ground, at the base of the stump where Colin had had his attack.

Could she see something moving there now? Or were her eyes trying to convince her that the patch of blackness she was staring at was more fluid than it actually was? If there *was* something moving, then it was struggling feebly, like a child or a small animal caught in quicksand. She blinked rapidly several times to clear her vision, and looked anew. This time she gazed without blinking for thirty seconds and saw nothing at all.

Slowly she straightened, her reflection in the glass shrinking and drawing back. Perhaps this was all she had seen, a flicker of her own reflection. Or a stray moonbeam sliding on the stump's highly polished surface. Or even an animal darting across the grass. She stared at her reflection for a moment; it wasn't just because it was ghostly that made it look like an older, more washed-out, haggard version of herself. She sighed, rubbed her smarting eyes and turned her back on it. Right, she was going to make sure the house was secure, then she was going to check each room systematically, from top to bottom, before attempting to catch up on as much sleep as she could manage.

For the next few minutes she moved through the house like an automaton, checking windows and doors. She went through every room on the ground floor, including the snug where she'd spent most of the evening, then she switched the landing light on and went up the stairs, treading purposefully, making no attempt to stifle her footsteps.

The first room she looked in was Miles's, whose door was ajar. She looked in the wardrobe and under his bed, and then, leaving lights on behind her, she checked out the other rooms on that level.

Ellie's room had a cluttered dressing table, cds and magazines scattered across the bed, and a stack of posters of movie actors and pop stars eager to be blu-tacked to walls that were awaiting a new coat of paint; the toilet was too small to contain a hiding place for anything bigger than a spider; and the room that Bridget intended to turn into a fitness room contained her exercise bike, rowing machine and step equipment, as well as a four-high stack of boxes whose contents were intended for other rooms that were currently being prepared for them.

One wall of this latter room comprised the sliding mirrored doors of a fitted wardrobe unit. Bridget opened each in turn, but found only her yoga mat and blocks, a selection of rackets and balls, hanging clothes draped in plastic shrouds and other paraphernalia.

The third floor—hers and Colin's bedroom, the bathroom, the spare room—was equally devoid of intruders. That left only the low-ceilinged attic room which Colin had appropriated as his study.

Bridget tramped up the stairs, her eyes on the door at the top. It seemed hard to believe that her conversation with Colin about the missing knives had happened less than sixteen hours ago. She wondered what Colin was doing now. Was he sleeping peacefully? Were his dreams untroubled? The door to the attic room was slightly ajar. Nothing sinister in that. He had probably just pushed it carelessly to behind him when he had come down for his sandwiches earlier.

The door creaked when she pushed it open. "Inevitable," she murmured. Her outward insouciance was belied, however, by the tension she could feel in her limbs and stomach as she stepped up and into the room.

She looked left and right, but the long room with its low, sloping ceiling coveted the darkness it was steeped in. Even the light on the landing below her made little impression on layers of shadow so thick they seemed substantial as dust.

Once again, Bridget reached to her left to locate the light switch. This time, however, its hollow click brought not relief but realisation. There were no bulbs in the ceiling's two light fittings. Colin had peered at the rusty, dust-caked fittings on their first day and said, "Very dodgy. I'm not going to risk putting bulbs in these. They look as though they haven't been used in years."

He had managed with his angle-poise lamp and whatever daylight had managed to squeeze in through the small skylight. He had talked of wall lamps and velux windows—none of which helped Bridget at this precise moment. If she was going to check out the attic room—and she wouldn't rest until she had—she was going to have to brave the dark for the dozen or so paces it would take to walk across to the desk and switch the lamp on.

Nothing to worry about except a few spiders, she told herself, wishing she had the courage to say the words out loud. She took a deep breath, then wished she hadn't. The mustiness of the room snagged in her throat and made her chest lurch with a bout of coughing she tried instantly to stifle. She didn't know why she was taking such pains not to draw attention to herself. There was no one but her in the house, and even if there was someone hiding in the shadows, they would be staring at her right now, silhouetted in the doorway, framed clearly by the dim light behind her—unless, like sharks and spiders, they located their prey not by eyesight but by homing in on the vibrations of sound and movement.

"This is stupid!" she told herself, and this time she *did* speak out loud. She marched across to the desk, her feet clopping on the wooden floor. She had taken maybe eight steps when something on the seat of the typing chair partly tucked beneath Colin's desk shifted and rustled. It sounded like a brittle-furred cat turning over in its sleep. The blood seemed to drain from Bridget's legs and rush to her heart, which began to pump wildly.

Her mouth was suddenly so dry that she couldn't have spoken even if she had wanted to. She stood, fists clenched and legs rigid, staring at the vague arch of blackness a few feet in front of her that was Colin's chair back. The chair, his desk and the items on his desk were so ill-defined in the darkness that Bridget was not even certain she was seeing them at all, but merely *remembering* them, her mind creating the shapes and edges and perspectives that she *knew* were there, but could not see.

Was she, therefore, imagining the spindly, ragged shape that was now rising slowly over the back of the chair? Was her brain simply trying to make sense of the scraping, scratching, *creaking* sounds in front of her? With small, stumbling steps she began to back towards the door. She didn't know whether the ragged breathing she could hear was her own, or whether it was coming from the thing that appeared to be trying to raise itself from Colin's chair.

It was only when the thing fell from the chair to the floor with a sound like a tumble of dry twigs that Bridget turned and ran. In the second or two that it took her to reach the door and slam it behind her, she fancied she could hear its scuttling, disjointed pursuit. She raced down the three flights of stairs, gaining speed as she went, having to grab the hand-rail on a couple of occasions to prevent herself from pitching headlong. Not until she reached the ground floor did she turn briefly to look behind her.

If whatever had been in Colin's study was giving chase, it was at least a flight above her. The fact that she couldn't even hear it was scant comfort; her drumming heart and panting, panicked breath was blotting out all other sound. She dithered for a split-second, wondering what to do, then ran into the snug and grabbed her bag from the armchair where it had been lolling for most of the day. She ran along the hallway, then out of the front door, slamming it behind her.

When she turned to face the night, she saw that there were things moving in the front garden.

"No," Bridget moaned, and made herself look away. She ran across to the car, unzipping her bag and rooting inside as she did so. "Come *on*," she muttered, hovering by the car door as she searched for her keys. "Come on, you fuckers."

She was on the verge of giving up hope, and beginning to wonder how far she'd be able to run in the darkness without stopping, when her fingers touched the familiar leather fob. The jangle of the keys as she tugged them free was drowned by her harsh cry of triumph. She separated the car key from the rest with fingers that felt as if she were wearing cricket gloves, and pressed the button in the centre of its black grip. The car responded with a flash of its lights and the satisfying *chunk* of disengaging locks. Bridget tore the door open, scrambled inside, then slammed and locked the door behind her. She was trembling and shaking, and made the car roar by over-revving it when she twisted the key in the ignition.

"Calm," she told herself. "Calm, calm, calm." She put the car into gear and coaxed it smoothly down the drive, if only because she was terrified of lurching and stalling. As she drove away from the house, her headlights bleaching the hedges and the rutted road ahead of her, she tried to deny the image that her mind was filled with. She hadn't really seen feebly struggling shapes at the bases of the stumps in the front garden, had she? And even if she had, they must have been foxes or hedgehogs or badgers, because there was no way they could have been composed partly of twigs and roots, and partly of the earth that appeared to be giving birth to them.

13

"Are you *sure* you saw what you thought you did?"

Bridget looked at Ruth through eyes that felt as if they'd been rubbed with salt, then rinsed in hot water. She had had so little sleep in the past two nights that she felt as though she was living in a dream sequence from a 1970s horror movie. The world seemed full of strange, distorted angles and echoing, exaggerated sounds. Her brain was a thick, lumpy stew from which she was finding it increasingly difficult to extract the words and phrases she needed to articulate her experiences. Her body felt jittery and brittle as though she and it were not quite in phase, as if she—the essential she—might slough away from it at any moment, leaving her flesh as dead and empty as a dropped glove.

The strip lights in the roadside cafe hurt her eyes, reflecting in a glare off the formica table tops, the off-white walls and even off Ruth's skin. Bridget closed her eyes for a second, and immediately the swirling blackness that had been hiding from the light surrounded her, swaddled her, threatened to drag her into itself. When Bridget felt damp heat on her forehead, she wondered dreamily why she'd suddenly started sweating, then realised her head was drooping forward, lowering itself towards the steam from her mug of paint-stripper tea.

Rousing herself with an effort, she stared at Ruth. "Don't you believe me?"

Ruth reached out and took her hand. It seemed to Bridget that her friend's arm stretched over a vast distance before their fingers touched. When Ruth spoke, each individual word was like a rock dropped into a pool so viscous it didn't even make a splash.

"Of *course* I believe you. I wouldn't have driven all the way down here at four o'clock in the morning if I thought you were telling me porkies. What I'm trying to find out, Bridge, is what you *actually* saw as opposed to what you *thought* you saw. I mean, look at you. You're tired and emotional. You've hardly slept for two days. I'm not saying you're barmy, but the mind can play tricks when it's been under the kind of strain that yours has been under recently. Now, I want you to think hard and tell me *exactly* what it was you think you saw. Do you think you can do that for me?"

Bridget stared at her friend for a long moment, then wearily nodded. "I didn't really see anything in the attic room. It was too dark. I *thought* I could see a sort of…hunched shape in the chair, but…I don't know…maybe my brain was just trying to see what it thought was there. I heard it, though. I definitely heard it. It was dry and scratchy, like…well, I don't know what it was like…old twigs or something. And out in the garden I thought I saw things moving around the stumps."

"You *thought* you saw them?"

"Again, it was dark, and I didn't want to look too closely…I was scared."

"Bridge," said Ruth softly, "do you think there's any chance you might have imagined all this? I mean, do you think it's possible that, say, an animal got into the house and you just kind of…freaked out?"

Bridget was silent for a long moment. Apart from herself and Ruth and the dumpy, grey-faced, middle-aged couple behind the counter, there was only one other person in the roadside trailer with the hand-written CAFE sign on the door, and that was a vastly overweight man whose articulated truck had caused the trailer to rattle as if in an earthquake as he had pulled up outside. Bridget watched the man pushing toast through the slot in his wiry black beard with tattooed hands, then she sighed and said, "I don't know. I just…I can't think straight. The whole thing seems like a bad dream now."

Ruth squeezed Bridget's hand. "I know," she said softly. "I think the best thing to do is go back to the house and have a look round." Though Bridget hadn't been aware of it, Ruth must have felt her tense, because she said more urgently, "It's light now, so there's nothing to be afraid of. And I'm going to be with you, and I'll stay for as long as you want me."

"What about work?" said Bridget weakly.

"Work can wait. Friends are more important."

Bridget looked at Ruth, still sporting the bruise above her eye where the two of them had clashed heads a couple of days ago. With her defences down, she felt emotion rushing through her, unchecked. Her throat closed up, tears began to pour from her eyes. She slumped forward over the table like a doll that had lost its stuffing.

"Hey, hey," Ruth said softly, "I know the prospect of having me hanging around is pretty unbearable, but crying about it won't help."

Bridget couldn't speak. She wanted to pour it all out to Ruth, wanted to tell her what an incredible friend she was, wanted to express her gratitude for the way Ruth had responded to her garbled, hysterical phone call.

Within three hours of wrenching her from sleep, Ruth had been beside her. Bridget knew that her best friend must have driven like a maniac to get to her in such a short time. The two of them had met in the car park of the pub which Bridget had pulled into in order to call Ruth on her mobile. By the time Ruth arrived, it was full daylight, and Bridget was curled up across the front seats of her car, slipping in and out of consciousness, her body desperate for rest but her fear trying to keep her alert. Ruth had coaxed Bridget out of her car and into her own, then had driven round for a while until she had spotted the roadside cafe. Bridget had tried to keep her emotions under control, but for the first half-hour or so had still been a gibbering wreck. It had been Ruth's calmness and understanding and reassurance that had encouraged Ruth to step back from the mental precipice she'd been teetering at the edge of and into at least some semblance of coherence.

Together, the two women left the cafe and walked across to Ruth's car, Ruth with a protective arm around her friend's shoulders. Bridget was happy for the time being to be treated like a child, found comfort in being looked after, in having her seat belt put on for her and a jacket draped across her knees. She closed her eyes and snuggled down in her seat as Ruth started the engine. She felt sleep rising from the darkness to claim her again, and wished she could drift for hours, enclosed in the womb-like warmth and safety of the car, wrapped in the soothing chug of the engine. She wished she could sleep away her troubles and wake refreshed on the other side, her problems solved, reality restored.

"Bridge." The voice spoke softly, but was still a harsh intrusion into her dreamless drifting. "Bridge, we're here."

Waking up was like sinking rather than rising, like feeling a great, burdensome weight settling inside her. Her body seemed full of wet sand, her thoughts an oppressive mass of dark cloud. She groaned and scowled, and at first her eyes refused to open. Despite the fact that Ruth had sacrificed sleep and work and who knew what else to be here with her, for a few moments Bridget hated her friend for hauling her back into a world she wanted no part of, a world whose fear and uncertainty and heartache was enervating, debilitating.

"Leave me lone," she mumbled. "Juss wan sleep."

She was vaguely aware of something moving on her head, then realised it was Ruth's hand, gently stroking her hair.

"Do you want to stay here while I go in and look round? I don't mind."

Bridget didn't know what alarmed her most—the thought of being left in the car or the thought of Ruth creeping around the house on her own.

"No," she muttered, forcing her eyelids apart. "No, mustn't do that. We go together."

"Okay," Ruth said, "whatever you say. You just come to. Take your time. We'll go when you're ready."

The first thing they did when they got out of the car five minutes later was check out the stumps in the front garden. Despite what Bridget thought she had seen last night, the ground around the base of them seemed undisturbed. There was nothing to even suggest that a mole or a fox had passed this way.

"So far, so good," Ruth said. "Now for the house."

In the sunlight the house looked as welcoming and picturesque as it always had. Bridget sighed and trudged heavily after her friend, who was crossing the lawn to the front door. She didn't know whether to feel relieved or disappointed at the lack of evidence so far. She certainly didn't want some scuttling, hideous *thing* to emerge from a dark corner, but neither did she want to come across like a hysterical, half-crazed idiot, seeing things that weren't really there.

Ruth turned on the threshold and said, "The door's open." Then she gave it a push to demonstrate.

Bridget watched the swinging door slowly reveal the hallway and the stairs down which she had fled a few hours before. "That was probably me. I might have left it open when I ran out of the house."

Ruth stepped into the house, Bridget behind her, her chest feeling like a delicate shell that could barely withstand her increasing heartbeat. She didn't realise she was scowling until Ruth said, "Are you all right? You look really angry."

"I resent being made to feel afraid in my own house," Bridget said. "I love this house. I don't want to be scared of being here."

Ruth looked equally defiant. "Then let's prove there's nothing to be afraid of."

Just as Bridget had done last night, the two women moved systematically through the house. They found nothing out of place, heard nothing except the faint music of birdsong, and, at one point, the drone of a jet engine which it seemed hard to equate with the tiny black dart and its creamy tail cutting through the clouds high overhead.

At last they were standing at the foot of the stairs leading up to the attic. They could see the bottom half of the door up there, which appeared to be firmly closed. Bridget's heart was now hammering so fast that her entire body seemed to be jittering in echo to it. She licked her lips constantly, but couldn't seem to stop them sticking together. When Ruth turned to look at her after contemplating the closed door above, the smile that Bridget attempted felt like a mass of facial tics.

"You okay?"

Bridget's instinct was to nod, but then she said, "Not really. A bit nervous."

"Do you want to stay here while I go up?"

Bridget had an image of Ruth pushing the door cautiously open, then of something yanking her inside and the door slamming shut again.

"No," she said, repressing a shudder, "we'll go up together."

"Okay, but I'll go first. We'll stick close together."

Bridget nodded, and stealthy as cat burglars the two of them began to ascend.

At each creak of the steps, Bridget winced and clenched her fists, and held her breath for a moment as she listened for a reaction from above. If she *had* heard anything, she had no doubt that she'd have been down the stairs in seconds, fleeing the house as she had done last night. And despite all her words of encouragement and reassurance, Bridget felt sure that Ruth would have joined her. Ruth was only acting the pragmatist now because she had been thrust into the role. In truth, she was generally the more gullible of the two of them, the more willing to believe in the presence of ghosts and demons and UFOs.

They halted outside the door, glancing at each other as if unsure what to do next. Then Ruth leaned forward and placed her ear to the wood, brow furrowed in concentration like a master safe-cracker.

"Hear anything?" Bridget whispered.

Ruth shook her head. "Not a sausage." She took a deep breath, gathering herself, then placed a hand on the door handle. "Here goes nothing," she hissed, and pushed the door open.

Bridget's shoulders hunched and her legs stiffened in anticipation of an attack. When Ruth, blocking most of her view of the room, drew in a sharp, hissing breath, she had a vertiginous instant when she thought it had come. Then Ruth murmured, "That is weird," and stepped forward into the room. Bridget sagged for a moment and held on to the hand-rail, wondering if she was going to pass out. It took a few moments of blinking and swallowing and breathing deeply before she was able to follow her friend.

In the daytime, the attic room, despite its lack of light, was welcoming, cosy. It was a place where you could cut yourself off, a peaceful retreat from the world. The motes of dust spiralling in the band of sunshine that connected the skylight to the floor projected an air of languidity, a sense that up here, within touching distance of the sky, life need never be frantic or cluttered or complicated or stressful.

Bridget blinked and turned her head as slowly as the room's ambience seemed to be urging her to. Ruth was bent double, examining something on the floor. The gloom made it look to Bridget as though a strip of the wooden floor, stretching half-way to the door from the desk, was charred.

"What is it?"

Ruth dropped to a squat, stretched out a hand to the charred area, then, evidently thinking better of it, folded her arms. "I think it's ashes."

"Ashes? What do you mean?"

Ruth squinted up at Ruth. "It looks as if someone's taken a load of ashes and bits of burnt wood out of the fireplace and scattered them across the floor."

Bridget looked at the thick trail of black flakes and brittle chunks of charred matter and shuddered. "Why would someone do that?"

Ruth looked at her steadily, her face composed, unreadable. "You tell me."

14

Shaun brought the children back at ten o'clock that morning. "Hullo," he said, unable to hide his surprise when Ruth answered the door. "Is Bridget knocking about?"

"She's sleeping," Ruth said.

"Ah. Probably for the best. She's had a tough few days, poor old girl."

"Yes, she has," said Ruth, then smiled and held out her hand. "You must be Shaun. I'm Ruth, Bridget's friend. I've come to help out for a day or two. Bridget told me you'd be dropping the little horrors off this morning."

Shaun grinned and turned to watch Ellie and Miles clambering out of the car with their bags. They were taking a long time about it, giggling and gossiping with their new-found friends, apparently none the worse after the nightmare that Bridget had told Ruth yesterday's barbecue had become.

"Our two will be sad to see them go. Been getting on like a house on fire. As will Claire and I. Be sad to see them go, I mean. Charming children. They're a credit to their…um…"

"Parents?" suggested Ruth.

"Yes, quite. Absolutely." Shaun inclined his head conspiratorially and murmured, "Any news on Colin?"

"Not yet," said Ruth. "As I said, Bridget's sleeping at the moment. I'm sure she'll phone the hospital when she wakes up."

"Oh, I don't doubt it," said Shaun, as if Ruth had inferred that he thought Bridget didn't care. "Well, keep us informed, and if there's anything else we can do to help, don't hesitate to let us know. The children are welcome any time—as is Bridget, and indeed you. Oh, and Colin, of course, when he's better. Well, cheerio. Nice to have met you."

"You too," said Ruth.

The day passed uneventfully. Ruth wondered whether she ought to ring the hospital so that she could give Bridget the latest bulletin on Colin when she woke up. In the end she decided against it, not because she didn't think it was her place, but because she wouldn't have wanted to give her friend anything other than good news. Late in the afternoon, she took the vacuum cleaner almost defiantly up to the attic and hoovered up the trail of ash that she and Bridget had found. She felt a savage satisfaction in the task because the stuff had been bothering her all day, and because it meant that she no longer had to tell herself that the reason she had put off dealing with it was because she hadn't wanted the sound of the vacuum cleaner to wake Bridget up.

If that *was* even part of the reason, she needn't have worried. Bridget slept solidly for over ten hours, only emerging at around seven o'clock that evening. Ruth was washing up after serving herself and the kids with pizza and salad when Bridget shuffled bleary-eyed into the kitchen.

"Hi," Ruth said, her hands encased in soap bubbles, "how are you feeling?"

Bridget switched the kettle on, then sat down. "I've come to a decision," she said as if she had spent the day thinking rather than sleeping. "I'd like to speak to Jean, the old lady who we bought the house from. Tonight if possible. I want to try and get to the bottom of what's going on here."

15

The village, less than ten miles from the Morgans' new home, seemed to consist of nothing more than a tea shop, a garage, two pubs and a couple of dozen cottages, each of which would not have looked out of place on a picture postcard. Bridget was sitting in the passenger seat of Claire's car outside a white cottage whose front door suggested it had been designed for children or midgets.

"Jean's rather frail, and she can get quite confused at times," Claire said after switching off the engine.

"It's okay, Claire, I'm not going to give her a hard time," replied Bridget.

Claire flushed slightly. "No, I know. It's just I feel responsible for her, and I know how anxious you are about Colin—understandably so, of course."

"Are you sure she didn't mind meeting me?"

"Not at all. In fact, she said how nice it would be to meet one of the people who had moved into her old house."

They got out of the car and walked up the path to the front door, between flower beds riotous with colour. Claire knocked, and the two women stood silently for half a minute, until the door opened and a mouse-like old lady with snow-white hair peered out at them.

"Hello, Jean," Claire said, reaching out and gently squeezing the old lady's hands, "how are you?"

"Oh, I'm tip-top, my dear, tip-top. Come in, come in." Jean scrutinised Bridget keenly as if she were some exotic creature. "And this must be your new neighbour."

"I'm Bridget," Bridget said, holding out a hand which Jean sandwiched in both of hers.

"Lovely to meet you, my dear. Well, come through, don't let's be standing about in the hall. It's lovely to have a bit of company in the evenings. Most nights it's just me and the folk from *Coronation Street*."

Bridget followed Claire and Jean into the lounge, ducking through the doorway so as not to bump her head on the lintel. She was only five feet six and relatively trim, yet the dimensions of the house made her feel large and ungainly. Despite the mildness of the summer evening, there was a fire crackling in the grate, two thigh-thick logs propped against one another, spitting angry sparks up the chimney as they blackened beneath coiling serpents of orange flame. Instantly Bridget felt her head beginning to swim, and plumped down in the nearest floral-patterned armchair, leaning back in order to distance herself as much from the oppressive heat.

"I'll be mother, shall I?" said Claire, and poured tea into three willow-patterned cups from a matching, already-prepared pot. The lounge was crammed with darkly Victorian furniture which had evidently had more breathing space in Jean's previous home. Bridget couldn't help feeling guilty despite knowing how absurd this was, as if she personally had forced the old lady to move. The crown of a grandfather clock was a hair's breadth from the ceiling and filled the room with its sonorous ticking; various surfaces were cluttered with ornaments as if there had once been twice as much furniture to accommodate them.

Bridget spotted what she had been looking for on the mantelpiece—a photograph of Jean's husband, Harry. However, if she had been expecting it to reveal something of the man, she was disappointed. The photograph was old enough to be sepia-tinted, and depicted the couple on their wedding day. Harry was wearing some sort of military uniform and grinning a toothy grin. The oil plastering his hair to his head was so thick that she could see the comb-strokes in it. He didn't look capable of cruelty or sexual deviance; he looked, in fact, like George Formby.

"Sugar?" said Claire, looking at her so pointedly that Bridget felt sure her thoughts must somehow be apparent from the expression on her face.

"Erm…no, thanks," Bridget said, and accepted the cup that Claire offered her. She also accepted an individual apple pie from a plate loaded with cakes and biscuits, though she didn't feel hungry. As Claire and Jean exchanged pleasantries, she nibbled the pie whilst feigning interest and wondered how she could steer the conversation round to asking what she wanted to know.

In the end, it was Jean who did it for her. During a natural pause that came at the end of a discussion about the hip replacement of a woman called Betty Blackshaw, the old lady turned to Bridget and asked, "So how are you settling in, dear?"

"Oh…fine, thanks," Bridget said, so taken aback that she almost blew her chance. She swallowed the morsel of pastry that was dissolving sweetness onto her tongue and blurted, "Although I must admit we've had a few problems. Not with the house, though. The house is fantastic. We love it."

There was a silence. Jean looked at Bridget quizzically as though waiting for more. Bridget in turn looked at Claire, hoping for some moral support. Claire gave a little moue of resignation and said, "Unfortunately, Bridget's husband, Colin, is in hospital at the moment, Jean."

"Oh dear," said Jean, and turned back to Bridget. "Nothing serious, I hope?"

"We're not sure," Bridget said. "He's having tests. The thing is…and this may sound odd…but we're not sure whether his…his illness is something to do with the…the…" All at once she realised that she couldn't think what to call the stumps. The word 'stumps' itself seemed somehow belittling, and of the other alternatives that sprang to mind, 'sculptures' sounded too grand (and possibly misleading), and 'things' too vague.

She knew she was becoming redder as the heat rose to her face, felt her thoughts twisting themselves into tight, strangling knots.

"What Bridget is trying to say," Claire said, not unkindly, "is that Colin seems to have been adversely affected by the wooden structures in the garden."

Bridget nodded vigorously. "Ever since touching one of them, he's been having mood swings, blacking out. I just wondered whether you could shed some light on what the...the structures actually are?"

She looked hopefully at Jean, and was unnerved by the slack, glazed-eyed look that suddenly seemed to have appeared on her face. Disquiet turned to shock a moment later when tears started flowing down the old lady's cheeks.

"Jean," Claire said. "Jean, are you all right?"

Jean's expression didn't change, but her lips parted slightly. Then she whispered what sounded to Bridget like, "My children."

"What did you say?" Bridget asked, leaning forward. But before the old lady could answer, Claire moved from her armchair by the window to sit beside Jean on the settee.

"Hey, Jean, come on," she said softly, putting an arm around the old lady's shoulders, "don't upset yourself."

Jean was trembling, gazing into the middle-distance, tears still flowing down her face.

"Jean, did you say that the structures were your children?" said Bridget urgently. "Is that what you said? Can you tell me what you meant by that?"

"Bridget, please!" Claire said sharply, flashing a scowl at her. "Can't you see she's upset?"

"Sorry, Claire, but this is important." Bridget's stomach was curdling with an anxiety bordering on desperation.

"Not important enough to risk upsetting Jean further."

"How can you say that? Colin's sanity could be at stake here. The whole key to what's wrong with him—"

"What's wrong with him is that he's got some sort of psychological disorder. I mean, come on, Bridget, you can't honestly believe that

Colin's whole personality has changed just because he touched a lump of wood."

Bridget felt her voice cracking, her own tears threatening to break through. "If that's what you really think, why did you agree to bring me here?"

"Because…because I wanted to help. Because I wanted to give you the opportunity to explore every avenue and come to your own conclusions."

"You think we're both mad, don't you?" Bridget said. "You think I'm as crazy as my husband!"

"Of course not. I think Colin's had some sort of breakdown and needs help—which, hopefully, he's now getting—and I think you've been under an enormous amount of strain because of it."

"You probably think we're always like this. You probably think a couple of nutters have moved in next door."

"Of course I don't, Bridget. I *know* you're not usually like this."

"How can you know? What makes you think we weren't raving mad before we came here?"

"I know because the children have told—" Claire's voice cut off abruptly and she flushed.

"Have told you what? That Colin and I had been having problems? That we moved because I had an affair?"

Claire's eyes widened, and immediately Bridget knew she had said too much. "N-no. Nothing like that. I was going to say, they…they told us what loving, wonderful parents you were, and how they'd never seen Colin behave like that before, and…and how they hoped he'd get better."

Bridget sagged, wishing she could retract her outburst, knowing it was too late. She felt weary and embarrassed and confused. Was Claire right? Was it merely the terrible strain she'd been under that was distorting her perceptions, sucking her in to a fantasy world?

"I'm sorry," she mumbled. "I…I know I'm being unreasonable. And, under the circumstances, you and Shaun have been fantastic. I just hope I get the chance to make it up to you. That Colin and I both do."

Claire, evidently touched, was about to respond, when Jean, still gazing tearfully into space, the conversation between the two women having apparently passed over her head, murmured something that slipped beneath the crackling of the flames and was lost.

Instantly Bridget craned forward once more, though on this occasion tried to reign in her needy anxiety, to appear not bullish, but composed, coaxing.

"Can you repeat that, Jean?" she asked. When Jean didn't respond, she felt the familiar tension attempting to splinter and harshen her voice, and fought to prevent it from doing so. "Jean," she cooed, "Jean." At last the old lady looked at her. "Can you tell us again what you just said? Is it about the structures? About your *children?* Can you tell us about them, Jean? It's very important." And then, without even realising she was going to say it, she added, "I need to know how to look after them for you."

Instantly a look of hope blossomed on the old lady's face. Her eyes sparkled. "Would you do that for me?"

"If I can," said Bridget. She glanced at Claire to gauge her reaction, and was encouraged to see that Claire looked wary, though not disapproving. "If you tell me how."

Suddenly the old lady was animated again, though this time there was a brittle fervency about her that Bridget recognised and responded to. "I didn't want to leave them. That was the hardest thing for me. You must believe that. I'm not a bad mother, but I had no choice, do you see?"

"I know, I know," Bridget said soothingly. "You don't have to explain to us. We understand. You did everything you could."

"Yes," Jean whispered. "Yes I did." She seemed to lapse back into her own thoughts for a moment, then abruptly she blinked up at Bridget. "Tell me, dear, are my babies happy?"

For a second Bridget was lost for words, then she saw Claire give an almost imperceptible nod. "Yes," she said decisively. "Yes, they're very happy."

"Oh, I'm so glad. I couldn't bear the thought of them being miserable."

Tentatively Bridget asked, "Jean, where did the…your children come from?"

The old lady gazed at her with utter incomprehension. "Whatever do you mean, my dear?"

"Well, what I mean is…who made them? Originally?"

Still Jean wore the expression of someone who couldn't quite believe what they were hearing. Slowly she said, "Well, of course...*I* did, dear. That is, Harry, my late husband and I did." She leaned forward and hissed conspiratorially, "*In the usual way.*"

Bridget stared at her blankly. Jean gazed back as if Bridget was the one who was being obtuse. It was left to Claire to say, "Well, thank you, Jean. You've been more than helpful. It's lovely to see you looking so well."

Jean half-turned towards Claire, and though her eyes were still rheumy with spent tears, she smiled as broadly as she had on their arrival. "You too, dear. You must bring your children to see me next time—if they can stand the boredom, that is."

As the conversation drifted back into the exchange of niceties, Bridget was left with her head faintly reeling. Had she actually learned anything here tonight? Was the old woman simply a bit doolally or was there some hidden meaning to what she had said? She sat, barely contributing to the rest of the conversation until it was almost time to go. Then, as Claire was rising from her seat, she blurted, "Can I ask just one more question?"

Both Jean and Claire looked at her as if they had forgotten she was there. Taking their silence as affirmation, Bridget said to Jean, "I just wondered...are the...children...well...*dangerous* in any way?"

There was an instant of silence, then Jean gave a silvery laugh. "Oh dear me, no. The very idea of it." She stopped laughing and her voice suddenly became serious, but comforting too, like a mother reassuring a fretful child. "There's nothing to worry about, dear. They're all as gentle as lambs." She squeezed Bridget's hand to emphasise her point. "Not a single one of them would hurt so much as a fly."

16

I couldn't live here, Ruth thought, staring out of the kitchen window. The lack of street lamps made it look as though there was a void beyond the glass, made her feel completely isolated, as though a cordon of darkness had been thrown up around the house which allowed no-one either in or out.

Like Bridget before her, Ruth stared at her reflection staring back at her, and suddenly wondered if there was something watching her out there in the blackness. She stepped back from the window with a shudder, thinking of the trail of ash up in the attic. If she had experienced what Bridge claimed to have experienced, wild horses wouldn't have been able to drag her back to this place.

As far as Ruth was concerned, her best friend was caught in a trap from which there appeared to be no escape. It was easy enough for Ruth to say that if she was Bridget she'd never come back, but she hadn't sunk a ton of money into the house, had she? She didn't have a family to think about. She didn't have a husband in hospital.

Whether or not Bridge *had* seen some sort of…creature up in the attic, there was no wonder she was at her wits' end. This was supposed to be a new beginning for all of them, the fulfilment of a dream. Instead it was turning into a nightmare.

Ruth glanced at the window again, then away with another shudder. She had come to make herself some tea, but now decided that she'd prefer something stronger. As she opened a bottle of Chilean red, she wondered, not for the first time, whether she was drinking too much. Barely an evening passed these days without the ritual uncorking, which she had come to regard as permission to relax. She *deserved* to relax, of course—running the business was stressful and exhausting, and involved being *responsible*, a concept she had never been happy with—but maybe sinking booze like it was going out of fashion was not the way to go about it. Perhaps if she only had a glass or two it wouldn't be so bad, but most nights, whether she had company or not, she polished off an entire bottle without too much difficulty.

Tonight, of course, was different. Tonight she was more than entitled to a drink. Tonight a glass or two was not only desirable, it was essential. But it *would* only be a glass or two, she promised herself. Just enough to calm her nerves, mellow her out a little bit.

Bottle in one hand, glass in the other, she hurried out of the kitchen, glad to get away from the great blank eye of the window. She turned off the kitchen light and pulled the door firmly shut as if that was sufficient to cut off all avenues of pursuit. Then she all but scampered across the hall, pausing only briefly at the bottom of the stairs to tilt her head towards the upper landing. If the kids were still awake she couldn't hear them. She wondered whether she ought to check on them, then decided she'd do so a bit later, once she'd got some Dutch courage inside her. After all, it was only 10:30; it hadn't been dark for much more than half an hour. They might still be reading, or doing something in the privacy of their bedrooms that they didn't want her to stumble in on.

Half an hour and almost three glasses later, Ruth's eyes were drooping. She wasn't renowned for being an early bird, but thanks to Bridget she had been up since about 4 a.m. She wondered how much longer Bridget was going to be. She'd been gone for almost three hours now. Ruth had *thought* she was coming down to give her best mate some much-needed moral support, not spend most of her time acting as a glorified babysitter.

No, that was unfair. If she hadn't been here, Bridge wouldn't have been able to catch up on her sleep, wouldn't have been able to go and see the house's previous owner without once again palming the kids off on to people she barely knew. Ruth wasn't here simply as a sounding board, or a safety net, or a counsellor, or whatever Bridge needed personally, she was here to help in any way she could. And if that meant holding the fort while Bridge went off and did other things, then so be it.

It wasn't until she had jerked awake that Ruth realised she had drifted off to sleep. Immediately she wondered what had woken her, and then, as if in reply, heard a series of thumps coming from upstairs. Instinctively she looked up as if she half-expected the ceiling to become transparent. The thumps continued, intermittent and uneven. What were the kids *doing* up there? Clog-dancing?

It didn't occur to her that something might be wrong until she went out into the hallway and saw the front door standing open. She blinked at it stupidly for a moment, then a feeling of dread overwhelmed her and she spun towards the staircase. She tried to shout out the names of the children, but her throat felt clamped. Her inability to speak didn't stop her legs from moving, however. She raced across the hallway, hurled herself at the stairs, and pelted up to the first landing.

The thumping sounds were coming from Miles's bedroom, the door of which was ajar. Utterly terrified but knowing she had no other choice, Ruth raced across to it and shoved the door all the way open.

The interior of the room was a confusion of shadows and movement. Ruth saw something flailing on the far side of the bed, something so bulky it was almost shapeless, that appeared to possess more limbs than it ought to. From the centre of the thrashing shape came a hideous gurgling, choking sound. With the room itself seeming to pulse juicily in tandem with the thumping of her heart, Ruth scrabbled for, and found, the light switch.

If anything, the light revealed something even worse than she had imagined. The bulky, gurgling creature resolved itself into two struggling human beings. Ruth took in the scene in a horrifying, instantaneous rush. She saw Colin, hunched and bestial, face contorted with insane rage, hands encircling his son's neck in a white-knuckle grip, crushing the life out of him. She saw Miles, face purple, tongue protruding, eyes bulging and bloodshot, waving his weakening arms like a drowning man, feet drumming the ground in a spasmic, unco-ordinated dance.

The sheer horror of the scene tore Ruth's voice out of her. *"Noooo!"* she screamed, the sound itself seeming to propel her across the room. She cannoned into Colin, who at first seemed not to even notice her, grabbed his right arm and wrenched it with enough force to free his hand from its death-grip on Miles's throat.

The next few seconds seemed to Ruth like a series of flash-images. She saw the livid fingertip-shaped bruises on Miles's neck. Heard a rattling whoop as he inhaled a lungful of much-needed air. Saw Colin's arm swing towards her, too swift to avoid. Felt fresh pain exploding in the still-tender swelling above her eye. For a moment saw only white lights cascading across her vision as she fell backwards to the floor.

Then she was up again and launching herself at Colin, raking at his face with her fingernails. She heard someone screeching before realising with astonishment that she was doing it herself.

"Get off him, you bastard! Leave him alone! He's your son! What are you doing? What the hell are you doing?"

Her hands were balled into fists now and she was punching Colin in the face, pummelling him, a whirling dervish, arms a blur of movement.

She only realised Colin had let go of Miles when she saw the boy's legs fold beneath him, saw him fall half on to the bed, then slide to the floor.

"Bastard!" she was screaming. *"Bastard! Bastard! Bastard!"*

She heard Colin roar, saw him duck his head like a bull and charge at her.

The battering ram of his head struck her in the mid-riff, knocking the air out of her, carrying her half-across the room. Legs kicking out, clutching at his hair, she fell backwards again, hitting the floor with a crash and half-dragging him down with her, not feeling a thing because of the adrenaline surging through her system.

Then he was standing over her, blood oozing from the scratch-marks on his face, teeth bared and slick with drool. His manic eyes rolled in their sockets. His voice was guttural as though he was regressing, devolving.

"You stupid fucking bitch. He's trying to wheedle his way back in. Can't you fucking see that?"

Ruth's stomach hurt and her lungs toiled for air, but she managed to croak, "Who is?"

Colin half-turned and stabbed a finger towards the bed, or rather towards Miles's supine form lying out of sight on the floor beside it.

"*He* is! *He* is! Who do you fucking think?"

Ruth glared at Colin. He looked as crazy as it seemed possible to look, but she felt no fear, only contempt. "That's your son!" she spat at him. "That's Miles!"

He shook his head like a dog with something in its ear; spit flew from his mouth. "No, that's a trick. That's what he wants you to think." Then his eyes narrowed and his lips drew back in an almost *Grand Guignol* expression of cunning. "But maybe you know that already. Maybe you want him here. Yes, that's it, isn't it? That was the plan all along."

Before Ruth could answer, there was a scream from the doorway. She twisted around to see Ellie in a pair of red pyjamas, fists pressed together and clenched protectively beneath her chin.

"Dad, what are you doing?" she wailed.

For a moment no one spoke or moved, though Ruth saw myriad emotions chasing themselves across Colin's face. There was guilt, shame, defiance, confusion; he even briefly held out his hands like Karloff's monster, begging forgiveness and understanding.

Then he made a sound somewhere between a grunt and a howl and blundered from the room, Ellie stepping smartly out of his way as he passed. She looked in distressed bewilderment after her father as he stumbled down the stairs, then turned back to Ruth and said almost accusingly, "Ruth, what's going on?"

Ruth started to shake, and for a moment didn't know whether she was about to laugh or cry. She felt bubbles of emotion rising up through her, which, with a gargantuan effort, she managed to stifle.

"Ruth," Ellie said again, "will you please tell me what's happening?"

Ruth felt jittery but enervated, as though a thousand frantic tics beneath the surface of her skin were sucking energy from her core. She tried to stand, but her body would not respond. Since Colin's departure her heart beat had actually increased, so much that she could only gasp out her words as if she had just run a race.

"I heard…a noise…came in and…found your dad…attacking Miles."

Ellie stared at her with something like revulsion. "Attacking Miles? What do you mean?"

With a leaden arm, Ruth pointed. "There…behind the bed."

Ellie shot her another incredulous look, then followed her pointing finger. When she rounded the bed and saw Miles, she jumped back with a little scream, then stumbled forward, dropping to her knees beside her brother.

"Oh God, Miles," she wailed, hands fluttering in front of her, uncertain whether to touch him, "Oh God, Miles." She flashed Ruth a stricken look. "He's not dead, is he? Please say he's not dead."

On all fours, Ruth crawled over to Ellie. She hadn't seen Miles since he had bounced off the side of the bed and hit the floor. When she *did* see him now, her first feeling was one of relief. He was unconscious, and there were plum-coloured fingerprints all over his swollen neck, but his face had returned to something like its normal colour, and even from here she could see his chest rising and falling.

A high-pitched giggle escaped her, which she immediately smothered with her hand. Then she put her arms around Ellie and hugged her tight. "No, he's not dead. He's breathing, look. He's going to be fine."

Even as the words left her lips, she wondered why she was saying them. How did she know that Miles was going to be fine? What if he'd suffered brain damage? What if the swelling in his throat became so bad that it blocked his air passages?

"What's happened?"

Because of its unexpectedness, the voice from the doorway made them both jump. Still clutching each other, they twisted in unison to see Bridget, wide-eyed and rigid with tension. Ellie broke free of Ruth, ran to Bridget and flung her arms around her.

"Mum!" she sobbed. "Mum! Mum!"

Bridget instinctively clutched at her daughter, holding her close, but she was looking at Ruth. "Ruth, what's going on?"

Ruth felt as if she wanted to break into pieces, shatter like glass, but she forced herself to remain composed. "Colin was here. He attacked Miles, tried to strangle him. I managed to fight him off."

Bridget looked at her, bewildered. "Colin? But he's in hospital."

"He must have…" Ruth had been going to say 'escaped', but then remembered that Colin hadn't been in a lunatic asylum, even though in her opinion he deserved to be "…discharged himself."

"So where is he now?"

"I don't know. He ran away."

"And where's Miles?"

Ruth, still on her knees, looked down at Miles, lying on the floor beside the bed, unseen from the doorway. "He's here."

"Oh my God!" Bridget disengaged herself from Ellie and flew across the room, dropping to her knees beside her unconscious son. When she saw the bruises on his neck, her face crumpled and her voice became shrill and tearful. "Oh my God, oh my God…"

"He's still breathing," said Ruth, putting out a hand to calm her. "He's going to be fine."

Bridget, bottom jaw trembling, eyes shining with tears, did not respond. She continued to stare down at her son, and for a moment Ruth thought she had withdrawn into herself, that it had all become too much for her. Then, abruptly, Bridget looked up, and Ruth saw something in her face—perhaps a new resolve, a determination to end this once and for all.

"Right," Bridget said, "I want the two of you to take Miles to the hospital. Ellie, can you remember the way?"

"Yes, I…I think so."

"Good."

Bridget stood up. Anxiously Ellie said, "What are you going to do?"

"I'm going to go after your dad."

"You can't," Ruth said.

"Yes I can."

"Bridge, don't be daft." Rather unnecessarily Ruth leaned away from Ellie and lowered her voice. "It's dangerous."

"He won't hurt me," said Bridget stubbornly.

"Why not?"

"Because I won't let him. I'll go prepared."

"How can you prepare yourself for something like this?"

Bridget pursed her lips. "He's my husband, Ruth. And he's ill. I'm worried that if I don't go after him, he'll hurt himself. And despite what he's done, I still love him. I still feel responsible for him."

"But by going after him, you'll only be making the situation worse," said Ruth. "Can't you see that?"

Bridget's expression remained obstinate. Ruth tried a different tack. "Why not let the police deal with it? They have special people who can handle these sorts of situations."

"No! I don't want the police involved."

"But they'll get involved anyway once we get Miles to the hospital and everyone sees what sort of state he's in."

"I know, but until then just let me do things my way."

"It's a stupid way."

"Look," Bridget said, "we're wasting time. Miles needs to go to hospital, and I need to go after Colin before he gets too far away."

"But you don't even know where he is."

"I've got a pretty good idea."

Bridget started to move towards the door.

"*Bridge!*" Ruth called despairingly.

"Just get Miles to the hospital," Bridget said. "I'll see you soon."

Then she was gone.

17

Prepared? Bridget thought scornfully as she trampled corn that had been struggling to right itself in the two days since she had last trod this path. *Is that what I am?* If she thought that arming herself with a torch and possessing enough blind faith and determination to believe that her troubled and possibly psychotic husband would listen to reason if she spoke to him calmly and reassuringly enough, then prepared was what she guessed she must be.

Seeing Miles lying on the floor with those terrible bruises around his throat had finally and irrevocably convinced her of one thing: she had to end this. It was no good *hoping* that things would sort themselves out, no good relying on other people; she, herself, had to be proactive, had to face her fears and do her absolute utmost to shout them down.

If she didn't, if she just stood by and hoped for the best, or turned her back and fled as she had done last night, then she would be faced with only one certainty—the disintegration of her world, of all that she had striven for, of all that she held dear. The attack on Miles, a glimpse of every mother's ultimate nightmare, had lit a fire in her belly that would not now be extinguished until she had seen this through.

Small creatures scurried unseen from the light as she shone the torch ahead of her. The corn stalks picked out in its beam looked parched, ashen; they cracked underfoot like sapless twigs. Each time she directed the coned beam at the dark block of woodland ahead, it seemed to flinch back like a single living entity. As if to demonstrate her new fearlessness, she shouted, "Colin, are you there? Can you hear me?"

The expected lack of response did nothing but encourage her to set her face more grimly. As soon as she arrived at what she thought was the place where she had entered the wood two nights ago, she stepped off the path and into the trees. She swept the torch left and right, its yellow light making the foliage look sickly, jaundiced, its beam fractured by the different perspectives of the limbs of trees it chose to highlight. During the day the wood would doubtless appear crammed and burgeoning with life, but now it seemed merely tangled, suffocating. She shone the torch on the ground in front of her and began to march forward as though her feet were desperate to reach the ever-elusive spotlight. Wherever the light touched it, the ground seemed to swell as though something under the earth was eager to rise into brightness. Trees that the torch-beam captured sprang forward, brandishing their multi-appendaged limbs. More than once, Bridget had to duck to avoid whip-thin, head-high branches that seemed to spring out of nowhere.

She checked her watch at regular intervals so that she knew precisely how long she had been walking, and could roughly gauge the distance. With light and time at her disposal, she could retain at least the illusion of being in control. Every few minutes she stopped, shone the torch around, and called Colin's name. Now and then she heard rustling in the undergrowth, which invariably turned into a frantic flurry of retreat when she attempted to pin the source of the sound with light.

For twenty minutes she walked in what she considered to be a straight line. She wasn't sure, but she reckoned the wood to be about two miles square. Given the terrain, that meant she could probably walk from one side to the other in—what?—thirty minutes? Forty? If so, then she must now be as close to the centre as she could get.

Turning in a complete circle, the torch thrust aggressively out in front of her, she shouted Colin's name again. The shadows between the trees seemed all the darker because of the way the foremost trunks soaked up the light, producing a flicker-show, an illusion of darting movement. "Colin, it's me, Bridget. If you're there, please come out. I'm not angry with you, I'm worried about you. I just want to talk."

Silence.

And then…the tiniest *tap* of movement. Immediately Bridget spun, jerking the light towards the sound, but before she had even completed her turn there was another *tap* from behind her, and then another over to her left.

For perhaps a second, Bridget felt a stirring of panic threatening to undermine her new-found resolve. Then she felt a dash of wetness on her cheek and realised what she was hearing. Rain! The first rain for several weeks. She shone her torch upwards and saw glittering jewels descending from the heavens, patting the leaves and the branches and the earth and her.

Great, she thought. It was typical for it to start pissing down just at the point when she was furthest away from home and wondering whether to turn back. And yet there was a sense in which she felt exhilarated. In a strange way the rain felt like a unifying force, making her not separate from the wood but part of it. Despite herself, she tilted up her face and closed her eyes, and exulted in the warm, wet spattering on her cheeks and brow and lips. She wished the rain could wash her clean, wash her troubles away. Within moments its clamour was all around her, like the dancing steps of a thousand tiny feet. It was the sudden thought that the rain could provide an effective screen for anything that might want to creep up on her that made Bridget open her eyes.

She glanced around quickly, but nothing independent of the twitching foliage appeared to be moving. Reflected by torch-light the rain was entrancing; as Bridget made the decision to walk just a little further before turning back, she felt as if she was enclosed within her own personal dome of falling riches, as if she had been singled out for the privilege.

She moved forward, the ground becoming squelchier underfoot. If truth be known, she was beginning to lose hope of finding Colin, was beginning to doubt that he had come this way at all. The idea had seemed to possess a certain symmetry, a certain *rightness* back at the house, but now, as if the rain had cleared her head, she realised how illogical it was to assume that she could understand her husband's increasingly wayward thinking enough to predict his movements.

Five minutes further on, she stopped again. It was raining hard now. Her fringe was plastered to her forehead; her clothes were getting heavy. More crucially, the light from her torch was not as bright as it had been when she'd started out. If she didn't turn back soon, it would fail before she was out of the wood, and she would be in the same predicament she was in two nights ago, blundering in the dark, the shadows feeding her imagination and her panic.

The trees no longer looked harshly jaundiced now, but sepia-toned and therefore unreal. The slashing rain added to the illusion, making her surroundings look like an old, badly-scratched film. One more sweep of the torch, one more plea for her lost husband to make himself known to her, and then she would turn back.

"Colin!" she shouted dutifully, turning in a slow circle. "Co-lin!"

Something flashed to her right as the torch beam swept over it. She blinked, surprised. It was as if something at ground level had deflected the light back into her eyes. Slowly she moved the torch back to where the flash had come from. There. But what was she looking at? Had someone broken a mirror and rammed the points of the largest shards into what appeared to be a hummock of earth so that they stood upright from it? But if so, why? Was it some sort of crude animal trap?

Cautiously she moved forward. As she got closer to whatever was reflecting her torch light, she became aware of a smell. It was faint, deadened by rain, but the first time it touched her nostrils she flinched back from it. It was a vile smell, putrid. It was like nothing she had ever smelled before, and yet it made her think of rotting meat, of slimy, cloying decay. She put her hand over her mouth and nose and took several more tentative steps forward.

All at once, as if a dial had been adjusted in her mind, pulling her thoughts abruptly into focus, she realised what she was looking at. She gasped and felt a judder of shock pass through her. Suddenly she wished she was anywhere but here.

The jagged shapes reflecting the light were not shards of glass at all—they were the blades of knives. *Her* knives. Her missing kitchen knives. Now that she was close enough, she could see not only the parts of their blades that were not buried in the ground, but also their jutting black handles.

But why would someone—Colin?—bring her knives up here and ram them into…into what? She had thought it was a ridge of earth, but she now realised that that, in fact, was on the near side of what appeared to be a slight depression in the ground, and that the knives were sticking out of what the depression contained, which seemed to be a tangle of rags and roots.

She took another step closer. The smell was worse now, making her feel sick. She stepped up on to the ridge of earth beside the depression in the ground, felt her foot sink a little as the mud compacted beneath her weight.

She shone her torch into the depression. For a moment what she was seeing seemed to swirl and blur, as if her brain was protecting her from the sheer awfulness of the sight. She stared hard at what the torchlight, brownish now, was illuminating, yet it was several long seconds before she was able to make sense of it.

And then all at once it seemed to come sharply into focus and she realised that it was a hand. A withered, almost deflated hand. It looked peculiarly unreal, like the hand of a corpse made for a movie with a minuscule special effects budget. With surprising steadiness, her own hand directed the torch beam up an arm that was clad in a stained, soil-spattered sleeve, and from there to a head.

The head was tilted back, its jaw yawning open as if to fill itself full of life-giving rain. Because of the soil, turning to trickling mud, that was packing its mouth and eye sockets and that was clotted in its hair, the head seemed to possess more an approximation of a face than a face itself.

So stunned was Bridget by what she was seeing and having to accept that for a few seconds she felt calm, almost indifferent to the appalling sight in front of her. Then the torch slipped from her fingers and thudded to the ground beside the makeshift grave, and, as if the darkness had prompted it, suddenly, piercingly, she began to scream.

She whirled away from the grave and ran back in the direction she had come. Whether she was terrified of the corpse itself or whoever had dug it up merely to pierce its sunken body with her set of stolen knives she had no idea; the panic that had hold of her was blind and all-con-suming—it left no room for rational thought.

She ran and ran, all control gone, light and distance and time flying away from her, irrelevant. Around her the rain continued to beat down, and now it no longer seemed an ally, but an impediment. It dashed her eyes; it stung her skin; it turned the ground to a quagmire. She slipped and stumbled, flinched from unseen branches that tore at her, drawing blood. Her mind raced with thoughts so terrible that she shied away from confronting them.

Something flashed in the trees to her right. She saw the harsh white disc of a torch beam maybe thirty yards away, bobbing, coruscating, as its silhouetted owner bore down on her. Was he shouting something? She wasn't sure because of the drumming rain and her own ragged breathing. Almost hysterical with terror she altered direction and fled, too exhausted to scream. She had no doubt that the man with the torch was the same one who had dug up the body and stuck a dozen knives into it, which meant he was probably also the same man who had killed whoever had been buried out here in the first place.

Oh God, she intoned silently as she slipped and stumbled away, *oh God, oh God, oh God*. Was this how it was all going to end? Was this how *she* was going to end? Terrified out of her wits, floundering in mud, hunted down like an animal?

She risked a look behind her. There was no sign of her pursuer now, nor of his flashlight. Had he turned it off so as not to give himself away? She turned back and it was as though her question had been answered.

Abruptly, horribly close, a giant eye of light suddenly blinked open and glared directly into her face. Bridget veered away, but too late. Blinded, her foot skidded away from her and she went sprawling. Her knee hit the ground first, then she fell heavily onto her side, shoulder striking the sodden earth with a splat. Before she could stand, she saw a bulky figure looming over her, felt a hand close around her arm.

18

"What's the word for something that becomes active at night?"

"Nocturnal?"

"Yes, that's it. That's me. I'm becoming nocturnal."

Ruth half-smiled, unsure whether the comment was intended as a joke. "How are you feeling now?" she asked.

Bridget's expression might have been the same if Ruth had asked her, 'How does the world work?' The look in her eyes seemed to suggest that the answer was too vast and complex for her to even attempt. Certainly she didn't *look* good. She looked hollow-eyed, haggard, as if she had lost too much weight too quickly.

When the police had found her in the wood, Bridget had been hysterical. This much Ruth had learned from speaking to WPC Summers, who had stayed at the house with the two women whilst the rest of her colleagues dealt with Bridget's gruesome discovery. So far Summers— who, to Ruth, didn't actually look *that* much older than Ellie—had remained tactfully unobtrusive. She had put Ruth in the picture when Ruth had gone into the kitchen a couple of hours earlier to make the first of several pots of tea, and afterwards had stayed in the background, keeping an eye on things but not interfering.

"She's going to need a lot of patient handling and a lot of support," Summers had said. "She's been through a terrible ordeal, and at the moment she's in shock, which means that although she may seem calm now, it could hit her really hard later on. That's when she's going to need her friends around her. She may have mood swings, become unpredictable, get very depressed."

"Don't you worry, I'll be here for her," Ruth had said. "I won't leave her side until I'm sure she's ready."

"And at some point," Summers had said, managing to sound both firm and apologetic, "and it's going to be sooner rather than later, I'm afraid, we'll need the whole story. There's evidently been a lot more going on here than we've been told so far."

"Well, I can tell you most of it now," Ruth had said, and whilst the kettle was boiling had given Summers a potted, third-hand version of what had befallen the Morgans since they had moved into their new house.

Afterwards, dropping her voice still further, she had asked, "So do you think Colin killed this person that Bridge found in the woods?"

Summers' face had given nothing away. "It's too early to speculate."

"But if he did, what would happen to him?" Immediately Ruth had rolled her eyes and rapped on her own head as if knocking on wood. "Sorry, stupid question. He'd go to prison, wouldn't he?"

Summers had raised her hands and said in a voice that brooked no argument, "Look, Ruth, let's not even go there, okay? There's too much we don't know yet. I certainly don't want you mentioning any of this in Bridget's presence."

"Of course not!" Ruth had said indignantly.

She had finished making the tea in silence, then had hesitated a moment before grabbing the brandy from the cupboard above the sink.

"Thought it might calm Bridge's nerves," she had said, reddening. "It is okay for me to give her some, isn't it?"

"A drop in her tea won't do her any harm," Summers had replied. "Don't let her drink too much, that's all."

"I won't." Ruth had proffered the bottle to Summers, but the policewoman had politely declined. She had picked up the tray and walked towards the door, then on the threshold had turned back. "What about Miles? What's Colin likely to get for trying to strangle his own son?"

Summers had regarded her levelly. "Again it's not for me to speculate. There are going to be a great many factors to take into consideration."

Ruth had nodded. "I suppose so. It's just…well, I'd like to have an idea what to expect, that's all. It's not looking too good, is it?"

Summers had sipped her tea, evidently weighing up her words. In the end, she had merely conceded quietly, "No, Ruth. I'm afraid it's not looking too good."

The two hours which had crawled by since Ruth's conversation with the policewoman had passed mostly in silence. Bridget had seemed content to spend her time sitting and staring into space, her arms tightly folded. Ruth, on the other hand, had been restless, wanting and yet not wanting something to happen. She was also anxious because she didn't know how best to handle her friend's reluctance to communicate. Should she try and get Ruth to talk about what she had seen, or would mentioning it only upset her? On the few occasions when Ruth *had* tried to instigate a conversation, Bridget's replies had been either abstract enough to intimidate Ruth into silence, or merely monosyllabic.

Ruth had spent her time drinking without getting drunk, making endless cups of tea, switching the TV on, then off, then on again, looking through Colin and Bridget's cd collection, and performing numerous bitty, trivial tasks that she hoped gave the illusion that she was being busy, purposeful. At one point, maybe an hour after their initial conversation in the kitchen, she had sought out Summers and had asked her how best to handle Bridget.

Summers had not been particularly helpful. "Just be open to her, be receptive."

"But should I *talk* to her?" Ruth had wanted to know.

"If Bridget wants to talk, yes. If not, just leave her be for the time being, let her have some space. Believe me, Ruth, Bridget will be expected to do plenty of talking before long."

Ruth's last proper conversation with Bridget, before Bridget's comment about being nocturnal, had occurred when Ruth had put down the phone after calling the hospital.

"Good news," she had said, brightly enough to realise immediately how crass she sounded. Adopting a slightly more sombre tone, she had crossed to the armchair that Bridget seemed to have melded with, and had knelt in front of it.

"I've just been on the phone to the hospital, Bridge. They've told me that Miles is going to be fine, that he's sleeping peacefully now and is expected to make a full recovery."

Bridget looked up as if she had woken unexpectedly and was still half-entangled in a dream. "I should have been with him," she said.

Again Ruth wasn't sure how to respond. She grabbed her friend's limp hands in both of hers and squeezed them tight. "It's okay. Don't worry about it. He's going to be fine. *Fine.*"

"I should have been with him," Bridget said again, and Ruth had been alarmed to see the growing distress on her face. "I shouldn't have abandoned him like that. He needs me."

"Bridge, you *didn't* abandon him. You left him with me and Ellie. You knew he'd be safe with us. And he's going to be fine, Bridge. We'll go and see him tomorrow, yeah? Me and you and Ellie. We'll all go and see him, take him something nice. Okay?"

"Ellie," Bridget said, panic tightening her voice. "Where's Ellie?"

"Ssh, she's fine, she's fine. She's staying over at your neighbours' again. I thought it'd be better there for her, what with the police here and everything."

"The police?" said Bridget, confused. "Why are the police here?"

"They found you in the wood, remember. You were...you were upset. They brought you home."

"But how did they know where I was?"

"I rang them," Ruth confessed, grimacing in anticipation of her friend's reaction. "I'm sorry, Bridge, but I had to. I couldn't just disappear and leave you to go off on your own. I was worried about you and...and Colin. I was worried about what might happen to you."

Bridget had looked at Ruth as if Ruth was a child who was finding it hard to grasp a very simple idea. "Colin wouldn't hurt me," she said. "Colin loves me."

"I know he does, Bridge. I know. But Colin's not himself. He's ill. He's confused."

"Colin wouldn't hurt anybody," Bridget said urgently, as if she needed Ruth to believe it, to agree with her, "not really, not on purpose."

What about Miles? Ruth wanted to say, but she forced herself to smile. "No. I'm sure he wouldn't."

Bridget looked anxiously around as if once again she had no idea where she was. "Where is he? Where's Colin?"

"They're looking for him, Bridge. They'll find him soon, don't worry."

Abruptly Bridget slumped back into her seat, closed her eyes. "I'm tired."

Ruth stroked her hand. "You sleep for a bit now. It'll do you good."

Nothing more was said until Bridget opened her eyes twenty minutes later and asked, "What's the word for something that becomes active at night?"

Taken aback, Ruth said, "Nocturnal?"

"Yes, that's it. That's me," said Bridget. "I'm becoming nocturnal."

Ruth looked at her friend, aware that if Bridget wanted to talk she ought to encourage her, but unsure what to say next. Feebly she asked, "How are you feeling now?"

Bridget looked at her as if she couldn't believe what she had been asked, and Ruth couldn't help but think that she had just made a faux pas in some kind of verbal game. She was wondering how to redeem the situation when there was a knock on the front door.

"Colin," Bridget breathed.

Both women began to rise from their seats, though Ruth did so primarily in response to Bridget. Before either of them could take so much as a step towards the door, however, Summers appeared in the doorway, hand raised as if on traffic duty.

"You two wait here."

Ruth thought that Bridget would disobey, but she slowly sank back into her seat. Ruth heard Summers ask, "Who is it?", which was followed by a muffled response, then the sound of the front door opening. There was a brief murmured conversation, then the rap of more than one set of footsteps approaching the snug. Summers entered first, followed by a red-faced policeman made bulky by his jacket. The way that the policeman looked hesitantly at the two women made Ruth think absurdly of a nervous boyfriend about to be introduced by a teenage daughter to her parents.

"Bridget," Summers said softly, "would you mind if Sergeant Brand here had a word with you?"

Ruth felt tense, though wasn't sure if the feeling was transmitting itself to her from the two police officers or whether she was merely apprehensive because of what Brand might be about to reveal.

"Have you found Colin?" Bridget asked with a calmness that seemed almost naive.

"Not yet," Brand said, and sat down heavily on the end of the settee. Ruth noted that he had left muddy footprints on the carpet and found herself thinking that it was a good job Bridget and Colin hadn't had a new one laid yet.

"What then?" Bridget said as if nothing else was worth her time. "What do you want to talk to me about?"

"I need to ask you a question," Brand said, "and I want you to think about it carefully. I'm going to say a name and I want you to tell me whether you've heard it before, whether it means anything to you."

"What's the name?" Ruth asked, clutching her knees hard.

"Jason MacNeill."

For a moment the room seemed to spin. Ruth felt sure she was pitching forward and shot out an arm to clutch the chair for support. The strange thing was, she didn't recognise the name straight away— or rather, she did, but she couldn't immediately place it.

She heard Bridget's voice as if it was echoing up from the bottom of a well. It was eerily calm, almost deadpan. "Yes."

"Yes?" said Brand. "Yes, you know the name?"

"Yes."

"Can you tell us anything about Mr MacNeill, Bridget?" asked Summers.

It was at this point that it all came rushing back to Ruth. *Oh my God*, she thought, *oh my God.*

"I used to work with him," Bridget said blandly. "We were…friends."

Brand frowned. "You used to work with him where exactly?"

"Where I used to live. In Yorkshire. At the Leisure Centre."

Ruth stared at her friend with a mixture of fascination and horror. She wondered whether Bridget had twigged yet. From her manner it didn't seem so. Or perhaps on some level she had, and the realisation had sent her so deeply into shock that her emotions had become unreachable, reducing her—on the surface at least—to an automaton.

Ruth saw Brand and Summers exchange a glance. Brand leaned forward as if he didn't want to allow a single syllable of what Bridget might say elude him.

"Bridget, when was the last time you saw Mr MacNeill? Please think carefully. This is very important."

Bridget blinked, and Ruth wondered whether the truth was finally filtering through into her best friend's fuddled mind. Bridget, however, merely sounded mildly indignant when she replied, "Not for over a year now. He went away. We're not friends any more."

"And he hasn't tried to contact you at all during that time?" Brand asked.

"No. I wouldn't have wanted him to."

"Oh? Why was that, Bridget?"

Bridget looked suddenly flustered, as if she had been manoeuvred into a corner. The glance she gave Ruth was full of child-like desperation, a clear appeal for help. Ruth's thoughts were zipping about like pinballs in her head, but the calmness of her own voice surprised her.

"Do you want me to tell them, Bridge?"

Bridget gave the faintest of nods and lowered her head, as if in shame.

Brand and Summers turned their attention to Ruth. They looked infinitely patient. Ruth said quietly, "Bridget and Jason MacNeill had an…a relationship. It didn't last long. She and Colin were going through a bad patch and it just…happened."

"I see," said Brand. He looked thoughtfully at Ruth for a moment, then turned back to Bridget and asked, "And who ended this relationship, Bridget?"

"I did," Bridget whispered.

"And how did Mr MacNeill take it?"

"Okay. It was all just a bit of fun for him. More than anything, I think he was relieved."

"Relieved why?"

"Because it was getting too heavy. Because Colin had found out."

"And this prospect frightened Mr MacNeill, did it?"

Bridget smiled a slow, dreamy smile. Her responses to Brand's questions were lucid, but hesitant. She was looking not at the policeman, but gazing into space.

"He wasn't frightened of what Colin might do to him, but he didn't want a scene. That's why he left."

"Left? Left his job, you mean?"

Bridget shrugged. "I turned up for work one day and he wasn't there. I found out later that he'd sent a letter saying he was leaving straight away."

"Did no one think this was odd?"

"I don't know."

"But didn't anyone come looking for him? Friends? Family?"

"No. He didn't get on with his family. I don't know why exactly. I think there'd been some kind of falling out. He didn't talk about it much."

"And you didn't try to contact him?"

"I didn't want to. He'd made it clear he didn't want to have anything more to do with me. And I'd decided that I wanted to save my marriage, that it was worth saving."

"So as far as you're concerned, he simply disappeared off the face of the earth?"

Another shrug. "I suppose so."

"And you have no reason to suspect that he might have followed you here or even previously re-located to this area?"

Even this failed to spark Bridget into life. "No."

"Hmm." Brand looked at Bridget as if trying to decide whether or not she was telling the truth. Bridget seemed oblivious to his scrutiny, but Ruth was indignant. She was debating whether it would help Bridget's cause to tell Brand in no uncertain terms that her friend was *not* lying when Bridget astonished her by saying blandly, "Jason's dead, isn't he? It's his body I found in the wood?"

Brand too seemed momentarily taken aback, but quickly recovered. "We won't know for certain until a post mortem has been carried out, but we have reason to suspect so, yes."

Bridget nodded slowly. Her face was set, mask-like. "And you think it was Colin who killed him, don't you?" she murmured.

19

Half an hour later, Bridget sighed and said quietly, "Colin *did* kill him."

After Brand had left, the three women had remained seated and silent, as if, in the wake of the sergeant's bombshell, conversation had been trivialised to the point of redundancy. Ruth hardly dared look at Bridget for fear that her best friend would see in Ruth's eyes her willingness to believe that Colin had killed Jason MacNeill, and would construe it as betrayal. Ruth had felt embarrassed for Bridget, and desperately, achingly sorry for her, but she could not bring herself to rise from her chair and go across and put her arms around her, could not swallow what she truly believed and make herself tell her friend that everything would be all right, that Colin couldn't possibly have done it.

So they sat in terrible, ringing silence, and even Summers who was supposed to be trained to handle situations such as this barely said a word. Indeed, in Ruth's eyes Summers seemed younger than ever, out of her depth, a teenager in fancy dress. After ten tortuous minutes, Ruth slipped out of the room, mumbling about tea, and once in the kitchen she gripped the edge of the sink and started to cry. She turned on the tap to drown the sounds tearing themselves out of her, and afterwards she doused her face in cold water, hoping it would hide the evidence, knowing it wouldn't, hoping that Bridget would be too preoccupied with her own thoughts to notice.

Ruth was back in the snug and contemplating pouring herself a third cup of tea even though her stomach was sloshing with it, even though it was an effort even to swallow, when Bridget spoke. For a moment afterwards there was silence, as if the voice had come from nowhere and stunned them all. Then Summers leaned forward.

"What makes you say that, Bridget?"

When Bridget looked at Summers, Ruth wondered whether her friend had inadvertently given voice to her innermost thoughts. Then, in the measured, seemingly indifferent manner that was beginning to freak Ruth out, that almost made her wish that Bridget would break down just so that she could comfort her, Bridget said, "There's no other explanation. Colin killed Jason and buried him up there in the wood. Then, two nights ago, he dug him up and killed him again."

"Killed him again?" Ruth said. "What…" Then she saw Summers motioning her to silence in the manner of someone using stealth to catch a dangerous beast, and the question died on her lips.

Bridget went on as though Ruth hadn't spoken, her voice quiet and mesmerising, like a hypnotist's, her eyes unfocused, gazing into space. It was as though she wasn't speaking to them at all, but merely vocalising her thoughts as a way of ordering them, making sense of them.

"Colin must have gone round to Jason's flat and confronted him and ended up by killing him. I'm sure he didn't mean to, I'm sure it was an accident, but somehow it happened. It must have been a terrible strain for him, keeping it to himself, but he wouldn't have wanted to upset us, would he? He wouldn't have wanted to upset the children. So he wrote letters pretending that Jason had gone away—one to work, maybe one to Jason's landlord, one to his family—and then he brought the body all the way out here, far, far away from home, and buried it."

She paused a moment, and although she didn't exactly start weeping, Ruth saw that her eyes were suddenly shining with moisture. She was about to interject, but Summers caught her eye and gave the tiniest shake of her head. After a moment, her voice even quieter now, Bridget went on.

"Do you know how we found this house? Colin told me he'd got lost. It was just after he'd found out about Jason. Things were bad between us and he said he needed a break, he needed time to think, to sort out his head. He drove down to London to see his agent, and then he told me he was going to stay the night with an old school friend in Kent. When he got back he was…different. More positive. Almost buoyant. He said he wanted to make a go of things, and talked about making a fresh start. He said he'd got lost on the way to his friend's and had seen this house with a For Sale sign outside it, and had fallen in love with it, and just thought, 'Why not?' He drove to the estate agent's and he got the details. When we were going through our terrible time, having all the counselling, it was like…like something for us to aim for. The light at the end of our tunnel. Our golden fleece."

She lapsed into silence. *Sick*, Ruth thought, *sick, sick, sick*. If truth be told, she'd always thought Colin a bit weird, a bit edgy, but she'd got on with him because he and Bridge had been good together, and because he'd been a great dad to his kids. Now, though, all her long-held reservations seemed finally to have been borne out—not that that gave her even the slightest shred of satisfaction. On the contrary, she was overwhelmed with horror at the thought of a man who would kill a love rival, take the body hundreds of miles away, and then move his family to within a mile of where the corpse was buried.

What did that say about Colin's state of mind? That he was stupid and insensitive at best, dangerously psychotic at worst. It was obvious that Bridge wanted to think of her husband as a victim of circumstance, but

Ruth found it hard to see him as anything other than a cold-blooded killer. For Jason MacNeill's disappearance not to have aroused suspicion before now, Colin must have planned the aftermath of his death with cold, calculating precision. And then to view the house that overlooked his victim's resting place as some sort of prize to be won at the end of a long, hard road was ghoulish in the extreme. It was almost as though, by moving in, Colin had been celebrating not merely the saving of his marriage, but also the ultimate physical vanquishment of what he evidently perceived as the catalyst for the obstacles he and Bridget had had to overcome.

Maybe that should have been the end of it, but something—whether within Colin or some extraneous, unpredictable factor—had refused to let the ground lie. And so there had been an exhumation of sorts, an eruption of phenomena, be it real or fanciful, that had eventually forced the truth into the light. *Killed him again?* What had Bridge meant by that? Had Colin been forced to somehow kill Jason for a second time because the first time he had not stayed dead? Had Jason been *haunting* the Morgans? Had it been his *spirit*, his *ghost*, that had sent Colin over the edge? Dead man's revenge, Ruth thought, and shuddered as she remembered the trail of ash leading half-way across the attic floor from Colin's chair.

"When did you know?" she found herself asking, despite Summers' warning frown.

Bridget gave her a vacant, faraway look. "What?"

"When did you know that Jason's body was buried up in the wood? Did you know before tonight?"

Bridget frowned as though Ruth was deliberately confusing her. "No, how could I?"

"Ruth," Summers warned.

"But you said Colin killed him again. How did you know Colin had killed him the first time?"

"I worked it out," Bridget whispered, "because of what I saw."

"What you saw?"

"Ruth!" Summers said again, more forcefully.

Ruth turned to her in exasperation. "This is *important.*"

Summers' face was taut with anger. "Maybe, but this isn't the time or the place. Bridget has been through a terrible ordeal. She doesn't deserved to be harangued like this."

"I'm not haranguing her, I'm—"

"*Shhhh.*"

The sound came from Bridget and was as fierce as escaping steam. Ruth and Summers looked at her, startled. Bridget looked blandly back at them.

"Jason had been there for a long time," she said. "Colin had dug him up and used all my kitchen knives on him. He was like a butterfly."

"A butterfly?" said Ruth, confused.

"Pinned into place. Tethered to the earth."

Ruth looked at her in horror. "You mean…what…so that he couldn't move?"

"So that he couldn't *walk*," said Bridget.

Suddenly Ruth remembered Colin's rant after attempting to strangle Miles, or the gist of it anyway:

He's trying to wheedle his way back in.

Who is? Ruth had screamed at him. *That's Miles!*

No, that's a trick. That's what he wants you to think. But maybe you already know that. Maybe that was your plan all along.

"That's why he tried to strangle Miles," Ruth breathed.

"What?" said Summers. "What are you talking about?"

Ruth turned to her. "Colin thought that all his…his problems were caused by Jason. Jason coming back to haunt him, to take revenge. That's why he went up to the wood and dug up the body and attacked it with knives. Like Bridge says, he was trying to pin it to the earth, to prevent it from coming after him again."

There was a moment of silence, then Summers' lips curled in scornful disbelief. "I'm sorry, but are you suggesting that the body of Jason MacNeill has been rising from its grave like a…a *zombie*?"

"Of course not," Ruth snapped. "I'm just telling you what Colin believed. Aren't you listening?"

Abashed, Summers raised her hands. "I'm sorry, go on."

"Okay, so to do what he did, Colin must have been getting pretty desperate. He attacked the body, but before he could bury it again, he was disturbed by Bridget here. That's probably why he seemed okay for a day or so afterwards, Bridge. Maybe he thought he had the situation under control again."

Bridget gazed at her as if enraptured by her story, but she didn't respond. Summers said, "So what set him off again?"

"It was at the barbecue, wasn't it, Bridge? You said he went off the deep end when Miles and his friend touched one of those stumps." Ruth was thinking on her feet now, trying to make sense of it as she went along. "So Colin must have thought the stumps were linked to Jason in some way. He must have thought that Jason was…I don't know…imbuing them with some sort of power, some energy. Maybe he thought because of what he'd done to Jason's body the power couldn't get to him, that it was latent, trapped in the stumps. Maybe he thought that all he had to do was get rid of the stumps or destroy them and it would all be over. But when Miles touched the stump, Colin must have thought that he'd released the energy, that it had gone into him, possessed him. Yes!" she said, warming to her theory. "In fact, he said as much to me. He attacked Miles because he thought Miles was no longer his son, but someone else. I didn't know who he was talking about at the time, but now I do. He thought Miles was Jason."

She finished breathlessly, her cheeks flushed, eyes flicking from Summers to Bridget. Summers looked shell-shocked, but Bridget wore the expression of a proud mother whose daughter has just delivered a word-perfect performance in the school play. Ruth felt that her assessment of Colin's twisted reasoning was pretty much water-tight, though she was all too aware that none of this explained the things that Bridget, and to a lesser extent, she herself, had seen.

"Have you finished?" Summers said heavily.

Ruth thought about it, then nodded. "Yes, I think so."

"Have you ever considered a career in criminal psychology?" Summers asked, still deadpan.

Ruth started to smile, then suddenly remembered what the circumstances were, and was appalled at her lapse. She turned to Bridget, dreading to think what her reaction would be, readying herself to apologise, but just then the attention of all three of them was caught by a flare of light from outside, so bright that it was visible even through the thick red curtains at the window.

"What the hell was that?" Summers said, jumping up from the settee. She ran to the window and pulled the curtain aside, and her face was immediately illuminated by what to Ruth looked like a pillar of flame in the garden. "Oh my God."

Instantly Ruth realised what she was looking at—the stump closest to the house in the back garden was on fire. For one absurd moment she thought that she was somehow the cause of it, that her unravelling of the truth had acted as a destructive catalyst, prompting the stump to spontaneously combust.

Then, bathed in orange light from the flames, she saw a capering figure, its face fixed in an expression of maniacal glee, its mouth moving as if it were chanting some incantation. In its hand it was carrying what she thought at first was a small suitcase, then realised was a petrol can.

"Colin." Ruth didn't even know Bridget had risen from her chair until she heard her say her husband's name behind her left shoulder.

Summers was already speaking urgently into the radio that was clipped to her breast pocket, calling for back-up; she referred to Colin as the 'murder suspect'. Outside, Ruth saw Colin run down to the stump that was furthest away from the house and splash petrol on it. Then she half-turned, and so was only peripherally aware of this stump too gouting into flame, as Summers said sharply, "Please stay here, Bridget. Don't go out."

Bridget was already at the door, an obstinate look on her face. "He's my *husband*," she said without breaking her stride.

"Bridget!" Summers ran after her.

Ruth glanced out of the window, saw Colin, a flapping, scarecrow-like figure, running back towards the house, swinging his petrol can, then she too ran out after the two women.

Bridget was already hurrying down the hallway towards the back door, Summers in pursuit. The door leading into the back garden was locked, and it was while Bridget was fumbling with the key that Summers caught up with her and put a hand on her arm.

"Bridget, this is *not* a good idea. I can't allow you to go out there."

Bridget twisted away from the policewoman's grasp. Colin's reappearance had energised her, imbued her with a new sense of urgency, but her eyes still seemed vacant, unfocused.

"I have to talk to him. *I have to.*"

"It's too dangerous, Bridget. Colin's confused, unstable."

"He won't hurt *me*."

"He might. He might hurt you without knowing what he's doing."

"He won't. He loves me."

"He loved Miles too, didn't he?"

Ruth winced, but Bridget just looked confused. "That was different," she muttered, then shook her head. "Anyway, I'm going out. You can't stop me."

"I can if I have to," Summers said almost apologetically, "but I don't want you to make me have to, Bridget."

"Look, why don't we all go out?" said Ruth, trying to be helpful. "Bridge and I can stay behind you."

Summers scowled. "No, none of us are—Hey!"

Bridget had taken advantage of the momentary distraction to wrench open the back door and plunge out into the night. Summers made a grab for her, but missed, almost stumbling over in the process. "Shit," she snarled as Ruth helped her regain her balance. The two women ran out after Bridget, who, presumably because she had been unable to see Colin in the back garden, was now heading for the path that ran up the side of the house to the front.

Already the heat from the burning stumps was tremendous. The hungry, twisting pillars of flame gave the impression that the blackened shapes they were devouring were somehow alive and writhing in agony. As Ruth and Summers followed Bridget, Ruth saw that the stump jutting from the ground on this side of the house was on fire now too, the light of which made the path which had been doused by the recent rain gleam like orange glass. Running past the stump took them close enough to it for pearls of sweat to spring like a rash from the exposed skin on Ruth's arms and face, and for the air that she inhaled to be sauna-hot. She hoped the house would be okay, that the soaking it had received earlier in the evening would be enough to prevent it catching fire too.

Bridget was maybe a dozen steps in front of them. As Ruth looked up, already beginning to pant, she saw her friend turning the corner that would take her onto the front drive. Seconds later, Summers, several steps in front of Ruth, turned the corner too. Instantly Ruth heard her shout, "Bridget!" and was simultaneously aware of the glow coming from the front of the house. As Ruth too emerged onto the drive, she saw the twin fires raging on the front lawn, already so intense that they seemed to merge and pulse with heat in front of her eyes, like the beat of a giant, incandescent heart.

Colin, bathed in luminescence, was already dancing around the third of the stumps, shaking his upended petrol can at it, releasing glittering fans of fuel. The heat haze and the constantly moving light made his form seem indistinct, made it seem to shimmer and falter, as if *he* was the ghost.

Bridget was moving across the lawn towards her husband, who seemed oblivious to her presence. Her right hand was raised in front of her, fingers spread, palm facing him, though whether this was intended to calm him or a feeble gesture to ward off the heat Ruth was not sure.

The policewoman's shout had intended to halt Bridget in her tracks, but Bridget was not listening. "Bridget," Summers shouted again, her voice raw-edged, "come back here *now*, do you hear me?"

Again Bridget failed to respond. Instead, she called out, "Colin. Colin, it's me." Her voice, thin and reedy, was consumed within the crackling of the flames. If Colin heard it, he treated it in the same way that Bridget had treated the order from Summers—as an irrelevance, or at best a minor irritation.

The moment that Colin struck a match and flung it with a bared-teeth grin at the third stump, Summers ran forward and dived at Bridget's legs. Bridget went down, felled by a perfect rugby tackle. As the two women struggled on the wet ground, a coil of flame engulfed the third stump with such speed and ferocity that Ruth was reminded of a predator rising from below to seize its prey. She saw Colin hurl his can to one side, then fling his head back and scream his crazed triumph at the sky. Then, gleefully, he began to leap up and down, to wave his arms, to laugh and rant, and though the roaring of the flames drowned out his words, Ruth gained the clear impression that he was jeering at the stumps, taunting them.

Because Summers and Bridget were preoccupied with their sodden tussle, it was only Ruth who witnessed what happened next. Afterwards her mind would try to convince her that she couldn't have seen what she thought she had, and later, when the police asked her to recount what she had witnessed, she would feel embarrassed, and would subsequently furnish them with a version of events that she knew they would find acceptable.

However, what she saw—what she initially *thought* she saw—was this: as Colin continued to caper and gloat, something—or rather, three somethings—seemed to swell, to mushroom, from the base of each of the stumps. At first Ruth thought that the incredible heat was simply causing the stumps to split and blister. All the same, that didn't prevent an additional notion from entering her mind, which was that each of the stumps looked to be giving birth. She pulled a face, slightly repulsed by the idea, then gasped as the three sacs of burning matter appeared to tear themselves free not only of the bases of the stumps, but also of the rapidly scorching ground beneath.

When she saw the breakaway sections of the three stumps uncurl and elongate, still encased in flame, she told herself that no, she couldn't be seeing this, it couldn't possibly be happening. What had appeared at first to be shapeless lumps of matter now looked like burning children. Only vaguely, admittedly, but the more Ruth looked, the more she became convinced that she could make out a charred dome of a head, a blackened torso and twisted, stick-thin limbs within each of the swirling white-yellow vortexes of bellowing flame.

What made her think—what made her *hope*—that she might be hallucinating was that Colin seemed oblivious to the presence of these…these *offspring*. She would tell the police later that he had simply ventured too close to the flames, that he may even have allowed himself to be set alight deliberately, but for a long time afterwards, whenever she closed her eyes, she saw something different, something altogether more terrifying. In unison, and with astonishing speed, she saw the creatures turn and flow towards Colin. She saw them pounce on him, savage him, bring him down. Saw him, at the last, dig his hooked fingers into the soft ground and try vainly to drag himself away.

Most of her attention still taken by the sight of Colin's thrashing, burning form, it took Ruth several seconds to realise that Summers was screaming her name. Tearing her gaze away from the terrible sight in front of her, she turned and saw the policewoman sitting on Bridget's back, pinioning her arms to her sides. It was clear that Summers' attention had been fully occupied by her struggle with Bridget, because it was only now that she glanced up and saw what was happening to Colin. The shock on her face made her look younger than ever. Ruth quite clearly saw her mouth the words: *Oh fuck.* Feeling as though she was moving in slow motion, as though her body was not quite her own, Ruth loped over to Summers. Kneeling down beside the policewoman felt like a prelude to collapsing. Summers tore her gaze away from Colin, who was now so immersed in flame that he and his attackers had become indistinguishable from one another, and began to shout in her ear. Yet despite her proximity, Ruth couldn't at first hear what Summers was saying. She was not sure whether the policewoman's voice was being drowned out by the fire or by the buzzing in her own head. "What?" she shouted, tilting her left ear closer to Summers' mouth and clapping a hand over her right.

"I said give me a hand with Bridget. I want to get her back inside before she sees…what's happening."

Ruth nodded, and together the two of them managed to keep Colin's burning, still feebly jerking body out of Bridget's eye-line as they turned her around and lifted her up. Moving at an almost-run, they frog-marched her back down the side of the house and in through the back door. Several times Bridget tried to dig her heels in, but on each occasion Summers roughly urged her on. "Sorry about this, Bridge," Ruth kept saying. "Sorry, but it's for your own good."

Summers motioned them into the kitchen with a nod of the head and then to a chair, where they deposited Bridget. Almost immediately, Bridget started to rise, but Summers, clearly close to the end of her tether, pointed at her like a dog owner ordering a pet to its basket, and shouted, "No! You stay there! You've caused enough trouble already. Don't you realise what an appallingly dangerous thing you did by going out there?"

Bridget didn't answer, but after a moment she lowered herself back into her seat. Summers went to stand by the door to bar her escape and rubbed at her face with a trembling hand. They were all three of them greasy with soot and smelling of smoke. Both Bridget's clothes and Summers' uniform were plastered with mud.

Tentatively Ruth said, "Did anyone else see what happened out there?"

"Don't!" Summers warned, holding up a hand. "I don't want anyone to say a word. I want us all to just sit tight until reinforcements arrive."

Ruth sank down and lowered her head into her hands, and as if on cue, there came the distant but rapidly approaching blare of sirens.

EPILOGUE

"Tombstones?" exclaimed Ruth. "What do you mean?"

Claire glanced around anxiously and made a quieting gesture with her hand. "Shh, I don't want Bridget to hear. It might make her even more upset than she already is."

Ruth gritted her teeth in apology. Bridget was on the far side of the crowded room, nodding abstractedly at whatever tale of woe a tall, thin man with wiry grey hair sprouting from his nose and ears was stooping to regale her with. Ruth had promised her friend she'd look after her today, and felt a little guilty that she wasn't striding over there even now to extract Bridget from the tall man's clutches. However, regardless of the memories that Claire's words were threatening to stir into life, she simply had to hear the rest of what Bridget's former neighbour had found out.

"Two days after Bridget and I went to visit Jean…that's, um, the old lady who used to live in the house," Claire said, "I had a phone call from the hospital. Jean had had a stroke and was asking for me. Apparently she was getting in a real state, saying she had something important to tell me.

"When I arrived she was in a bad way, poor old girl. She was very weak and her left side was paralysed. She could just about talk, though, through the right side of her mouth. When I sat down, she grabbed my hand as though she was worried I'd leave before she could tell me everything that was on her mind, and as if this would be the last chance she'd have. It turned out she'd had the stroke because she'd been so upset at what had happened at the house. Some insensitive old biddy had gone along to see her, bursting with local gossip—though I suppose Jean would have found out sooner or later."

Claire paused and looked around again. Despite the adverse publicity, Colin's funeral had been well-attended, and not predominantly by the ghoulish or the curious. Whatever they thought of Bridget's husband, it seemed to Claire that the majority of the attendees had come to support Bridget in her grief and to offer their genuinely heart-felt condolences. Bridget had been flanked by her children and by Ruth throughout the ceremony, and it was only back at the house for the

wake, which—despite the amount of alcohol that was being consumed—was a sombre, low-key affair, that Claire had come forward to
pay her respects.

Bridget had been gracious, dignified, albeit in a distracted, shell-
shocked way. She had thanked Claire for coming, for driving all the
way up to Yorkshire, and only once had she given an inkling of how she
was really feeling. This was when she had responded to Claire's hug
with one of her own, and Claire had felt Bridget's claw-like hand
clutching at her back and had realised how desperately her ex-neigh-
bour was trying to hold herself together. It was at this point that Ruth,
as though sensing Bridget was about to crack, had introduced herself.
"Hi," she had said, "I'm Bridget's best friend, Ruth. I met your husband—Shaun, isn't it?"

Claire had come not only to pay her respects, but also because she
felt she had no right to keep Jean's revelation to herself. Of course, she
realised that Bridget's previous desire to find out about the stumps had
stemmed from her need to understand her husband's increasingly irrational behaviour, a motive that subsequent circumstances had rendered
irrelevant, but even so, Claire knew that grief brought its own obses-
sions, its own desperate urges to unravel the hows and whys and where-
fores of death. What if Bridget *still* had a need to know, to find out as
much as she could? Claire wasn't entirely sure how the information
Jean had given her could possibly shed any light on what had happened, and yet she had nevertheless felt duty-bound to come here, to
test the water, gauge Bridget's mood.

As soon as she saw Bridget, however, she realised that she couldn't
tell her anything. Bridget looked brittle, on the verge of collapse. Claire
couldn't help but feel that what she had to say, unrelated though it may
have been to what had happened to the Morgans, might have shattered
her completely. She had all but resigned herself to keeping Jean's dis-
closure to herself when she decided to tell Ruth. Ruth was close to
Bridget. Since Colin's death she had been with her every day. If anyone
should decide how important it was that Bridget know the truth, Ruth
should. At least if Claire gave her the information, Ruth would then be
in a position to pass it on to Bridget if and when she felt the time was
right.

"The last time I saw Jean, which was the time that Bridget came with me," Claire said, lowering her voice still further, "Jean told us that the stumps in the garden were her children. She didn't elaborate on that, but she got quite emotional about it. She was upset and seemed rather confused.

"I knew she and Harry had never had any children, so I took it to mean that for some reason the things were her pride and joy, a kind of child substitute. That sounds silly, I know, but what she said didn't seem to make much sense, and I was more concerned with her not getting upset than I was with trying to decipher her ramblings. Bridget was being quite intense too, which didn't help."

Ruth looked as though she was bracing herself for something. "So this time Jean told you that the stumps were actually tombstones?"

Claire paused, then said, "Before I tell you what Jean told me, please understand that I'm not saying it's all true. On the other hand, I'm not saying it's a lie either. When I saw Jean in hospital, it seemed clear to me that she sincerely believed her own story. But like I say, she's old and she gets confused, and strokes can do funny things to people."

"I know," Ruth said, impatiently enough for Claire to say, "Sorry, I'm rambling, aren't I?"

"You said the stumps were tombstones," Ruth said. "Tombstones for who?"

"For her children," Claire said.

Before Ruth could respond, Claire said quickly, "I know I said that Jean and Harry never had any children, but that doesn't mean they didn't try. Jean told me that she got pregnant seven times, but each time she miscarried."

"Oh God," breathed Ruth.

"I know. It must have been devastating for her. I don't know the full story, because it was obvious when I saw her that she just wanted to talk, to get it all off her chest. I didn't ask questions because I didn't think it was tactful. I'm not sure, for instance, whether the miscarriages were natural, or whether they were…"

"What?" snapped Ruth.

"Or whether they were induced."

"Induced? You mean, brought on deliberately? By who? Jean?"

Ruth's voice had been rising and Claire made the quietening gesture with her hand again. "No, not by Jean."

"Her husband?"

Claire looked uncomfortable. "She didn't actually say it was Harry. It was more what she implied. She said that Harry didn't want any children. She said that she kept trying, but he wouldn't have them."

"So he made her abort?" Ruth breathed in horror.

Claire shrugged.

"How would he do that? By punching her in the belly? Inflicting violence on her?"

Miserably Claire said, "Oh, this is terrible. We're jumping to conclusions, speaking ill of the dead. It might not have been like that at all."

Ruth was silent for a few seconds, then she said in an oddly hollow voice, "So the…the foetuses were buried under the stumps?"

"According to Jean."

"God," Ruth breathed. "And Colin burnt them all. He burnt the graves of her children. No wonder she reacted like she did."

"Not all of them," said Claire.

"What?"

"Colin didn't get to all of them. He died before he could reach the one on the far side of the house."

"Big consolation," muttered Ruth.

Claire pursed her lips and quickly raised then lowered her eyebrows in a gesture that was partly in sympathy with Ruth's sentiment and partly an apology for being pedantic.

"So did the authorities know about this?" Ruth asked.

"I don't know how they could have done, do you?"

"But wouldn't Jean's doctor have suspected something? Or her friends?"

Claire shook her head. "It's a fairly isolated community. And things were different back then, remember. Jean might not have gone to her doctor. Harry might have persuaded her not to. And I don't think she's ever had that many friends. Besides, if she miscarried early in each case, no one need ever have known she was pregnant."

"It's horrible," said Ruth. "How on earth could she stay with a man like that?"

Again Claire shook her head. "Like I say, it was a different time back then. Divorce wasn't such an easy option. Besides, I think Jean still loved Harry in a way, despite everything."

Now it was Ruth's turn to shake her head, though *she* looked angry and disbelieving rather than melancholy. "So who actually made these…these tombstones? Harry?"

"I assume so. Jean didn't say."

Ruth looked momentarily too disgusted to speak. For a few moments the two women stood silently together, surrounded by the low burr of conversation. Finally Ruth asked, "Why exactly are you telling me all this?"

Claire sighed. "To be perfectly honest, I don't know. Probably because it's another piece of the jigsaw. And because before Colin died, Bridget was desperate to know what the stumps were. I suppose I wondered whether she still wanted to know. I suppose I felt terrible for her, and I had this idea that maybe I'd at least be able to ease her mind about *something*."

"I don't think it would ease her mind to tell her that there were the corpses of seven children buried in her garden."

Claire gave a watery smile. "I suppose not."

With an aggressive abruptness that made it sound like a challenge, Ruth suddenly blurted, "Do you believe in the supernatural?"

"I'm sorry?" said Claire, taken aback.

"The supernatural?" repeated Ruth, her scowl deepening. "Do you believe in it?"

"Well, I…I don't know. I suppose it depends what you mean by supernatural. Why do you ask?"

"The night that Colin died, I saw something. Something I haven't told anyone about. Something I've been trying to forget."

"What was it?"

Ruth snorted a laugh that contained no humour whatsoever. "My imagination probably. It's always been over-active. I'm the sort of person that believes anything. All these programmes on telly about ghosts and werewolves—I drink it all in, accept it as gospel. Do you know the word 'gullible' isn't in any dictionary?"

"I'm sorry?"

"Never mind. Joke."

"Ruth," said Claire quietly, "what did you see?"

"Nothing probably. Don't worry about it."

"All right, well if you don't want to tell me—"

"No, I *do* want to tell you. I do. It's just…" Ruth looked at her in anguish "…it scares me shitless just thinking about it. I've spent the last few weeks trying to deny it, trying to tell myself I didn't see anything. But the image is still there at the back of my mind. It's there when I close my eyes at night."

"Maybe it would help to talk about it," said Claire.

"Maybe. I don't know."

"Try," Claire suggested.

Haltingly, her face taut and pale as though each word was being torn physically out of her, Ruth told Claire what she had seen. Claire listened, crossing her arms tightly as if to protect herself from the story as it unfolded, or to contain the nervous judder in her belly.

"So what do you reckon?" Ruth said when she was done, once again over-compensating for her defensiveness by making her words sound like a challenge.

"I don't know," said Claire.

"I mean, in light of what you've told me…I swear I didn't know anything about this before…"

"No, I believe you. It's all just…it's probably best not to dwell on it too much."

"You know what I think?" said Ruth.

"What?"

"I think that place is cursed. I think there's something there that makes men kill, that drives them crazy."

Oh, thanks a lot, thought Claire indignantly. *I have to live next door*. Then she said, "But Colin killed Jason MacNeill before he moved there, didn't he?"

Ruth looked momentarily flustered, then she said, "Well…maybe the house attracts evil men then. Or maybe when whatsisname…the old guy…"

"Harry?"

"Yeah, Harry. Maybe when he killed his kids, or as good as, it created a sort of…energy. An evil energy. And when Colin came, the energy sought him out. Possessed him."

"Seeking a kindred soul?" suggested Claire.

"Sort of, yes. And then that energy set off another energy, an energy that wanted revenge. In the end the whole thing came full circle. Everyone dead."

"Well, not everyone," said Claire.

"No, I mean…everyone involved in the killings. It's kind of neat in a way, I suppose. Horrible but neat."

Claire looked across at Bridget, blank-faced and hollow-eyed. Miles was standing beside her now, his hand resting lightly on her arm, the bruises faded but still visible on his neck. She thought of Jean lying in a hospital bed, no family to visit her, a life spent mostly unloved, but still indomitable.

Was this neat? she thought. Was this the kind of conclusion where everyone went away happy and satisfied?

No, it wasn't. It was real life. Messy and tangled and unpredictable. There were no winners, no happy endings, just a constant struggle to come to terms with its cruel twists of fate, a fight to allay the inevitable.

"So what will Bridget do now?" Claire asked.

Ruth shrugged. "Sell the house. Move somewhere else. Maybe closer to me. I've offered her a job."

"Will she take it?"

"She's not sure yet. She says it's too early to make decisions. Time will tell, I suppose."

"Yes," murmured Claire, and saw Ellie step up quietly beside her mother and slip an arm around her waist. "Yes, it always does."

"I have to go now," said Ruth. "Thanks for…for coming, and for telling me what you know."

"Will you tell Bridget?" asked Claire.

"I don't know. Maybe one day. We'll see."

Ruth walked away. Alone, Claire turned and left the room without speaking to anyone. She walked out of the house that belonged to Colin's parents and down the crazy paving path bordered by flowers that nodded their heads at her, as if in sympathy. As she reached the gate that appeared to be attempting to conceal itself within the high, plump hedge that bordered the property, she glanced back.

The black-garbed mourners she could see through the many small panes that became one large window via the grid of their frames seemed no less distinctive nor animated than the shadows shifting in the restless hedge. The tall man still stooping over Bridget appeared vulture-like in silhouette. As Claire turned away and pushed open the gate, she was wondering sadly whether Bridget might decline from keeping in touch simply because seeing her would re-awaken too many bad memories when the thought was driven from her mind by the lurch of shock she felt at the sight of her car.

It had been broken into. Or at least that was her initial impression. As she hurried across the road to where it was parked, barely glancing both ways, she fully expected to see a glinting scatter of safety glass on the pavement and a black slot trailing wires where the radio had been.

To her relief, however, all the windows were intact, which, if she could close the yawning boot which had alerted her, meant that at least she wouldn't be overly inconvenienced. As she peered into the boot, she was trying to recall what had been in there aside from the muddied Wellingtons and scuffed football and bundles of old newspapers and the bin bag of clothes destined for Oxfam, and couldn't think of anything that was. Indeed, the boot contained more than she remembered, not less, because she was certain there hadn't been this amount of soil scattered over everything the last time she had looked. She could only think that Shaun had bought a bag of compost without noticing it had a hole in it, though if that was the case it would be the first time he had ever used his initiative where the garden was concerned.

Actually, now she looked more closely, the stuff in the boot was darker even than compost, so dark, in fact, that it more closely resembled ash. Could someone—kids maybe—have attempted to start a fire by throwing a chunk of burning wood into the car? But if so, why hadn't the newspapers caught? Maybe the kids, or at least one of them, had had second thoughts and either extinguished the burning object or fished it out before it could do any damage. Yes, that must have been it, because, now that she was aware of it, she could see that the ash formed a sparse but still distinct trail that led along the pavement from her boot before meandering across the road. Odd that the trail seemed to stop at the gate to Colin's parents' house, but perhaps the culprit or culprits had seen her go in and were checking to ensure no one in the house had observed their mischief.

For a moment she wondered whether she ought to go back and warn everyone to be vigilant about their own vehicles, then decided, not without a pang of guilt, that she couldn't face it. As she unlocked the driver's door and folded herself into the seat, she was suddenly and unexpectedly hit by the most intense wave of sadness she had experienced thus far. The Morgans had seemed like such a nice family. Three-quarters of them still were. She, and Shaun too, had been looking forward to becoming friends with a couple with whom they had initially seemed to have so much in common.

Starting the engine, she thought about what Ruth had said about the house attracting evil, or at least evil men, and told herself almost angrily what a lot of rot that was. Even so, as she eased the car away from the kerb at the start of a five-hour journey home that would leave sadness further behind her with each mile she travelled, she couldn't help wondering with no little unease what the next owners of the house would be like.